"I'm afraid the news is unpleasant."

Dr. Navarro paused a moment, then continued. "I'm sorry to have to tell you this. The results reveal that you are experiencing an unusual reaction. That is to say, an unusual immune response. I believe your body is developing antibodies to the implants that were inserted into your jaw during your reconstructive surgery. I'm afraid the implants must come out."

Charlotte's heart sank and she slumped in the chair. Oh, God, no, she thought, bringing her hand to her jaw. Did that mean she'd have to go through still another surgery to fix up her face? She never wanted to go through that kind of pain again. And how was she going to get the surgery done without telling Michael?

"Thank you, Dr. Navarro. I'm—I'm grateful you found the cause of all my complaints. I've been led to believe my symptoms were all in my head. But there's one thing I don't understand. If I'm having a rejection of these implants, what will they replace them with?"

"I think perhaps you don't understand," he began, shaking his head regretfully. "The implants... They cannot be replaced."

Charlotte blinked, uncomprehendingly. Surely she'd not heard right. This wasn't real. She was in shock. "What if I don't do it?"

He drew himself up in his chair and looked her straight in the eye. "You must understand, Miss Godfrey. These disorders get progressively worse. If you don't remove the implants, it is my opinion that you will get very sick. And die."

MARY ALICE MONROE

GIRL IN THE MIRROR

MIRA

ISBN 1-55166-451-8

GIRL IN THE MIRROR

Copyright © 1998 by Mary Alice Kruesi.

All rights reserved. Except for use in any review, the reproduction or utilization of this work in whole or in part in any form by any electronic, mechanical or other means, now known or hereafter invented, including xerography, photocopying and recording, or in any information storage or retrieval system, is forbidden without the written permission of the publisher, MIRA Books, 225 Duncan Mill Road, Don Mills, Ontario, Canada M3B 3K9.

All characters in this book have no existence outside the imagination of the author and have no relation whatsoever to anyone bearing the same name or names. They are not even distantly inspired by any individual known or unknown to the author, and all incidents are pure invention.

MIRA and the Star Colophon are trademarks used under license and registered in Australia, New Zealand, Philippines, United States Patent and Trademark Office and in other countries.

Printed in U.S.A.

This book is dedicated to
Oscar Rogers Kruesi
A Man of Ideas

Acknowledgments

Each book is a journey. First and foremost I'd like to thank my agent, Karen Solem, for sharing my vision of where I wanted to go and taking hold of my hand. I'm indebted to Julie Beard and Diane Chamberlain for reading an early draft and giving me a surer sense of direction. For encouragement and advice all along the way, I offer heartfelt thanks to Nora Roberts. Marguerite Martino Abramson discussed the themes of this book with me on an almost daily basis for months and gave me more insights than I can ever thank her for. I am especially grateful to Dianne Moggy and Amy Moore at MIRA for believing in the book from the start, and to Randall Toye and Candy Lee for their support. Most especially, Martha Keenan earned my sincere appreciation for her sensitive editing. I'd like to thank Marisel Vera for her help in developing Hispanic issues in the story, and Alice O'Neill for answering my countless questions about the Hollywood scene. I read many inspiring books for research, in particular the works of Lucy Grealy, Richard Rodriguez and Earl Shorris. Finally, without the enormous help, medical research and support of Drs. Oscar and Markus Kruesi, this book couldn't have been written. Thanks all, it's been a great trip.

Part One

Beauty is in the eye of the beholder.

—Margaret Wolfe Hungerford

One

April 1996

If all the world was a stage, it was time once again to play her part.

Charlotte sat in the green room of the television studio while outside, strains of the talk show's theme song intermingled with audience applause. She had promised Vicki Ray this interview, and there was no choice now but to endure the hour or suffer months of bad press. She'd had enough bad press lately. Now her plan was set. Freddy had seen to every detail in his usual compulsive manner. How had he put it? "Interview, marriage, surgery. Bim, Bam, Boom."

The only booming she felt right now was in her temples, a rhythmic, tympanic beat. How hot the room was! Bringing a fevered hand to her forehead, she noticed with alarm that it was trembling. And her lips, so parched. Oh, please, she prayed, holding her fingers tight, steadying them. Don't let the symptoms come back now. Maybe one more pill, she decided, quickly fumbling through her purse. Just in case.

Three brisk knocks sounded on the door.

"Charlotte?" Freddy Walen walked in without waiting for a response. Although not a big man, his dominating presence filled the room, causing Charlotte to shrink inside. His eyes, as hard as the diamond on his pinkie finger, assessed her with a proprietary air.

"Good...good," he said, stroking his neatly trimmed mustache, observing every detail. Her swanlike neck was unadorned, her golden hair spilled loosely around her shoulders, and her eyes, her large, luminous blue eyes, shone with an icy, mesmerizing luster. It was a look that Freddy referred to as "the brilliance of a star." He'd taught her that her public expected Charlotte Godfrey to be dressed in understated elegance, and she never disappointed them.

"What's that you're taking?" he demanded.

"A painkiller. I'll need it to get through the interview." She stared at the white pill in her hand, then raised her eyes, worry shining clearly. "Freddy, cancel the interview. I'm not well enough. The symptoms are returning, my hands are shaking, and taking another pill is not the answer."

"You'll be fine," he said in a gruff manner, patting her shoulder. "Buck up. We can't cancel now. Besides, we need this interview to settle a few rumors. Then the press will be off our backs so we can hustle to South America and get you well. Zip up this show and we'll be out of here. I promise. Now, take that pill."

Charlotte poured herself a tumbler of water. "I don't trust Vicki Ray. She's tough. Crafty. What if she suspects?"

"Forget it. Vicki doesn't have a clue. If she did, I'd know about it."

"Miss Godfrey?" From outside her door came the high, strained voice of an usher. "Are you ready yet? It's *really* time."

She understood his panic and took pity. Besides, she

couldn't stall any longer. "Yes," she called, quickly swallowing the medicine. "Of course. Right away."

"Remember," Freddy said, grabbing hold of her shoulders. "It's just another part. Follow the script, babe, and you'll be great."

Charlotte shook off his hands. "Don't be a fool, Freddy. There's no script with Vicki Ray." Opening the door, she met a panic-eyed young man who guided her down the hall with the speed of a police escort, past a series of attendants who smiled at her with starry eyes. She'd become immune to that rapt expression during the past few years, knowing better than to be flattered. They knew nothing about her, the woman behind the face. She walked quickly by with only a nod of acknowledgment.

They reached the stage just as Vicki Ray launched into her introduction. She mentioned several of Charlotte's film roles and the meteoric rise of her career. Charlotte listened keenly, compelling herself to become on camera the woman being described: a woman of legendary beauty. An on-screen phenomenon and an off-screen recluse. The new Garbo.

There was a minute's silence, one brief moment to raise a hand to her brow and collect her wits. Charlotte took a deep breath, willed her hands to appear relaxed at her sides, then dug deep to deliver the mysterious, sultry smile that was her trademark.

The Applause sign lit. With a jarring flash, the lights bore down on Charlotte as she stepped out on the stage. To her, they were like prison searchlights blocking any avenue of escape. She walked with studied grace across the shining floor, then settled herself in the isolation of a single white chair in the center of Vicki Ray's stage.

Under the glare of lights, she felt like a laboratory specimen being scrutinized. She looked out at the sea of faces and saw in the eyes of women the familiar flash of envy, and in the men's, desire. It was always this way, she thought, feeling again a twinge of loneliness.

Then, decisively discarding the last remnants of her identity, Charlotte Godowski transformed herself into the role she'd painstakingly created and played so well: Charlotte Godfrey. It was a useful device, yet she felt a little more of herself die each time she employed it. Still, it was necessary to shield herself from the rest of the world. To create an armor that was impenetrable. She allowed no one to pierce it. Not even Freddy. Especially not Freddy. Only Michael... At the thought of him she felt a chink in the armor.

The interview began easily enough. During the first half of the show, Vicki screened a number of film clips. Charlotte peppered the clips with anecdotes, especially about her handsome co-stars. The audience lapped it up, never for a moment suspecting the struggle within the actress. She appeared relaxed, loosening her knotted fingers, uncrossing her legs, even venturing to laugh at the occasional silly question posed by the audience, usually about her well publicized love life.

"Water," she almost begged when the break came. With miraculous speed, the usher delivered Perrier and lime, which she sipped gratefully. Her lips felt cracked, and she sweltered in the glowing heat of her fever.

As the signal flashed that the show was continuing, Charlotte discreetly dabbed at her brow with a Swiss embroidered handkerchief and marshaled her wits. At the last second, she remembered to catch the eye of a cameraman and wink. He returned a crimson grin. Freddy had taught her tricks on how to get flattering camera angles. This charade was easier to manage if she took control.

"Welcome back," began Vicki. "We were talking about your upcoming marriage." Turning to the camera, she continued, "Freddy Walen, for those of you who don't know, is not only Miss Godfrey's fiancé, but her agent as well."

"What can I say?" Charlotte replied, offering a slight gesture with her hand. "He's wonderful. Supportive. He's always there for me." She glanced offstage. Freddy was standing with his feet wide apart and his hands clasped before him, the captain of a ship in unsteady waters.

He gave her a smile. Freddy looked formidable in the dark gray double-breasted suit that complimented his salt-and-pepper hair. She knew he was listening intently to every word she uttered because his pale blue eyes glowed with approval of her answer. He didn't seem to mind that she refrained from saying she loved him.

"Walen discovered you, didn't he? Some say he built your career."

Charlotte shifted in her seat. "He believed in my talent, and any good agent advises his client. Isn't that his job?"

Vicki smiled. "But in your case, it's been said that Walen has a Svengali-like obsession with your career. And you."

Charlotte had the presence of mind to laugh. "Is that what they say?"

"I suppose it's natural for any man to be obsessed with you," Vicki added magnanimously. The audience chuckled and mumbled in agreement. Charlotte shrugged her slim shoulders with seeming humor.

"So many men..." Vicki added with a devilish glint. The cameraman winked at her.

Charlotte knew where this was coming from and couldn't blame Vicki for the insinuation. Freddy had carefully orchestrated her public image, hiding her natural shyness as a star's reclusiveness and arranging numerous dates with her co-stars, then leaking to the press that she was having affairs. It was nothing new, an age-old publicity ploy, but the press and the public bought it, again and again.

"Now there's only Freddy," she replied without guile, and the audience responded with heartfelt applause. She imagined Freddy backstage, his chest expanding. He loved the spotlight, especially when it hinted at his virility.

"Your kind of beauty is the stuff that legends are made of. But some consider it to be a curse. There's Helen of Troy and, of course, Marilyn Monroe."

Charlotte paused. Beauty again... *Is that all they see when they see me? Doesn't anyone see anything else of value?*

"I don't think Marilyn's beauty itself was a curse," she answered with care. "The curse was that no one could look past her beauty to take her seriously."

"You're referring to the old 'She's beautiful so she must be stupid' myth."

"It's hard when only your beauty is prized. I know."

"Couldn't the same be said then of an ugly woman?"

Charlotte felt a dart of anguish and looked at her hands clasped white in her lap. "I'm sure," she began with hesitation, "that it is the secret dream of every ugly woman that someone will discover the beauty within her. Redemption through love, isn't that at the heart of fairy tales?"

"But life isn't a fairy tale."

"Unfortunately," she said, trying to keep the bitterness from her voice. "Both legend and reality bear out that men want women who are physically beautiful, as proof of their power and worth. The dream dies in an ugly woman. It withers, as any fruit withers on the neglected vine."

"But...doesn't beauty wither, too, in time? What happens then?"

Charlotte swallowed hard. "Desperation."

"So beauty *is* a curse?"

"I..." She thought again of Michael and sighed in resignation. "Yes. Perhaps it is. As is ugliness."

"I don't know if I buy this. I mean, aren't women changing now? We talk about a woman's worth, intelligence and goodness. Don't these attributes constitute a woman's beauty?"

Charlotte wanted to agree, oh God, how much. She thought of those days, in the garden, when she'd believed such a thing was possible. When, like a blossoming flower that reveals the delicate core, she'd been ready to give everything up for a single dewdrop of that ideal. But Michael had crushed that belief with the heel of his conceit. She'd learned that no one would love her for her intelligence or for her goodness. Without the beauty, no man was willing to even give those qualities a chance.

"Plus ça change, plus c'est la même chose."

"Are you endorsing this attitude?" Vicki Ray interjected. Her tone was sharp, angry. Nearing fifty, she exuded the confidence of success. Yet Charlotte saw in her eyes the quiet panic of a woman who could not stave off the inevitable decline of her looks, and as a talk show host, possibly her career as well. "Do you believe women today should do everything they can, anything they can, to be as attractive as they can?"

Charlotte's lids fluttered imperceptibly as she dredged up her personal history to answer this question. *Everything…anything…for beauty?*

"I do," she replied firmly, each syllable sounding in her ear as a death knell. "Yes, absolutely."

She heard the disapproving rumbling in the audience. Several women were now wildly waving their hands. Vicki, delighted, hurried to deliver the microphone.

"So what did you do to look so great?"

Charlotte exhaled a stream of air, then smiled. She wanted to say she'd sold her soul to the devil, but no, she couldn't do that.

"*I* didn't do a thing," she lied with feigned nonchalance. Then, hinting at the truth, she added, "Don't forget, legions of experts labor hours to make me look this good." The woman chuckled and seemed to forgive Charlotte for her beauty.

"Have you always been this beautiful?" Vicki asked

through narrowed eyes. Her microphone swung in her hand from left to right, like a club. "Confession time!"

Charlotte gripped the arms of her chair tightly. "Well…"

"Don't you ever wake up with bags under your eyes or a pimple on the tip of your nose?" The audience laughed.

Charlotte put her hands together and looked at the ceiling. She felt like she'd just dodged a bullet. Should she tell them that she woke up every morning in raw pain? And with the knowledge that this marvelous facade was crumbling under the surface?

"I'm no different from anyone else," she replied, wishing it were true.

"Were you a pretty little girl?"

The question pricked Charlotte, deflating her balloon of confidence. Her head felt woozy, and, slipping back in time, she saw the face of the little girl she had been. The sad eyes, the thin, gawky figure, and always, that face. A leaden weight was pulling her down, deeper into the memory, till she experienced again the stark loneliness of her childhood. She remembered how she used to stroll through the wealthy neighborhoods, the kind with the big houses and the manicured lawns, waiting for her mother to finish cleaning. It was so far and foreign from the noisy, close-set apartment buildings on Chicago's far west side, where she lived. She didn't mind waiting. She liked to peek through the windows at the people inside sitting on the pretty furniture. She'd thought they were so lucky to live where everything was so pretty, so content.

"Miss Godfrey?" Vicki's voice was strident.

Charlotte blinked heavily. "What? Oh, yes, I was trying to recollect," she said, struggling for composure. Lord, that extra medication was really kicking in. It felt like her brain was mush. "I…I don't remember much of my childhood. At least not how I looked." The lies were pounding in her head now. How much longer did she have to go on?

"What *do* you remember?" Vicki pressed.

Charlotte sighed heavily. "I can remember trivial things. Let's see—" she rubbed her temple "—I was a bookworm, especially for Charles Dickens. I always wanted a garden and, of course, I remember the games." She swallowed again, her throat dry, recalling how often she'd been the target of cruel games.

"The gossip that always surrounds a celebrity is difficult to live with," Vicki continued, changing topics. "But you seem to attract so much gossip. You've been on the cover of almost every magazine and seem to be a favorite of the tabloids."

"I can't imagine why. I live a rather boring life."

"Maybe it's because they're attracted to the unknown. Your quest for privacy is as legendary as your beauty."

"Is it? I just prefer to keep to myself. What do they think they'll find that's so interesting? When I'm not working, I'm pulling weeds in my garden."

"Well, for starters—" Vicki flashed a smile "—isn't it true that you were released from your last film? Rumors circulated on the set that you were loaded with drugs. Perhaps even had a breakdown of sorts?"

Charlotte took a deep breath, knowing without looking that Freddy's smile was gone and he was leaning forward, waiting for her answer, deliberating on damage control. She decided to face the truth head-on.

"I *was* sick," she admitted. She saw Vicki's brow rise in anticipation of a coup. "I had a terrible case of the flu that I ignored." Vicki's smile fell and Charlotte knew she wasn't buying the story. "The role meant a great deal to me. My mother taught me that illness is a weakness to be worked through. Unfortunately, the flu progressed to pneumonia." She shrugged slightly. "I'm told I had a serious case, and I have to admit I was frightened."

"You disappeared." Vicki's eyes were hard.

"Yes." The image of Michael again flashed in her mind.

His touch, his eyes, his love—they were for her like the sun, soil and air were to the garden. Her smile cracked. She wanted to disappear again.

She brought a shaky hand to her face, but a warning glare from Freddy caught her before she betrayed herself. With a clever tilt of her palm, she gracefully settled her long fingers along the exquisite curve of her jaw.

Vicki waited with the patience of a pro.

"I didn't really disappear," Charlotte continued. "That sounds so glamorous. All I did was spend some time in the country, alone, to regain my health."

"Like in *Camille*? You won an Oscar for that role."

Charlotte laughed lightly, determined to regain control of the interview. "Yes, I suppose so. Life imitates art...or vice versa." She kept her smile firmly in place. "My health," she said, emphasizing the word, "was the reason I requested a release from my last film. The pills I was seen taking were prescription. And it is common knowledge that I adhere to a strict regime of vitamins and herbs." She lifted one hand and flicked her fingers lightly. "I swear, one can't take a vitamin anymore without being tagged a drug addict."

Vicki smirked, and Charlotte realized the host was removing her gloves. All bets were off. Charlotte felt betrayed, trapped. As her headache pounded in her temples, she felt the beginnings of a wave of chills. Her hands formed fists in her lap, digging moon-shaped dents into her palms as she fought for composure. She wasn't up to this. She had warned Freddy. Oh, God, she prayed fervently, don't let me get sick now, on national TV.

"Can you respond to the rumors of a breakdown?"

Charlotte offered a steely smile. "I thought I just had."

"Oh, surely you can't pretend not to have been upset by your breakup with Brad Sommers?"

This time Charlotte genuinely laughed out loud. Freddy's

press releases had done their job. "Vicki, really. Give me a little credit. Brad and I are friends," she lied.

"If not Brad, then—" Vicki quickly checked her note cards "—what about Michael Mondragon?" she asked, raising her eyes with a gleam of triumph. "Some say that behind your tall, ivy-covered walls you were in fact hiding a torrid love affair with your gardener."

Charlotte sat back in her chair, dumbstruck. How did Vicki know about Michael? How dare she call him a gardener? How? Nausea rose up to choke her, forcing her to swallow hard, appearing to the camera, she knew, overwhelmed by the question. Guilt by silence.

Her gaze flew to Freddy standing just offstage, a mute appeal in her eyes. Please come out, her eyes entreated. You set this up. Or...are you setting me up?

Her pal the cameraman obliged and shifted the camera focus to catch a glimpse of Freddy, arms now clasped tightly across his chest. He bore a hard grin, but his eyes were flashing. Freddy remained resolutely silent, only waving the camera away. Vicki made a discreet gesture and immediately the camera returned to her.

"Michael who?" Charlotte finally blurted. She sat straighter in her chair, angry at Vicki for digging into her personal life, angry at Freddy for leaking the information, angry at herself for not having enough courage to walk off the stage. "Me and my gardener? Really. This is too much."

She couldn't help herself; her hand rose to cover her eyes. The tremors were returning. She felt weaker, dizzy. Poor Michael. If he heard what she'd just said it would hurt him deeply. But what choice did she have? What choice had he left her?

"These kinds of rumors are why I choose to keep my private life private," she added, raising her eyes. Anger made her strong. She didn't realize her hands clutched the arms of her chair. "When Freddy and I are married we're going to take a long trip, away from public view, so I can regain my health. When I come back I'll be as good as new and ready to face whatever.''

Vicki retreated, moving into the audience. A sweet-faced woman, obviously a fan, flagged Vicki. ''Is there another film we can look forward to?''

Charlotte mentally blessed the old woman. ''Oh, yes,'' she said, with a smile that lit up her face. ''I'm very excited about my next project. I've always wanted to play the lead in *Tess of the D'Urbervilles.*''

''Another demanding role,'' chided Vicki. ''You're known to become the character you play, but you won't let yourself die like poor Tess, I hope?''

While the audience chuckled, Charlotte caught her breath. Did Vicki suspect? Was Dr. Harmon right and Freddy wrong? Who should she believe? It was clear she was getting sick again. Worse than ever. She could hardly get through a day without collapsing.

Despite the dizziness that blurred her vision, Charlotte focused on the answer by force of will. ''Goodness, I hope not!'' She flashed a megawatt smile straight at the cameras. ''I hope you'll all come see it.''

Vicki seemed satisfied, and the audience showed their approval with their applause. In the wings, Freddy was nodding with paternalistic pleasure. Everyone was smiling. Charlotte leaned back in her chair and quickly glanced at her watch. It was over. She'd made it through the interview without the truth slipping out. For a few tense moments, she'd thought Vicki had the scoop and would press her hard for a confession, breaking her down like a guilty witness on the stand. What good TV that would have been: the end of a career.

No matter, she thought, pretending not to feel the wrenching of her stomach. In a few minutes more, she could go home to her big four-poster bed, cuddle up under her down comforter, take another dose of her herbal remedy and pray for the illness to pass.

"We only have time for one more question."

A man in the audience rose. There was something familiar in his towering height and the breadth of his shoulders. Something about the neatly clipped black hair brushed back from his forehead that caught her attention. A chill shivered through her. Her breathing grew shallow as she squinted through the haze of lights to focus on the man. He was moving forward now, down the stairs toward the front stage. Toward her. Each step he took was measured by her gasps. Each inch closer brought her further to despair.

Vicki, sensing something amiss, followed the man who boldly approached the stage. She opened her mouth to speak, but either instinct or memory hushed her. She stilled the security guard with a flick of her wrists and expertly allowed the tension to spread throughout the audience. While the camera whirred, one by one the hands dropped and the heads turned toward the handsome, dark-haired man who now stopped at the foot of the stage and stared with bruising intensity at the frozen actress. Silence reigned.

"Charlotte Godfrey," he said, piercing the quiet with a voice that carried the clarity of conviction. "You are a fraud."

A collective gasp surged through the room, and from somewhere she could hear the angry shouts of Freddy demanding that this moron be removed.

Charlotte stared back into the piercing dark eyes that silenced her. No words came for her response. She had no lines, no script. She was rendered mute with confusion, struck dumb by her blinding hatred for this man. And more. Oh, yes. That other, deeper, more excruciating pain. For she loved no man more than Michael Mondragon.

Vicki was talking now, rapidly closing the show, promising the gaping audience that she would schedule a follow-up. Freddy was being forcibly held back, but she could hear his garbled shouts rise up over the din. Mustering dignity, Charlotte stood up, catching hold of the chair to steady herself. Then, turning on her heel, she walked with her chin high, away from the blinding lights, away from the shouts of Freddy, and most of all, away from the tangible pull of Michael Mondragon. He called after her, more a demand, but she ignored him. Faster she walked, almost a trot, back to the seclusion of the green room.

"Don't let anyone in," she ordered the guard. He nodded and straightened his shoulders as she filed past him, locking the door behind her.

What did she do now? she asked herself again and again as she paced the floor, holding her flushed and fevered face in her hands. Throw something? Run? But where could she go?

"Charlotte!" Michael roared outside her door. He pounded, shaking the wood. "Open the door. We need to talk. I won't let you die!" The door shook. "Charlotte!"

Then Freddy's voice. Now both of them were calling her name. She threw herself on the sofa, covering her ears. Outside, they took to shouting at each other, like two territorial dogs defending what was theirs. Oh, God, were they fighting? She heard the muffled sounds of fists against muscle, grunts, followed by shouts of alarm from Vicki.

"Go away," Charlotte screamed at the two men, at everyone. "Please just leave me alone!"

She curled up on the sofa, bringing her knees to her chest, shivering. Each bone in her body ached, every muscle trembled. "Go away," she moaned, over and over, crooning as the chills and fever racked her. She couldn't go on like this. She wouldn't. No more listening to Michael or Freddy.

Wasn't it *her* face, *her* life that was at issue here? She had to make this decision alone. She had to think, to remember, to go back to where it all began.

Her eyelids felt like heavy weights and she could no longer fight off closing them. As soon as she relinquished resistance, she felt blanketed by a languid, drifting blackness. Her mind called out to the ghost of the child evoked earlier during the interview. As she slipped deeper into the darkness, from somewhere she heard the high-pitched, singsong voice of a little girl saying over and over, "I told you so...."

September 1976

Charlotte sat on the periphery of the playground. Her yellow dress hung limply around her knees as her feet dangled over the bleachers. Humming a nameless tune, she watched the other kindergarten children cover the ground, laughing, playing the many silly, exciting games that she knew by heart: hopscotch, jump-rope, cat's cradle. But no one invited her to join, so she sat, swinging her legs, and watched.

Suddenly two young girls she knew well darted past her to hide behind the bleachers. Charlotte sat up, tense with anticipation. She marveled at how their pretty cheeks were pink with excitement. Their voices were shrill with feigned alarm.

"Come back here, Charlotte," one of them whispered. "They'll see you and guess our hiding place. Hurry!"

Charlotte jumped up with a rush of joy to join them.

"Me? You want me to play?" No one ever wanted her to play.

"Hurry up!"

They were playing with her! Charlotte scurried around the green wooden bleacher and huddled with the other girls, her hands tight against her chest in excitement. She imagined her own cheeks were as pretty and pink as theirs.

When the group of young boys spotted them, they pointed and charged. The girls took off, squealing in the chase.

Charlotte's heart pounded gleefully as her little feet soared across the hard-packed grass of the playing field. She was running with them and, oh, she was fast! She could feel the wind kiss her smile and flap her dress hem against her thighs as she sprinted. Behind her she heard heavy footfall, and, feeling cocky, she looked over her shoulder teasingly. She knew she was smarter in school, and now she knew she was faster, too. The boy who chased her flushed and frowned furiously.

Charlotte's laughter pealed and she ran harder. As she began to tire, she sensed a subtle shift in attitude. Them against her. Instead of one boy chasing her, now there were three, and they were frustrated and closing ranks. Where were the other girls?

"Hey, you're fast," one boy shouted with resentment.

"Like a horse," called out another.

"Yeah, she does look like a horse."

"Hey—Charley Horse!"

The boys burst out laughing, holding their sides and bumping shoulders as their pace slackened. They used the spontaneous nickname as a rallying call.

"Get Charley Horse!"

Little Charlotte Godowski ran hard then, as far as she could from the sound of the cruel nickname that poked fun at her face. It was hateful to be so mean. Mean, mean, mean.

Charley wasn't her name. Her name was Charlotte. A beautiful name. Did she look like a horse? She couldn't help how she looked...why would they say that? The name hurt and they knew it. They kept hurling it at her like stones as they chased. Charlotte felt a little afraid now, but she dug deep and ran faster. When she spotted the bleachers, she made a beeline for them. She would hide like before.

It was a dumb thing to do. She knew it the moment she

ran behind them and saw that she was trapped by the chain-link fence. Like a pack of dogs they came after her, one from around the left side of the bleachers, two from the right. With cunning, they cornered her.

Charlotte moved away from the fence, instinctively allowing herself space. The boys clustered together, their young chests heaving, panting like dogs after the chase. As they stared, she saw conceit gleaming in their eyes.

The boys gathered closer. She could smell the candy on their breaths. Billy's Keds were smeared; he had stepped in dog manure. The wind gusted, hurling the foul scent toward her. Charlotte shivered, wrinkling her nose, and searched through the slats of the bleachers to where the other schoolchildren were playing. Their high-pitched voices soared in the sky like birdcalls. They seemed so very far away. Suddenly, she felt very alone. She wanted her mother, her teacher. Where were the other girls? She didn't like this game anymore. She didn't want to play.

"Okay," she said, putting out her palms. "You guys win." She laughed, but it sounded queer, too high.

The boys looked at one another, nervously shifting their weight. Then one boy, Billy again, spoke. His voice was raspy. "If we catch you we get to pull down your pants."

Charlotte paled and she sucked in her breath. She hadn't heard this rule. She'd never have played the game if she'd heard this rule!

"Uh-uh, dog-doo foot," she muttered, shaking her head and backing away with her palms turned outward against them. It was a big mistake, she thought, because she saw Billy's eyes turn mean. "I didn't mean it, Billy. I'm sorry. I quit this game. Okay? Please?"

Billy took the lead now. He was determined to show power.

"Let's see if she's as ugly down there."

Her breath stilled. Surely she hadn't heard right. She looked at Billy with uncomprehending eyes. Ugly? How could that be? Her mama told her she was pretty. Just last night, at her bedside, her mama prayed to St. Levan for her to be pretty. No one had ever called her ugly. No! They were just being mean.

And yet... From some as yet unvisited place in her heart, Charlotte heard the whispering that it was true. For the first time in her life, at five years of age, Charlotte came face-to-face with her ugliness. Her arms slipped to her sides and she stared back at them with vulnerable eyes.

Sensing her new weakness, they were on her, pulling her to the dirt. Charlotte was filled with a panic she'd never felt before. She kicked her long, spindly legs blindly, with all her might, satisfied when she heard muffled *umphs* and grunts of pain. She fought hard but there were too many of them. With their sticky hands they held her down. She began to cry and beg them not to.

"No... Please... No!"

Their short, blunt nails scraped her hips as they pulled the pink flowered cotton down around her thighs. Then they looked, really looked, with their mouths hanging open, surprised that they'd actually gone through with it.

When the school bell pierced the air they all jumped back, startled, frightened by the reality of what they'd imagined. Charlotte instantly curled into a ball, tucking her thin yellow dress tight around her knees. With her face in the dirt, she hiccuped, tasting the salt of tears and the minerals of earth. She hated these boys. In the harshest jargon of a five-year-old, she shouted out, "You're *bad!*"

Knowing what they'd done was wrong, the boys scuffed their shoes in the dirt in an embarrassed silence. From her level, Charlotte saw the manure still smeared on Billy's Keds. When she looked up, she caught Billy's expression before he turned heel and sped across the field to join the rest of the class as they filed into the school. Charlotte thought Billy had seemed horrified. It didn't occur to her five-year-old mind that the boy may have been guilt stricken at his own behavior. All Charlotte thought was that maybe she *was* ugly—even down there.

Mortified, her tears cascaded down her grossly sloping chin to pool in the dirt. She hated boys. They were mean and not to be trusted. And she didn't like the girls, either. Why didn't they help her? She would have helped them. They had to know…

Lifting herself from the dirt, she spied a dandelion whose stem had been crushed by the heel of a boy's shoe. Charlotte bent over the broken flower and tried to straighten the yellow head, shoring up its sides with dirt. "Poor little flower."

Charlotte didn't go back to school but stayed behind the bleachers until the teacher came out to fetch her and scold her for not following the bell. Charlotte told the teacher that she was sick and wanted to go home. The teacher looked at her tearstained face and believed her. It wasn't really a lie, but Charlotte told God that she was sorry for the sin, anyway.

But she wasn't sorry for hating the boys. She promised herself she was never going to let them hurt her again.

Two

December 1991

Charlotte, weary after a five-hour dress rehearsal of *A Christmas Carol,* unlocked the door of the four-room apartment she shared with her mother. The paint was chipped around the door handle and the single bulb in the hall cast a seedy pall. A home fit for Scrooge, she thought, with a resigned chuckle. She rubbed her sore throat with her mittened hand. What a hectic day. Her voice was hoarse from shouting replies to the harried director and from prompting lines to the actors, who seemed unable to memorize a single scene of dialogue. Charlotte couldn't understand how they could be so lazy. She knew everyone's lines; her memory was razor sharp. Everyone depended on good ol' Charlotte to deliver. Perhaps that was part of the problem. As the stage manager, it was her job to make things easier for everyone else—and she was very good at her job.

Not that she expected to be cast in a role herself, as much as she would have loved it. She would have to remain behind the scenes. She'd accepted her fate years ago, when she accepted her deformity. The theater was in her blood, however, even if only as part-time stage manager for the local company. She was in charge of all the details no one else liked to do, a satisfying enough position for a detail kind of person like herself. She arranged dressing rooms, kept the scripts in order, stepped in for rehearsals when an actor didn't show, and generally made nice-nice to keep everybody happy. She didn't mind being in the background. With her looks, it was her lot in life. Her greatest, most secret thrill, however, came during the actual production when she stood offstage, her face upturned in the lights, and whispered the lines of the play with all the feeling and heart that was lacking on stage.

"Mama, I'm home!" she called out, dropping her coat on the bench by the door. She went first to her room, closed the door behind her and switched on the music, delighted with a few minutes all to herself, with no one calling her name. After undressing, she collapsed on her bed, relishing the soft comfort she had no intention of leaving till it was time to go to Sunday mass the next morning.

"Charlotte, you're home so late!" Helena called out. The large Polish woman's broad shoulders, already humped over from years of cleaning other people's houses, stooped a little more in relief at seeing her only child safely home. At forty-seven, Helena Godowski's face was as pale, trans-lucent and crackled as a piece of her treasured bone china. But she was strong enough to lift the bulky dark wood armoire that housed the fragile dishes, and her physical strength paled when compared to her stern will.

"I know, I know, I'm sorry!" Charlotte hurried to erase the frown from her mother's brow. "Rehearsals were crazy today, and I had to stay until everyone had their lines down pat. It's always like this before an opening." She ran a hand through her hair, shaking it out. "I'm pooped. I think I'll go to bed early tonight."

"Go to bed? But you can't!" Helena raised the purple-and-pink plastic container that she carried under her arm. "Tonight there is nice party!" she said, her eyes bright.

"See, I brought my makeup. We will try something pretty, no?"

"Oh, no," Charlotte groaned, her eyes closed tight in misery. Her stomach did a flip and she lost her appetite. "The office party. I'd completely forgotten. Mom, I'd rather stay home. *A Christmas Carol* is on tonight. The old one with Alastair Sim. It's the best one. And," she added, thinking fast, "I'm so tired."

"Movies," Helena grumbled. "Movies and plays. Always this. You are a watcher. Day and night and never go out, except to that silly theater that doesn't pay you enough for train fare. This is not good for you. You must live in real world, Charlotte. You can not always hide in your room. You'll never find a husband like that." Helena bent to pick up Charlotte's clothing from the floor and folded the articles into a neat pile on the bed.

"Oh, Mama. I won't find a husband at the office Christmas party. All I'll find is a drunk." She shuddered, rubbing her bare arms at the dismal prospect of another party of long hours sitting alone, enduring snide remarks. "Oh, all right, I'll go," she conceded when she saw her mother's disappointment. "But only because Mr. Kopp sent a memo that implied we all have to show up—or else."

"Your boss, he won't let anything be too wild. You'll have nice time. You'll see."

The image of "Fast Hands" Lou Kopp flashed through Charlotte's mind. Her boss was the very one women worried about most. "I'll try to have a good time," she said with a sigh of resignation. "If I can find something to wear." She dug through the dingy, cramped closet stuffed with old shoes, worn suits and a collection of dusty hats. Her mother never threw anything out. Everything had a little life left in it.

Making things do was the modus operandi for Charlotte and her mother. Their apartment was small and devoid of any charm, but it was located on a convenient bus line and the rent was cheap, so, like everything else, it had to make do.

If it wasn't pretty, however, at least it was clean. Not a spot marred the old linoleum or the bland brown carpeting. Neither was there a stain on Charlotte's old skirt or a button missing from her blouse. The pale green Formica in the kitchen might have been ugly, but it sparkled. As did Charlotte's unpolished nails and polished shoes. And anyone who entered the narrow lobby on Harlem Avenue would tilt his head and sniff with closed eyes toward the delicious scents simmering behind apartment 2B.

"I have a good feeling about this party. You might meet someone," Helena said with smug satisfaction. "I prayed to St. Jude."

Charlotte rolled her eyes and turned her back to slip into an old red wool dress.

"A woman needs a man to look after her," her mother continued, intent on pursuing this line of conversation. "And she must take care of him and his home. And his children. Matrimony is a holy state. A sacrament. Yah...I pray for that for you." Her voice rose with emotion. "I don't want for you to be alone and unhappy."

Charlotte tensed, squeezing her hands into tight fists around the hanger. In the mirror she saw herself as her mother refused to see her: an ugly, thin, twenty-year-old destined to be a back room accountant and live with her mother in this dingy apartment for the rest of her life.

"Mom," Charlotte said, wrapping an arm around her mother's shoulder. At just this moment, she needed to receive comfort as much as give it. "Don't worry about me. I can take care of myself—and you. We won't be alone. I love you."

She bent to kiss her mother's cheek, thinking that each time she did so, there was less fullness to her face. Her mother stiffened, patted Charlotte's arm, then gently pushed her away.

"You better get dressed now. Pretty, okay?"

Charlotte pulled back quickly. "Pretty…" she repeated, scorched by the word. She slipped the dress over her head, groaning as the tight waistband barely squeezed over her bust then cinched her waist. Either the wool dress had shrunk or her bust had grown, because the bodice felt like a vise around her chest. Looking up she caught the grimace on her mother's face.

"You no can wear *that* dress to party!"

"It seems a little small, I know…." Charlotte tried stretching the fabric out from her chest.

"A little? I can see your…you know!"

"What?" Charlotte spun around to look at herself in the full length mirror. The dress clung to her long slender frame like a second skin, outlining her full breasts in scarlet, voluptuous detail.

Her mother flushed, pointing frantically. "Ach. The tips! They stick out—like coat hooks!"

Charlotte flushed as red as her dress. Her nipples did indeed protrude from the fabric. A man could hang his hat on them. Mortified, she hunched her shoulders forward, but it was no use. Her breasts would not be concealed. Oh, Lord, Charlotte sighed with exasperation. Why did she have to have such big ones? In the dim light of a vanity lamp, she studied her figure, appalled. Her breasts were full and her waist was small; a figure most women dreamed of.

But she was unlike most women. Her figure was her nightmare. It attracted male attention—until they raised their eyes.

"You must wear something else."

"I don't have anything else! Except my church dress, and I'm not going to wear that old brown thing to a fancy party. I just won't go."

"No, no, you go. Maybe a jacket. To cover yourself. Is a sin to provoke."

Provocation was the last thing she wanted. When Charlotte tried on a somber black suit jacket over the offensive dress, her mother visibly relaxed and nodded in satisfaction.

"It will do. You can wear jacket so nice. Like your father."

"I hope he didn't have a chest like this," she muttered.

"Don't talk like that about your father! He was a fine man. A fine man," her mother repeated, smoothing out her sweater like ruffled feathers. "From a fine family in Warsaw. What grand house they had. And servants! And his mother—oh, such a lady. There was a woman who never had to lift a finger."

Charlotte turned away and slipped off the jacket. It didn't flatter the dress but, like everything else, it would have to make do. She had nothing else. They were poor now. They had always been poor. What value was there in coming from a family that had once upon a time been wealthy? It was just another fairy tale.

"You are so like your father," her mother continued wistfully, happy in her memories.

"But I don't look like him."

"What you know how he looked?"

Charlotte shrugged. Even as a child she'd thought it odd that there were no photographs of her father. All her classmates had albums full of relatives. She hadn't even one.

"You told me he was handsome." Her comment floated between them, like a challenge.

"You are smart like him," her mother amended, picking at her sweater. "And you have his nose. A strong, noble nose. Still, you have my eyes, your grandmother Sophie's eyes."

Listening, Charlotte's gaze traveled in the mirror up from her full chest, beyond her thin shoulders and long neck to her face. It wasn't often that she suffered the study of her own reflection and she was momentarily stunned. Staring back were the large, wide, vivid blue eyes under dark, finely arched brows that resembled her mother's. And the long, narrow nose of her father.

"But from whom," Charlotte asked bitterly, "did I get this grossly sloping chin and these drooping lips? Who do I have to thank for these fine features?"

"Hush, Charlotte," her mother pleaded, her face ashen. "You got your looks from God."

Charlotte swallowed her retort and lowered her head, ashamed for the angry thoughts she'd just had about God. Besides, she didn't want to upset her mother with useless anger. After all, what choice did her mother have but to accept her only daughter's ugliness as God's will? Charlotte's own daily prayer was that she herself could accept the face.

"Someday," her mother said, beginning the phrase that was more a prayer in this Polish Catholic house than the Our Father. "You will meet *Someone*. A fine man who will love you for all your good qualities. And you *are* a good girl, Charlotte."

Charlotte pressed her lips together and turned away from the mirror. There would be no *Someone*. Not for her. "The jacket won't fit under my coat," she said crisply, her lip trembling. "I'll carry it."

Her mother closed her mouth and looked wearily at her hands clenched in her lap. "Yes," she said softly, maintaining the charade. "The jacket will be fine. Nice girls don't need to advertise."

Charlotte forgot her jacket. In her mind's eye she could see the black wool lying on the bench beside the front door. How could she be so forgetful? she thought, mentally kicking herself. One minute of stupidity meant hours of agony.

She had to go back home, she decided. She'd wave at her boss, enough to let him know she was here, then duck out. Charlotte peered in through the entrance of the banquet hall. Round tables, decorated with garish faux silk poinsettias festooned with glittering red and green ribbons, were assembled on an enormous revolving floor.

"Come on in!" someone shouted from the crowd. Charlotte took a small step into the room, clutching her coat close to the neck. Beyond, revelers slowly traveled a three-hundred-and-sixty-degree tour of Chicago's skyline and Lake Michigan to the tune of "A Holly Jolly Christmas."

Everyone was there, from the top management to the lowly file clerks. McNally and Kopp was a small accounting firm, but when you multiplied that number times two, it didn't take great math skills to know that at least one hundred people were assembled tonight to celebrate the holidays. And from the sounds of it, most of the guests were already on their second or third drinks.

In the far corner, a group of men in suits gathered at the bar. Between laughs and swallows, their eyes scanned the room with the hungry look of animals on the hunt.

"Charley!"

Charlotte cringed at the name she still hated. Looking up, she saw Judy Riker, her office manager, approaching wearing a peekaboo dress of red sequins and straps that barely held her together. Boy, oh boy, Charlotte thought with a smile. Her mother would be shocked to see so much of Judy's "you knows" exposed. The men at the bar noticed, too, and Charlotte saw them lean over and comment to one another as Judy passed.

"I was just leaving," Charlotte said as Judy walked up.

"Leaving? Nonsense. You've just arrived. Come on, don't be such a wallflower. It's time you had some fun." Judy coaxed a reluctant Charlotte out of her coat. "My, what a nice dress," she said, barely disguising her surprise. "You look nice in red, Charley. You should wear it more often instead of that baggy black and gray you always wear. People always ask if you're in mourning. With your long blond hair, red is definitely your color."

"It's Christmas," she responded, blushing.

"Well, Merry Christmas, Charley! Come on. Let's go get a drink. It's a cash bar, those cheap bastards. You'd think they'd spring for Christmas. What the hell, it's my treat. Let's tie one on for Ol' St. Nick."

Judy bought Charlotte a white wine and, with typical efficiency, directed her toward her assigned seat. Then, her job as hostess done, she disappeared into the crowd. Alone again, Charlotte clutched the stem of her wineglass like a lifeline and tracked her path to the table. Her heart sank. She had to walk past the bar.

Charlotte had learned early in life that an ugly face drew as many comments from a group of guys as a pretty one. Maybe more. Hunching her shoulders forward, she let her hair slide over her face in a practiced move of camouflage. She imagined that she was on stage, marked her point across the floor, then, eyes on the point, she proceeded in a straight line across the floor to the backbeat of "Babes in Toyland."

As she passed the bar, the rowdy men quieted. She held her breath and invoked St. Anthony the Great to protect her from swine. Hurrying her pace, her hands clenching and unclenching the stem of her glass, she found her seat and slunk quickly down into the vinyl upholstery. Just when she was muttering thanks to St. Anthony, she saw a man swerving toward her. She sucked in her breath and averted her face.

"Excuse me," he said at her side. "Have we met?"

It was her boss, Lou Kopp. A chill ran down her spine and she sunk farther into her seat, bringing her hand to her face. From the bar she heard the jeers: "Way to go, Lou."

She felt like a trapped animal, but years of ridicule had taught her never to show fear. Taking a deep breath, she turned her head slowly to face him, and, as she looked up, her hair fell back from her face. Lou Kopp's face registered woozy confusion, then shock as his smile slipped.

"What the hell—"

Charlotte winced as though struck. "My name is Charlotte Godowski," she said, willing her voice to remain even. "You might remember who I am. I'm an accountant in your company."

Now the voices from the bar turned to hoots of laughter. "Wow! Tonight's your lucky night." "Hey, this is Christmas, not Halloween!"

After each outburst they broke into a renewed round of drunken laughter that riddled like bullets.

Charlotte's defense was to pretend not to hear them, or the sympathetic *tsks* from the women within hearing distance. Yet inside she felt like a slip of paper that had burned, curled and turned to ash. If only she could blow away.

She knew, as she saw Lou Kopp swagger back to the bar to be welcomed with sympathetic slaps on the back, that tonight would be no different from all the other parties she had ever attended. No different from the lunchrooms at school. Now the naughty boys had a target upon which to vent their frustration against all the beautiful girls who'd scorned them.

Charlotte stood straight and filed past the boozy comrades at the bar. They drunkenly nudged and snickered as she crossed their line of vision. Judy Riker hurried to meet her at the door.

"Charlotte, I don't know what to say. Maybe if—"

"Please," she responded, holding up her hand to stop the other woman's babble. "Merry Christmas, Judy. Good night."

It just wasn't in her to muster a smile. Turning on her heel, she quickly collected her coat, covered the now despised red wool dress, then pressed the elevator button. The bell rang promptly and she moved quickly into the box, punching the lobby button, then closing her eyes in relief at being alone. Just as the doors swept shut, a man hurried in. The door bounced from his shoulders then quickly slid shut behind him.

Looking up, she saw Lou Kopp.

"Going to the garage?" Lou asked, pushing the G button.

Charlotte didn't respond. Her heart pounded and her breath came quick. Now she was truly trapped. Silently, she began praying. *Hail Mary, full of grace...*

"Listen. About what happened earlier..."

Blessed art thou among women and blessed is the fruit of thy womb...

"I'm sorry."

Her prayer halted. Did he say he was sorry?

"Hey, it was a terrible thing we did in there. Some of the guys were drunk. Not that that's any excuse," he hurried to amend. "And, as your boss, I take full responsibility. Please, Miss Goz... Well. Accept my apology."

Charlotte hesitated, looking up to gauge the expression in his eyes. Lou Kopp wasn't a good looking man by most standards. *Slick* was the word that best described him. His eyes were his saving grace. They were a sunny sky blue that brightened when he smiled, as he did now. You're the last person who should judge a person by looks, she scolded herself. She accepted his apology with a brief nod.

"How can I make it up to you?"

"You've said you're sorry," she replied, eyes straight ahead. "That's enough."

"No, it's not. How about I buy you a drink? Wanna go for a drink?"

"No. Thank you."

"How're you getting home?"

"I'll take a cab. It's not far." She was planning on taking the train.

"You'll never get a cab. It's the holidays—a Friday night. No way. Hey, I'll tell you what. I'll drive you home. What d'ya say? It's the least I can do."

"That's not necessary," she replied, almost stammering.

"Sure it is. I'll drive you home. It's no big deal. Besides," he added, "I'm your boss. I should take care of my employees, right?"

She didn't have time to respond. The elevator doors opened on the fourth floor and a tall man, conservatively dressed in a long navy wool coat, stepped inside. The elevator seemed to shrink in size and Charlotte, mesmerized, grew acutely aware of everything about him. She stole a quick glance.

He had the most beautiful skin, she thought. The rich color of terra cotta. His cheekbones were high and pronounced, and he had a strong Mayan nose that gave him a distinguished, even stern appearance. Although his thick black hair was long and fringed along his starched white collar, it was so neatly cut that it was clear the length was by choice, not neglect. Most arresting of all, he bore the indefinable manner of a gentleman, which always set a woman at ease, knowing she had nothing to fear. The scent of sandalwood cut through the stale air of the small compartment.

As they descended, he stood with his dark, long, unadorned fingers clasped before him. In contrast, Lou fingered coins in his pocket. When they reached the lobby and the doors slid open again, the tall man stepped forward and paused to hold the door for her in an age-old gesture of chivalry. Charlotte, flattered, moved forward. Suddenly she felt Lou Kopp's hand on her arm. She paused awkwardly. The stranger's dark eyes flashed to meet Charlotte's, then flicked to Lou's hand on her arm before quickly snapping back to her, his brows knitted in question.

"Did you want to get out?" he asked. His voice was low and polite, yet she heard in the undercurrent the clear indication that he would help her if she needed it.

"I said I'll drive you home." Lou's voice sounded insistent, and she felt his grip tighten on her arm. He was her boss and Charlotte responded instantly to the authority in his voice.

"Thank you," she said to the stranger. "I'm fine."

The man's gaze probed like an eagle's, then without another word, he nodded politely and stepped aside, allowing the doors to hum shut between them.

"Lousy spic," muttered Lou. "What did he think he was doing?"

Being a gentleman, Charlotte thought to herself as she dropped her gaze to her shoes. She felt suddenly and inexplicably lonely.

Lou Kopp and Charlotte rode down the one floor to the garage in silence. Neither did they speak as she followed him along the freezing ramp of the dimly lit, deserted garage. The cement walls were dingy and smeared with graffiti, and the frigid air was heavy with the acrid smell of gasoline. At last they reached a large gray Oldsmobile parked in the corner. He opened the doors and slid into the front seat. Charlotte followed suit.

Lou fired the engine but it coughed, chugged and stalled in the bitter cold. "Damn, but it's cold. Can't barely touch the metal."

Charlotte didn't respond but curled her chilled toes in her shoes.

Finally the engine turned over, sputtering unevenly and rocking the car like an old beast of burden roused from its hibernation. "Good ol' American car," Lou said with a gleam of triumph while rubbing his hands vigorously. Long streams of vapor flowed from his lips and the scent of stale brandy hung heavily in the air. Charlotte ducked her nose into her collar and tucked her icy fingers under her arms. Tonight was one of those arctic Chicago nights that froze the hair in one's nostrils.

"Yep. Cold tonight," he repeated, glancing her way with a spark in his eyes. "Wind chill brings it below zero."

"Feels like it," she responded shyly, shivering in the

darkness. The lights from the garage were dim and made their skin appear sallow and gaunt. "Maybe we should wait inside till the engine warms up."

"Nah." Lou reached into his vest pocket and pulled out a small flask. The silver flashed in the yellow light. "Always be prepared," he said, unscrewing the top with a wink. "This'll warm us up, eh?"

Charlotte's eyes widened and she shook her head no.

A shadow of a frown crossed his brow before he wrapped his lips around the flask and took a swallow. When he finished, he released a long sigh and glanced her way. "You don't think I'm trying to get you drunk here, do you, honey?"

"Of course not, Mr. Kopp," she replied quickly, embarrassed that he thought her such a prude. Of course he wouldn't be trying to make her drunk. What man would?

"Just trying to warm you up a little. Spreadin' some Christmas cheer." He lifted the flask to his mouth and drank heavily. "How about some music?" He reached over and flicked on the radio. "A Holly Jolly Christmas" played again.

"Isn't the engine ready yet?" she asked, her voice high with tension.

"Nope. Engine's not idling. It's colder than a witch's teat out there." His eyes shifted to her chest. "Speakin' of which, that was a very pretty dress you wore tonight. You're a regular wolf in sheep's clothing, if you know what I mean."

Charlotte shrank into the upholstery.

"Never noticed you before," he continued. "You're a real nice girl, you know that? Real nice. What's your name again?"

"Charlotte. Charlotte Godowski."

"Charlotte..." He said the name slow, rolling it with his tongue. "Charl..." He stopped and smiled a surprised grin. "Charley?"

She looked out the window, catching her horselike reflection in the glass.

"Well, how come they all call you Charley when you've got such a pretty name? Charlotte is so, I dunno, elegant. You know?"

"The name doesn't exactly match the face," she replied.

"Hey, what kinda thing is that to say?"

Charlotte was momentarily surprised by his defense and responded to his backward compliment like a dry sponge to a droplet of water. She loosened her grip on the door handle.

"So, how'd you get to be called Charley?"

"One boy thought of it and the name just stuck." *Get Charley Horse!* In a flash she recalled the many times she'd lifted her desktop to find carrots or bits of sugar inside, followed by explosions of giggles and laughter.

"Well, Charley's a decent enough name, I guess. Here," he said, handing a capful of brandy her way. "Merry Christmas, Charley."

He was smiling at her, being nice to her, and she wondered if perhaps she'd misjudged him after all. Perhaps he was just like her, teased and tormented by co-workers and merely seeking out a friend on a lonely holiday night. She knew he was no longer married, and this made him safer in her mind.

"Maybe I will," she said, feeling adventurous. She took the small cap from his hands with a shy smile.

"You have a real nice smile, Charley."

Her heart skipped at her first real compliment, and she could feel the heat of a furious blush across her face. Charlotte bent her head and brought the icy cap to her lips, desperately trying not to look like a horse with a feed bag. The liquid was smooth and burst like a flame in her belly, warming her all over.

"See? I was right. Told you it'd warm the blood." He smiled, refilling the cap. "Get your juices flowing."

Charlotte braved another smile and swallowed more, closing her eyes. She *did* rather like it. It tasted of fermented plums mixed with fire and something magical that tickled her nose and tingled her tum. When she opened her eyes, Lou was still smiling at her. She searched his crooked features with a forgiving eye, seeking signs of integrity and goodness, qualities she may have overlooked before. No, he wasn't a handsome man, not even a good looking one. But she never expected the attention of a handsome man. If his heart was kind, wasn't that enough?

"Aren't you getting warm in here now? Why don't you take off that heavy coat? We're having a little party here."

"No," she blurted. "No, I'm still cold."

"Let me warm you up." Lou swooped down to press his mouth against hers.

The sudden move took Charlotte by such surprise that she was frozen in shock. Then it dawned on her. *My God, she was actually being kissed!* For years, she'd only imagined the poetic experience of flesh on flesh. And now it was happening to *her.* She'd begun to believe it never would. She ought to discourage him, push him away, but what harm was there in one kiss?

In the cool, blanketing anonymity of night, the spinster analyzed the sensations with studied detachment. His lips felt dry and chapped and tasted of brandy. Yet it wasn't so bad, she decided. As she relaxed more she felt a queer sensation, a tingling, that spread through her bloodstream like the brandy had. It left a fiery sensation in her belly, then, yes, lower in that secret place. Charlotte felt wicked and thrilled that she was experiencing a kiss, a real kiss—at last.

"There now," he murmured with satisfaction, slipping the coat off her shoulders and shifting his body so that he was leaning over her. He smiled at her sweetly. She half smiled in return. "You should wear clothes like this more

often,'' he said, his voice rich with praise. ''Shows you off.
Shows these off.''

His gaze traveled from her shoulders down to her chest.
He encircled her breasts with his hands, weighing their fullness over the stretch of red wool. He sighed lustily.

''Oh, you're big. And it's all you, too. We weren't sure
it could all be you.''

He lowered his mouth to hers again, and she soon discovered how he got the name Fast Hands. Charlotte was
awash in new sensations and asked herself again and again
if she should stop. But surely this was all harmless. She'd
heard the girls in the office talk about this sort of thing all
the time. Why shouldn't she experience this, too?

Suddenly, Lou lifted himself back with a jolt, unbuckling
his belt. As the cold air settled between them, she saw him
fumble with his zipper. Charlotte realized in a snap that
they'd gone too far. She didn't want anything that had to
do with unzipping trousers.

''I think we should stop now,'' she said firmly, pushing
up on her elbows.

''No...no, not yet. We haven't even started having fun
yet.'' The zipper hummed loudly in the darkness.

''I said that's enough.'' Her voice was as crisp and cold
as the night.

''Whoa, baby. Not so fast. You're a wild one, aren't
you? I'm ready for you, though.'' He grabbed hold of her
hand and thrust it against his penis. ''Feel that? Huh? What
d'ya think? I'm as hard as a rock for you, baby. Oh, yeah.
I'm gonna give you a real nice Christmas present.''

She wrestled her hand away from his grasp with a cry
of alarm. Where was the spark of kindness that she thought
she'd detected? How could she have been duped into trusting him against her better judgment. Her dreams had exploded, and Lou Kopp was transformed into some crazed
monster. Evil. Sinful. Fear replaced pleasure in a sudden
rash move. She fought against him, but he wrestled her legs

wide, maneuvering one up onto the seat while the other dangled uselessly to the floor. When his hand moved to slide under the waistband of her panty hose, Charlotte felt doomed.

She screamed but he cut it off with his palm. "I'll bet I'm the first one, right?" When he saw her eyes widen in horror, he laughed. "Thought so. Didn't think a whole lot of guys would be lining up. You got a great body, kid, but I swear, I oughta put a bag on your head."

Tears instantly flooded Charlotte's eyes as she felt a despair deeper and more raw than any caused by a physical blow.

"Don't cry, baby. You're gonna love it." Opening up his pants, he pulled out his erection. It was large and full. When he saw her eyes widen again, he laughed a low, vulgar sound.

Charlotte bit his palm, digging into soft flesh, then threw her head back and screamed as loud as she could. "No!"

He hit her then, hard, stunning her.

"Shut up," he said in an angry growl. "You'd better play along or you'll lose your job. Besides, you're so ugly, you should pay me for it."

Lying there, feeling the tug of fabric roll down her hips, buttocks, then thighs, Charlotte felt detached from her body once again, only this time it was in helpless terror. She flashed back to the time long ago, in kindergarten, when she'd felt the same brutal pulling down of her pants. Now it was happening again, she realized with unspeakable shame. She was lying here, on this smelly car seat in this dirty garage, letting Lou Kopp do it to her all over again.

Something snapped in Charlotte. All the anger and shame that she'd felt lying on the dirt behind the bleachers came back to her in a rush. Fifteen years of remembering that incident, wishing she'd fought harder, screamed louder. Years of anguish from cruel jeers and taunts from boys while she just sat back and took it all, came rushing to her.

Suddenly, in a brilliant flash that lit up her dim dismay, Charlotte remembered the promise she had made herself back behind the bleachers.

She flashed open her eyes to see Lou Kopp lean back, clear his throat and spit into his palm. "There. That'll make it easy."

Consumed with fury, indignation and resolve, she was strong. Charlotte bunched her hand into a fist. "N-o-o-o!" she screamed, and swung up to meet his jaw with a resounding crack.

Lou cried out, falling back, slapping his spit against his jaw. Seizing the moment, Charlotte raised her right leg and with righteous power kicked like a horse, making direct contact with what he'd been so proud of moments before. Lou howled in pain and doubled up.

Not wasting a second, Charlotte yanked open the door with her hand. Pushing hard away, she fell back out of the car, losing her shoes and landing in a heap on the hard, cold pavement. Scrambling to her feet, she yanked up her pants, grabbed her purse and ran, shoeless, toward the stairs. She allowed herself only one quick backward glance at Lou Kopp. He was still moaning and cursing, hunched over in the front seat. A wounded wolf howling at the moon.

Vindication surged through her veins as she raced to the door. *She'd fought back!* No more cowering. No more whimpering. Never again would she allow someone to take advantage of her. She was through feeling sorry for herself.

Running out of the garage to the sidewalk, Charlotte gulped the air and felt invigorated by its crispness. The icy cold burned her chest, cleansing her. It awoke her to the stars that flickered in the sky overhead. Standing in her stocking feet, with her coat and purse dangling at her side, she lifted her face to them.

"I *matter,*" she called out to the stars. Then farther into the heavens, she called out to God. "I do not accept this fate you've given me. I swear by all that is holy that I will find a way to change it. And if you have any mercy at all for me, your lowliest of creations, you will not stop me.'' She took a deep, trembling breath, afraid of the new feelings that rumbled inside her breast, demanding to be heard.

"And if you do try to stop me," she cried, shaking her fist in the sky, "I will defy you!"

Three

---◦◦◦◦◦---

Michael Mondragon paused at the hotel lobby door. The look in that woman's eyes as the elevator door closed stayed with him. As well as that huddled-shoulder stance that he saw so often in women when they were feeling shy or insecure. A gut instinct told him that he should have pressed further, made sure that she was all right. But she had said no. Any more interference would have been seen as aggressive.

Certainly the sour looks from that other man told him to back off. Michael's lips curled. He knew the type: a real sleazebag out for a good time. Another reason why he didn't feel comfortable leaving a seemingly naive girl with him. There was something about her. Not beauty. It was a shame about her chin.... She had lovely, silent-movie-queen eyes that spoke for her. And they spoke eloquently of an innocence that men like that creep preyed on. And that men like him defended.

Michael blew a steady, calming stream of air from his lips, trying to shake off the guilty feeling. She'd said no, he reminded himself. These days women knew their own minds and didn't appreciate unasked-for chivalry.

"No good deed goes unpunished," he muttered, closing the case in his mind and pushing open the glass doors.

He stepped straight into a frigid blast of wind that gusted from Lake Michigan. It took his breath away and whipped his long hair back from his forehead.

"Damn this Chicago weather," he cursed. The Windy City was aptly nicknamed, and this close to the lake, the gusts were strong enough to push along even a man as big as he. He'd never get used to it. Michael hunched his shoulders, turned up his collar and rammed his hands into his pockets before joining those few foolhardy enough to walk the sidewalks this arctic night. He thought of the warm breezes of California and fingered the envelope in his pocket.

Michael quickened his pace to Michigan Avenue where, with luck and a piercing whistle, he might catch a cab. He'd just ducked out of a small wedding reception for a fellow architect at city hall. Frank and his bride seemed so happy, so sure of their decision to spend the rest of their lives together. Their happiness left him feeling hollow, reminding him how empty his own life was. As the wind nagged, another question nagged with even more ferocity.

Michael fingered again the envelope in his coat pocket. He had received the letter from his father early today and carried it with him, rereading it several times. His father hadn't written him more than three letters in his whole life. Most of the letters he'd received were from his mother. Her English was better, and she would kindly include his father's opinions. "Your father and I are proud of your good work at school." "Your father sends you his love." "Your father and I wonder why you don't come home more often."

His father, however, rarely lifted a pen to write a letter. Michael never judged him harshly for it. Truth was, he understood that his father was too exhausted from lifting a shovel all day to even consider lifting a pen into his large worn and callused hands.

He had received his first letter when an essay he'd written on the Constitution was published in the local newspaper. The second when he graduated from the University of California. "A college graduate!" his mother had crooned, her breast as puffed as a hen's. The first ever from his family. Michael's entire extended family had gathered to celebrate the occasion at a noisy fiesta with plenty of singing and laughing. He remembered with chagrin the suspicious glares from the "gringos" neighbors. And now this one. In this third letter, his father, Luis, had called Michael home.

"My hands," he had written in his own hand. "They are bad now. They no do what they must do. And the customers, they are not happy. So many young men come with new ideas. Ha! They know nothing of the soil. Of the plants. But they draw pretty pictures for *los gringos* who know even less nothing than they do.

"I need you *now*," he wrote, underlining *now*. "To help the family. You know how to draw those fancy pictures. You know how to talk the English good. Most of all, you know the soil. I need you. *Tu.* Miguel. My son."

Michael shivered as a cold blast shot down his spine. *Mi padre.* He loved his father. And he missed him. Yet his father was asking him to give up his career as an architect to return to California and the landscape business that his father had started thirty years earlier. Asking him to return to his roots.

Michael closed his eyes against the memories. Roots. The soil. Black dirt under his nails. He ground his teeth. What did he want with roots? He was an architect. He built skyscrapers. *Madre de Dios,* he swore under his breath. He strove higher and higher into the sky. Miles—years—away from the soil. Away from the time he was scurrilously considered just another spic with a shovel. Wasn't that why he'd left California? To sever the roots? To break with the culture that grounded him?

Michael lifted his chin and laughed loudly into the bitter

wind. Fool, he was! Such roots could not be severed. He would return. He knew it. Like poison ivy, the roots of his family were invasive. They dug too deep. No matter how he fought to deny it, he was Mexican. It was his culture, his blood. It was who he was. And, more, he was a Mexican man. *Machismo*. A Mexican male could not be weak or cry about his pain. Machismo required that he honor his father. Machismo demanded that he remember the family.

To remember it all.

The Michigan Avenue office of Dr. Jacob Harmon was as glittering and impressive as his reputation. The waiting room had the cool, smooth elegance of crystal, and as with fine crystal, Charlotte felt afraid to touch anything. But her eyes took in everything: the forced paperwhites in a pine-cone basket, the lovely petit point upholstery, and a pungent, silvery eucalyptus wreath for the holidays. Even the artwork was original, not like the cheap prints and peeling posters on the walls at McNally and Kopp. It made her feel that she'd come to the right place. She held her hands tight against her thighs, not willing to so much as move a single up-to-date magazine in the plastic-protected covering from its precisely ordered line. In the corner, her blue wool coat hung in shabby contrast. It embarrassed her just to look at it.

"Miss Godowski? Come this way, please."

The stunning brunette nurse led her to a small, shell pink examining room to take a thorough medical history. Then she was transferred across the dove gray carpet and left to roost in Dr. Harmon's office. She thought all the glass and shiny chrome was rather cold and hoped it didn't reflect the doctor's personality. Charlotte was exceedingly nervous about the interview. She knew that the doctor's psychological exam was as important as the physical one in determining if she was fit for surgery. And she just *had* to have the surgery....

After what felt an interminable wait, the office door swung open and Dr. Harmon came sweeping into the room with a billowing white coat, followed by another model-perfect nurse. Charlotte's mouth fell open. The doctor appeared more a boy. He was short, small boned, with amazingly smooth skin for a grown man. How old could he be? she wondered. More to the point, how many operations had he done?

Dr. Harmon delivered a quick, piercing look as he passed her, then moved to sit behind the huge desk that only dwarfed him further. The nurse appeared attentive, even fawning, to Dr. Harmon as she presented him with the chart and a coquettish smile. She left without so much as a nod of acknowledgment to Charlotte.

Charlotte's heart began to pound. She slunk far back into the chair and peered out at Dr. Harmon with a guarded expression. He appeared unaware that she was even in the office. He leaned far back in his leather chair and began reading her chart, flicking pages with sharp, quick precision. She thought of a sparrow picking at seed. Good hands for a plastic surgeon, Charlotte decided.

Gradually he lowered the manila chart and raised his gaze. It was as though a searchlight had been flicked on and was scouring every inch of her eyes, her nose, her lips and the awkward line of her deformed jaw. Charlotte didn't feel embarrassed by the scrutiny because Dr. Harmon studied her with the cold focus of a clinician.

Then, as suddenly, his expression changed. The intensity dissipated, and a slight, practiced smile politely took its place on his face. Charlotte sat up. The interview was about to begin.

"Good morning, Miss…" He looked again at the chart. "Godowski."

"Ah, yes. Thank you. Miss Godowski. Your general health seems to be in fine shape. I'll give you a complete exam, but I don't anticipate any worries there." He looked up again at her with a benign expression. "Suppose you tell me, in your own words, how you would like me to help you." Dr. Harmon folded his hands neatly upon the desk and looked at her with a bemused expression.

Looking at his face, a face so baby smooth she wondered if hair ever grew on it, Charlotte was at a loss for words. "I..." She stammered and looked away. "I would think it's obvious."

The doctor only offered that same faint grin in reply.

She clenched her hands tightly in her lap. What could she say that he didn't already see? He cocked his head as a prompt. Taking a deep breath, Charlotte blurted out the truth that hovered at her lips.

"I want to be beautiful."

He furrowed his brows and pursed his lips in concern. "I see," he replied.

Charlotte flushed. Of course he saw, all too clearly, and no doubt he thought she was crazy. She shifted her weight, mortified to have released her innermost secret. "Well maybe," she amended, plucking at her dress with trembling fingers, "maybe just sort of pretty?" She could hear her mother saying, "We'll make her pretty, no?"

Dr. Harmon's expression altered to reveal compassion. "Maybe," he conceded. "In fact, quite possible." Studying her face like an artist would a blank canvas, he continued. "There are changes I could suggest, but I'd like to hear your thoughts first. What specifically would you like to see done?"

Charlotte took a deep breath, blinking. Had she heard right? He hadn't laughed at her. He hadn't said her dream was impossible, rather, he'd said "possible." Did he have any idea how much hope he had just given her? Her heart was pounding wildly in her chest, and it was an effort to keep her mouth moist enough to speak.

"Well...I guess...let's see..." she stammered out. Then, raising her gaze to meet his, she said firmly, "My chin."

"What about your chin?"

"I want one," she said more boldly. "A real one that curves out from the jaw and rounds out under my lips. And now that I mention it, I'd like a jaw, too. One that rolls at a right angle from my neck. A separate entity, not the mountain slope that I have now."

"And the rest? Your nose, your eyes, your cheekbones?"

Charlotte thought a moment. "No," she replied. "God gave me those. They reflect my mother and my father, and I accept those as part of who I am."

"Very good."

He smiled, and Charlotte felt enormously relieved. That was obviously a right answer. She began to relax a bit, unclenching her fingers. She was aware that Dr. Harmon noted in that steel trap of a gaze every movement she made.

"How long have you been unhappy with your chin?"

"Forever. I used to think God shortchanged me on my face."

"Shortchanged? That's an interesting way to put it."

"When I was a little girl, I believed that God made each of us separately, like a sculptor. The rest of me is just fine." She blushed and laughed shortly. "I figured God ran out of time and had to push me through, leaving my chin unfinished." She looked up, relieved to see an amused smile on Dr. Harmon's face. "A child's reasoning, I know," she continued. "But I haven't found another excuse yet. It just feels so…unfair."

She paused, choosing her words. "I'm not looking to change all of me, Doctor," she said in earnest. "I'm just asking you to finish what God started."

Dr. Harmon didn't speak for a moment. He seemed moved by what she had said. At the very least, Charlotte could tell he had listened because his eyes took on that special gleam eyes do when the brain is clicking.

After an interminable silence, he spoke. "I'm pleased to

hear that you do not want me to change everything. That would be unrealistic. What you have is a congenital flaw in your jaw. It's a rare condition, and correction will involve a long, sensitive procedure. The jaw might be cut and repositioned, bone grafts will be considered, and in extreme conditions such as yours, artificial implants are inserted to augment size and thrust of the jaw and chin. Simply moving bone is not enough. And perhaps, follow-up with an orthodontist. It is, however, doable, and frankly, you have come to the right doctor. I specialize in craniofacial surgery."

"I heard that. I also heard that you were the best."

A flicker of satisfaction crossed his face, but he had the grace not to confirm the compliment.

"How does your family feel about the operation?"

"Family?"

He glanced at his chart. "It says here you live with your mother."

"That's right."

"Is there anyone else important to you? A significant other?"

Charlotte sighed. "There's only my mother."

He raised his brows, determined that she would speak.

"I haven't told her yet."

His brows rose higher. "Why not?"

"I don't believe she'll approve."

"Sometimes relatives don't understand how important it can be for someone to have a particular operation. Nonetheless, it is important that you discuss it with her if only to determine the degree of support you can expect."

"I can do this alone."

"Miss Godowski, after any operation there is a physical and psychological stress that may affect both your stamina and mood. That is only natural."

"I'm very fit. I have great stamina."

"By this I mean many people feel blue and down for a

while. You will need some support. I encourage you to talk to your mother. Honestly and frankly.''

Charlotte nodded in compliance. ''I'll try.''

''You will let me know her reaction?''

Charlotte nodded again.

''What if your mother opposes surgery? What will you do?''

Charlotte looked up and met his gaze squarely. ''I will still have the operation.''

Dr. Harmon narrowed his gaze. ''This operation means so much to you?''

''Yes. It means everything.'' She forced herself not to shrink away from his questioning gaze.

''Why?'' he pursued. ''Why now? Usually women who are born with your condition have surgery at least by their adolescence. You are—'' he again checked her chart ''—twenty. What prompted you to seek help now?''

The image of Lou Kopp flashed in her mind. She couldn't tell him that. Definitely not. And if she was honest with herself, Lou Kopp wasn't the only reason why she wanted change. Truth was, he was just the tip of the iceberg, the proverbial last straw.

''I guess it just took me longer to grow up than those other women,'' she replied slowly. Then, thinking of her old dreams, she added, ''I used to believe that beauty was in the eye of the beholder. I had to. If I didn't, I'd have to give up the dream that someday, someone would see beyond this face and love the person I am inside.'' She looked at her shoes and her shoulders slumped. ''I finally figured out no one will give me a chance with this face.''

''By give you a chance you mean…''

''Love me.''

''Ah, I understand.'' Dr. Harmon tapped his fingers together and blew a stream of air through pursed lips. ''And you believe that this operation will make someone love you?''

"No," Charlotte replied, wise to the trap. "I know my face alone won't make someone love me. That's why I said 'chance.' All I want is a chance."

"That's a fair answer. So, in general, would you say that life treats you pretty well?"

She gave another crooked smile. "To be totally honest with you...no. This face hasn't made life easy."

"Have you ever seen a psychiatrist, or any other mental health professional?"

"I'm ugly, not crazy." Charlotte dropped her hands and sighed. "I know you have to ask all these questions, Doctor." She looked up. "But I'm not asking you for some cosmetic repair here, like a nose job or a face-lift. I have a legitimate deformity. You said so yourself. I'm physically well. I exercise, eat well and have no known ailments. I'm a prime candidate. And though my life has been dull, Doctor, it has been stable. There are no skeletons in my closet. I assure you, I am not crazy."

"No one is suggesting that you are. You must realize, however, that a surgery such as this, that can dramatically alter your appearance, will require psychological adjustment, too. It will take time—weeks, perhaps even months—for you to accept your new appearance. You may even experience a personality change."

"I'm not afraid, Doctor. I'm ready for a change. I've waited for twenty years."

Dr. Harmon was listening intently. She could tell by the way he tilted his head and stroked his chin that he was making far more than superficial observations.

"Very well, Miss Godowski," he said, closing her chart. There was no warmth in the gaze he offered, but she hadn't come here for that. Shining in Dr. Jacob Harmon's eyes were the bravado and conceit of a supreme surgeon who had made a decision, who knew he could get the job done—and done better than anyone else. Charlotte sat straighter in her chair. Her excitement could barely be contained. She sensed that he meant to do the operation.

"One more question, Miss Godowski, and we'll be done. Tell me. Do you believe that this surgery will change your life?"

She raised her gaze to his and told him exactly what he wanted to hear. "I don't believe surgery will change my life. But it will make it better."

Dr. Harmon allowed himself a smile then and she knew she'd passed the exam. When his smile broadened and his eyes twinkled, she knew she'd scored an A.

"Well then," he replied, laying down his pencil and sitting up in his chair. "In that case, I don't see why we can't proceed."

Jacob Harmon swiveled in his Eames chair while pouring over the computer images he had designed for Charlotte's face. On the table beside him dozens of photographs of her face and body that he'd shot over the past week lay in scattered piles, along with X-rays, dental models and other diagnostic studies. He magnified the computer images and traveled the hills and valleys of her cheekbones to the gaping nostril hollows, then north to large blue lakes of eyes and the broadening plains of the brow. The doctor punched in coordinates and brought the whole face back again to gain better perspective of his new jawline design, the resulting curve of her lips and the triumph of her delicately curved chin.

Charlotte was a most challenging case. Her body... Remembering it now still gave him pause. If he had not known better he'd have sworn she'd been well worked over by teams of surgeons to achieve such perfection. It had everything. Symmetry, proportion, smoothness, color. Even her skin was perfect, like polished alabaster.

Still, she had something more that compelled him toward absolute perfection. She possessed an ethereal quality that brought her beyond mere mortal beauty. Charlotte's eyes—they mesmerized him. Past her veil of shyness, Charlotte's eyes held mystery.

Jacob returned to his sketches with renewed vigor. His fingers itched to work. Surgically, Jacob knew what had to be done. He'd reached the point where the physician's work ended and the artist's work took over. Crossing this line was what made his work poetry and so many other surgeons' efforts merely adequate. He chuckled to himself, delighted at the concept of himself as an obsessed artist at work on his masterpiece.

For that was what she would be—his masterpiece. He knew that body image was a view of the body through the mind's eye. But this girl wanted to be beautiful. And he would make her more beautiful than even she had dreamed possible.

Charlotte's visit with Mr. McNally a week later was quick and businesslike. As she coolly told her former employer the reason why she was quitting her job, she watched McNally's usually ruddy face pale and pinch. As she stammered out the sordid details, his lips thinned and his eyes narrowed in silent fury. At the end of the discussion, Mr. McNally did not call in Lou Kopp, as she had worried he would. He calmly assured her that she would be spared any further discomfort, then asked if she'd like a cab home.

As soon as Charlotte left, Mr. McNally hurried to his phone and dialed his lawyer.

"George, Kopp has been at it again. I had some girl in my office threatening to sue for sexual harassment."

There was a long, rumbling sigh on the other end of the line. "What did he do this time?"

McNally briefly recounted the events, including the job threat.

"I think it would be better if we settled this one

quickly," the lawyer advised in a somber tone. "The other one may still go to trial."

Charlotte was delighted later that the amount offered for settlement was enough to cover the cost of her operation. Charlotte's lawyer had suggested more, but Charlotte wasn't greedy. In fact, she was so relieved by the amount that she had to stop herself from thanking Mr. McNally.

"I only want one assurance," she said as they shook hands.

McNally raised his brow.

"I want assurance that Mr. Kopp won't do this to someone else. He's plagued the women in that office for years."

"I think we can take care of that."

That was enough; she was not out for blood. Although she did break out in a grin when, a few months later, she learned that Mr. Kopp had left the company for "personal" reasons.

Four

❧❧

On Christmas Eve, Michael Mondragon eased his rented Mustang convertible onto Interstate 5, stretched his arm over the car seat and began whistling along with the Christmas melodies playing on the radio. He had to admit, Christmas Eve was always best when spent with family. And he'd be home in time for Mama's Christmas Eve dinner.

As he pushed beyond the gray tentacles of Los Angeles into the vertical green of the mountains and valleys that surrounded his home, he felt the long trip's tension slide off his shoulders like rocky boulders. Chicago seemed a million miles away. An hour's drive out, he turned off the main road to an obscure side road, barely fit for travelers. Those with money and sense kept to the main road that led to plush resorts and well maintained camping grounds. Only the adventurous few ventured along these roads that wound past small townships and farms and through forests of white fir, cedar and piñon, ponderosa and Jeffrey pines. He knew the names of all the trees and vegetation. It was, after all, the family business.

The road angled sharply, then dipped lower as he entered the familiar lushness of the valley he called home. It had rained recently; the road was slick and black sage lent a purple hue to a whole mountainside. The rain-scented wind stung his face and he could taste its sweetness. Michael drove steadily down the same road that, years ago, he'd driven trucks along from the Mondragon nursery to the yards of California suburbia.

Memories passed through his mind like mile markers as he drove by familiar landmarks of his youth. At a favorite lookout point, Michael slowed to a stop and turned off the engine. Dusk was setting in; the birds were calling. From his high vantage point, the valley lay spread before him as open and lush as a willing woman. He breathed in deeply, his chest expanding. Damn, but she smelled sweet, too.

Deep in the valley, the dark vegetation reached up to the sky, as though to grab the pale evening clouds that hovered low. "The hems of the angels," he'd called them as a child. Michael had always felt that at this languid hour, at this mystical spot, he was within reach of heaven.

He sighed, running his hand through his thick hair. So many old memories stirred. It was here that he first found love in the cab of a Mondragon truck. Here that he'd made his decision to defy his family and take the Harvard scholarship. Here that he'd sworn that someday he'd leave these mountains and never return.

And he did leave. His life in Chicago was more than the few thousand miles away from his Mexican-American family. It was a world apart. Yet there lay the irony. Why was it, he wondered, that no matter how far he traveled or how much he changed, when he returned home he slipped back into old, familiar patterns? Like following a bad script of an even worse play. He knew that when he drove through the Mondragon gates, he would no longer be Mr. Michael Mondragon who'd graduated magna cum laude from Harvard, who'd earned a hard-fought-for position at a well connected architectural firm in Chicago, who'd billed more in one year than his father dreamed of billing in a decade. No, in a few moments more he would be poor little Miguel, the brooding outcast who'd dared to leave the family fold.

His large, manicured hands molded over the gearshift, tightening in resolve. He'd worked too hard, come too far, to play any more roles. When he saw his father, mother, sister and brother, he would make them see, this time, who he was. Now. Michael took a last look at the fading sunset, then shook his head as a bittersweet smile hovered at his lips.

He might as well try to catch the hem of the angels.

Once he passed the borders of his father's property, he saw visible signs that the business had taken a bad turn. The outbuildings were slipping down, the stock was sparse and what was left didn't have the luster and vigor that Mondragon plants were known for. His brow knit, but he traveled without pause past the hilly slopes of viburnum, euonymous and evergreens to the small stucco house with the red tile roof a hundred yards beyond. His father's 1989 Chevy pickup was parked in front beside a few newer, full-size American cars. He recognized his sister's wedding garter hanging from her Mercury's rearview mirror.

The house looked pretty much as it always did. Mama's bright yellow front door was trimmed with fresh pine boughs and holly, and behind Mama's lace curtains, the lights were blazing and Papa was playing mariachi music. His heart skipped with anticipation—no, he had to admit, eagerness. No sooner had he pulled the car to a stop than the front door of the house flung open and his father stepped forward, both arms stretched wide and a toothy grin on his weathered face. Michael felt childishly pleased knowing that they'd been on the lookout for him.

"He's home!" Luis boomed, his voice like thunder in the valley. "Everyone. Come out. Miguel, he is home at last!"

Behind him came the high-pitched welcomes of his mother and his sister, Rosa, and behind them, Rosa's children. More slowly, his brother Bobby sauntered forward.

As he embraced them one by one, he could smell the heady scent of a Mexican Christmas on their clothes, in their hair and lingering in their kisses. Dark chocolate, vanilla and oranges.

Once inside, he was tempted to walk around the family home, to peek into bedrooms and closets, to see if he still had a room. He felt nervous. Out of place. The family clustered around him, however, chatting amiably, reminiscing over events that were far sweeter in memory. After a few minutes the conversation slowed, but this was to be expected. After all, it'd been several years since he'd been home. His ear was quick to pick up the soft, intimate sounds of Spanish, the language of his family. Michael could feel his tongue stumble around the vowels and consonants as he struggled with his broken replies.

"Little Francisco speaks better Spanish than his uncle Miguel," his mother teased. Michael felt his heart lurch but only smiled. This was an old stalemate that had begun when Michael, the only Mexican in his suburban first grade class, announced one night at family dinner that he would only speak English as the nuns had instructed him to. His mother, hurt and confused, had ceased her fluid flow of Spanish and met his announcement with obedience. "If the nuns said so…"

His father had responded typically, exploding in anger and casting him off to his room, where Michael preferred to be, anyway. It was the beginning of the unraveling of his ties to his family. The first step in the distance he was to create between them.

Tonight there was no criticism in Luis's eyes, however. He beamed at his youngest son.

"Rosa," Luis boomed to his daughter. "Settle your children. I want to talk to Miguel alone for a moment," he called out, then guided Michael to the large family kitchen. Closing the door, he paused and sighed a bit theatrically. "Ah, some peace and quiet, eh? If I could harness the energy of those bebés, I could live forever! But—" he shrugged with his whole body, arms and palms lifting upward "—I'll settle for a small glass of beer."

"Ah, Mama," Michael said, accepting a bottle and sniffing the air. The familiar scents of Mexican cooking, mingled with the sounds of children laughing and grown-ups talking in Spanish in the room next door, was like a soothing balm, restoring his sense of place. He was home. It didn't matter so much that there was little to say. "Smells like heaven."

Marta said nothing, but her skin flushed with pleasure as she hovered over the huge stove covered with simmering pots. He and his father leaned against the wood counter in the delicious-smelling room, arms crossed, bottles held in fists as they began the awkward conversation that always followed months of separation.

"So," Luis began. It was more a clearing of the throat. "How are you?"

"Fine…fine," Michael responded slowly. He hoped he didn't sound cautious, and took a long swallow of beer. "Real good."

"What you doing in Chicago?"

He shrugged. "Same old, same old. Mayor Daley wants more trees planted, so when we finish a building, we plant him more trees." Father and son exchanged glasses over their bottles and shared a mutual laugh.

"Glad to see you're still planting something."

They tried hard to maneuver their conversation into friendly territory, and the occasional quips Marta offered as she stirred at the stove helped. Yet it was clear to Michael that his father was pining to talk plainly but didn't want to push his son hard the moment he stepped in the door. Luis was a tall, big-fisted and broad-shouldered man with a voice to match. Seeing him stutter over inanities was like watching a bull stumble in a china shop. Michael decided to make it easier for him.

"The nursery looks hard hit," he opened, going straight to the point.

Luis's face revealed surprise, immediately followed by relief. He began to nod his burly head widely. "Yes, yes, exactly!" he boomed, stretching out his arm in agreement. "The drought last year, aieee! We lost so much, and what is left—" he shook his hands to the heavens "—it's not fit to live. Son of a bitch drought. Grass burn like hell, and the people call and say, 'No cut.' When we no cut they no pay. Do they care? No! 'No cut' is all they say." He shook his head. "So much dies."

"I heard it was bad. I'm sorry you were so hard hit."

Luis shrugged. "Will of God, no?"

"Perhaps…" He took a long swallow of beer, avoiding a religious debate. In the Mondragon household, life's twists and turns were all part of God's infinite plan. To be endured. "How is Manuel doing?" Michael didn't know his brother-in-law very well. He seemed a decent sort of fellow, but the man would have to be a saint to live with his hot-tempered sister, Rosa.

His father shrugged noncommittally. "He does okay cutting the lawns. The men they like him, but…" Luis rubbed his jaw. "It's not just drought. He no can draw the land pictures like the people want now. They want something special, you know? And if you can draw the pictures, you can sell stock, too. Draw for free sometimes, just to get the job."

"I know what you mean, Papa. It's common now. Why didn't you hire someone? A designer?"

"Why I go hire someone when my son is best there is?"

Michael's sigh rumbled in his chest. "Perhaps because I'm an architect in Chicago? Papa, I build skyscrapers. High in the sky." He ground his teeth and said softly, "I don't dig in the earth anymore."

"*Madre de Dios.* How can you like working away from the soil? What you want to play with concrete blocks for in Chicago when you can have all this fine California earth? This precious land. I ask you!"

Michael heard the pleading hidden in the boisterous exclamation and it broke his heart. His father was a proud man, raised harshly as an orphan by his relatives in Mexico. At twenty-two he brought his family to America because a bachelor uncle had died and left a small piece of California land to his only living nephew. From the moment he'd seen the fertile valley, Luis Mondragon's life had had purpose. He'd turned a deaf ear to the many lucrative offers for the land and held on tight to his future—a risky move for a poor Mexican with three hungry children.

When he'd saved enough money, Luis had moved his ragtag family to the suburbs and established a modest lawn maintenance company. He slaved in suburban yards from dawn till sundown seven days a week, like a huge bull in the harness. Luis hated the suburbs, but Marta had wanted the good "gringo" schools where the nuns would teach her children the same things as white children. Besides, what could he do? The suburbs was where the money was. The people liked his wit and strong back, and his business thrived. When the boys grew older they helped run the mowers and hedge clippers, working for a pittance.

Though his father may have been cheap with a dollar, he was very generous with his knowledge. Like his precious nursery, he nurtured his boys, teaching Roberto and Miguel about the soil, stock and the family secrets for a vigorous plant. Every spare penny earned went back to the land. When at last he could begin a nursery, he sold only a few select plants, just the ones his customers were likely to buy. Then, slowly, with his twinkling eyes and infectious laughter, he teased his customers to "try something a little bit different, no?" Plant by plant, Luis built the reputation of the Mondragon nursery, and Michael knew it had to break the old man's heart to see a lifetime of struggle strangled by heat, drought and competition. Looking at his face now, he saw how the drought had coursed new crevices in his father's handsome face as well.

"What would you have me do, Papa?" he asked simply.

His father searched his face, then relaxed with a satisfied, proud grin. "Ah, Miguel. You are a true son to me. *Sí!* I see so much of me in you."

Michael stepped back from the bear hug, rebelling against the comparison. He wasn't like his father. Not at all. "Papa..."

"You see, Marta?" Luis interrupted, tightening his possessive arm around Michael's shoulders. The force of his will flowed through him. "I told you my son would help me. I have *one* good son."

Michael met his mother's gaze over his father's head.

"No, Luis," she replied somberly. "You have *two* good sons."

When the feast was prepared, the family gathered around the long, dark wood table while Marta served the family favorites with pride. Ceviche, roast leg of pork in adobe sauce, corn pudding and green rice. For dessert, Marta insisted on no less than four cakes with fresh strawberries and cream.

"Sit down now, Marta," bellowed Luis. "Enough! You run like a rabbit. It makes me tired just to watch. Sit! It is time to eat."

Clucking her tongue while scanning the table for any missing salt shakers, butter or salsa, Marta reluctantly took her seat beside Luis.

While Luis led the family in prayer, Michael studied the faces collected at the table. His family reflected Mexico's rich and diverse history. His father was still a virile, handsome man. Tall, with dark hair boldly streaked with gray and heavy, bushy brows. His mother, Marta, had skin as fair and glowing as the Madonna in the May holy card pictures she adored. Her brown and gray hair, rolled smoothly back into a bun, accentuated the delicate, patrician features that reflected her Spanish descent.

His brother, Bobby, was the most like her. His hair was as blond as hers once was, his skin as light and his frame as delicate. His cocky smile carved deep dimples into a face already over-blessed with good looks. His sister, Rosa, was also fair. But to her lifelong dismay, she was tall and wide in the shoulders, like himself and their father, a large woman able to lift heavy machinery and do a man's day of work. Luis had often complained bitterly to Marta that she had somehow gotten the genes between Bobby and Rosa mixed up.

Michael grew up knowing that of all the family, his features were the most Indian-like. Unusually tall, like his father, his skin was the darkest, his hair the coarsest and his face as severely chiseled as any Mayan statue. Of the three Mondragon children, only he'd been given a nasty push from behind by the local suburban boys after school.

"We do not come together every Christmas," began Luis, his dark eyes gleaming white against terra cotta skin as he stood at the table, a glass of wine held in a toast. "We are together—as a family should be." His gaze scanned the family, one by one, settling firmly on Michael. *"A la familia!"*

"To the family!" Michael replied in English, covertly catching Bobby's amused glance.

"You look good," Bobby said later, his eyes openly appreciating Michael's black jacket, crisp white shirt and knitted silk tie. Bobby had always been the sharp dresser and used to chide Michael pitilessly while growing up. "Armani, huh? Where are the worn jeans, the mismatched socks, and God...remember the leather jacket?"

"Of course," he replied with a wistful smile. "Wish I still had it."

When he was young he'd always worn a shirt, even in the summer, so his already dark skin wouldn't darken more.

He could still remember how hot and sweaty he got working in the yards, covered up, while watching pale-skinned boys run and play in cool T-shirts. He'd saved every penny he earned, not buying a candy or seeing a movie, in order to buy himself that leather jacket, and it had become a second skin.

"Man, I loved that jacket."

"Maybe, but that one's not too shabby. *Los gringos* in Chicago finally taught you how to dress?"

Michael smiled, refusing to rise to the bait. Truth was, clothes didn't matter to him in the least. As long as it was well cut and black, he was satisfied. What mattered to him was how pale and thin his brother looked. Bobby's clothes hung from him as limply as from a wire hanger.

"You feeling all right, big brother?" Michael leaned over and asked, concern in his lowered voice.

A shadow flickered in Bobby's eyes, then, as quickly, disappeared. "The flu," he replied with a casual smile. His gaze darted to his mother. "It's been going around."

"*Sí*, it is terrible," Marta exclaimed. "Everybody is getting it. One of those terrible new bugs. From China." She crossed herself. "Be careful, Miguel, you don't get it, too."

"Ha!" Bobby barked out a laugh.

Luis glared at him, his spoon halted before his tightly closed lips. Bobby's smile quickly vanished and he seemed to withdraw inwardly.

After the four cakes were served and the coffee was poured, the family gathered around the tree, as they did every Christmas Eve, to hand out a few special "parent-child" gifts.

"Bobby, you are eldest. You be Santa's helper," ordered Luis.

"Glad to, Papa," Bobby replied with enthusiasm.

Michael watched with affection as his elder brother donned a red Santa's cap and let loose a hearty round of "ho-ho-ho's" before handing out the gifts. Although he made a pitifully thin Santa, Bobby was not above playing up the part for the sake of his niece and nephew. The children squealed with delight.

"Enough! Don't be a fool, horsing around," Luis barked.

Bobby's shoulders drew back, but he smiled urbanely and tilted his head. "God bless us, everyone," he said, with sarcasm in his voice that Michael knew disguised his hurt. "Even you, old Scrooge."

Luis grumbled as he shifted in his seat.

Bobby pressed on with enthusiasm, shaking the children's gifts and making them guess. Everyone, save Luis, laughed and clapped as the children unwrapped their treasures. Instead, he sat with a bemused expression, watching as a king would his subjects.

Later, when the children were playing with their toys, the adults cast surreptitious glances at the remaining few packages under the tree. Just as when they were children, they wondered what gifts their parents had selected for them this year.

An awed hush fell in the room when Bobby opened his wrapping to find their great-uncle's pocket watch nestled inside, the same revered uncle who'd left Luis the prime California land. Rosa and Manuel were equally surprised and delighted with the set of china that had been in Marta's family for generations. Eyes were wide. These were not the usual token gifts: a camera, perhaps a new sweater. Tonight their parents had passed on the few family treasures they possessed. Now all eyes turned to Michael. Bobby searched under the tree but there was nothing left. Michael lifted his brows.

"Poor Tío Miguel didn't get a gift," said Maria Elena, wrapping a small, thin arm around his shoulders in consolation.

"I guess I was a bad boy," he quipped, giving Maria

Elena a hug. He smiled, but inside felt a sharp pang of disappointment.

At that Luis rose with great ceremony and walked before the fireplace. From the mantel he took an envelope, and after a dramatic pause, he delivered it to Michael with an expression of enormous pride.

Michael searched his father's face for some clue, then quickly darted to the faces of Bobby, Rosa and Manuel. Their expressions were curious…guarded. Apparently no one knew what the envelope contained.

With a nod of gratitude he took the envelope from his father's hands, opened it and read the legal documents enclosed. The color drained from his face.

"This is a promissory note."

"I am a man of my word. I ask you to come to California to help and you came. He came!" Luis exclaimed to the others, turning his head to meet their gazes. "He has proved himself a son and now he will prove himself a Mondragon. He will rebuild the family honor in this valley. Michael will draw the designs, we will start again, as a family. I know this and it brings my old heart great joy to see."

He moved closer, placing his hand upon the shoulder of his seated son with as much pride and dignity as any king would place a sword upon the shoulder of his champion knight. "I promise to you the land, the business, everything! In you I place the future of the Mondragon name."

The burden of the honor was heavy on Michael's shoulders. Unwelcome, unspoken promises were tied up with this promissory note: A promise of loyalty, of continuance. A promise to marry, to settle on the land, to produce an heir. Looking into his father's eyes, he saw Luis's determination to collect each promise.

"Father, how can you do this?" cried Rosa. She was the first to break the stunned silence and her bitterness rang clear. "Manuel and I, we've slaved for you all these years. Years that Miguel was away. We always understood…"

"Understood what, *querida?*" asked Luis, his voice strained in warning. Slowly he turned toward his only daughter, his back to Manuel. He was smiling but his eyes flashed. "You will always be part of the business. But *your* name is not Mondragon. Your son's name is not Mondragon. *This* is what is understood."

Rosa flushed as bright as a poinsettia, and she cast a furious glance at her husband. "Speak up, Manuel. Why must you always sit there like a beaten dog and let me fight your battles?"

Manuel flushed and his jaw set, forcing his lips into a tight line. Without a word, he rose and hurried from the room.

"What about you, Roberto?" she charged, turning to face her elder brother.

Bobby paled but managed to raised his glass to his lips with an urbane shrug. "It's Papa's land to do with what he wants. And—" he paused, taking a sip "—Papa wants to give it to Michael."

"You are the eldest son! It should be yours!"

Michael saw pain flash in Bobby's eyes, but it quickly was doused with wine. "I paint murals, Rosa. What would I do with a landscape business?"

"Enough, all of you," Michael said, standing in the middle of the tightening circle, unaware that he'd just sounded exactly like Luis. He silenced Rosa with a sharp glance, then turned to his father. Looking him in the eye, he handed back the papers. "Papa, this is a great honor." He paused. "Too great an honor."

"You are *fuerte,* no?" Luis replied, pushing back the papers. "Strong. In heart and character." He patted his son firmly on the back, and it shamed Michael to feel such joy in his father's pride. "You will not turn your back on me. You will help the family, no?"

"Help, yes. You need me, that's true. And I'll do what I can. But I didn't ask for all this in return."

"Ask? Miguel, I give you everything. The lawn maintenance company, the nursery, the spring, everything! I give you freedom. Your own place makes you your own man. Nobody to tell you what to do, to make you feel small. With this a man with skills such as yours could be rich."

He exaggerated, but to some extent, Michael knew it was true. The land was very valuable now, and the springwater could be tapped for untold amounts. He was humbled by the enormity of the gift. But at what price?

"*Gracias,* Papa. Truly. However, I need time to think this through."

"Think? Think?" Luis's eyes were wide with shame and embarrassment that his most precious gift was refused. He swung his hand down like a machete. "You always need to think. Sometimes you think so much you don't see with your heart. It turns to stone."

Father and son stared at each other across a familiar impasse. It was always this way between them. Hot temper versus cool stone. Luis abruptly turned toward the Christmas tree. The lights were flashing green and red against the white and black of his father's hair. His eyes were mournful. Michael thought he looked like a great bull that had just received the sword.

"Papa." Michael moved to speak.

Luis cut him off with a backward wave of his hand. He glanced sharply at Marta. She stood quietly with her small hands clasped meekly before her apron, her eyes cast downward. Then, with a shrug of his wide shoulders, he turned and stomped from the room.

"So, you think this is fair, little brother?" Rosa said, her sharp voice breaking the brittle silence. "Is this why you came home? To get it all?"

"Rosa!" Marta exclaimed, horrified.

Michael, saddened and insulted by her bald-faced resentment, met her sharp gaze evenly. She was hurt, he knew this, and she was very angry to be ignored by her father. Poor Rosa, she would never be happy filling the traditional female role in their culture, despite their mother's determination. She was too bold, too smart. She deserved better treatment than this. But so did he.

"First off," he began, his voice low, trembling with control, "I only came home because our father asked it of me. Second, I don't want any of this." His hand angrily slashed the air. "And if you'd listen instead of shout, you'd have heard me turn it down. Third, and pay good attention, *hermana.* If you paid half your mind to building up that husband of yours instead of tearing him down, perhaps Manuel *would* be able to take over the operation.

"As it stands, Papa is right. I *am* the only one in this family who can rebuild this nursery, and if you'd quiet your waspish tongue long enough to consider it, you'd realize it's true. I didn't come here to take anything from anybody. I came here to help my family. And I intend to honor that promise. But when I'm done, I'm out of here. It's clear nothing has changed. I'm still 'pobre negrito' in your eyes. Undeserving. But I've learned something in that wide world out there. I deserve everything I work hard for."

He scanned the faces of his family. They were flustered and silent. Then he followed his father out to the front porch.

He found Luis standing, one foot before the other, leaning against the porch railing. His eyes stared out at the dark, swelling earth of his beloved nursery. Michael knew it must seem to the old man that in rejecting the land he rejected him. Was it true? he wondered, gazing at the fertile property stretched out before him. Was he rejecting his father or the land?

"I will give you one year," he said aloud. "This I will do out of love for you and my mother."

"One year is not enough. We cannot rebuild in that time. Two. I need two. We can do much in that time."

Michael set his jaw, realizing that a two-year leave would jeopardize all he'd worked for. Yet his father was right. Two years would be enough time to begin again.

"Agreed," he replied. "If you promise not to hound me about my decision. After that—" he placed the papers firmly back into his father's hand "—we will talk again."

His father turned his head and studied Michael, staring intensely into his eyes, as though to catch a loophole. Whatever he found must have satisfied him because he nodded, squinting, and at last accepted back the papers.

"Starting when?"

"March. In time to complete orders for the spring."

"Not soon enough! I begin in two weeks."

"Mail me the materials. I'll do it from Chicago."

A loud, boisterous laugh burst from Luis's lips and he wrapped his arm around his son's shoulder, squeezing possessively. "How can I lose?" he asked in a voice gruff with emotion. "I know my land. She is like a fine, fat woman. All fertile and sweet smelling. You will plant your seeds in her and she will make you hers. See? I know you, too. You are my son. You are machismo. You will never turn your back on her that you love most."

In Chicago, Ascension Church was ablaze in light and song as the jubilant congregation celebrated midnight mass. Though it was packed to the rafters, Charlotte and Helena sat in the reserved section near the altar, a boon for spending the day decorating the church. Charlotte looked with a proprietary air at the yards of crisp white linen trimmed in green embroidery, the six handsome balsams twinkling in white lights, and clustered around them the scores of fresh red and white poinsettias.

"Beautiful," Charlotte sighed.

Father Frank offered them a wink of approval from the altar.

Charlotte's heart was filled with thoughts of beauty this Christmas. Dr. Harmon had presented his final plan and, though she was shaken, the composite of her new face was so beautiful he could have wrapped and tied it up with a bow as a gift.

She'd stared at the sketches. "I can't believe that will be me," she'd said, breathless.

"Believe it. I can make it happen."

"But the nose. You've changed it. It isn't mine."

"It will be," he replied, persistent.

"I don't know. My mother, she won't like to see me so changed."

"How do *you* like it, Miss Godowski?"

Her gaze lingered on the beautiful curve of the jaw. "I love it." She then slipped a piece of paper over the face so only the eyes were left showing. "Is it still me?"

"Of course it is. And how clever of you to look at the eyes, Charlotte. That, my dear, reveals the real you."

I wonder, she thought to herself. Yet, she had agreed to the design, refraining from telling her mother about the nose. Her new face was her gift to herself. Her gift to her mother was her new job. Dr. Harmon had kindly offered her the position of accountant for his practice at a handsome salary. Now her mother wouldn't have to worry about the money coming in. She'd surprise her mother with the news when they broke the fast after mass tonight.

When the choir began singing "Joy to the World," Charlotte joined in, singing loudly, joyfully—meaning every word. Her world was beautiful, full of joy and hope. How could her heart contain such happiness?

Five

❦

Three months later, Dr. Harmon methodically removed the bandages that wrapped Charlotte's head while she lay motionless upon the hospital bed. Like a high priest and a mummy, she thought, staring out from an open patch. A mummy come back to life. Three men and a woman in their late twenties, cloaked in white jackets and clutching clipboards, all inched closer, their eyes focused on her face. They were residents in cosmetic surgery, Dr. Harmon had told her. Her case was particularly interesting, and over the past few weeks, they'd stopped by frequently to check her vitals, ask the same questions and read over her chart. Dr. Harmon allowed no one but himself to direct this case. Charlotte sensed from the residents and nurses that he'd taken an especially keen interest in her case, and within the walls of Six West, where Dr. Harmon ruled, she felt like a queen.

Two weeks had passed since her operation, weeks of desperate arguments with her mother as to whether she had made the right decision, a moral decision. Weeks of praying that the operation would be a success while beating her breast in worry if she even had a right to pray, now that she'd "defied God's will," as her mother claimed. Charlotte felt again the prickly surge of resentment. She was *not* her mother's sacrificial lamb. How easy for her mother to condemn her decision, to pity her ugliness. Helena had a pretty face.

Charlotte didn't blame her mother, however. Charlotte was simply past the point of being able to accept her ugliness as God's will. To her mind, God gave her this life and it was up to her to make the best of it. Whatever it took.

Well, she thought, tapping her foot against the bed's cool metal rail in a dance of anxiety. This was the moment of truth. There would be no more waiting. As the bandages were unwound and gathered from around her head, she could smell the oddly sweet, pungent odor of dried blood and her stitches. Loosened from the constraints, her jaw throbbed, the nerve endings tingled. Within, her heart pounded with anticipation.

"Just a few more..." muttered Dr. Harmon. The seconds seemed an eternity as his delicate fingers twisted and unwrapped the bandages.

When at last the final layer was removed, Charlotte's face felt tingly and raw, exposed to the elements. Dr. Harmon examined her, touching her face with confidence. It stung where his fingers met skin. When he was done he cradled her head in his nimble hands and studied her with his pale, piercing eyes. Time seemed to stand still as she searched his face, his eyes, for some sign of his approval or distress. But his face remained impassive.

"Are you ready?" he asked at length. His tone was fatherly.

She couldn't speak. Very gingerly she brought her fingers to her jaw and palpated the soft flesh. It felt squishy and swollen, like a partially deflated balloon. Yet even in its fullness she detected the unmistakable curve of a jaw and, traveling farther forward, a jutting of bone that could only be a chin.

She glanced at her mother, gauging her reaction. Helena

was peering down, her eyes squinting and her mouth working silently. She looked appalled.

Charlotte swallowed hard. Her throat was as dry as a desert.

"Mirror?" Dr. Harmon asked a nurse.

Charlotte tried to smile, but she couldn't manipulate her swollen face. Then she took a deep breath. It took a Herculean effort just to sit up. The room spun and nausea rose up her throat, but she fought it back down, determined to sit. In an odd way, she felt as though she were about to meet someone new. Someone important.

"Now, remember that you will still see swelling and some bruising. That will be with you for quite a while, but gradually your face will appear normal."

She felt alarmed. He sounded very tense. Had something gone wrong? She tried to speak, but the incisions inside of her mouth and the swelling made it hard to move her lips. "Normal?" she mumbled.

A resident piped in. "He filled it in nicely, but it's so early yet."

"What do I look like?"

"Why don't you see for yourself." Dr. Harmon handed Charlotte the mirror.

Charlotte held the mirror in her hands for a long moment, gathering her courage. Then she manipulated the glass, peeking first at her forehead and eyes, old friends that remained unchanged. Then slowly, hesitatingly, she tilted the mirror.

"Charlotte?" Dr. Harmon moved closer. "Are you all right?"

No, she wasn't all right! She was afraid. Terrified. Charlotte set down the mirror with agonizing slowness and laid back upon the bed in degrees, closing her eyes. The world was spiraling. She felt as though her spirit had risen from her body and floated in the air, into some other dimension, like some people described near-death experiences. Hadn't she died in a way? Wasn't she some wandering spirit?

For there was no doubt, the Charlotte she had been was no more.

Helena huddled beside her daughter's bed, her fingers speeding over the rosary beads and her lips moving silently in prayer. The hour was late; the lights were lowered to a dim green in the small, bare hospital room. Someone was moaning in the next room, a low keening sound that failed to arouse the nurses, who were busy preparing for the eleven o'clock shift change. They made eerie shadows on the wall as they passed the door. Throughout Six West there was an uneasy loneliness in the night quiet. Patients and nurses alike shared an unspoken understanding. Everyone was simply trying to get through the night.

Helena shivered and returned to her prayers. She hated hospitals, would rather die in the streets than return to one. Outside the room a pair of nurses were discussing Charlotte's case: bandages off today...swelling normal... Percodan for pain on demand. After the medical report, the tone lowered to personal mumbles. Helena's mouth twisted in annoyance. No doubt they were nattering about Charlotte's transformation. Everyone on the floor was talking about it.

Helena shifted her weight, showing the nurses her back, and brought her face within inches of Charlotte's. Where was her daughter with this new face? She bunched her fist. Who had the right to change it? Certainly not that pompous Dr. Harmon. Guilt rose up like a wave as she recalled her consultation with the doctor prior to surgery. Helena winced, recalling his barely concealed fury.

"Why haven't you pursued surgery for Charlotte before now?" he had asked her, his eyes glaring and his tone bordering on an accusation. "These techniques are not new. Certainly she could have avoided years of—" He waved his hand, searching for a word that could possibly describe what Charlotte had endured. No word sufficed. He set his mouth in a grim line.

She replied with the usual simpered excuses: no money, no insurance, ignorance. Dr. Harmon had shook his head with pity.

"True, yes, it was all true," Helena told the sleeping Charlotte, clutching the thin mint green hospital blanket. Helena's reserve crumbled and she lowered her head upon her daughter's hand. How effective these little truths were in obscuring the one big Truth. So much more effective than lies. But God knew, she scolded herself, beating her breast. God knew that she was a sinner. And the scourge for her sin had passed on to her daughter.

"The sin was mine, Lord, not hers," she prayed. "The blame belongs to me. Perhaps I should have told her. But how?" Her thin fingers, worn dry and brittle by cleaning solvents, spread out to cover her eyes as she wept. "My sin...my sin..." she mumbled. "Mine and Frederic's, so long ago."

The first moment Helena saw Frederic Walenski, she knew she loved him. At twenty-six, unmarried and isolated on her family's farm, her prospects were slim. Life was hard in the late 1960s in Poland. Food prices were rising and salaries were falling. The economy was in an uproar. Helena remembered those years as a time when they struggled just to keep their livestock and family fed.

Her village sat at the edge of the Carpathian Mountain range, and on weekends young men and women from the cities would flock to the mountains to hike. Helena wasn't flirtatious, nor did she seek out the attention of the young men who strolled through the village. This Frederic, however, was different. He was more stocky than tall, with thick blond hair and large, insolent eyes. He had a bearing that bordered on haughtiness, that spoke to her of the city, of privilege and of a worldliness unknown in her provincial town. She spotted him while he hovered with his friends over a map, backpacks tilting from their shoulders. While the others pointed and argued what route to take, this handsome man glanced her way. Helena, shocked by her own boldness, didn't avert her eyes. He returned a knowing glance and a slow, simmering smile. Her blood roiled. She felt a rush like she'd only read about in books.

Falling in love was easy in the mountains. The air high up was thin and sweet, far from the haze of industrial smoke and revolutionary politics that hovered over the cities. Every weekend Frederic returned to court her, and eventually, Helena did not refuse his kisses. Frederic was so different from anyone she had ever met. Unlike herself, who took the vocational tract in school, Frederic was educated at the University of Warsaw. Where she was politically passive, he was passionately anti-Communist, a rebel who allied himself with protesting students and political organizers who resented Communist attacks on the church and intellectual freedom. On summer nights after making love on the fresh hay of her father's barn, he wooed her with promises of a golden future, together, in a new Poland. By December, when they sat together near the warmth of the hearth, he murmured in her ear that he loved her. Helena, happier than she'd ever been in her life, believed everything.

Then late December of 1970 the dream went wrong. She didn't know exactly what had happened. Frederic's voice was frantic, and his explanations were garbled and rushed during his last phone call from Warsaw. Something about worker riots over food prices, gunshots and a bomb. He had to leave, quickly. His family had connections and could whisk him out.

"I must go, Helena," he'd said urgently, while her hands shook on the telephone. "I must. Now, or risk prison."

"No! No, Frederic, you can't go."

"I'll send for you in America. As soon as I can, I will arrange it."

Helena clutched the phone while her heart slammed against her chest. "No! I'll come with you. I'll leave right away."

"Goodbye, Helena."

There was a click and she knew he was gone.

She'd waited for him as loyally and diligently as any wife would await a husband away at war. For that's how she saw it. They were married in their hearts, weren't they? Each day she ran to meet the post, and each day brought a new torrent of tears to find the box empty. One month, two, and not a word came from America. Not a single postcard telling her that he had arrived safely and was waiting for her. At first she convinced herself that he was just being cautious lest the authorities track him down. As the months pushed on, however, she grew more desolate. These feeble excuses would not explain away the growing child within her belly.

"You disgrace the family!" her mother wailed when she could hide her pregnancy no longer. Devout Catholics, her family couldn't reconcile the shame, and soon afterward, Helena was sent to the Nuns of the Holy Sacrament in Warsaw.

The nuns at the convent were kind and sympathetic to her situation. Their eyes blazed with fervor as they assured her that God would forgive her for the sin of fornication if she prayed hard, showed remorse and vowed to sin no more. During the following two months a new calm settled within, one that grew as her baby grew.

It was then that Father Oziemblowski from her village came to see her. "Good news!" he'd announced. He'd found a family that would adopt her baby. After the birth, Helena could discreetly return home and not another word would be mentioned of this unfortunate affair.

"You must trust our guidance in these matters," Father had told her. "For your child's sake, if not for your own."

Helena listened with eyes wide and meek, but in her heart, she balked. Give up Frederic's child? Unthinkable! Her child was *not* a bastard. If Frederic was here, they would be married, in a church, blessed by God. Maternal instincts flared, making her cunning.

As soon as she found an unsupervised moment, she sneaked from the cloister and took the bus to the old section of the city where a row of flat-faced, four-story buildings in stages of disrepair stood shoulder to shoulder before a park, like ancient grand dames sitting in the splendid shade of trees in full bloom. The Walenski apartment was in one of the larger buildings with a grand entryway. After a brief wait, a stylish stocky woman answered the door. Immediately, Helena recognized the same regal haughtiness she had once admired in Frederic, and the same strong, aristocratic nose.

"I am a friend of Frederic's," Helena said, standing tall in her shabby, oversize raincoat. "I was hoping you could help me find him. It's urgent."

Mrs. Walenski was on guard. "I don't know where my son is."

"Wait!" Helena pushed her hand against the closing door. "Just one moment. What I have to tell you should be spoken in private."

Mrs. Walenski's eyes narrowed in scrutiny, and Helena read dismissal in their flinty coldness. "I don't allow strangers inside my home. What is this about?"

Standing on the front stoop, Helena stubbornly held her ground. She unbuttoned her long coat and slipped it open, revealing the rounded belly of a woman in her fifth month of pregnancy. She felt tawdry beside the elegance of her surroundings, ashamed of her predicament, but for her child's sake, for Frederic's, she would not back down.

"I am carrying Frederic's child."

"You are lying," Mrs. Walenski whispered, quickly ushering Helena into the foyer and closing the door. "Do you think you are the first girl to try to trap my son in such a vile manner?"

While Mrs. Walenski moved through the rooms with sharp precision, Helena wandered as though she were walking in a dream. The house was a blur of splendor, such a contrast from the ramshackle farmhouse her family squeezed into. As she gazed around the room, she noticed details rather than the whole: a gold filigreed clock, the rich carpet, a crystal chandelier of princely proportion. What must it be like to be the mistress of such a house? she wondered. If she were Frederic's wife, would she live here as well?

"Tell me who you are," Mrs. Walenski demanded.

"I am Helena Godowski and I am not trying to trap your son. Don't you think it's the other way around? I am carrying his child. Your grandchild. Frederic promised he would send for me from America, but as you can see, I can't wait any longer. My family is shamed and I can't return home, either. I've nowhere else to turn. The nuns want me to give away my child. Did Frederic never mention me?"

Mrs. Walenski was blinking heavily and shifting in her seat. "No, never. What do you want?"

"I want Frederic. I want to be with him."

"That's impossible! I don't know where he is. Really, I don't. He cannot write, you little fool. The authorities are looking for him, surely you understand that? You don't want him to go to prison, do you? You can't want that."

"No, no, of course not." Helena was flustered now, her face flushed with joy. If Frederic could not contact his mother, then surely he could not contact her, either. He had not forgotten her. He loved her! She was sure of it.

"I love Frederic," she said. "I wouldn't do anything to hurt him, you must believe me."

Mrs. Walenski's shoulders lowered. She nodded, and a new sadness entered her eyes.

"I need help," cried Helena, encouraged by the sympathy she now sensed. She looked at her belly. "Frederic doesn't know about the child. He left before I was certain. Before I could tell him." Raising her eyes, she leaned forward. "Please, if you could tell me just the name of the city in America he's in, I'm sure I can find him. Please, you must believe me."

Mrs. Walenski stared at nothing for a long time. Her hand had risen to her cheek and she sat as though frozen in thought. When she brought her hand back to her lap, her eyes were focused on Helena and the curve of her belly.

"I do believe you," Mrs. Walenski replied at length. "And now you must believe me. All I know is that he went to a city called Chicago in a province called Illinois. There is a large Polish population there."

"Perhaps you can give me the names of your relatives, or friends. Someone I can reach when I arrive. I know no one in America. And I'm already five months along."

"I'll write a letter of introduction to a friend of mine. She will help you. And I will give you money to purchase an airplane ticket. One way." She cleared her throat. "And there will be enough to give you a new start in America."

"Oh, thank you," Helena exclaimed, her hands covering her face as she sobbed in relief. She had never hoped for so much.

"Don't thank me. You don't know my son as well as I do." Mrs. Walenski seemed to shrink inside herself as she continued. "Frederic is a selfish boy. Perhaps it's my fault. I've spoiled him." She fingered a rosette of garnets in her ear for a moment, then dropped her hand with a vague gesture. "If you should find him," she began, pausing, searching for the words. "Please know that he may not welcome you. I don't say this to hurt you, but you see...you are not the first girl he has placed in this situation. Frederic is very determined when he wants something. Obsessed. And...sometimes cruel. His father can be like that, you see. The other girl was from a small village, like you.''

Helena looked away, afraid the worry in her eyes would betray her.

"He never mentioned your name to me, not once," Mrs. Walenski continued. "Do you understand what I'm trying to tell you?"

"I must find him," Helena replied in a strangled voice.

"Very well. I shall see to the arrangements. One more condition, however. If you do not succeed in finding my son, you will promise not to declare your child a Walenski.''

The affront took Helena's breath away. "But the child *is*...''

"I must insist on this point," she interrupted.

Helena lowered her head. "I promise." With two words, Helena whispered away her child's heritage.

Mrs. Walenski was true to her word. Within the month a young, very pregnant Mrs. Helena Godowski arrived in Chicago. Helena learned quickly that a woman alone in a foreign country, especially a pregnant one, had no friends. So close to term, and with no English skills, the best that a letter of introduction got her was a baby-sitting job, earning enough for room and board. Whenever she could, Helena searched for Frederic.

She searched everywhere, begging the help of the close-knit Polish community for any word of a Frederic Walenski from Warsaw. One man had seen him, soon after his arrival, but had not seen him since. It was generally believed that he'd left town.

When her water broke, Helena realized she was about to give birth, alone, without a husband, or a mother, or even a friend. Her dream of finding Frederic in time was over. It suddenly became very clear to her that she was in this alone.

"Do you speak any English?" the nurse at County Hospital asked her. She spoke very loud and slow.

"N-no English," Helena stuttered, her mouth dry with panic.

The nurse rolled her eyes. "Oh, boy. I've got a prima here with no English. We're in for a ride. You just take it easy, honey. I'll take good care of you."

Helena stared at the peeling ceiling as she was wheeled past rooms filled with moaning women. They parked her in a small, pale green room where men and women dressed in uniforms took turns spreading her legs and poking cold fingers in her. She felt so alone, so afraid, so vulnerable. But she had to be strong for her baby.

The pain came in waves now, mounting high, roiling through her abdomen, then crashing against her lower back. The graphs on the strange beeping machine they hooked to her belly arched high and dipped low. Rhythmically, one after the other. Her sweat glistened. Sweet mother of God, why had no one told her? Was it like this for every woman, or was this a special punishment, just for her? She had no one to ask.

Suddenly she felt a strange, overpowering sensation to push. She cried out in Polish, "My baby is coming. Hurry! He's coming!"

Suddenly three people in white surrounded her, shouting instructions she couldn't understand. Gritting her teeth, she pushed till her breath squeezed out of her and tiny gray dots blurred her vision. Then again, and again, like a snarling, spitting animal tearing at its bindings, seeking to be free. "Frederic!" she cried out.

Then with a gush of relief, the pain suddenly was gone, and over the din of voices she heard the lusty wail of her baby. She tried to hoist herself up on her elbows but slipped back down, too exhausted. Tears, this time of joy, sprang to her eyes as she caught glimpses of the people in white bending over her bawling infant, talking excitedly. It seemed to take forever for them to finish fussing over her baby. At last they handed into her arms a baby swaddled as tight as a pierogi.

Helena's breath stilled as she stared at the face of her newborn, nestled in the pink blanket. The baby's face was puckered, and large blue eyes blinked heavily with wonder. But something was wrong. Very wrong. Now Helena blinked, and her attention zoomed in on the baby's chin and jaw. They slid down into the neck, like a mudslide she had once seen in the mountains.

She shot a worried glance at the nurses standing beside her. Their eyes reflected pity, and without a word being spoken, Helena instantly understood that this was not normal. Like a madwoman she tore open the blanket to investigate the rest of the baby's body. Exposed to the cold, the baby began to howl and kick while Helena's gaze devoured the child. Everything looked normal. Ten fingers, ten toes. And it was a girl.

Helena looked again at the deformed chin on that little, scrunched-up face in her arms. She could not ignore it, nor wish it away. This deformity would not improve with time like the funny wrinkles or the pressed nose that she already knew would resemble Frederic's.

Helena turned her head away. So…God had not forgiven her after all. She quietly wept. She hated the nurses who patted her arm and spoke garbled words of sympathy. Why didn't they leave her alone? Didn't they understand? This was her punishment—her cross to bear. Her pain went far beyond mere hopelessness and despair. Helena was like the dog that had been beaten so many times it no longer hid from the club. Her last vestige of hope faded. She resigned herself to her fate. Her one consolation was that at least she had Frederic's child. She was not alone.

Twenty years later, Helena again sat in a hospital room and studied the face of her daughter. This new face. This stranger's face, she thought. What was done to her child was a travesty! Heartbreak flared anew.

Where are you, Frederic? she asked herself. The scars were expertly hidden. Soon they would be invisible and there would be no trace of what deception was committed here. Unnatural thing! *His* nose... There was nothing left of Frederic.

Now, she thought bitterly, I am truly alone.

In California, the spring sun beat hard upon Michael's neck as he watched the twenty-two men that made up his crews gather together at the Mondragon compound to kick off the new season. The men were mostly Americans, from their twenties to their fifties, most of them married, with children. There was one group of Mexican men, clustered together, separated by language and choice. These were men who came to the Mondragon nursery every spring to work especially for Luis. They all came in one single rusting truck that belched fumes and grunted like an old man.

Some men of the crews were more experienced in the business than he was, Michael knew. They'd worked for his father for as long as he could remember. A few were greenhorns and had to be trained. Like Cisco, his nephew. He was only nine years old, but he was here at Michael's invitation, earning a good wage. It pleased Luis to see another generation in the business.

Young or old, experienced or green, citizen or not, it didn't matter. As long as they put in an honest day's work they were paid an honest day's wage. They all understood this as Michael stepped forward and began outlining his plans for change in their routines. It was also understood that Michael was a Mondragon. And Luis had made it clear to all that *this* Mondragon was now in charge.

While Michael spoke to the men, he noticed that Bobby was translating his words to the small cluster of Mexican men who stood apart from the rest. They listened to Bobby, but they kept their dark eyes on him. He felt an old uneasiness rise up, the gnawing ambiguity that he couldn't speak his father's language well enough.

"Is good what you say!" Luis complimented him when he was finished and the crews had dispersed to begin their work. "You are *El Patron* now, eh?" His dark face was flushed with pleasure, and his eyes sparkled as brightly as the sun overhead. "But now is the real test. Now you must go out to work with your men. Make your soft hands work, eh? Shovel. Rake. Real work." He slapped his back and laughed. Then, calling out to his foreman, Luis hurried away, boasting loudly to anyone who would listen.

"You're really enjoying this, aren't you?" Michael said to Bobby, who was smothering a smile behind his hand.

"Hey, better you than me."

Michael looked at his brother's long, thin frame and his linen trousers flowing in the breeze and realized that what he said was true for many reasons.

"I'm doing the designs and managing this place," he replied gruffly. "Papa's got another thing coming if he thinks I'm wielding a shovel out there. I'm through with dirty nails." He wiped the back of his neck, feeling the beginning of a sunburn. He muttered a curse under his breath for forgetting to wear a hat.

"Whatever you say, *bracero*." Bobby reached out and placed his floppy-brimmed panama hat over Michael's head, laughing.

Later that evening, Michael hobbled into the Mondragon office, clutching his back and limping like an old man. An old, enfeebled man.

Bobby looked up from his paperwork and his face broke into a grin of pure pleasure. "Hey, *El Patron.* I thought you weren't going to do any hard labor," Bobby teased, tilting on the hind legs of his chair.

"There was this tree root—" Michael waved his hand "—never mind. Give me a beer."

The icy liquid flowed down his throat, feeling like spring rains after a drought.

"I'd forgotten what it was like out there." He wiped his brow with his sleeve. After a brief pause, a sheepish grin crept across his face. "You know, it felt good to use my body like that again." He stumbled over to the old sofa and collapsed upon it, stretching his long legs out before him. "Look at my hands," he groaned, holding his palms before his eyes. Blisters were already forming where he'd grasped the shovel and pickax. He smiled, remembering how an old-timer had come up to him and told him he was doing it all wrong, then proceeded to show him how to save his energy—and his back.

Michael drank down his beer in a few chugs, then let his hand droop, his fingers barely balancing the bottle on the floor.

"Why don't you go home and take a hot bath?" Bobby asked. "You earned it, *bracero*. And you could use it. Whew."

"Yeah, yeah, I will. I'm just going to close my eyes for a minute. Just for one minute."

In that short space of time, his hands loosened, the bottle tilted and rolled to the floor, and he was out.

Bobby rose and walked to his brother, picking up the bottle and resting Michael's hands up on his belly. A bittersweet smile flickered across his face when he noticed the mud in Michael's manicured nails.

"Welcome home, *El Patron*."

Part Two

She walks in beauty, like the night
Of cloudless climes and starry skies;
And all that's best of dark and bright
Meet in her aspect and her eyes.

—George Gordon Byron, Lord Byron

Six

~∞~

It had been a long year of recovery. Charlotte's progress had been slow and agonizingly painful, full of medication and examinations, months of orthodontics and adjustments. There was a brief time of panic soon after the surgery when she'd had a bad reaction to the sutures, but she'd endured it without complaint, dreaming of the day when she'd begin the next phase of her plan.

And that day had finally arrived.

"You're moving *where?*"

Charlotte's hand hovered over the kitchen sink. Soapy water trickled in rivulets down her forearm to soak in the sleeves of her rolled-up, starched white blouse. Turning her head to look over her shoulder, she saw that her mother had thrown back her shoulders and her eyes were like sharp daggers of fury. Charlotte squeezed the sponge hard, draining it completely.

"C-California," she managed to stutter out.

"Do you know how far that is away from Chicago? From all you know? From your mother?"

Helena snapped the blue-and-white-striped kitchen towel against her thigh. The crack ricocheted in Charlotte's ears, causing her to jerk her head away and avert her eyes. She kept her gaze riveted to a thin streak of soap that floated above the white breakfast china in the sink.

"What you know about going far from home? It is hard and cruel for a young woman who travels alone. People, they take advantage." Her eyes grew bright with hysteria. "You don't know what you're talking about."

"I—I wouldn't be alone. Dr. Harmon gave me the name and address of a big agent in Hollywood. Dr. Harmon's writing a letter of introduction."

"Dr. Harmon again?" Helena's eyes glittered with hatred as she pronounced his name slowly. "Always it's Dr. Harmon with you."

"Mother, please. Let's not start that again...." Charlotte saw her mother's face harden against her and it frightened her.

"You take his word over mine. It doesn't matter anymore what I think. I'm only your mother. I only gave you your life, and give you a roof over your head and food for your belly. What right have I to have opinion? You change your face, your job, and now you want to change how and where you live? In California!" She grunted, shook her head and placed her hands on her hips, caught in a private thought. "A letter of introduction? Ha!"

She felt her mother's will push down on her, suffocating her. "I've always wanted to act."

Helena slapped the air. "Ach, you are no actress, Charlotte. You just do a little helping at the theater. Stop dreaming. Why not you just be happy as an accountant? It's a good job. That is enough for people like us. You can't do something like be an actress."

"Mama, I *can* do this! Why do you always tell me what I *can't* do?"

"Because I know better. And I don't want you get hurt."

"I want to try."

Helena raised herself up, tossing the towel upon the spotless counter. "No," she declared sharply, making the decision for both of them. She straightened her broad shoulders and clasped her hands before her on her belly. "You will *not* move to California where they make movies and live wild life." She began wiping her large hands on her apron, as though the very idea was dirty.

Then she speared Charlotte with an accusing look. "And you will throw out that ridiculous list that you hide in your room. Yes, yes, I saw it. You write down how you want to change *everything*."

Charlotte paled and her breath shrunk in her breast, thinking of the list she kept hidden in her room, her list of wishes, goals, dreams. The small room of the apartment she hated was growing smaller, trapping her. "You're going through my things now? In my room? That's…that's private! That's unforgivable. I'm not a child. How could you do that?"

"Don't you dare raise your voice to me. I'm your mother! This is my home. I can do what I want in my own home!"

Charlotte was white with anger. How long had she handed over her paycheck, willingly, to support her mother? Only to be told she didn't even have the right to privacy in her own bedroom? She didn't have the right to make her own decisions? God, the pain was raw. She felt so exposed. Naked. Her list was her most private secret. Except for…

She flushed, realizing that her diary was also in her drawer. Lifting her hands from the cooled, greasy water, she glanced quickly at her mother. Helena was watching her with arms akimbo.

"You read my diary." It was an accusation.

The truth glittered in her mother's pale eyes. Her guilt was written on her rising blush and the nervous tapping of her fingers.

Charlotte couldn't look at her. She felt physically ill.

Drying her hands quickly, she asked in staccato, "You know what happened to me? About Lou Kopp?"

"Ach, dirty. That filthy man. I hope to think you learned your lesson."

"*My* lesson?" she cried, hearing the hurt she felt come through. "The only lesson I learned is not to let anyone take advantage of me ever again. *Anyone*, Mother."

Helena's pale blue eyes iced over, like a lake caught in a bitter chill.

"I can't continue like this," Charlotte cried. "I've made up my mind. I *am* going to California."

"Ungrateful slut!" her mother called out, the vehemence of it forcing Charlotte to slam back against the kitchen counter. "You turn your back on me? After all I've been through for you?" She shook her head back and forth like a dog with a biting flea in the ear. "You were my punishment. I knew it from the first I saw your face. But did I turn my back on you. No!"

"*Your* punishment? Mother, how can *my* face be *your* punishment? I'm the one who suffered. Not you."

"You know nothing!" Helena snapped back. She caught her breath, staring madly at her as though considering whether to stop now, to hold back. But fury had already broken the bounds of control. Helena took two steps forward, aggressively invading Charlotte's personal space.

"You think you know so much?" she charged on. "You want to change your life, do you? Then you should know it all." Her eyes narrowed and she pointed a finger at Charlotte with accusation.

Charlotte shrank back, instinctively knowing a hurt was coming.

"Your father he never married me. Because of you I had to leave my family, my homeland. I leave everything to come here and live alone. To have you. You! I come with nothing but lousy letter of introduction. It did nothing for me. Yes, I suffered!" She buried her face in her hands and wept piteously. "Your face it was my punishment for my sin. Sin of having child out of sacrament of marriage."

Charlotte's mind whirled with the news. She felt like she was riding a carousel, going round and round with macabre music playing in the background and the barker crying out, "Bastard. Bastard." She felt dizzy. She couldn't think straight.

"That is why I say no to surgery," Helena moaned. "May God's will be done."

"God's will? What about your will? And mine?" Charlotte pushed away from the Formica. All further words tumbled and spilled unspoken from her mouth in a soft whimper. She turned to leave, stumbling away.

"If you go to California," Helena called at her back, "you will never be welcomed here again. If you leave, you are not a Godowski!"

Charlotte stopped, tilted her head, then slowly met her mother's unyielding gaze. She felt as squeezed dry as the sponge in her hand. "Apparently, I'm not a Godowski, anyway," she replied in a low voice. "I don't know who I am. But I assure you, Mother, I intend to find out."

Charlotte arrived in Los Angeles two days later. As she stepped from the cab, bag in hand, she hoped no one passing her on the street could hear the pounding of her heart or see the trepidation blazing across her face. She quickly glanced at the dog-eared business card in her hand. Yes, this was the right address. The office of Freddy Walen, Talent Agent.

The ghost of the little girl she once was materialized in her mind, tugging at her thoughts, telling her this was much too much a dream for her to go after. *Who do you think you are, anyway?*

Charlotte chewed her lip as she craned her head far back to stare up the tall granite building. Well, wasn't that the very question she had to answer? she asked herself. Scoot-

ing the little girl from her mind, she entered the building
with long strides, marched through the plush marbled lobby
and rode the elevator to the top floor where a shiny brass
plate indicated the offices of Freddy Walen. A young
woman with enormous breasts and lips gave her the once-
over when she walked in.

"I'm here to see Mr. Walen. He's expecting me."

"Your name?"

Charlotte braced herself for a laugh or a rolled eye as
she said her new name.

"Charlotte Godfrey."

"You may go in now," drawled the secretary without
raising her eyes. "He's expecting you."

Charlotte's heart began pounding anew, and the butter-
flies flapped in her stomach. Be calm, she told herself, determined to gain control. You're prepared. You *can* do this.
She tucked down her jacket, lifted her chin, then passed
the secretary, entering Walen's office after a brisk three
knocks on the door.

The room was determinedly masculine with its brown
leather chairs and sofas and heavy, square-cornered dark
wood desks and tables. A spectacular marlin arched over
the sofa and golf clubs slouched beside it. Golf trophies
were placed at prominent positions throughout the room.
Freddy Walen was a man with an ego.

Charlotte scanned the black-framed photographs that
filled the opposite wall. Some of the stars in the frames she
knew. Some big names—mostly long forgotten names, either dead or has-beens. Had she not been an old movie
buff, she'd never have recognized a few of them. There
were a number of character actors with familiar faces but
names she couldn't remember. Nowhere was there a Wi-
nona Ryder, a Brad Pitt or any other young, hot actor.

Charlotte pursed her lips and, shifting her gaze, noticed
other telling details: the worn leather, the dust bunnies in
the corner, the dying dieffenbachia by the window. This

looked more like an office of someone on the way down, not up. After all, it was hard to kill a dieffenbachia.

"Welcome to California, Miss Godfrey" came a voice from the corner.

Turning her head, she saw a barrel-chested man nearing fifty years of age, leaning casually against the wall studying her. He was handsome, in a polished, older sort of way, she thought. The kind of man who wore slip-on shoes, flowing, tailored slacks and cashmere sweaters that showed off his muscular chest and arms.

"Sit down."

Charlotte startled at the brusque command, felt her color rising, then told herself to remain calm. Play the part, she ordered herself, then strolled to the sofas with a practiced elegance that Grace Kelly would have envied. In her mind's eye she could see what he saw: the too-wide lapels on her suit jacket and her out-of-date heels. She'd considered purchasing new shoes, but thought it best to eat instead. She walked, however, as if she were wearing couture. It's not what you wear, but how you wear it, she remembered reading in a magazine one day.

The sofa sighed as she sat on the leather and carefully tucked her skirt beneath her thighs. Mustn't perspire and stick to it.

A smile curved his lips, raising his black mustache, making her suspicious that he'd guessed all this was an act and was playing along. To humor who? she wondered. He had dark blond hair interspersed with gray and wore it slicked back. It was his facial hair, however, that gave him such an intimidating appearance. His thick dark brows and mustache contrasted with his blond hair and accentuated the paleness of his blue eyes like bold punctuation marks. When he looked over his dominant nose to stare at her, Charlotte felt pinned.

"You're tall, have a beautiful face and you've got nice teeth," he said as an opener, striding across the room. He

sat on the sofa directly opposite her, leaning far back into
the cushions, spreading his arms out across the cushions in
a position of command. "But your feet are big, and you
walk like a man." He flipped his palms up. "All in all, I'd
say Harmon was right. You have potential."

Charlotte's mouth slipped open and her mind went blank
except for the vision of her big feet.

"You're from Chicago, right? Good theater there. Says
in the letter that you did quite a bit of off-Broadway kind
of stuff."

"Yes, that's right." Sort of, she thought to herself, tightening her hands in her lap.

"Lessons, studio work?"

"Of course. I have my portfolio with me." Charlotte
bent at the waist to shuffle through her bag.

"Just set it on the table. I'll get to that later." He brought
his hand to his face, stroking his jaw while he studied her.
Then he asked her a few basic questions about roles she'd
played, her range, her methods. Questions she'd prepared
for on the long flight from Chicago to L.A. She answered
carefully. Dr. Harmon and she had agreed that her plastic
surgery would remain private. She didn't want to be just
another Hollywood makeover, or worse, a freak. Dr. Harmon had warned her that if the gossipmongers found out,
they'd never take her seriously as an actress, they'd be so
occupied searching for scars.

"Come, come, this isn't the time for nervousness,"
Freddy said, mistaking her hesitation for shyness. The corners of a smile emerged from under his mustache and his
eyes sparked. "Your voice is good, too. Very sexy."

She shifted, a slight movement that created distance. Was
he trying to pick her up? Most men did when they met her
these days. Young and old alike, they lit up like Christmas
trees. Freddy Walen wasn't looking at her breasts, however,
or moving into her personal space. He looked at her the

way Dr. Harmon had—clinically, professionally. He looked directly into her eyes.

"I've been told that before," she replied coolly.

"I'll just bet you have. And a lot more." His smile disappeared as quickly as it had come. "But it doesn't matter if the guy who bags your groceries, or your hometown boyfriend, or even your parish priest thinks you're the greatest thing since white bread. In this town what matters is that the right person—a connected person—thinks you're special and introduces you to other right people. It's all who you know. And—" he leaned back in the cushions and crossed his legs; his eyes delivered a challenge "—it helps if you have talent."

Charlotte leaned back in her sofa and met his gaze straight on, accepting the challenge. On this point, she felt supremely confident. "I have talent."

Their gazes met and held.

He was keenly interested.

She was eager.

He had the resources.

She had the ability.

The tumblers clicked.

He stroked his chin for a moment, then picked up his phone and buzzed his secretary. "Has Melanie Ward found a new roommate yet? No? Tell you what. Call her now and tell her I've found one for her. Charlotte Godfrey. Yeah, the lady here. Give Mel the details and tell her I'll drop her by soon. Good. Get right on it."

Charlotte heard all this with widening eyes. Even if he didn't sign her as a client, at least Dr. Harmon's letter of introduction had secured her a place to stay.

"Got a nice place lined up for you," Freddy Walen said, hanging up the phone. "It's a small rental house up north. You'll have to lease a car, but then again, welcome to L.A. Melanie's a little loose in the attic but all right. She's one of my clients. Been around for a long time. She might not

be smart in the bookish kind of way, but she's smart in
things that you need to learn about. Things like publicity,
promotion, who's who in town. She's not doing so well in
her career right now.'' He shrugged. ''Things are slow for
aging starlets. So she could use a roommate. Works out
well for both of you.''

''I see. Thank you.'' She cleared her throat, ashamed for
the question she had to ask. ''Excuse me, but how much is
the rent?''

''Don't worry about it. Jacob's got you covered.''

''Dr. Harmon? Why…'' This was the first time she'd
heard of this arrangement. Pride kicked in. It would be the
last. ''No,'' she said in a clipped voice. ''That's not right.
He…''

''Look, honey, it's done all the time.''

''Not by me, it isn't,'' she snapped, putting an end to all
speculation about casting couches or whatever kind of lure
he was using. ''I'll pay my own rent, thank you.''

Freddy cocked his head and took her measure. His eyes
took on that peculiar, amused gleam again, a sparkle of
interest and something else that she hadn't quite figured out
yet. ''No problem,'' he replied easily. Again that look.
''It's between you and Melanie, then.''

She nodded, outwardly appearing much more sure than
she felt inside. ''Thank you, Mr. Walen,'' she began,
choosing her words. ''If I could prevail upon you one more
time. I—I need a job. Right away. Any job that's decent
and provides minimum wage. I'm trained as an accountant
and I can get you excellent references. But, in the meantime, I can do just about anything. Secretarial, phones…''

''What's all this talk about accounting? What do you
think this is, an employment agency? You came to me as
an actress. Are you one or not?''

''Of course,'' she blurted out. ''It's just that, well, I
thought…'' She took a deep breath. ''I don't have any illusions.''

A smug smile crossed his face. "Illusions are my specialty."

He sat forward in his seat, looking at her with unabashed interest. Not sexual. More the way she'd once seen track betters study fillies before the race at Arlington Park. No, she corrected herself, Freddy Walen wasn't a gambler. He was a handler. Maybe even an owner. Yes, she thought, sitting up in her seat, gaining insight into the question she'd asked herself all afternoon about this man. What she'd thought was amusement in his eyes was in fact the thrill of possibilities.

"Tell me, Miss Godfrey, do you like to work? Work hard?"

"I'm a very hard worker," she answered honestly.

"Good. Because what I have in mind will require not just long hours of hard work, but dedication. Total commitment. Are you ready for this, Miss Godfrey?"

Charlotte was long past ready. She nodded her head as hope stirred in her breast.

"Here, give me your hands." He unfolded, stretched out his arm with a spark of excitement in his eyes. She hesitated for a fraction of a moment, then leaned forward, stretching across the low table, and placed her hands in his. It was a large hand, very smooth, with long, elegant fingers that wrapped around hers in a possessive grip. She felt a strong, abiding kind of connection with this man. It flowed between them like electricity.

"There's something about you," he said. He squinted, as though seeing something far off in the distance. Then, squeezing her hands, he burst forth with renewed enthusiasm. "You will have to learn how to walk, how to talk, how to dress, how to smile...yes, especially that. A slow, seductive smile to match that husky voice." He gestured with his hand, as though picking an apple from the sky and bringing it to his lips. "I can create something very special with you."

He must have noticed her expression because suddenly he laughed out loud. "Look, your hands are shaking! Are you afraid?" His eyes narrowed. "How old are you?"

"Twenty-one."

"Ah, the age of consent. Don't frown. I'm old enough to be your father. But I'm not. I'm a businessman. People are my business. I see you as an investment. When I die, people will remember that I gave you to the world. Do you believe I can do this?"

She did. Completely. How could this be any more of a miracle than what Dr. Harmon had done with her face? He couldn't possibly understand how complete a transformation she'd already undergone. This was the second time in her life a man wanted to create something special from her. She nodded, unaware that she was holding her breath.

His eyes flashed as they bore into her. "You must promise me that from today you will do what I say. Swear it!"

"I swear," she replied with reverence. She didn't believe Freddy Walen would make this offer to ugly, shy Charlotte Godowski from Chicago. No one wanted *her*. Offers like this only came to beautiful, strong-minded women like Charlotte Godfrey.

"This kind of arrangement goes beyond a mere contract. It's a commitment. Heart and soul."

Charlotte felt a gush of excitement, an impulsiveness to grasp for the ring. But her guard was up now. She had a new wariness, a savvy that she wore like a shield against her sentimental, romantic nature.

"You're asking me for a leap of faith, Mr. Walen. Let's just say, I'm no longer a believer. As you said, this is business."

Freddy smiled openly now, appreciating her intelligence and straightforward manner. "Miss Godfrey, has anyone ever pulled the wool over your eyes?"

"The whole blanket, Mr. Walen. Let's just call our arrangement mutual consent."

He laughed heartily and stuck out his hand. "Then it's a deal?"

"Mr. Walen," she replied, shaking his hand with a strong, committed grip. "You've got yourself a deal."

"Babe," he replied, releasing a pleased, crooked smile but keeping a firm grip on her hand. "Deal is my middle name."

Freddy drove Charlotte along the crowded freeway, whizzing out from the city, pushing on past the suburbs, climbing the inhospitable terrain of a steep mountain toward a house that she would soon call home. The powerful Mercedes looped around countless curves, past looming cypress and pine, ending the forty-minute journey with a sharp turn into a dirt driveway barely wide enough for his large black car. Gravel crunched beneath the wheels as they continued up a sharp incline for another twenty yards. Charlotte looked around, breathing deep to calm the pounding of her heart.

The lot was as scrubby as the coarse wild grass that filled it, and straight ahead, perched on the ledge of the cliff, squatted a sixties tract house, skimpily constructed of a soft beige stucco that looked like someone spilled cottage cheese over it. A wide, rotting wooden pergola overrun with thick twisting cords of wisteria tilted over the front door.

"Here we are," Freddy announced, yanking up the emergency brake on the steep incline. "Doesn't look like much, I know, but it's a good place. Let's take a look around."

Walking up the pebbled path, Charlotte saw that the little house was poorly maintained. The yellowed paint was chipping on the small, square windows, dirt and debris littered the corners of the tiled front patio and the screen on the front door was torn and curled at the edges. She might have felt disappointed by its shabbiness if she'd had prior expectations. But she'd had none. To a girl who'd spent a lifetime in a dingy apartment on a bus route, this was a *real* house. She sniffed the air. Spring, with its warmth and color, was only a breeze away. Birds sang in the greening trees, and hearing them, Charlotte felt welcomed. Her left hand tightened its hold on her suitcase, and with her right, she pressed a bouquet of daisies close to her heart.

At the entrance, Freddy made a fist and banged the door three times. After a short wait, a sexy, kittenish woman with pumpkin-hued hair and large hazel eyes opened the door. When she saw Freddy, she leaned against the door frame in an insolent pose, exposing a slim midriff under a baggy T-shirt.

"Freddy... Long time no see."

"Melanie Ward, meet Charlotte Godfrey."

Charlotte offered a polite smile, thinking Freddy was accurate if not gallant.

"So, you're my new roommate," Melanie said, arching one dark brow while she openly assessed Charlotte. Her voice was unreal, very high and breathy. "Haven't had one of those since college—at least not a female one. And don't even ask how long ago that was. I don't believe in age."

With that pronouncement, she released the door and extended a delicate hand with long, coral-tipped nails and three rings, one of them on her thumb. "Well, Charlotte Godfrey. Welcome to L.A."

Regardless of whether Melanie believed in age, Charlotte immediately knew that Melanie was older—and most certainly wiser in the ways of the world—than she was. But it was anybody's guess just how old the beautiful bombshell was. Melanie was dressed as though they'd just interrupted her aerobic session. Her eye-popping body was as taut as a young girl's and she had a streetwise manner. It was in her eyes, however, eyes that were edged with telltale lines, that Charlotte saw a warmth that could only come from a big heart.

Charlotte, as grateful for the warm welcome as a desert for a sprinkling of rain, dropped her suitcase and shook her hand with relish.

Melanie was taken aback by Charlotte's heartfelt reaction. Screwing up her large, pouty lips, she looked carefully into Charlotte's eyes. "I'll have to do your chart," she said in earnest.

"My chart?"

"Horoscope. You know, Gemini, Aries…the alignment of the moon and the planets. The stars never lie. Unlike men," she added, casting a loaded glance toward Freddy.

"Yeah, well I'm getting Cancer standing out here in the sun," Freddy retorted. "So if you don't mind, can you girls go on with all that New Age stuff later after I'm gone? I've got some important phone calls to make." He turned toward Charlotte, ignoring the obvious bristling of Melanie. Her feelings didn't seem to matter much to Freddy, a fact Melanie seemed well aware of.

"I have a couple of possibilities that I want to follow up on. I'll be back in a couple of days and we'll talk specifics. Till then, Melanie here will show you around, help you get your bearings. Won't you, Mel?"

"Sure, Freddy."

"It's gonna be great, babe. I promise. Take good care of her," he called over his shoulder to Melanie, then walked down the path toward his powerful car.

Melanie let loose a low whistle and shook her head, looking at her with a look of wonder mixed with envy. "Mmm…mmm…mmm, girlfriend. That hound has caught the scent."

Charlotte could only blink heavily. The jet lag, the anxiety over the move and the hours without sleep began to hit her as forcefully as the sun overhead.

"Never mind, honey. In time it'll all become perfectly clear. Come on in and make yourself at home." She stepped aside and allowed Charlotte in.

"Here, these are for you." Charlotte handed Melanie the rather sad-looking bouquet of daisies as she passed. "I didn't have much to spend, but I didn't want to arrive empty-handed, either. I'm afraid they're a bit wilted."

Melanie's face softened and her guard slipped as she plucked at the straggly leaves. "I can't remember the last time someone bought me flowers."

She pressed them to her nose. Charlotte knew the daisies had no scent and suddenly wished they could have been roses.

"You know, Godfrey," Melanie said with a crooked little smile. "I think this might work out just fine."

Seven

~~~~~~~~~~~~~~~~~~~~~~~

Charlotte never knew time to fly by so fast. Spring, summer, fall, winter, she worked for Freddy Walen as she'd never worked before in her life. She wanted to prove to him that she was committed. A winner. For so many years it was easy to blame her failures, her shortcomings, her insecurities on the simple and undeniable fact that she was ugly. How much simpler to own up to the physical imperfections than the ones dealing with intelligence or character.

Each morning she rose at six, drank a cup of coffee, then traveled in her rental car to various acting, voice and modeling lessons in Los Angeles, to Freddy's office or, when she was lucky, to an acting gig. Freddy worked hard for her as well. She gained a lot of experience and exposure working for minimum scale on several small films—independent, low budget, documentaries. He also secured bit parts in two major motion pictures. She was making enough to pay her bills and still squirrel some away in a savings account.

Her friendship with Melanie grew stronger every day, but she couldn't explain why she preferred to stay home instead of going to parties or bars. She was still gun-shy about meeting new people, especially new men. Men who not so long ago might have made snide remarks. She was more comfortable spending time alone; it was what she knew. Home, books, solitude, a sense of purpose—these were cherished old friends that she needed at the end of a harrowing day.

Yet, each day she said a prayer of thanks for her new friend. Melanie was the sunshine that forced itself through the dark cracks. She kept Charlotte on her toes, laughing to inside jokes that only roommates can share, teaching her the newest dance steps, buying bright red dinner dishes or painting her nails, helping her, in everyday ways, from slipping into her shell.

So the months passed while Charlotte kept her mind focused on her training, gearing all her physical and mental energy toward the big deal Freddy promised would arrive.

After ten months in California, Freddy's big deal came down.

"It's all arranged," he said over the phone, his excitement ringing. "It's a real part, not a blink-and-they'll-miss-you kind of thing. Here's the deal. The preproduction was all done for this film, but there've been some casting uproars. Suddenly, there's a juicy part available that has to be filled quick. I tell you, every agent worth his salt was out gunning for this one. My old pal Dave Dolezal is in charge over at Miramax now. He's a crony from my days at CAA. He's willing to meet with you." She envisioned him grinning over the phone. "I want them to get a good look at you. He's setting it up for dinner tomorrow."

Charlotte's mind went blank. "How? I mean, it's so fast."

"In this town, baby, it's all who you know."

"But what do I do? What do I wear?"

"That's my job. I've got you lined up for the whole treatment. Afterward we'll buy you some pretty things to wear from Giorgio's. I've got to go. Just called to tell you the good news. Now, close your mouth before you catch a fly. All you have to worry about is being ready to roll first thing tomorrow morning. I'll send a car for you. And no booze or anything else tonight, not even to celebrate. I don't want any puffiness or anything. Tomorrow's our big day.''

"Dinner with Dave Dolezal?" Melanie squealed in her unreal, breathy voice.

They were standing in her bathroom, where she was giving Charlotte lessons on how to use an eyelash curler—something that looked to Charlotte more like an instrument of torture. Melanie's bathroom was a warehouse of beauty paraphernalia—creams, lipsticks, applicator wands of all sizes, liners, an eyebrow tweezer and an acreage of jars of vitamins and pills. It was a shrine to cosmetic beauty.

"He's pulling out some big guns, sweetie," she explained to Charlotte. "I don't know what he said, but if I know Freddy, I'm sure they'll ask you to read for a part."

Charlotte began feeling a little faint and reached for the counter.

Melanie pulled out a stool and indicated with her coral-tipped fingers for Charlotte to sit down on it. Charlotte did so, tucking her hands between her knees and exhaling heavily.

"Calm down, honey, you're a little pale. Keep doing breathing exercises and I'll make you a special herb tea to calm the nervous system." She returned a few minutes later with a steaming cup of chamomile tea sweetened with honey. "Here, drink this down. Then maybe a little blush. You look like death warmed over."

Charlotte sipped gratefully, feeling the warmth of the tea coat her frazzled nerves.

"You need to calm down big time. There's no way you're going to get this organized in that file cabinet of a mind you have. This is Hollywood. It's free-falling."

"I like knowing what to expect. To be prepared. I've waited for this moment all of my life. Now that it's here,

I feel like I'm going to throw up.'' She gave a nervous laugh. ''I feel like I did when I was in school and I found out there was a big test that I hadn't studied for.''

''Oh, yeah, I have a dream like that all the time. I'm standing outside this classroom, right? My arms are loaded with books but I can't force myself to go in.... I'm like, motionless with fear because I didn't study.'' She rolled her eyes. ''Probably because I never *did* study in school and in real life that kind of thing happened to me all the time.''

''Not me. I was a nerd.''

Melanie reached out to pat Charlotte on the back. ''Kinda figured you were. Well, for you this horrible dream is coming true. Welcome to Lala Land. Where nothing is quite the way it seems.''

Charlotte gulped her tea and said nothing.

''If it were me about to be trotted out before studio bosses,'' Melanie continued, dabbing at her cheeks with blush, ''I'd be starving myself to lose that extra pound, fretting about my hair. Hell, I'd probably call my plastic surgeon for a quick tuck somewhere.''

Charlotte's ears perked up at the mention of plastic surgery. ''Why? Have you had surgery?''

Melanie laughed and poked through her box of shadows till she found the right shade of brown. ''Me? Oh, sure. Are you kidding? What the good Lord didn't give me I bought for myself. Besides, at my age, which you'll never know, I like to think I have some defense against gravity.'' She picked up the blush and lazily applied a streak of pale pink to her high cheekbones. ''I remember when I first made a splash, I—'' A shadow flickered across her face, but she brushed it away with a wave of her hand. ''You don't want to hear about me.''

''Sure I do.'' Charlotte leaned back against the counter. She really didn't know much about Melanie's career, other than it had taken a downward slide. As Freddy succinctly put it, "Her fifteen minutes are over."

"No, not now. I don't want to go into ancient history." Her voice turned hard-edged with an annoyance she was trying to disguise. "Look. Let's keep this upbeat. I'm busy enough trying hard not to hate you right now."

Charlotte looked at her hands. "I'm sorry. I didn't mean to pry."

Melanie sobered. Picking up a case of eye shadow, she began dabbing her brush in it. "Don't be. Mine's a common enough story here. You might as well know the way it is. I had lots of work when I first came here, but that started dwindling as I got older and well—" she leaned forward and applied a layer of cocoa shadow to her lid "—now I'm not so hot anymore. Most of us plod through year after year, taking a part here and there whenever we can find work. It's not so much a thing where we get to decide if we want the part. Shit, it's not even that Freddy is worried about what part I take. I'll take *any* part, for any money, and say thank you. He knows it, too."

Melanie shrugged and brushed back her hair, revealing fine lines at the corners of her eyes. "Ups and downs, euphoria and depression. The only thing that's steady is unemployment. Mostly, though, it's a little bit here and there, just enough to keep us hanging in there."

Charlotte regretted having brought it up. She hadn't meant to make Melanie feel badly. "Oh, I'm getting ahead of myself, anyway. Freddy has all these plans for me, but it doesn't mean they'll pan out."

"They will." Melanie took a deep, shuddering breath, then raised her large, heavily mascaraed eyes to meet Charlotte's. "I knew it the moment I saw you standing outside my door with those soulful eyes. Freddy saw it, too. Everyone will see it."

Charlotte squirmed under the scrutiny.

Melanie's gaze sharpened and she pointed a finger at

Charlotte. "Just understand this, girlfriend. When you're out there, the men may fawn over you, but the women will be maneuvering to stab you in the back. Beauty is power, especially in this town. So use your beauty. While you can. It doesn't last forever."

"You look like a goddamn Merchant–Ivory star," Freddy said approvingly when he stepped into the hair salon the following afternoon. Several stylists encircled her, smoothing out a wisp of hair, patting her cheek.

Freddy regarded them with disdain, knowing that as soon as he and Charlotte left the premises there would be a cat-fight among them as to who was responsible for the trans-formation of one apparently gawky girl into this goddess. By tomorrow the buzz of a New Girl would be on the street—as well as the news that she belonged to Freddy Walen.

He had to admit they did a miraculous job on her. Char-lotte's pale gold, baby fine hair was trimmed but kept long and curled just enough to give her a classic sleekness that evoked memories of a young Lauren Bacall or Greta Garbo. Freddy liked that, not only because it smacked of Holly-wood, but because it possessed that "look but don't touch" elegance he was after. Everyone knew that only a woman with the absolute, unquestionable beauty of Charlotte God-frey could carry that look off.

"Real classy. Now, pull your shoulders back and raise your chin a notch. You want to walk like a star so people will think you are one. If you slouch, people think you don't have confidence or you're a nobody. Now, walk back and forth a little. That's right, chin up," he admonished as she took coltish strides across the salon. She had moments of natural grace, like an untried, untrained Thoroughbred. "Great," he replied, waving her over. "You're a quick study. I like that."

He took her elbow and guided her to the back room of

the salon, a small sitting room for the employees to take breaks in. She looked around the cramped and dingy room with its few vintage sixties pieces of furniture and wondered why the employees always got stuck with such poor conditions. Even in a glamorous salon.

"We have to get a move on," Freddy said, his voice gruff with tension. "We've fallen way off schedule and dinner's been pushed up to seven. Dolezal is bringing along a few of his cronies." He took a swift look at the large Rolex on his wrist and scowled. "Damn. That hardly gives us enough time. Definitely not enough time to go across town to the hotel and back. So take your shoes off and rest here for a little while. I've arranged with André to let us use this room to relax in. I've ordered some food in, too."

"Food? You just said we're going out to eat soon."

"No. We're going to an *interview* soon. Food is immaterial. I don't want you thinking about what you are eating tonight. I want you focusing on the questions and how you act. Remember, when you circulate at large parties or small luncheons, you're 'on.'"

Freddy began pacing back and forth in front of her, gesturing in his typical broad manner. She slipped off her shoes, accustomed as she was now to the signal that one of his long lectures was about to begin. She sat back in her chair with a fluidity of motion made easier by months of exercise.

"I'll remember, Freddy," she replied in rote style.

"When we're in the restaurant, don't eat. And definitely don't drink. Stir your food around the plate a little bit, and if you must, consume a little. When I take you to dinner parties, then you gotta take a few bites. You don't want to insult a hostess, after all, but better to let them think your art is your nourishment. Most certainly don't eat when you are in a circle of women. Just look straight into their eyes and flatter them. Tell them they look beautiful." Here he jutted his finger. "And never flirt with their husbands. Trust me. It's never worth it."

Charlotte, who had been looking out the window with an aloof expression, turned her head toward him, uneasy. "It all seems so artificial. So fake. Why can't I just be myself?"

"Because, my angel, they will naturally envy you, and you must do what you can to avert their hostility. Looks like yours make other women edgy."

She nodded, tapping her lips in thought. Melanie's words came back to mind. If beauty was power, especially in this town, then she had better pay attention. She'd never wanted beauty for the purpose of power. In truth, she wasn't quite sure what her new beauty qualified her for. Everything was new and different. Suddenly she was noticed, fawned over. In this town, her beauty made her somebody. Yet, rather than give her identity or even satisfaction, this unsubstantiated appreciation left her feeling adrift, without a mooring and in need of an anchor.

Right now, Freddy was that anchor. She focused again on his words, listening more carefully. Taking mental notes.

"Keep your distance from people as a general rule," Freddy continued, slowly gaining steam as he clicked off his list of instructions. "Stay close only to me. Don't trust anybody but me and don't make close friends."

"What about Melanie?"

"Melanie...okay. I trust her to keep her mouth shut, and she can advise you if you get into any kind of minor trouble. But for the big problems, and the big decisions, you come to me."

"You I can trust..."

"If not me, who?"

She had to give him that. "Okay, go on. But first, when's dinner coming? I'm starved."

"It'll be here any minute. Now, where was I? Oh, yeah. Keep your distance and don't go accepting help from every corner. I'll get you whatever you need. Be independent. Move fast. Moss doesn't grow on a rolling stone and all that. When you receive an invitation, tell me. I'll let you know which parties you should attend and which you should not.''

Charlotte felt a sudden chill. Memories of earlier parties in her life crept back into her consciousness. Parties where she was mocked and teased mercilessly. ''Promise me you will come with me.''

He stopped his tirade suddenly to look at her. Stubbing his cigarette out on the marble floor, he came to her side and took her hand.

''Baby, baby...you're not scared, are you?''

She raised her eyes to his and he was struck by the genuineness of the emotion he found there. Looking into her eyes, so brilliant a blue against her pale cream-colored makeup, he was suddenly reminded of the cerulean skies of his homeland against white cirrus clouds. He was reminded of the robins' eggs he'd collected as a boy. He was reminded of so many things....

Freddy frowned. What the hell was the matter with him? This fixation with the girl was becoming an obsession. It was worrisome. Irritating. But he was powerless to stop it. Like her, he'd committed to ride this train all the way.

''Don't worry,'' he replied, surprised by the tenderness he felt. ''I'll always be beside you.''

Five days later, Charlotte sat quietly on a stool in the shadows of a very large screening room at Universal. She was here to read for the film *American Homestead*. Her thick makeup and elaborate Victorian dress felt stiff and stifling, even in the deep air-conditioning. In the center of the room there was a circle of lights and cameras, and beneath them long, thick cables entwined like pythons. She didn't know the names of most of the equipment, or what it was used for. Freddy did, however, and was out there in

the middle, talking animatedly with the lighting cameraman, Josef Werner. Earlier he'd introduced her to him,
nudging her forward while whispering in her ear how she
always wanted to have the cameraman on her side. Now
he was out on the set arguing the angles, determined that
they get the lighting right.

Charlotte's hands were sweating, her breath came short
and she couldn't seem to drink enough water to keep her
mouth moist. The scene she was scheduled to read was not
the one she had prepared for. Freddy was elated that the
studio execs were so enamored with her during the dinner
that they were asking her to read for a bigger part. She'd
found Dave Dolezal, with his alcoholic sheen and his not-
so-subtle sexual advances, abhorrent. It had been easy to
follow Freddy's admonitions and merely push her food
around her plate. What wasn't easy was to not stab Dave's
sausagelike fingers with her fork each time he grasped her
hand.

Freddy was elated with Dave's response to her, however,
and whispered in her ear after dinner, "A good man to have
on your side."

Which side of the bed? she'd wondered.

She'd received the new script last night by special messenger. Even though it was a push to study the scene in
time for today's reading, she felt much more empathy for
this character. Her name was Celeste. She was the beautiful,
slightly neurotic bride of a possessive brute of a man who
kept her virtually imprisoned on their estate. It was a small
role, but significant. What Freddy called "a juicy part." A
get-noticed kind of role beside big, billable stars.

"Okay, let's do it," called out the director.

Charlotte's heart pounded loudly in her ears, but she
managed to slide from the stool to walk to the center of
the room. Her legs and arms felt stiff, her head was balanced on her neck like a ball on a stick. Once in the center
of the cameras, she couldn't find her mark. Her knees felt

watery. She looked around with vague, uncomprehending eyes. The cameras and lights began to blur.

Freddy, sensing her panic, hurried forward and gently guided her to where she was to stand, murmuring soft reassurances, handling her as carefully as a trainer would a spirited racehorse at the gate.

"There are only two things you have to keep in mind," he said, holding on to her shoulders and forcing her to focus on his steady gaze. "First, you must be aware of the period the character is living in. This is 1897, New York, with Victorian morals, and you are very, very rich. Second, you must be aware of who the character is. It's simple. It is *you*."

"I don't know who that is."

He shook her shoulders lightly. "You are Celeste."

She stared at him with the dawning of understanding.

"Off the set. Let's go!" called the director.

"You can do it." Freddy looked into her eyes, straight through to *her,* and repeated, "You can do it." He released her and hurried from the set.

Charlotte closed her eyes and shut out the cameras, the lights, Freddy, Josef, everyone and everything. She traveled down the velvety blackness within herself to that secret place in her heart where Charlotte Godowski felt most comfortable and secure. It was in this private place that she stored her favorite books and music, her cherished memories, her most precious dreams. It was to this place that she went whenever she'd been teased as a child, or hurt as a teen, or neglected as an adult, to nurture whatever it was that was unique about herself.

She realized with a burst of sudden clarity that from these carefully wrapped units inside of herself, which she'd lovingly tended all these years, her strength as an actress would come. Like an actor rummaging through old costume trunks, she'd find her inspiration here.

She felt suddenly free and light-hearted. She knew this

place so well. Yes, she could do this! A small smile curved her lips. It didn't matter what style her hair was in, or how elegant her clothes were. When the camera lights were on and the film was rolling, it was, in the end, up to her.

Charlotte Godowski slipped deeper into herself, shrinking very, very small. She was skilled at doing this, had done this so many times all her life. Then slowly, tentatively, she allowed the character of Celeste to emerge. She opened her eyes and blinked heavy lids, like one awakening from a deep sleep, then with smooth steps, took her position under the lights. Her mannerisms, her voice, her inflection, they were all Celeste.

And Celeste knew exactly what to do.

There was absolute silence on the set as though everyone else sensed that they were witnessing a remarkable transformation. The director gave the cue, the cameras whirred and with her beautiful, clear voice, Celeste began to speak.

Freddy watched the rushes with Sam Bonnard, the director, Dave Dolezal and a few other men, including Josef Werner, who insisted he see the dailies. After her entrance on the scene, there was a gasp followed by an intense hush. Charlotte on film was even more illuminating than Charlotte in the flesh. It had something to do with the skin. It had a luminous quality that only a few others had: Greta Garbo, Marilyn Monroe, Uma Thurman. The camera loved her; she literally lit up the screen. Her voice was low and seductive with a natural cadence. He was right about her eroticism, too. Paired with her innocence, it was a lethal combination. Looking at the men in the room, he could tell she was having the same effect on all of them. They stared at the screen, transfixed. A few shifted uncomfortably in their seats.

Freddy faced the screen again, filled with glee. He wanted to laugh out loud. Charlotte was the one he was waiting for. His instincts had been correct. She had it all, beauty *and* talent. She was going to be big. Very big.

And nobody was going to get to her—except through him.

Freddy Walen returned to his large Mediterranean-style home, locked the door behind him and dropped his briefcase on the floor. The sound reverberated through the empty house. He moved on to the large, sterile kitchen, stuck a frozen low fat dinner into the microwave, poured himself a Scotch and water, and went straight for the phone and dialed. One thing he'd learned in this business: be fast. After a few rings, he reached John LaMonica, a deal maker.

"I saw her," LaMonica said. "I want her."

Freddy smiled and swirled the ice in his glass. "Everybody does, John."

"I've optioned this book," he said, excited. "I've got bound galleys coming to you by rush messenger. Read it, then we'll have lunch at La Scala. Already some big interest in the project. Major capital infusion. Michael Bay directing. And get this—Schwarzenegger. We're getting preproduction started and we all agreed. We'd like to see Charlotte as Nancy."

"Nancy? Who the hell is Nancy? I don't know what that means, John."

"Nancy as in the lead," he replied, smugness ringing across the lines.

Freddy sat down on a flimsy little iron chair beside the mosaic-and-iron kitchen table, one of the few pieces of furniture his wife had left him after the divorce. Cleaned him out, the bitch, but it could have been worse. She got most of the cash, the furniture, the summer home up north and every damn stick of furniture and piece of china or crystal they'd accumulated in their ten-year marriage. He got the house and his sanity.

Freddy wiped his face with his hand. Who the hell cared about that now? Now he had Charlotte Godfrey.

"You've got backing?"

"As I said. Really deep pockets, as in Korea and Germany. Look, read the book. You'll see why she's perfect for the role. If Garbo was alive, we'd a wanted her. But this girl. Damn if she might not be better."

John was flattering him by building up his client, but a little kiss-ass was expected in this business. He smiled, thinking how good it felt. It'd been a long time since anyone had bothered.

"Sure I'll look at it, John. If you like it, and Arnold, well, I'm sure it's great. I'll call you as soon as I finish it."

He hung up the phone and stretched his arm out on the counter, resting his head. He was tired, heaving like he'd just run five miles uphill. He removed his sunglasses, rubbed the bridge of his nose and said a short but fervent prayer of thanks to God for giving him Charlotte Godfrey. LaMonica was interested in her? He wanted to weep.

With his left foot he kicked the other iron chair, a bistro chair Ali had called it, and sent it flying across the room. Fuck this cheap furniture, he thought, feeling exuberant. Fuck his ex-wife. And her new husband who was loaded, though part of him loved the guy because he didn't have to pay alimony anymore. Ali had married again and was already pregnant with her second child. Freddy swallowed the Scotch, feeling the burn slide down his throat. Yep, that's what she always wanted. A kid.

And it was the one thing he couldn't give her. An injury years ago, as a young man, had rendered him impotent. "Shrapnel to the groin will do it every time," the doctor had said with a laugh. Freddy never saw the humor in that.

Ali had been a good sport, he'd give her that. She'd really tried to make the marriage work. On those rare occasions, like tonight, when he could get past his bitterness, he could forgive her for dumping him.

The microwave's high beep let him know his pasta Alfredo was done. He grabbed a mitt, pulled out the small orange box and carried it to the single chair in his living room. He swallowed a forkful of the Alfredo, then another, but the runny, tasteless, overcooked noodles didn't match the excitement of the day. Setting the box on the floor, he nursed his Scotch instead.

Maybe it was seeing the future in those crystal clear eyes of Charlotte Godfrey on the screen that had set him off tonight. He had dreams again, after such a long streak of bad luck. Ten years back, this house was buffed and polished, dressed to the nines. He and Ali had had some good parties here. Now the place could use a good face-lift—like most of his clients. The carpet was peeling back, the floors needed refinishing, and here and there molding was sheared off. The place was the size of a small palace and it took every penny he had just to keep it in bad shape.

If all went as he hoped, he'd be popping those champagne corks in this house again. He just had to hold on long enough to milk his new cash cow. Lord, and did she have the udders. Then no more dodging bill collectors, double tightening the water faucets, turning off lights and being on a first-name basis with appliance repairmen. And he'd pick up some new furniture, too. Hell, maybe even hire one of those decorators Ali was so fond of.

He leaned back in the threadbare wing chair and looked out the window, slowly swirling the ice in his drink to the moody tempo of Chopin. Down in the street some supernanny was pushing one of those old English prams while beside her a little girl was pumping away on a pastel tricycle. She was a sweet little girl, with long blond pigtails and her gingham dress flipping back over chubby legs as she pedaled. He felt a short stab of disappointment that he and Ali never had a kid. It was an old, familiar pain, but one he'd not felt in a long while. He liked kids, liked to think he would have been a good father if he'd had the chance. Their little girl would probably have looked a lot like that one, with Ali's German blood and his Polish blood. As it was, one explosion and he was the last of his line.

He downed the rest of his Scotch in a gulp, then leaned forward to close the blinds. He wasn't about to fall into that self-pitying trap again. In this town a loser could be sniffed out at twenty paces. It was survival of the fittest, supermen able to leap major deals in a single bound. He had the smarts, the contacts and the drive. Most of all, he had a sweet little girl all his own.

He had Charlotte Godfrey.

Eight

❧❧❧

Surely nothing more could happen in a lifetime, Charlotte thought blithely. At least nothing significant. She chuckled in the early summer wind. At least not today, certainly. For today she was on vacation, the first she'd taken in ages. No classes, no fittings, no makeup, no nothing. She meant to do something fun and free, and for no other reason than the pure pleasure of it. Something just for her.

Today she would begin her garden.

She pressed her foot on the accelerator of her new car, anxious to arrive at the nursery. She wanted to put some distance between herself and the strange new thing her life was becoming.

Her first supporting role in *American Homestead,* was "in the hopper," as Freddy liked to say, and she felt flush with the compliments from the director and the cast alike. Even though it would be months before the film would be released, Freddy said there was a buzz about her name now and he'd lined up her first co-starring role in a major independent film.

The screen test went as Freddy had predicted it would. Signing a big contract in the immense office, shaking hands, laughing at the pop of a champagne cork—it all happened so quickly. Suddenly she had money.

Not a lot of money, but enough to really begin the life she'd charted for herself such a short time ago. She patted her purse, amazed that a few Ben Franklins were actually nestled in her wallet. After so many years of hanging around Abraham and George.

She laughed again, feeling more free than she could remember, and pushed the accelerator again. Her navy sports car pushed past the city, past thoughts of work, Freddy and the film she would soon be starting. She wanted to keep moving, to keep memories far behind her. Today was her day to think about flowers and the sun kissing her face, and to sing out loud with *La Traviata* blaring from her CD player.

Melanie had claimed she was crazy to spend her money on a flower garden. Why fix up the place, she'd argued, when you don't even own it? You'll only raise the rent. What did she care? she'd argued back. She'd pay the difference; it was worth it to her. So she'd picked a nursery from the phone book—the Mondragon Nursery—because she liked the name. She'd be there soon. Small green-and-white signs, freshly painted, pointed the way.

At first she leisurely strolled through the rows upon rows of blooming flowers. She didn't know the names, but she refused to feel overwhelmed. She had a fine memory, especially of things she loved. It would only be a matter of time till she had a handle on this gardening thing. Something was here for her, she felt certain.

She was touching the smooth, chubby leaves of a begonia when she saw him.

He was standing surrounded by a trio of women, each with a potted flower in her hand, each with eyes fixed on his long, handsome face. He was being kind; it was obvious by the fixed smile and the way he tilted his head while he listened, as though he couldn't bear to miss a word. His black hair was the color of a raven's wing, his shirt as white as the clouds above. Beneath it was the smooth, terra-cotta-colored skin she remembered so well.

From somewhere a bird called. She thought it was her sigh.

He looked up and briefly looked her way, then turned back again to the ladies. She held her breath. Slowly, as though he saw something he wasn't quite sure of, he turned his head again in her direction. His brows furrowed, as though he was trying to place her.

Charlotte couldn't move, not her feet, nor her hands, not even her mouth or eyes. It was him. The stranger she'd met in the elevator on a cold, fateful night in Chicago. It was as though all she'd experienced, all her decisions, all the roads she'd traveled since that night had led her to this moment.

He didn't seem to recognize her, yet she felt certain that he sensed some connection, too, because he straightened and returned her study with the same open-eyed wonder she was sure she wore.

He cocked his head and squinted. *Who are you?*

She smiled. *Yes, it's me.*

The trio of women around him, realizing that they'd lost his attention, silenced and turned curious gazes her way. She saw them as scenery, a mere backdrop to the action between her and him. He apologized to the ladies, oblivious that their faces dropped in disappointment, and signaled for an assistant to come over. Then he walked toward her, eyes on her face.

She didn't move, couldn't move, but gauged his progress toward her with her breaths. His hair was longer now, tied back at the nape of his neck. Thick dark brows formed a serious line over eyes shining with intent. He seemed a formidable mass, all black and white, rolling toward her, like thunder. She was powerless to stop it now.

"Do I know you?" he asked, stopping before her.

It was the same voice, the same dark undercurrent she

remembered as if it was yesterday. They both knew the question sounded too much like a pickup line. Charlotte stared at the gravel, wildly wondering whether to answer yes, and explain all her history. Or to simply say no, and start anew.

"No," she replied, then smiled tentatively.

He searched her eyes, his own large, brown eyes probing under heavy brows like an eagle. "I thought I might. There's something…" He shook his head with some embarrassment. "It doesn't matter. My name is Michael." He paused, extending his hand. "Michael Mondragon."

She nodded, making the connection to the nursery. "I'm Charlotte." She took his hand. "Charlotte Godfrey."

His hands were strong and slightly callused, and the touch of them sent a tingling up her arm. She'd wondered about his hands so many times during those many lonely nights in Chicago. She'd seen them in her mind's eye: long-fingered, tanned, scrubbed.

He took back his hand and tucked the tips of his fingers into the back pockets of his jeans. "Well, Miss Godfrey. Can I help you?"

His eyes held the sparkle of interest, though his demeanor was very proper. She remembered his chivalry in the elevator. She remembered that she'd held back that night and said no. This time, her answer would be different.

"Yes, thank you," she replied, picking up a white lily and examining it very carefully. "I'd like your help very much."

"Would you like to look around?" he asked, extending his hand.

They strolled in a companionable manner through the rows that Charlotte had walked through before. Each felt that this was a special moment in time. Each tried to pretend that it was not.

Michael pointed out specific plants, reaching out to touch the leaves of flowers as he described them with great detail.

It impressed Charlotte how much he knew about so many things: the soil, the plant's requirements. Every plant had a story. When she mentioned this to him, he laughed and indicated a little white plastic tab stuck in the dirt of each plant.

"A cheat sheet," he said, pulling one out and showing her how each one had the plant's name and care instructions on the tab.

"Thank goodness for those," she replied. "Even someone as lost as I can figure out a picture of a full or a half sun."

"I take it you don't know much about gardening?"

"Not a thing. But I'm a quick learner. I have a nice piece of land that has lots of potential and lots of sun. It could be something special. To me, anyway. It's the first piece of land I've ever lived on."

"I'd be happy to help. What kind of plants are you interested in? Perennials or annuals?"

"Is that full sun or half sun?"

He laughed. "Annuals live for one season, then die off. Perennials come up every year. I'd recommend mostly annuals if this is your first season in your garden. It will give you color and lots of show while you get to know your garden better."

"There's so much I don't know," she confessed after their tour of the nursery garden shop was completed. "I thought this would be so easy. Just go to the nursery, pick out what you liked, sort of like a dress, then come back and stick them in the ground. I'm sure you've figured out by now that I'm your worst nightmare."

All he could think was that she was his dream come true.

"It's not that overwhelming. You just have to decide where to begin."

"Where would you suggest?"

He smiled. This was going far too easily. "With your garden space," he replied casually. "Where do you live?"

* * *

They arranged for Michael to come for a site visit on the following day. As far as Charlotte was concerned, tomorrow wasn't soon enough. She went directly from the nursery to her local library, emerging an hour later with an armful of gardening books. The ones she chose had scores of pictures of blossoming flowers and shrubs; she needed pictures. She didn't know the names of any of them. When she got home, she sat at the kitchen table with a tuna fish sandwich and a cup of coffee and did what she hadn't done in years—crammed for a test. She wasn't about to let Michael Mondragon think she didn't know a begonia from a petunia.

All night long she tossed and turned, waiting for the morning. Never in her twenty-two years had a man come to see her at her home. A pitiful state of affairs, and if she admitted it to herself, even this was business and not a date. But it was the closest she'd ever come to one.

When the sun finally rose the next morning, she'd worked herself into a frenzy of anticipation.

"What are you all freaked about?" Melanie asked in a sharp tone. She was wearing a skimpy thong bikini of fluorescent pink, carrying a bottle of suntan lotion in one hand and a tall iced tea in the other. A paperback book was tucked under her arm. She obviously had her morning planned.

"I just want everything to be right," Charlotte replied, smoothing back her hair.

"It's probably why you were an accountant." Melanie scrunched up her face and walked across the patio straight to a lounge chair. Once settled in, she immediately began lathering on a coat of lotion. "This is your madness, not mine. I'm not about to work into a sweat just to impress some gardener."

Charlotte felt stung by the nasty tone of Melanie's voice. Michael Mondragon could hardly be called just some gardener. Melanie was snapping a lot lately. Like she was sitting on a burr.

She looked at Melanie as she lathered the lotion onto her already deeply tanned skin. In the bright morning sun, her hair appeared even more brassy. Melanie had changed her hair color to blond, a shade suspiciously close to Charlotte's own. Melanie was borrowing her clothes a lot lately, too, and when she bought new ones, they were very much in the sleek style that Charlotte preferred. Not at all like the colorful, formfitting styles that were Melanie's trademark.

She rubbed her neck, feeling the heat of the early morning sun prickle. Maybe her fears were right; Melanie was jealous of her recent success. Melanie's career was in a downward spiral. That was a lot of pressure for them both to bear. They didn't dance much anymore.

"You're not upset that I'm going ahead with this? The last thing I want to do is start pushing you around in your own place."

"No, no, don't be silly. It's just as much your place. More, if you consider how much cleaning and organizing you've done." She paused and took a long breath. "Honey, if you want to grow some pretty flowers, go right ahead. I'll only get upset if you ask me to pull any weeds. Flowers and bugs are just not my thing. Cooking on the other hand..." She turned her head, listened for a moment, then flopped a hat over her face. "There's the doorbell. It must be your gardener."

There was no time to change into the outfit she'd finally picked out, or comb her hair, or even wash her hands. The doorbell rang again. Oh, well, she thought as she trotted through the living room to the front door. What did it matter, anyway. This wasn't really a date.

After taking a deep breath for composure, she swung open the door, hoping that despite her muddy jeans and old oxford shirt, the expression she'd placed on her face was gracious.

Seeing him again literally took her breath away. She felt the same way she did as a child at Christmas when she opened a wrapped present to find that the gift she'd desperately wanted was actually there. He was every bit as imposing in his dark good looks as she'd remembered. He was wearing jeans and an immaculate long sleeved white shirt—what seemed to be a uniform for him. The formality suited him, she decided.

He was inspecting her with the same intense scrutiny. When his eyes rested on her forehead, he smiled, amused.

"What?" She reached up to touch her forehead.

"May I?" With his eyes crinkled, he reached up to brush some dirt from her forehead.

"I was in the garden...." She was mortified and began rubbing at her forehead furiously.

"A streak of mud is a badge of honor in our business," Michael said gently. "And you wear it well."

She felt a blush rising. "You were early."

"I hope you don't mind. We weren't sure how long the trip would take." *We were eager,* he thought.

"No, of course not," she blurted. "I've been waiting for you." Her toes curled. *Was that too obvious?*

"My brother is here to help take measurements. He's already walking around to the side lot." He turned on the step toward the yard.

Charlotte hid her disappointment that they wouldn't sit first to discuss her plans, perhaps over a cup of coffee, with some thick cream and one of the doughnuts she'd purchased especially for him. She'd imagined showing him all the books she'd read, pointing out the pictures of flowers she liked best and now knew the names of. "You're a quick study," he might say. She'd demur. Perhaps they'd even laugh, get to know each other a little better. Why did she always have such hopes, she scolded herself as they walked outdoors in single file. She was such a romantic. Why did she think this was anything but business?

She followed Michael's long-legged stride around the house to where she spied a tall, very thin young man with equally long legs and a wide-brimmed hat standing in the shade of a cypress, reading a small paperback novel. Michael called out to him as they approached. He looked up, waved briefly and tucked the book into his jacket pocket. Closer, she noticed that his skin, though a darker shade than her own, was still much fairer than Michael's deeply tanned color. Yet, it still looked pale in an unhealthy way. Dark circles shadowed his eyes under the floppy hat, but the smile he offered her when she drew near was warm and open.

"This is my brother, Bobby Mondragon," Michael said. Then turning to his brother, "Our new client, Charlotte Godfrey."

Bobby reached out to shake her hand with one that was surprisingly soft for someone who did outdoor labor. "Ah, yes, Miss Godfrey," Bobby said in a tone that implied he'd heard plenty about her already. He slid a telling glance at his brother, brows arched. "A pleasure."

Charlotte murmured some pat phrase, wildly wondering what had been the topic of conversation in the truck on the way here. Michael frowned, confirming her suspicions.

"Will you help design the garden?" she asked Bobby.

"Good heavens, no. I leave that kind of high brow scribbling to Miguel, here," he replied genially, nodding toward Michael. "I like to use what the nuns called my 'native intelligence' and throw paint on the walls of abandoned buildings in the city."

"Don't mind him," Michael said. "He's very proud to be a muralist." He looked with affection at his brother. "And I'm proud to say he's one of the best. The park commission hired him to paint two more city buildings this summer."

"What kind of murals do you paint?"

"No cacti or coyote," he replied, teasing her. "I'm a mere step higher than a graffiti artist."

Michael shook his head, chuckling. "We should get to work."

For the next half hour Bobby and Michael walked the lot taking measurements, discussing where a few shade trees might be placed, where the best sites for future flower beds would be, and how to achieve privacy from the road. Charlotte felt the excitement of building something new. In contrast, Bobby was bored. He'd done this a million times before.

Later in the morning, Michael worked alone, noting in his book the sun's patterns on the property, taking soil samples, getting a feel for the way the house sat on the lot. He walked to stand on a small rise that gave him full view of the expanse. Cragged rocks below met smooth, grassy plateau and a sea of blue sky. The small, defiant house perched on the cliff caught his imagination. The landscape only interested him as far as it augmented the structure.

He missed working with buildings. Cement and mortar. Wood and tile. Yet his father was willful. After the two years, he felt more and more sucked into his father's plans. His father had successfully eked out another season from his promise. "Build your own house here!" Luis prodded. "Get married. Raise beautiful Mexican children." Michael looked over to where Charlotte was holding the measuring tape along the ground for Bobby and felt a sudden lurching of his heart. Such times as these, the idea of staying in California was very appealing indeed.

He looked back at the house, away from the girl. But it could never be. He would give his father this final season. Then he'd return to Chicago and the architectural firm that waited impatiently, that promised he'd rise as fast as any of the skyscrapers he helped design.

Charlotte looked up from the measuring tape and saw

Michael standing alone on the small rise. The man seemed a part of the scenery as he stood, hands on hips, his hair whipped by the wind like the meadowsweet at his feet, his jaw set like the granite rocks.

"He must love his job," she said to Bobby.

Bobby looked up and followed her gaze to his brother, standing alone and studying the house. "His job?" He offered a smile filled with irony. "Yes. I suppose he does. Pity."

Charlotte looked at him, puzzled.

Bobby pulled back the measuring tape and tucked the pencil in his pocket. "We're all done here. Let's go catch up with Renaissance Man and see what he's been scheming. Yo!" he called out.

Above, the gulls arced and cried out in reply.

"You've got the worst house and the loveliest site," Michael said when they reached his side. "You could do a lot with it."

Charlotte glanced at the square structure with a questioning face. "*I* can't do anything with it," she corrected him. "Since I don't own it. An old widow owns it, and I think she's just holding on to it for sentiment's sake. She doesn't want to do any repairs or even paint it, so I doubt we'll get her interested in renovations."

"Too bad. There aren't many opportunities like this available anymore."

"Forget the house," Bobby said, coming up from behind. "She didn't ask for an architect. The lady just wants a garden."

"I realize that," Michael conceded, shaking his head. "I can't help but mention what seems so obvious to me. I'm just tossing out ideas." He smiled at Charlotte with what she could only interpret as flirtation. "No charge, of course."

"My brother," Bobby confided loudly enough for Michael to hear. "He's mad for houses. He's an architect, did you know that?"

"An architect?" Charlotte replied, confused, looking at Michael. "I thought…"

"I design gardens now," Michael replied firmly, cutting off any further discussion on the topic. He glared at his brother in warning.

"He's stubborn, too," Bobby added with another laugh. Michael's discomfort only seemed to add fuel to his teasing.

"I'll remember that," she said, catching Bobby's eye. She liked him, though he really was a rascal.

They were laughing when they reached the front patio.

"Would you like some coffee? Some water or something?"

"Water would be nice."

She led them through the house toward the kitchen, stopping dead when she entered. Melanie was shredding lettuce in the sink, still in her bikini. Her incredible body, all bronzed and slick with oil, was displayed like a feast. Michael coughed as he entered the room.

Melanie turned her head and smiled, totally at ease in her attire.

"Sorry to bother you, Melanie," Charlotte said, a little embarrassed. "We're just passing through."

Melanie, however, had eyes only for the two tall, handsome men who stood regarding her in silence. She offered a coy smile of acknowledgment.

"These are the men from the nursery I told you were coming. Michael and Bobby Mondragon."

Melanie's gaze flickered over Bobby, then rested on Michael, swallowing him whole. "Well, hello there," she drawled in her breathy voice. "So, you're the gardeners?"

Charlotte saw Michael stiffen and he pursed his lips, as though holding in a retort.

Bobby, who had a fine sense of the absurd, bowed slightly.

Melanie had a fine-tuned instinct herself where men were concerned. She arched her back as she turned from the sink, offering a full view of her ample bosom and generously curved hips and thighs. Charlotte glanced nervously at Michael and Bobby. Michael's face was unreadable. Bobby was smiling, obviously very amused.

Charlotte thought now seemed an excellent time to offer drinks.

"I told Charlotte that I thought it was ridiculous for her to make you come all the way out here just to draw up a design for a flower bed. She has all these grandiose ideas, but she has no idea what she's getting into."

"And you do?" asked Bobby with a thin smile.

"Oh, sure. Did I mention that I once had a very large garden? With a pool?"

"How very fortunate for you," Bobby replied with an urbane air. "We can recommend some very reputable pool companies."

"What? No," she hurried with a small frown. "We certainly don't want anything so grand here. We're both, how shall I put it, in transit. I hope Charlotte hasn't been giving you the wrong impression. We're in between films."

"You're an actress?" Michael directed his question to Charlotte.

"I'm Melanie Ward. You don't recognize me?" There was an unmistakable hurt in the tone.

"You look familiar," Bobby hurried to reply. "But I don't see many movies."

Melanie's face fell as her shoulders slumped.

"Melanie's been in loads of films, but she's a character actor," Charlotte rushed in, trying to patch things up. "Everyone knows her face. Didn't you see *Crazy Girls*?"

"Oh, yes, of course," Bobby replied, smiling weakly. Everyone knew he hadn't. An awkward silence fell.

Michael kept his questioning gaze on Charlotte.

"I'm just beginning," she hedged, aware of Melanie beside her. "I've done a few small films. Nothing's out yet. I'm still a nobody. You wouldn't know me." Her cheeks ached from holding on to the starched smile.

"Her first major role starts next month," Melanie prompted with pride in her voice.

"Next month? Then you'll want this design in a hurry. I'll work on it right away and call you, what? Tomorrow?"

"Tomorrow would be fine," she replied.

Melanie gave off an unladylike snort and slipped her sunglasses back on as though to punctuate her remarks. "I said it before and I'll say it again. I don't know why you're going to all this trouble. It's just a rental, you know."

"So I've been told," Michael replied, seemingly unoffended. "However, I'm sure I can design a flower garden that will fit Miss Godfrey's budget." He turned to Charlotte again, ignoring Melanie completely. He smiled and looked at her as if she were the only one in the room. "And it's no trouble at all."

Charlotte was walking back to the kitchen, hoping to find out what Melanie thought of Michael Mondragon. She saw in her eyes that Melanie had found him attractive. That pleased Charlotte. She looked forward to flopping on Melanie's bed, laughing with her pal again and giggling about boys, the way she'd always imagined sisters or best friends did. The way she saw it done in the movies.

She was about to push open the door when she stopped, hand stilled in midair.

Melanie was standing before her bureau mirror, staring at herself. Her hands slipped down to encircle her waist while she sucked in her tummy and pushed out her ample chest. Then she pivoted from left to right, one shoulder up, the other down, her cheeks sucked in and her full lips pursed in a sexy pinup girl pose.

Charlotte caught her breath and stepped back, blushing. This felt too personal, like she was a voyeur or a Peeping Tom. She'd taken another step back when she saw Melanie slowly exhale. It was pitiful, like watching a balloon deflate. Her shoulders slumped, her breasts and stomach sagged, her head drooped and her mouth slipped into a frown. Melanie stood quietly and still before the mirror, her breath marking the rise and fall of her ample breasts. Suddenly, she hid her face in her hands and wept bitterly.

Charlotte winced and backed slowly away from the door, careful not to make a sound. Her heart ached for Melanie. She knew better than anyone the pain of not liking one's own reflection.

In the pickup truck, Bobby was not letting his little brother off the hook easily. He was merciless in his praise of Charlotte's beauty, her poise, her sweetness, anything he could think of, because the more he heralded her the more stone-faced Michael became. It was an old game they'd played years back when Michael was in high school and had dated scores of girls, but seldom the same girl for very long.

"*Madre de Dios*, the face of an angel she has," Bobby exclaimed. "Those wide-set eyes, such an exquisite color. I'd love to paint her in one of my murals. I'd call it *Venus on the Taco Shell*." He laughed, leaning far over the steering wheel. "Do you think she'd pose nude?"

Michael scowled. "Watch where you're going." He shifted in his seat. "And your mouth. Better yet, pull over. I'll drive."

"Not on your life, gringo. You've got your mind on that pretty little gringa, and there's no way I'm going to put my life in your fevered hands. Who knows what you'll be grabbing when you downshift. That Melanie, however." He whistled softly. "What is it with that one? If I was a betting man, I'd have lost five bucks that she was going to fall out of the bikini before we left.''

"It wasn't for lack of trying."

Bobby burst out laughing again.

Michael shook his head in disgust. "I can't stand women like that. So obvious. There's nothing left to the imagination."

"Oh, I dunno. I'd say there was a lot left to the imagination. X-rated, of course." He pushed the envelope. "You mean to say you weren't thinking of that gorgeous Charlotte Godfrey in that way?"

Michael swung his head to glare at Bobby, but remained silent.

"Ah, I see how it is," Bobby said, wonder mixed with a little pity. "No joking with that one, eh? Very interesting. Has cupid's arrow finally hit your heart? Well, well, well." He considered for a moment. "Papa won't like it. He has his heart set on you marrying a nice Mexican girl and having lots of little Mexican babies."

"Oh, no," Michael replied, laughing now. "*You* are the eldest Mondragon son. Not me. That's your job to fill."

Bobby grew very silent, strangely so. Michael saw his muscles tense as he leaned over the wheel, like a large cat, about to pounce. They drove a mile more as an awkward silence settled in the cab. Bobby lit a cigarette and turned to look at him from time to time, his expression changing from cautious to pondering to resigned.

"If anyone is going to produce Mondragon babies," he said, his voice assuming a nonchalance that rang false, "it'll have to be you, *hermano*. It isn't going to be me." He paused, flicked an ash. "I'm gay."

Michael felt the air whoosh out of him, all replies tumbling out with it. He looked straight ahead and rode out the news, his emotions rising and falling with the hills. He heard the words *I'm gay* again, but couldn't grasp them. Not Bobby. Not a Mondragon.

Yet, from somewhere deep in his mind, he had to admit that he wasn't really shocked. He'd always wondered about Bobby, but wrote it off in his mind. Bobby was eccentric. Bobby had style, good taste, culture. So what if he was thirty-one and didn't have a girlfriend? He just wasn't sexual. Better asexual than homosexual. Everyone in the family thought this, hinted at this, but dared not voice it directly. Such things were not discussed. Secrets, especially important ones, were best held close.

Michael's mind felt numb as the miles passed uncomfortably in his silence. He kept thinking of how he'd missed all the signs. Bobby's mannerisms, the tone of his voice, his having a lot of friends who were girls, but no girlfriends. He was careful with his dress but never flamboyant. His father had noticed this, too. He used to laugh at Bobby's double breasted suits, his fine leather shoes, his attention to detail. What did Papa call him? A man-about-town? But always with a hint of pride in his voice, that his son was so good looking. A Mexican man showing the gringos how it's done. Papa especially liked the scarf tied around Bobby's neck. Thought it was Mexican. Such fools they were. The scarf was not a bandanna. It was Hermés.

The clues were all there, but Michael had never taken the time to add them all up. Or had the courage to see the sum total.

"Does Papa know?"

"What do you think?" He took a long drag from his cigarette. "Haven't you noticed that Papa and I are—" Bobby searched for the word "—incommunicado?"

Michael nodded and cleared his throat. It felt very dry and his tongue felt thick; it was difficult to form words. "Sure," he replied uneasily. "He's never easy to get along with. I figured that he's still angry at you for not taking over the business."

"Oh, yeah, he was," Bobby replied, his sarcasm unable to disguise the depth of his bitterness. "Still is...especially

since you took off, too. It's sad.'' A long drag on his cigarette. ''Papa and I used to be so close. Once he was proud
of my murals, especially the ones about Mexican culture.
When he used to point them out to his friends, it made me
feel proud, you know? Like what I did had value. Even if
it wasn't the family business.'' He shrugged. ''I guess he
thought that I'd just give the murals up as I grew older.
Like my painting was just some little boyhood hobby.''

''You didn't tell him?''

''What? About being gay? Jesus, I told you I was gay,
not nuts.''

''He should know. It's nothing to be ashamed about.''

Bobby burst out laughing. ''Esse, you think I don't tell
him because I'm ashamed of being gay? Who is being naive here?'' His dark eyes were scornful. ''I'm gay. It's who
I am. I have no problem with that. But Papa?'' His expression turned bitter and his eyes glittered with scorn.
''You grew up in the same house I did. What do you think
would happen if I told him?''

''I can't even guess.''

''Well I can. First off, he wouldn't believe me. He
wouldn't even hear the words. And even if he did, well,
he'd probably beat me to a pulp. To get the demon out.''

''I wouldn't let him beat you.'' Michael ground out the
words.

''God damn it, Miguel,'' Bobby shouted back. ''I don't
want you fighting my battles anymore. I'm a man, too. I
don't need you to defend me to my own father!'' The car
swerved a bit, chewed some gravel, then settled back on
the pavement.

''Take it easy...''

Bobby's face was red and he was breathing hard. He took
a minute to gather his emotions, then said in a quiet, steady
voice, *''I don't want you to tell him.''*

''All right. I won't.''

''Swear it.''

"I said I wouldn't."

"Promise."

Michael sighed and leaned his head back. "*Sí*, Roberto. *Yo te promiso.*" He paused and rubbed the bridge of his nose. "It's your decision. It's just a damn shame that you can't talk to your own father."

"When could we ever?"

Bobby made the usual exit off the highway. When they hit the back roads, he reached into his pocket and pulled out another of those thick black cigarettes he favored.

"Does Mama know?" Michael asked more softly.

Bobby looked haunted but merely lifted his shoulders. "We never spoke about it, of course. But when the family gathers for Sunday dinners, birthdays, saints days, whatever, she doesn't ask me about my girlfriends anymore. She suspects but will never pry. She's afraid of the truth. No, little brother. She won't ask. *Mamacita* only wants to know if I'm going to church. To confession." He let out a short laugh and shifted a sideways glance. "Sodomy is a sin, you know. A mortal sin, eh?"

Michael refused to see the humor.

"They pushed the truth down so deep that they never had to deal with it. Or accept it. It's easier to tell themselves that I'm a crazy, good for nothing artist with an artist's ways."

"Roberto…"

"No, I mean it. They've never come to visit my apartment. Not once." He lit another cigarette in precise, angry movements. After a long drag he exhaled a steady stream. "It's a nice place, too. I have good windows," he continued wistfully.

Michael knew that Bobby was struggling to hold back the tears. To make this easier for both of them.

They pulled up to the nursery in deathly silence. Michael felt ashamed, like he'd let his brother down. He should have been here, to protect him, as he always had. He won-

dered what Bobby had to go through during the past years
while he was gone. Was he discriminated against? Mocked?
Or worse? He'd heard about gay bashing.

He looked over again at Bobby staring out through the
windshield. His face, like his secrets, was masked. Michael
felt a rush of compassion and affection. Bobby was his
brother. He'd go visit his brother's apartment, he decided.
Meet his friends. See his windows.

Bobby turned his head around and met his gaze, almost
reading his thoughts. His troubled expression lessened, and
his frown shifted into a crooked smile. Then, in the same
manner of their father, Bobby leaned over to wrap an arm
around his shoulder in a typical, masculine embrace.

Michael flinched. It all happened in mere seconds. A
simple reflex. An involuntary movement. One flinch, but
they'd both felt it. Bobby drew back, his face ashen as
though he'd just been slapped.

Michael was frozen. He wanted to take it back. He hadn't
meant it.

"Bobby..." he said, reaching out to him as Bobby retreated, opening the car door. He grabbed his shoulder.

Bobby shrugged him off. "I'm sorry if I repulse you."

Michael raised his empty hand to his forehead and
rubbed hard, swearing. His gut hurt as he cursed his own
stupidity.

"Bobby!" he called as he leaped from the car, slamming
the door and running after him.

"Leave me alone," Bobby snarled back, waving him
away.

"God damn it, wait," Michael shouted, hot on his heels.
When he didn't slow down, Michael reached out and
grabbed Bobby's arm, spinning him around. Bobby's eyes
glowed with anger, his jaw was locked with hostility.

"What the hell did you expect?" Michael ground out,
anger flaring. "You dump a load like that on me and expect

me to smile and say, 'Oh great. You're gay. Let's go get a beer'?''

"Yeah. Exactly."

"Bullshit. You knew that wasn't going to happen."

"Yeah, right again. I did. More's the pity. Call me an optimist, but I'd hope you'd be sympathetic. I didn't know you were so fucking homophobic."

Michael looked at his shoes, ashamed. Looking back up, he saw the hurt in Bobby's eyes more than the anger. "I'm not afraid," he replied, calmer now. "At least, I hope I'm not. I'm just a guy who wasn't ready to hear all that from his brother."

Bobby looked at him with a strained expression, as though he wanted to argue the point. He pressed his fingers to his lips, eyes squinting, then simply shook his head like a dog shaking off the tension.

"Well I'm just a guy who happens to be gay. It's your problem how to deal with being my brother. Not mine." Then he whirled around and walked away down the gravel path, disappearing into the darkness.

Nine

Charlotte woke up two days later to discover Michael Mondragon pacing the width of the lot outside her bedroom window. She was peeking out at the day's weather when her hand froze on the curtain. She gasped and the lace fell back across the window. She told herself it didn't matter what she wore, but she tossed away two dresses before she chose the simple mint green sheath, slipped into sandals, splashed her face with cold water and hurried out to meet him.

Michael smiled when he saw her, thinking the day just turned sunnier. She was a vision with her pale blond hair caught in the wind and her long, slender legs looking like they went on forever under that short summer dress. She took long, graceful strides across the lot. When she drew near, he was moved by the eagerness in her eyes.

"Hello," she said with a tilting glance, her hand smoothing her hair in the breeze. "You can't be finished with your drawings already?"

On another woman it might have been a coquettish gesture, but there was nothing intentionally come-hither about Charlotte.

"I am. Time was of the essence, since you're leaving in a few weeks. I should have called, but I spent most of the night finishing them and drove out here at first light. I doubted you were up that early this morning.''

"Just woke up now, as a matter of fact.''

He tucked his hands behind his back and stood erect, holding back his enthusiasm. His thick dark brows had a way of angling down to his straight nose in a serious, almost scowling manner. It made his boyish excitement all the more endearing.

"Well, let me see them. I'm dying of curiosity.''

He began to unroll the designs, but the wind tugged at the thin sheets of paper.

"This won't do," she called out, chasing after one and catching it midair. "Let's go inside. I'm desperate for a cup of coffee, anyway. How about you?''

"You're an angel of mercy.''

"How do you like it?''

"Strong and black, please.''

Of course, she thought to herself, glancing back. His lush black hair was tied back in a stubby ponytail again today. Thanking her stars that she'd scoured away Melanie's lasagna mess last night, she led him to the kitchen, where he spread out the designs for her on the hardwood table, using utensils as weights. The sugar bowl rested on the magnolia tree, a fork lined a row of rhododendrons, a spoon rested on the perennial bed, and a salt shaker held down a few Australian pines. Charlotte slipped down into the chair, her chin in her palm only a few inches above the wood, staring like a child at a picture book story.

The blue ink transformed the blocky terrain of her lot into a rounding, graceful living space filled with flowering bushes, a few well chosen trees and swirls of perennial beds, ground covers and tiered annual beds.

"It's more than you asked for, so don't get worried. I like to get a picture in my mind of what can be done, then we can pare down together what you want and can afford.

It's not a hard sell, believe me. It's only to give you choices."

"Who said I was worried? I'm just speechless. It's hard to believe it's the same lot. It's...wonderful."

His eyes sparkled in pleasure. "It's all about using space to its maximum. People don't need a lot of land to feel like they've got a beautiful place to come home to."

She'd always wanted a beautiful place to come home to. "What's this one?" she asked, leafing through the several drawings and pulling out one that included sketches for the house.

"You weren't supposed to see that one," he said, pulling the design sheet out of the pile.

"Please let me. I'd like to see your ideas for the house." She shrugged. "Even if it's way beyond the possibility."

He traced his long index finger around the blue lines that extended the house's left side to encircle the tile patio facing the cliff. The skin under his rolled up, long sleeved white shirt was deeply tanned and marked by tiny crisscrossed scratches from vines or maybe roses.

"I couldn't help myself," he explained, raking his hands through his hair in discomfort. "It's so painfully obvious to me what this house needs." He swept his fingers across the design, as though sweeping away the fantasy. "I know it's a rental, but I wanted to draw it out for my own pleasure. It's been a while since I've done an architectural drawing."

It was clear that the house, not the garden, held his heart. "Why did you leave architecture?" she asked.

His face clouded, and he placed another garden design over the house design. "I didn't. I'm working at the nursery for a short time to help the family." He paused, then added in a quieter, slightly troubled voice, "Sometimes, family needs take priority."

She felt more attracted to him for his loyalty to his family and his reticence to talk about his personal life. Michael

Mondragon had a quiet reserve, a holding back, that she resonated to. Like a dark, mysterious pond.

"Do you build houses?"

"I can," he replied easily. "But I prefer skyscrapers. To build something that literally scrapes at the clouds is thrilling. Uplifting." His excitement radiated.

"From the earth to the sky. That's quite a leap."

He smiled then, thinking in an odd way that this girl understood. Looking at the design, he asked, "What about you?"

"What about me?"

"You've just made a leap into movies. No mean feat that."

"If you only knew," she muttered, playing at a corner of the paper. "I've been very lucky. I always wanted to act but never believed I'd actually get the chance." When he looked at her quizzically, she added, "Let's just say I was a gawky child."

He laid down his pencil and sat down beside her. "Beautiful women always say that. How ugly they were as children. Why is that? It strikes me as a little phony sounding." He leaned back in his chair. "I can't believe you were ever ugly. I'll bet you came out of the womb perfect."

Charlotte forced a smile on her face and turned her head. Inside her stomach, the coffee burned. "Believe me, I was ugly."

He seemed skeptical. "The ugly duckling turned into a swan story."

Charlotte frowned, suddenly irritated. "Something like that." She swung her head around, her eyes defiant. "Why is that so difficult to believe? You tell me you can make that ugly space of land out there turn into this beautiful garden and expect me to believe you."

He held out his hands in surrender. "You win. I believe you were an ugly child."

Hearing the words took her breath away. She wanted

suddenly to be honest with him, to say, "Yes, that's right,"
then tell him all about her lonely life, the teasing, the cru-
elties. The surgery. Maybe, too, how she'd met him once
before. In the elevator. She was that ugly girl—did he even
remember her?

Impossible, she thought. He could never know that. He'd
think she was some kind of freak. She'd made her decision
back in Chicago. Charlotte Godowski was gone. She was
Charlotte Godfrey now. Charlotte Godfrey was the woman
Michael Mondragon knew. Pushing the shy, embarrassed
girl deep down inside of herself, Charlotte clenched her jaw
and focused on the garden designs on the table.

"I'd like the magnolia near my bedroom, so I can see
the blooms. My mother loved magnolias."

Resting his palm on the table, he leaned again to quickly
alter the design, moving a tree with a few sharp strokes of
his pencil. Her stomach fluttered as his shirt breezed against
her cheek.

"Done. And I think you should definitely do the annuals.
Here…and here."

His closeness was suffocating. She couldn't believe that
he didn't feel the intensity that their nearness provoked.

"You make it look so easy. I can't even draw a straight
line," she said, her voice raspy.

"I owe it all to the nuns and the Palmer Method of Hand-
writing."

She laughed, remembering the Palmer Method herself
and practicing row after row of loops.

"Where did you grow up?" he asked, trying to stimulate
a conversation.

Her laughter faded and she sat back in her chair. "Chicago," she replied cautiously.

"No kidding? Small world. Where?"

"Oh…" Her mind scanned possible locations that would
be vague enough, nice enough. Somewhere her mother
might clean houses. "Out in the western suburbs."

"Which suburb?"

He was nothing if not persistent. What would happen if she said, *Oh, actually, the western part of the city. On Harlem Avenue, in one of those apartment buildings an architect like you would just love. Right next to Burger King and Stella the Star Gazer. She tells fortunes for ten bucks a pop.*

She looked up at him as he waited for her reply. Would that make her any less desirable? she wondered. Would she want him if it did?

"Oak Park," she replied, coughing on the lie. "It's a city, actually. Just off the Eisenhower Expressway."

"Of course I know where it is. The Frank Lloyd Wright museum is there. Some great houses of his, too." He looked at his hand, then asked in a casual way, "Did you live alone?"

"No." She held back her smile when his brows knitted. "I lived with my mother. She needed me and I felt I should stay with her."

He couldn't conceal his pleasure.

"And you?"

"I live downtown. I still have a loft on Printer's Row."

She arched a brow. "That's a nice area. Very artsy and chic."

"It's convenient, close to the museums and the library. It suits me."

She imagined it did. Very well. "You must miss it."

He shrugged. "You must miss your mother."

"I do...I do." She thought quickly. "She's very active, has lots of friends. She had this lovely old house that she'd lived in forever, but it got to be too much for her, you see. Especially since I was leaving for California. So she had to sell it. Now she lives in a condo. It's very nice," she hurried to explain. "Everything she wants at this point in her life. Elevators, it's near shopping and the church. All her friends are close by. You know, a no-muss-or-fuss style of living. She's very active.'' Charlotte wiped her brow, feeling the beginning of a headache in her temples. ''I'm sure she doesn't miss me.''

''I find that hard to believe. I'm sure she must miss you very much.''

Tears threatened and she looked away. She didn't want to talk about her mother. ''Let's talk about the garden,'' she said, pursing her lips and squinting as she made a show of studying the plans. Then in sharp precision she pointed to areas of plantings.

''If I understand it right, we've got the annuals here and here by the front door...the magnolia here...I can wait on the ground cover...a few yews here, and oh, yes. I must have this bed of lilies. Done. How much is that?'' She raised her gaze to his, all business. ''With labor included. And, of course, whatever you need to bring the soil up to speed. Compost, peat moss, whatever. I want the plants I put in to thrive. I'd rather start small but with a good foundation.''

Michael wondered what he'd said that made her suddenly so cool and unapproachable. He hadn't meant to press. He thought he'd been careful. Still, he couldn't help but be impressed. She was able to make quick decisions, and her instincts were good. He'd have advised her to make the same choices.

''A three dollar hole for a one dollar plant, my father always says.'' He made a few notations on his designs while she watched, leaning far over the table, her face inches from his. Her hair smelled sweet, like shampoo. He closed his eyes and inhaled it, then cleared his throat.

''Would you rather I leave this here for you to look at? You can call me at the nursery if you have any questions. Or perhaps you'd rather Bobby called?''

''No,'' she replied quickly, sitting back in her chair. ''I'd rather you stayed.'' Their gazes locked, and she saw with some amazement that it wasn't only she who was feeling nervous. She'd never thought that someone like him might feel awkward, especially not with someone like her. She reached out to touch his arm.

"Stay, please. Do you think I would know what questions to ask?" she said through a small smile. "I think that I'd rather you explained it all to me. Very carefully. There's no hurry. I'll make that coffee. And I've got scones. Have you had breakfast?"

The morning lingered long past the point where she'd selected the annuals, added a few more perennials and changed to a cluster of rhododendrons near the front door. Michael had already decided that he'd do a large portion of the labor himself, at his own expense. It would give him a good excuse to be near her. Charlotte wanted Michael to add one small feature to the plan.

"I'd like a small kitchen garden, for Melanie. Tomatoes, herbs, those kind of things."

Michael cocked his head. "Are we thinking of the same Melanie? She made it clear she didn't want anything to do with a garden."

"Not flowers or bushes, nothing like that. But she loves to cook, and I'd like to do something special for her. Nothing that would require a lot of work," she added, thinking of Melanie's manicure.

"I'll do whatever you like, of course." He paused, scribbling. "The two of you are an odd pair," he said. "You're...different," he concluded.

"We are, I suppose. She can be very sweet. She knows about a lot about things I don't, like the smarts of filmmaking. And makeup." She looked at her own ruined manicure. The day after they were done she'd ruined her nails by scrubbing the floors with hot, soapy water. Melanie had taken one look at the chipped polish, hurried for her kit and wiped it all off. Charlotte smiled at the memory.

"I don't think you saw her best side the other day."

His eyes lit up. "I'd say she has any number of good

sides." Relieved that she chuckled, he considered the plan again. "I was thinking," he said, tapping the pencil. "What about pots on the patio? It's quick, easy, attractive. I think even Melanie would approve."

"Perfect! She can step out from the kitchen and clip them with scissors. She won't muss a nail."

"I have a few more calls to make today." He hesitated, then took the gamble. "Why don't we finish this later, over dinner? Say, about six?"

She couldn't believe he was saying the words. She reached for her coffee and took a small sip. "You don't have to do that," she replied, looking at her cup. "I don't expect you to work that hard just because I'm in a hurry."

He took her hand and studied her long fingers with their oval nails. Unpolished, unpretentious, like her. "It will be my pleasure," he said, gently rubbing her knuckles with his thumb. Then with a wicked smile, he added, "And I hope it won't all be work."

That evening, Michael picked her up, not in his red pickup truck with the name Mondragon emblazoned on the door, but in a sleek, dark and powerful convertible, his one indulgence for putting the rest of his life on hold and living with his family, he explained to her as they roared toward the city. She ran her hand over the buttery softness of the leather, thinking dangerous thoughts. The night was balmy so the top was down. She wound a silk scarf around her hair, enjoying the feel of warm air and soft silk against her face. He drove her to a charming Italian restaurant that faced the Pacific Ocean and had a great sunset view.

The maître d' at La Luna knew him by name and welcomed him with a wide grin of pleasure. When he spied Charlotte beside him, he pursed his lips in a silent whistle while shaking his hand as though it were burning. Michael discreetly lowered his brows and shook his head in warning, but it didn't do any good. By the time they were seated at his favorite table by the window, two busboys were circling Charlotte like buzzing bees, filling her water glass to the brim, piling a tower of pats of butter on her plate. When one moonstruck boy, an eighteen-year-old, offered to smooth her napkin onto her lap, Michael scowled dangerously and grabbed the napkin from his hand.

"I'm sorry," he said, offering her back the napkin. "It's not often they see a woman as beautiful as you."

"It's not your fault," she said, though she felt uneasy. She always found such displays uncomfortable. "I'm told I have to get used to it."

He raised his brows. "Ah, yes, the ugly duckling." He saw her frown and quickly gestured to the waiter, who promptly brought a bottle of Pinot Grigio to the table. Michael tasted it, then took the bottle, pouring her a glassful himself. She sipped it slowly, her long fingers with the pale nails curled around the crystal. Her skin glowed in the candlelight, and again he felt a powerful surge of desire for her. He'd have to be very careful with this one.

The waiters, eager to make amends, hurried to bring heaping platters of aromatic pasta, grilled eggplant, peppers and zucchini dribbled with extra virgin olive oil and rosemary, long coils of spicy sausage and samplings of pungent, creamy cheeses. Charlotte ate with abandon, savoring the delicious meal as she told him stories about her life.

For that's what she told him, stories. Fiction, peppered with facts as pungent and spicy as the food. Her mother was a widow living comfortably on the money left to her by her father. What did she do in her spare time? Well, she spent her time painting. She was very good, respected by her colleagues. But no, he wouldn't know her work. Her mother didn't show in galleries any longer. Her father died when she was young, but she remembered him well. He was handsome. A good, kind man. She'd loved him very much. There wasn't much left of the small fortune he'd left them, so her mother was prudent.

Charlotte went on to tell him how she loved to act and played principal roles in all her high school and college plays. Did he enjoy Shakespeare? She'd played so many roles: Juliet, Ophelia, Portia.

As the candles glowed low, she recited her life's story, her voice well modulated, the gentle music playing in the background. He asked her questions which she answered carefully, always with an amusing detail added, such as the time she missed her cue and left Romeo hanging on the balcony, or how her father loved to watch her run and dance herself into a frenzy as he played the Hungarian Rhapsody on the piano...the old family Steinway. While Charlotte Godowski quivered deep inside of her, Charlotte Godfrey came alive as she spoke, filling in the gaping holes in her background with tales that, in time, she'd claim as her own.

After all, she thought, what were memories? How different was this than the selective memories other children unknowingly created when they viewed the Super 8 mm films of their childhood? Those of Grandpa lying on the picnic blanket, Dad with a thick head of hair raking leaves in the yard, a slender, beautiful mother on Christmas morning? She was simply taking the initiative. These sentimental stories she wove tonight would become her own selective memories.

Michael sat back and enjoyed listening to her unusual, husky voice and watching her absentminded gestures as she spoke. He loved the way she toyed with her long, silky hair or reached out to tap his hand to punctuate a point. He especially liked the way she stroked his sleeve while recollecting some detail. While she spoke, she was totally unaware of her potent allure, so intent was she on the telling. Occasionally he'd glimpse a sadness in her eyes when she paused to consider her answer, but once she began speaking again her eyes came alive and were focused solely on him.

It was almost as though she were gauging his responses to her answers.

As the candles dripped low, he felt pampered by her attention, flattered and very aroused. He was aware, even if she was not, that her eye-blasting beauty was mesmerizing and had attracted the attention not only of Tony and the rest of the waiters, but of every red-blooded man in the restaurant.

By the time a bowl of fruit and chocolates arrived for dessert, it was already dark outdoors, two bottles of wine sat emptied and the candles were short stubs in their holders.

"Not another bite," she sighed, leaning back in her chair and tapping her fingers across her flat stomach.

"Perhaps just a plum?"

Sighing, she took the plum from his extended hand, their fingertips lightly grazing, then lifted the ripe fruit to her lips. He groaned inwardly when she bit into its fleshy sweetness, licking the droplets of juice from her lip with a rosy-tipped tongue. Blissfully unaware.

He straightened, signaled the waiter abruptly and, within moments, settled the bill. He offered her his hand. "Shall we go?"

She nodded and after dabbing her mouth with her impossibly huge napkin, placed it on the table and slowly, gracefully rose to her feet, her eyes on him.

They drove back to her house in a comfortable silence pierced only by the music from the radio. The moist California air was heavily scented with pine and wild honeysuckle. Atop, the stars shone bright above the thick canopy of trees, and around them, the night songs of insects serenaded them as they cruised the dark, winding roads.

When they reached her house he stopped, parked and turned off the engine. He heard her shift nervously in her seat and turned his head. She was looking forward, out the windshield. Her skin was luminous in the moonlight, and the color of her lips made him think of the two ripe plums they'd had for dessert. When she bit them gently in anxiety, he could almost taste their sweetness. Her long, thin arms were clenched tight around her waist, pushing her full, rounded breasts high upon her chest. Under her sheath dress he saw the outline of her long stretch of legs and slender hips. Every sense—his sight, hearing, smell, taste, touch— all of them wanted her, demanded that he take her in his arms and taste the tender sweetness she promised.

His senses told him, too, however, that she was cautious, even fearful. That she expected him to make a move—and dreaded it. He reached over and laid his hand on hers atop the leathery seat. She startled and he heard the sharp intake of breath. On instinct, he drew himself up, opened the door and climbed from the car. He didn't miss the relief in her eyes when he guided her from the car, then to the front door. Their heels clicked on the pebbled path.

When they reached the front door, he stopped, searching her face. She offered no invitation in her eyes. There were no coy mannerisms that hinted she might be persuaded to invite him in.

"The house is dark. Is Melanie asleep?"

"Perhaps we should say good-night here," she replied, her voice strained. "So as not to wake her." She offered him her hand, the image of proper deportment. "Thank you for a lovely dinner."

The disappointment was bitter. God, he wanted her. He ached for her and was grateful for the dark shadows that obscured the evidence of his desire. "You realize," he said, holding on to her long fingers, "I'll just have to come back tomorrow to begin work on your garden."

She gave a wry smile. "It is, as you say, your job."

Touché, he thought. He felt tongue-tied, unsure, unable even to conduct a decent conversation. He was, he knew, merely lingering for one good-night kiss.

"Well—" she swallowed, then cleared her throat "—I suppose then you'll need your sleep."

He leaned forward, bringing his lips close to hers. "I'm not at all tired." He was being too eager, like a schoolboy. He would have laughed if he weren't so excited by it.

All her composure fled. Her eyes darted left to right, her color heightened, and she, too, appeared absolutely tongue-tied. Perhaps even uncomfortable. That, he couldn't bear to see.

"Charlotte," he said softly, rubbing his knuckles gently along her jaw. "Why are you afraid of me?"

She tilted her chin downward, but he lifted it back up with his fingertips so that she had to look him in the eyes. Yes, there it was again. Fear—and, yes, desire. It inflamed him. He leaned forward. "Shhh, Charlotte. I won't hurt you."

She leaned back, far against the door, then could move no farther. He continued on course, gaining ground by millimeters, his breath warming, her breath coming quicker, then, so close now, her breath mingled with his. His nostrils flared, picking up her scent. He heard her soft intake of breath and paused one nanosecond more. Then, in one smooth move, his lips were on hers.

He was gentle at first, only slight pressure on her soft, dry lips. A gentle testing. She made no move against him, but he sensed her icy reserve beginning to melt. He pressed harder, holding back the fire burning inside himself. Whose lips trembled more, his or hers? Slowly, he brought his fingers up to cup her chin, tilting her mouth, sipping deeper her sweetness. She moaned, softly, opening her lips.

His mind blurred and he lost his reserve. Desire raged through him, and he drank from the kisses like a man dying of thirst. He lunged forward, crushing her against him, letting her know, feel, his urgency. She shuddered in his arms, or was she still trembling? He couldn't tell. His hands trembled, too, as they rounded her shoulders, caressing back and forth, then slid down the slim curve of her back and the gentle swell of her buttocks. Back up again to her shoulders, where he wrapped his arms tightly around her and held her against him, lips, chests, hips pressed tight.

He heard a whimper, a soft, high sigh that pierced his black cloud of passion the way a single ray of dawn breaks the darkness. His body stilled and his hold loosened. For a moment he listened to their breathing, coming hard and warm. He released the folds of fabric bunched in his fist by her thigh and he stepped back, giving her room. Cool air rushed between them.

He looked at her face, barely visible in the dim light. Still, he could see that her lips were swollen and magenta colored, the soft skin of her cheeks was chafed by the coarseness of his late evening bristle. She was looking away, so demurely he wondered if it was an act. He might feel like a teenager, but was far from it.

"Charlotte? Is anything the matter?"

She turned her gaze upward to meet his, and he saw with amazement, and some other fierce emotion he couldn't identify, that her modesty was sincere. Her wide eyes hid nothing. She seemed frightened, even distrustful of his desire. He wanted her then as he'd never wanted any other woman, and because he knew that this feeling for her went beyond mere carnal lust, he found it in himself to back off.

"It's late," he said. "I should go."

She tilted her head, then nodded.

"I'll see you tomorrow."

"Yes. Please." She paused. "I'd like that."

He felt a wave a relief. "I'll be here early, about nine?"

"I'll be waiting."

She'll be waiting, he thought. Maybe so, but not as impatiently as he would. He doubted he'd get any sleep tonight. It was unlike him to feel so unsure, so agitated. And she...she was looking at her hands, so calm and serene in the security of her incredible beauty.

He felt a moment of doubt. Was he being played for a fool? How could someone like her be so naive? No, he'd been wrong. She was a temptress. A tease. How many men had she led on like this? Tortured? How many? In which way? The thought stabbed him with the prick of jealousy. Still, he was like a man addicted. He didn't want to see the evening end, but couldn't think of anything to say or do to delay his leaving. The silence lingered too long and grew awkward. She seemed troubled, her brows were knitted together.

"Good night, then." He turned to leave.

"Michael," she said in a voice so soft he wasn't sure he'd heard it. Looking at his arm, he saw her hand lightly touching his sleeve. "Did you ever feel—" She paused to study the crease she was making in his shirt. "Did you ever feel as though one change—I don't know, perhaps one star shifting in the sky or one, single decision—one small change occurs in a life and it's like a pivotal piece is moved and suddenly everything falls into place? Everything is... different."

"Yes," he said, looking into her eyes with a sense of heightened wonder. Could she know that was how he felt when he saw her that day in his nursery? A new thought struck him. Perhaps this was all predestined. His father calling him home. His working at the nursery. All to bring him here, at this point in time, to meet her.

"Yes," he repeated. "Absolutely I believe that."

She smiled brightly then and moved her hand to cover his heart. His larger one covered hers.

"I hoped you'd say that, Michael," she replied. "Please. I want you to stay."

Ten

$\sim\!\!\text{\textcircled{}}\!\!\sim$

She led him through the quiet house, dark except for the kitchen light.

"Melanie?" he asked, looking toward the light.

"She's not here."

He didn't reply, but squeezed her hand.

It seemed a long way to her bedroom. For her, a journey of a lifetime. Twenty-two years. Her heart raced on ahead, eager to be there, in his arms, skin to skin. Her mind, however, was back out on the porch, closing the door, locking him out. No, her heart called back, singing. Come, hurry! It's your turn, it's your time. He's the one.

He *was* the one, she knew it in her heart. Other men didn't matter. Those who offered furtive glances—all so annoying and so forgettable. Only Michael mattered. Everything about him captivated her, but it was the details that evoked this newfound sensuality in herself. She loved the way he listened to her, leaning back in his chair, relaxed, attentive, even amused. She loved the way his eyes lit up under those heavy brows at something she said, the way he cocked his head, lifted his shoulders in a shrug, the way his beautiful hands stroked the wineglass. Yes, especially that. She was driven near mad staring at his middle finger tracing a watery path across the condensation on his water goblet.

That was when she knew she wanted him. The way a woman wants a man at night, in a romantic restaurant, over drinks and glowing candles and intimate conversation. Of course, she'd been terrified of the possibility that they would be together tonight, that her long-endured celibacy would come to an end. Still, the wanting in her core was a burning thing—the fingers stroking the glass hinted at what could be, his pouting mouth, pursed in thought as he considered, then asked, question after question.... God, she felt obsessed with desire for one kiss from that mouth.

And when he did kiss her, her fears melted like ice. An Antarctic glacier slipping into the ocean. No more fears, she told herself as she approached her room. No worries, no regrets.

Her room was dark when they entered. Her hand reached for the light switch, but Michael's hand covered hers and drew it away to his lips. Her heart fluttered as he kissed each fingertip.

"Your hands are like ice," he said, rubbing them under his breath. "Are you cold?"

She shook her head.

"Wait," he said, and walked to the windows, pulling back the drapes. A pale stream of moonlight flooded the room. The whiteness of his shirt was opaque in the shaft of gold light. When he turned, she could see the whiteness of his eyes as well, standing out against his bare, tanned skin. They shone with intent. He was a study of contrasts: dark and light; tender yet strong. She, standing a short distance away, felt she was a study of shadows and secrets. He would make it all right, she thought, thinking of the lies she'd told at dinner. She would tell him the truth soon.

The hum of a zipper sounded in the silence, startling her. Unbidden, the image of Lou Kopp flashed before her.

"Let's you and I have a little party." She shuddered and turned away.

Michael immediately reached out for her.

She balked and stifled a protest.

"Charlotte?" he called to her, his voice gentle and questioning. He held out his arms again and waited. He was magnificent in his nakedness, all lean and broad shouldered, his skin the warm color of amber, his thick wavy hair falling to his shoulders. "Charlotte, you're shivering. Come here, *querida*."

She looked into his face, so full of gentleness. The specter of Lou Kopp vanished. She walked into his arms and he wrapped them around her.

"Michael," she began, her lips against the soft black hairs of his chest. Beneath her palm, she felt his heart beating. "You should know..."

"Know what, my sweet," he replied, nuzzling her forehead, her cheeks, her neck.

She sighed and tilted her head back as his kisses sent tingling shivers down her spine. "I've never done this before."

His kisses stopped abruptly as he froze, then slowly he righted himself, and holding her shoulders with his hands, he bent at the knees to stare into her eyes. "What are you saying?" he asked in seriousness. "You've never..."

"No. I've never made love. I'm a virgin."

He stared at her, blinking once. It didn't seem possible. He played the words over again in his mind. Then slowly, a small smile tilted the corners of his mouth, changing to a wide grin of surprise. "My darling, I never thought. Are you sure?"

She giggled. "Quite sure."

"No," he replied, chuckling a little. "Are you sure you want to? Make love. Tonight. With me?"

She brought her hands up to cup his face like blinders so that he would stare only into her eyes. "Oh, yes. Quite sure," she repeated. "It's just that I'm not sure what to do. How to make you happy. And—" she giggled again "—I'm a little nervous. I'm ready, willing, hopefully able. But very nervous."

He pressed her head against his chest again and lay his lips to the top of her head, then just held her, squeezing her tight for a second. Then again. Charlotte felt cherished, treasured. Unafraid.

"We shall go very slowly" was all he said, but his hands trembled as he ran his fingers down her hair and traced her jaw. Moving steadily down, he unbuttoned the seemingly countless tiny buttons on her dress, released her new lacy bra and slid away her silk panties, first one leg, then the other. It was like a choreographed ballroom dance. Each step was performed carefully and skillfully. His hands never left her body, never broke the tender connection between them, turning her left, then right, as he undressed her, then, holding her hand, led her to the double bed. Before lying down he stepped back to gaze at her, still holding hands across the expanse.

"Don't be shy," he said when she ducked her head down. "Don't you know how beautiful you are?" Her skin was like polished ivory. Her breasts were high and firm, her nipples hard. She had the voluptuous body of a temptress and the innocence of a girl. How could such a thing be possible? he wondered. How could he be so lucky?

He was as good as his word. She sensed he was holding back, going very slowly for her sake. He laid her down on the sheets, then arched over her, his dark hair falling forward. She closed her eyes, waiting, her arms by her side.

She truly was inexperienced, he thought. She positively trembled beneath him. He wanted to be gentle for her. To be patient and hold back his desire. He lowered his head. His kisses alighted here and there across her face, her shoulders, her breasts, like a butterfly sucking nectar.

She was inexperienced, true, but even she knew that he

was being exceedingly gentle. Unlike Lou… No, she shook her head, clearing it. She wouldn't think of that night. "Michael," she whispered, wanting his name on her lips.

He answered her with his mouth, searing his name on her lips, his breath like a hot iron, branding her. She willed herself to relax beneath him as his clever fingers explored her body, encircled her breasts, then slid down her taut belly to skim her inner thighs. She gasped and stiffened when he cupped the tender area between.

"Relax, my love," he murmured. "I won't hurt you. Shhh…we'll take our time."

His fingers found a spot so tender that she arched against him in surprise. He caressed her there with the flat of his thumb in small, gentle circles, swallowing her sighs with his mouth. She felt as though liquid fire flowed from that spot through her veins, engorging her core where a small nut of desire was beginning to crack in the heat. She began to move her hips involuntarily in rhythm with his hand, around and around till she felt dizzy yet sharply focused on the spiraling within her. A soft, high moan escaped when she felt a first tumbling climax. It was as though she'd left herself behind and was traveling deeper into the blackness, spiraling toward that one spot that glowed like a red hot coal.

"Michael," she called again, this time in urgency.

He moaned, vying for control. He'd felt her sudden tightening and her gush of moisture like fresh spring rains. He'd heard her sudden intake of breath, and he was blinded by the lust fire that burned upward to his brain. It ripped away his rationale, making him feel like a raging animal, wanting all of her, now. With a groan he arched above her, creating some space between them. Baring his teeth against her shoulder, he closed his eyes tight in concentration and told himself, *Slow down.…* Holding his breath, he ordered himself, *For her.*

His body responded and he felt his control return in ebbs,

amazed that it had been so difficult. He'd never felt so excited, or unsure of his skills. He wanted this to be perfect for her. This joining was so much more than another sexual encounter. It was an honor. So many women he'd had, but she was his first virgin. He'd heard the stories. There would be pain, and blood. It was said she would remember him always.

At that another instinct flared, slamming his brain with a strange new arrogance. He stared down at her face, so pale and lovely, her eyes trusting, yet fearful. He felt this arrogance puff out his chest and boil his blood. *Yes,* she would remember him, he vowed, gritting his teeth. Forever. She would be *his.*

With feral intent, he lowered his mouth to hers again, tasting the sweetness he already was addicted to. *His* sweetness, he thought. He gentled her again with soft kisses along her jaw, her neck, suckling her breasts till she moaned out loud. Only *he* would hear her moan like this, he swore. His fingers slid inside of her, testing the waters. Even though she stiffened, her body was warm and moist. She trembled as he petted and stroked. Now, slowly, he told himself, breathing hard. She is ready.

Her skin and flesh were like pink flower petals, moist with dew. When she arched again her fragrance engulfed him. His vision blurred and his blood surged.

"Tell me you want me," he almost growled.

Charlotte flickered open her eyes to see him staring down into hers with a ferocity that excited her. Her lids fluttered, and she glanced quickly down at the narrow space between them. At him. She sucked in her breath and glanced upward again, suddenly unsure.

"You must tell me," he said in a strained voice.

"I want you," she cried, quickly reaching up and holding him fast around the neck.

He saw the fear in her eyes again, but it was time. He wedged his body between her thighs, wrapping her long

legs around him. Then, fearing the first stroke would cause
her pain, he thrust in slowly, stopping when he met resistance. Raising himself, he looked into her eyes and smiled.
And waited. At last, she smiled tremulously, assuring him
of her willingness.

He thrust again. She gasped and muffled her face in the
pillow.

"*Querida,*" he murmured, gentling her with kisses, unaware that he was speaking Spanish. Then when she relaxed again, he began moving within her. Advancing and
retreating, slowly at first, giving her time to take him in.
She was so hot and tight around him. He thrilled at her
high-pitched gasps as he lunged, and her soft sighs as he
released.

Charlotte knew her virginity was over, and she hugged
Michael fiercely in a triumphant welcoming. This was right,
she told herself. I give myself to him willingly. I will never
have any regrets.

The sensation of him inside of her was so deliciously
foreign. There was nothing in her sheltered experience to
compare it to. When Michael thrust, it felt as though he'd
pushed straight up to her heart, piercing it through. Then
higher still, to her mind, obliterating all thought. Everything
except for her senses. She could smell the pungent scent of
his skin, taste the saltiness of his shoulder, feel the scrape
of his jaw against her cheek. He stoked the fire crackling
inside of her relentlessly, making that little hard coal glow
hotter and hotter. Charlotte felt bits of her past peeling
away like old veneer under the flame. The ugly girl, the
shy girl, the insecure girl, they were all curling up and
turning to ash.

Pump, Michael, she begged in her mind, arching to meet
his thrusts. Make it burn hotter. Make it burn away those
memories. Make me new. Make me whole. Make me yours.

Something was happening within her. She was being carried upward in the heat, traveling in a tunnel. She was

climbing and clawing to reach that white hot coal, just there, almost within reach. She felt crazed, sweating and gasping, calling his name. Reaching. She heard him call her own name and she felt the blast of a furnace slam into her. The burning coal exploded into a million sparks. She arched high and shuddered, suspended in time. Then the white fire slowly drained through her veins like rivulets of lava, straight out of her limp fingers and toes.

Michael felt her shuddering climax and relinquished with a groan of triumph all the control he'd so carefully commandeered until that moment. He drove once, twice more and felt her fire spread throughout his own body like a blazing torch, cleansing him of all memory of those who came before her. Scorched clean, he felt like a virgin himself. Surely, lovemaking had never felt so pure.

His pleasure penetrated his bones and he collapsed atop of her. Her bones were slack beneath him.

Later, he felt her smile move beneath his lips. For a while, neither of them spoke. Their breathing gradually returned to normal, and when he could lift his arm, he gently stroked her damp hair away from her face as he looked down at her.

"Michael," she began in a voice so quiet he had to move his head to hear her. "I feel—" She paused, lifting a limp arm to smooth away the straggles of hair from his eyes. She wanted to see him clearly. "I feel like I've been baptized." Her voice was filled with the joy and delight she felt.

"A baptism by fire." He chuckled and shifted on the mattress, lifting her to his shoulder. He took the wrinkled, stained sheet and wrapped it over them. In the warm, moist cocoon of their lovemaking, he cradled her. "Sleep now, Charlotte," he crooned in her ear. "Tomorrow will be brand-new."

Charlotte awoke with the sun pouring in from her window directly on her face. Every muscle and bone in her body ached, but it was a delicious kind of ache. Her skin felt smoother, her lips fuller, she stretched taller. Yawning, she fluttered her eyelids open, feeling a little disoriented, as if she'd wakened in some strange room.

Suddenly she recalled everything and her eyes opened wide. "Michael…"

But when she looked for him beside her, he was gone. Her mouth fell open in a silent gasp. He couldn't have left her. She'd heard how some men didn't like to wake up with a woman after casual sex. God, no, she thought, running her hand through her tousled hair. He couldn't think what they'd shared was commonplace. The pillow beside her still bore his imprint, the sheets still held his scent. But they were cold, like her heart.

"Michael?" she called out. No answer.

She rose from the bed, spotting the red stains on her sheets. The red color flooded her cheeks. Grabbing her robe to cover her nakedness, she hurried to the kitchen, to the back patio, out to the yard. His car was gone. He was gone.

She felt a sudden chill and wrapped her arms around herself. What a fool she was, she chided herself, kicking a pebble in the driveway. Last night in his arms she'd felt beautiful. Truly loved and cherished. What was the matter with her? Why couldn't anyone love her? She knew the answer. It was because she was nothing but an empty shell. When he touched her deep inside he must have sensed that. Otherwise, how could he have just left? Not even left her a note to say goodbye?

Wiping her eyes, she turned and headed back inside. Just as she reached her front door she heard a crunching of gravel at the drive and two short beeps from a horn.

Roaring up the driveway was Michael's red pickup truck, looking more like a Parisian peddler's flower cart. The sides were overflowing with the large pink blossoms of a magnolia tree, dozens of flowering shrubs, and bursting at the seams with annuals and perennials of reds, blues, yellows and pinks. Behind him were two more trucks filled with tools, soil and men in green T-shirts emblazoned with the name Mondragon.

Michael leaped from the truck and hurried to her side, scooping her in his arms and planting a deep kiss on her mouth. When he released her he handed her an enormous bouquet of flowers.

"You weren't supposed to be awake yet. I wanted to be here when you opened your eyes."

The tears in her eyes flowed down her cheeks and she reached around his neck to hug him close. "Oh, Michael, I am awake. Wide awake. And I see you."

"That's not all I want you to see. Come! Look at what I've brought," he said, tugging her toward his truck with the excitement of a boy at Christmas.

He was a man accustomed to giving orders, and the men responded to him quickly and with respect. She lingered close behind him, admiring the flats and flats of flowers as they were unloaded.

"So many, Michael!" Her hands were on her cheeks; her mouth was grinning widely.

"That's just the beginning. Wait here."

He strode off in long, happy strides toward his men, then led them around the lot, pointing out the landmarks for his foreman and reviewing the blueprints. He spoke to the six workers in Spanish, joking with ease and friendliness. How efficient he was, she thought, watching him with pride mixed with admiration. And his crew was well organized. Within a half hour of their arrival, they'd begun outlining her gardens with string and the first shovels struck the earth.

"You've brought so much more than I ordered," she said when he returned to her side.

"I hope you'll allow me to give you gifts."

"But so many... I've given you nothing."

He moved to stand intimately close to her, running his

callused hand along her back. The silky slide of fabric revealed she was naked under the robe. His lips caressed the top of her head and he said in a gruff voice, "The gift you gave me last night was the most precious gift I've ever received."

She was deeply moved. The final insecurities she'd felt this morning evaporated in the sunlit sky like a specter at dawn. A small smile curved her lips and she moved them closer to his ear. "The pleasure was in the giving."

"*Dios,*" he swore softly, and moved his head to cover her lips with his own. He held her tight, leaving her no doubt that he was ready to comply. "You are a quick learner, *querida*. One night a virgin, the next morning a temptress."

"I had a good teacher."

"I'll give you another lesson tonight, my love. But for now—" his caress on her bottom became a firm pat "—I must get to work with my men. I've already stripped the crews from other jobs. There'll be hell to pay, I'm sure. So, if we're going to get your garden in before you leave to film your movie, it's got to be today. Besides, you really must go inside and get dressed. It would be a shame if I have to kill all those good men for sneaking looks at you in that skimpy robe."

She blushed furiously, unaccustomed as she was to such teasing. He loved her shyness, the fumbling on the sash of her robe, her long toes curling in the grass. She was in so many ways still a gawky young girl, all long limbs, bones and awkward blushes. Then she'd surprise him and assume a mantle of maturity, a depth of wisdom in those pale blue orbs that extended beyond her years. She was a quixotic creature, and he doubted he would ever grow bored. He reached for her again and cupped her small rear, pressing her close.

"Okay, break it up. You'll inspire a mutiny out there." Bobby sauntered to their side, his large panama hat fanning his smiling face. He was dressed in pale linen pants and a flowing mint shirt, certainly nothing to wear while working rocks out of the soil. He once told her that he went to sites "strictly as an adviser."

"They're looking at you like you're a bowl of juicy ripe strawberries," Bobby said to Charlotte.

She laughed lightly, feeling happy.

"Nice of you to show up," Michael said. He seemed aloof and dropped his hand from her. She tilted her head, wondering at the sudden tension. "Go around back and tell them to keep their eyes to themselves. I'll be right there. Please," he added, his voice cool.

Bobby's smile hardened. "You're the boss." He flopped the hat on his head, then with a worldly air, bowed to Charlotte, offered her a friendly wink and walked away, his heels clicking on the pavement.

"Shit," Michael swore, slamming his hands on his hips and scowling.

"What's going on?"

"Nothing." He was cutting her off. "Listen, I've got to see to things." He gave her a chaste kiss. "Later. We'll talk about those strawberries."

Her gaze followed Michael as he walked with purpose toward the side lot where his men were working and his brother was leaning over the blueprints, directing the placement of the plastic edging. What could have happened between those brothers that made them so estranged, she wondered?

The men finished packing up the tools into the truck and drove off before the sun set, eager to be home. They'd put in a long, full day. Bobby was the last to leave, presenting Charlotte with a hybrid tea rose plant as his gift.

"Yellow roses are for friendship," he told her, placing the pink-fringed yellow rose in her hands. "I'll leave it to Romeo here to give you the red roses. Long-stemmed beau-

ties. Like you. I took the liberty of creating a small bed for
roses over there by the far edge of the patio. The spot is
perfect and you'll catch the scent as you sit.'' He kissed
her on both cheeks. ''Welcome to California.''

''Don't feel you have to leave,'' she hurried to reply. ''I
was just going to serve some wine. Won't you stay for a
glass?'' She looked at Michael to add to the argument, but
he held curiously back.

Bobby glanced at his brother, then back at her with a
slight flush. ''No, but thank you for the offer. It's Friday
night and I have plans. I'll be back next week with a truck-
load of mulch, that is, if my brother doesn't bring it. Now,
why do I suspect he will?'' There was a gentle tease in his
eyes. Michael looked at his boots.

After he left Charlotte carried a tray of chilled glasses of
white wine and a bowl of fresh strawberries that she'd purchased at the market especially for tonight. Beyond them
the sky was shooting out spears of magenta, purple and
pink that rivaled the colors in her new garden.

And such a garden Michael had given her. She was overcome with love for him just to see it. The scrubby lot had
been transformed into a charming, informal garden that had
the exuberance of spirit that comes from a mixture of flowers and herbs against a backbone of select trees and shrubs.
Earlier, Michael had taken her hand and walked the gentle
sloping hills now dazzling with the extravagant colors of
verbena. She was delighted with his asymmetrical ap-
proach, curves blending one into another. It softened the
harsh lines of the landscape, flattering the house, creating
an oasis in which to relax.

On the patio he'd placed several immense terra cotta pots
for Melanie's herbs. Occasionally a breeze brought the
scent of rosemary or lavender, and the heady fragrance of
Bobby's rose.

''You've done too much,'' she said, gazing at the last

views of her garden in the fading light. "Do you always go overboard?"

"Only where it concerns you," he replied. "I intend to spoil you terribly so you'll be unfit for any other man."

"You've already succeeded. You can rest on your laurels."

"Hmm. I still have to plant a laurel bush."

"Stop, you've done too much already. They'll say I'm a kept woman and Mrs. Delaney will raise the rent."

He shrugged insolently and swirled his wine. "Tell her they're mostly annuals. If you leave, it will all revert to nasty weeds with long, stubborn roots in all that expensive soil I just put in. She should reduce your rent for improving the property."

"I don't care about any of that. I'm just so happy."

"I am, too," he replied, surprised to realize that for the first time in many years, it was true.

Part Three

Love built on beauty, soon as beauty, dies.

—John Donne

Eleven

So this is love, Charlotte mused. For one glorious summer Charlotte lived and breathed Michael Mondragon. His name was on the tip of her tongue while the sun was up, and filling her dreams when the sun was down. Her skin glowed with a rosy color, partly from joy and partly from the long hours she was spending outdoors in her garden. She liked to run her hands through the rich, black soil, relishing its coolness, thinking of the way she combed her hand through Michael's thick black hair when they made love. It seemed all of her senses were awakened and alive. The air smelled sweeter, the birds sang more clearly, the nerves of her fingertips were sensitive to hot and cold, smooth and rough.

Most of all, the woman that she saw in the mirror was no longer an impostor. Especially after lovemaking, after Michael had caressed every inch of her body and turned her feelings inside out. At those times, flushed with satisfaction, when she looked in the mirror she actually liked the face she saw smiling there.

It was the face that Michael loved.

Michael came to see her every day. They'd trowel together in the garden a bit, perhaps she'd toss in some peat moss, or he'd add a plant or two. Then she'd cook him dinner and he'd stay until late in the night. He was an insatiable lover and an incurable romantic. She discovered a sweetness and kindness that he hid behind his usual stern expressions and silent demeanor. Or perhaps it was a side that he chose to reveal to only a few people. She wondered this while watching him chop vegetables into professionally small pieces and talking animatedly. She giggled thinking that her stoic Michael could talk up a storm when alone with her after a heady bout of lovemaking. He had many sides to his personality. He was like the soil—dark, mysterious, sensual, grounded. The thought of planting roots in him appealed to her. Her love for him was everything. She couldn't imagine a future without him. She never thought she could feel so connected to another human being.

Which was why lying to him had become such a burden. The more he opened up to her, the more she found it necessary to close doors. At night, after they'd made love, Michael liked to draw her up to his shoulders. He'd punch the pillows behind his head, then hold her tightly in his arms, sometimes lightly stroking her hair, sometimes tracing patterns on her arm, while he talked about his family, his philosophies, his ideas. It was then, when she should have felt closest to him, that she felt the wedge of lies slip between them.

He told of the time his father, Luis, swam across the river into the United States one dark, starless night. Thigh-deep in water he'd met a pregnant woman struggling to cross with her three-year-old child. Luis carried the child on his shoulders as he swam the heavy current, then, after settling the child on the shore, he'd returned to help the woman reach safety.

He told of how every Saturday night, until puberty when he staunchly refused, his mother had treated his dark skin with a mixture of egg white and lemon juice concentrate as a remedy to lighten his dark skin. It was Marta's lifelong sadness, Michael said with a sad smile, that the potion never worked for him.

Lying on his dark chest, she loved to hear his laugh rumble beneath her ear as he spoke of his fiery sister, Rosa, a tomboy who refused to wear a dress, learn to cook or take dancing lessons like all the other girls. She was a home-run hitter on her softball team, liked strong coffee and Cuban cigars, was a whiz at math and science, and was stronger than most men he knew. Yet as a woman, she had fought with their parents to send her to college. College was unthinkable for a girl whose main job in life was to raise a family. A waste of money. So Rosa got married to Manuel quickly after high school and ran the business with their father. When Charlotte asked about Bobby, however, Michael was strangely silent.

He had so many stories to tell about his family, his boy-hood, his years away at college. He had opinions about everything: pollution, politics, religion, even the way she wore her hair. In turn, Charlotte ventured her own opinions about these subjects, flattered that he was a rapt audience. She prided herself on her intelligence. For most of her life, it was the one attribute she could hold out to the world without shyness or fear of being mocked. Now, when her brains tended to be overshadowed by her beauty, she was all the more appreciative to share ideas with Michael. They loved to debate loudly, heatedly, over anything at all, usu-ally ending their contest in a tangled, passionate pile on the bed.

When he asked about her childhood, however, she an-swered obliquely, shrugging away a lifetime with "Oh, there's not much to tell."

One night she came very close to telling him the truth. That the face he loved had been created by man, not God. That she was estranged from her mother, that her childhood had been hard and downtrodden. What did he call the story? The Ugly Duckling Who Turned into the Swan? Yes, she wanted to say to him. That was her story!

But he told her again how much he loved her face, how her beauty mesmerized him. How would he feel about her if she told him the truth? He would think she was unnatural. Some kind of freak. The truth died, unspoken, on her lips. So the lies endured, and the more days that passed, the more trapped she became by them.

All these thoughts were like thorny rambling roses in her mind as she dug energetically in the late summer garden, the one he'd created for her. The next day, she'd be leaving to begin filming *One Day in Autumn* in Maine. They had only today left before they'd be separated for two months. Their love was too new to test, she decided. She'd tell him everything when she returned.

"You should wear some gloves or your hands will get callused."

Charlotte startled, bringing mud to her shirt where her hand covered her heart. It was more than the surprise that made her heart jump and a hot flash sear through her. That feeling happened every time she saw Michael Mondragon.

"You scared me. I didn't hear you."

"You were a million miles away."

"Not really. I was thinking of you."

That answer pleased him. His eyes lit up and shone like the sunshine, and he gathered her in his arms as gently as if she were a bunch of flowers.

Freddy was eager to see Charlotte, eager to discuss the travel itinerary with her, eager to give her the good news of another pivotal project he'd just lined up for her. Production of *One Day in Autumn* was right on schedule. And he already had another project in the works. A big deal with big money that would eclipse anything she could have imagined. Another period piece. Charlotte's classic features were perfect, and combined with her remarkable ear for accents, a whole vista of film opportunities closed to actresses without her range lay open to her.

Then there was that book treatment on the horizon that LaMonica had sent over. It was a zany book, full of action, romance and humor and, most of all, memorable characters. If film could do the book justice, then it was sure to be a cult hit. Like *Pulp Fiction*.

He was coming from a meeting with LaMonica that had lasted from coffee and doughnuts in his office, to Ma Maison for lunch to cocktails at the Polo Lounge. There was a part in there for Charlotte that could really showcase her. Zoom her right to the top. He knew it, LaMonica knew it. The question was, for how much?

LaMonica kept saying, "We're also talking to Uma Thurman."

Freddy would counter with "Yeah, and we're talking to Begelman about another deal."

It was a game they were playing, shuffling the pieces like cards on the table. He knew that LaMonica wanted the script and the director to be the stars of this film. An unknown actress with an unforgettable face was what he was really after. And Freddy had her.

"Go fish, John," he said to himself with a smug grin as he pulled into Charlotte's driveway and yanked back the parking brake. He was in the works early on this one and was working like a dog trying to package the big deal. When he left LaMonica's office, it was all set except for Charlotte's signature on the line.

He grabbed the bottle of Dom Pérignon from the passenger seat, slammed the door and almost sprinted to the house. He was feeling buoyant, like he was full of helium and about to fly. What was that cornball saying? High on life, not blow? Whatever, it was true. When there was no answer at the door, he mumbled impatiently and trotted around the back.

En route, he looked around, puzzled. It dawned on him

that something was different since he'd been here last. The place looked pretty good. What was it? He craned his neck. The shutters and the front door were painted a bright turquoise color, there were some nice bushes by the front door, and hell, he was walking on an attractive winding gravel path that wasn't here before.

When he rounded the corner of the house, he stopped short, mouth agog. The whole frigging yard was transformed. It was like a fairy godmother had come, flicked her magic wand and changed the pumpkin into a coach.

"What the—" With his hands on his hips he took in the curves of flowers and landscaped walks, the blooming shrubs. It was like he was in a small park. Where the hell did all this come from? Who died and left these gals some money? He heard a soft, throaty laugh and turned his head toward the back patio. Under a pergola that wasn't there two weeks ago, he saw Charlotte on her knees digging some kind of leggy vine into the dirt at its base. Beside her knelt some dark-haired, dark-skinned man, no doubt the gardener. Freddy's heart skipped when he saw her in that funny little white straw hat and those cute little gloves. She was something, all right. What a pretty picture she made.

He lifted his hand in a wave and was about to shout out a hearty hello when he saw her raise her eyes to the gardener and, with a coy smile, reach up to tenderly brush a leaf from his hair. Her hand lingered by his ear, then slid down to cup his jaw in her palm while she gazed at him. The man's eyes burned into hers, then he turned his head to kiss her lightly.

Freddy's hand dropped to his side. His mouth turned dry and he felt the breath whoosh out of him like he'd been socked a good one in the solar plexus. What the hell was going on here? He stared for a few minutes more before getting the feeling that his eyeballs were going to burst into flames. He could understand her flirting a bit with the gardener. Hell, every estrogen-replaced woman in Southern

California licked her lips over those broad shouldered, tanned young boys who toiled in their manicured lawns. But Charlotte was a hot young girl with a world of prospects. She didn't have to bottom fish.

So could someone explain to him why she was in her backyard with some guy in stained khakis and dirty hands, both of them cooing and pawing each other like teenagers in a hormone surge?

His own blood began to bubble and he could feel his pressure rise. He wasn't about to sit back and watch his investment go down the proverbial cesspool. Gripping the champagne tight, he stepped forward.

"Charlotte!" he called out. "Come to Papa, baby. I've got good news."

Charlotte sprang to her feet, and he was pleased to see an embarrassed flush flame her cheeks. Yeah, he thought bitterly. Caught you in the act. He sauntered, even swaggered, to her side, arms outstretched. When he reached her, he pulled her into his arms and hugged her long enough, and with enough familiarity, so as to make it clear to the guy he wasn't just another acquaintance.

Charlotte stepped back from Freddy's embrace and eyed the young man at her side warily. From the corner of his eye he noted that the dark-haired man was standing very still, his broad shoulders thrown back over slim hips, and his dark, thick brows knitted over squinting eyes. Freddy thought he looked like a matador and despised him instantly for that glamour, that brutal power. He resented him deeply for making him feel like the goddamn snorting bull.

"Freddy," Charlotte said, her voice high with tension. "I'd like you to meet Michael Mondragon. From the Mondragon Nursery."

Alarms went off in his head. Nursery? So that was where all the flowers and stuff came from. Shit, he thought, looking around. What the hell did she do to deserve all this?

Freddy purposefully slighted him, dismissing him with a scant glance.

"Hmm, yes."

Charlotte flushed and the young man eyed him with barely concealed fury. Freddy added insult to injury by turning his back to the young man and addressing Charlotte.

"Can we go somewhere and talk? In private." He looked over at the man with deliberate disdain. "Tell your gardener to go home. It's past quitting time."

"He's not my..."

"I'm afraid you misconstrue the situation," the man said in a low, dangerous voice.

Freddy turned with insolent slowness, taking the man's measure in a trick he'd learned years ago from a five foot two, balding movie mogul. It was all in the straight shoulders and the sneer, and it almost never failed to intimidate.

"Oh, yeah?" he drawled, finishing the routine. "And just how do you know what I 'construe'?"

The man didn't back down. Rather, he smiled with a superior kind of mockery that set Freddy's teeth on edge. "I have no intention of leaving. I've only just arrived," he replied with a surprisingly urbane tone for a gardener. "My business with Miss Godfrey is personal. It's you, I believe, who keeps business hours with Miss Godfrey and it's—" he looked briefly at the red sun lowering in the western sky "—quite late. Kindly conduct your business and leave. We were just about to have dinner."

Freddy felt the doughnuts he'd had for breakfast, the mussels marinara he'd consumed for lunch and all the nuts he nibbled on with his martinis roil in his gut and threaten to choke him. His temper erupted and he took a step forward and pushed hard against the man's chest, shoving him back. "Listen, you lousy spic, I oughta..."

He couldn't finish. In a flash he felt a hand shoot out to grab him by the lapels. The man leaned into his personal space, his face just a few inches from his own, his eyes shooting fury like flame, and he ground out in a menacing tone, "Don't...ever...call...me...that...again."

"Michael, please," Charlotte cried to him, her trembling hands on his shoulders pulling him away. Her eyes were wide with panic. "Please. Let him go."

Freddy felt the scorch of shame hearing her plead for his release, but he had the good sense to keep his mouth shut. Besides, what else could he do with his face beet red and his breath cut off. In his heart, however, he was vowing himself to a plan of revenge.

The man she called Michael took a deep breath and dropped his lapels with that macho lifting of his hands Latino men were so good at—a gesture that implied to touch him any further would dirty him.

"Never attack a man unless you're prepared to back it up," Michael said, then turned his back and walked a few feet away, like a matador turning his back on the wounded bull after he'd made the fatal lunge. Freddy felt his pride drain out of him like blood.

"Freddy," Charlotte cried, "are you all right?"

Her solicitation infuriated him. Made him feel even more ashamed. "Yeah, sure I'm all right," he sputtered, elbowing her away and straightening his tie. "What do you think? That muscle man over there suddenly is some kind of fucking hero?" He let go of his tie and rolled back his shoulders. "Get rid of him before I call the police."

"I can't..."

"Get rid of him, I said," he shouted in fury.

Michael spun around, his fists clenched.

Charlotte jumped in front of Michael and blocked his path. "Freddy, stop goading," she called over her shoulder. "Go inside. I'll meet you there. I need to talk to Michael for a minute. Please, Freddy," she said sharply when he didn't budge.

Freddy bent over to pick up the champagne that was

lying in the grass, thinking sourly that he couldn't uncork it now or they'd be sprayed with the stuff after it was shaken up. This only added to his frustration, and he stomped toward the house, pounding holes with his heels in the soft, new gravel.

From the kitchen window he watched as Charlotte talked hurriedly to the man, her hands fluttering on the long row of buttons of his shirt. Shit, he thought, slamming his hands on the table. She was placating the son of a bitch. He had to put a stop to this. Quick. He rubbed the stubble on his jaw, grown after a long, hard day of negotiating this girl's future. His own future. Anger and frustration burned white in his brain, but he calmed down, telling himself now was the time for action.

Okay, okay, he said to himself. At least he was getting her out of town. Away from that Latin lover. She had this bit but juicy part in *American Homestead,* but it would get her out of town for a few weeks—a month at most. The film was already well under way and would be wrapped up soon. She'd be back in her garden with this guy in the dog days of summer. That was no good.... He'd have to pair her up with some big names, some handsome actors who would take her mind off that piece of meat out in the yard. She liked dark-haired guys? Hmm... Maybe Johnny Depp. Yeah. He looked like this guy, and what he didn't have in size he had in stature. Charlotte was tall and willowy. Depp's type. Maybe this would work out. He'd get right on it.

As he watched the two from the kitchen window, he saw Mondragon lean over and kiss Charlotte soundly on the mouth while his hands roamed her body possessively. Freddy's own mouth went dry again, this time in desolation. He closed his eyes, and in the blackness tried to imagine what it would feel like to run his hands over Charlotte, over those enticing curves that he saw in the mirror. He felt the desire burn in him, a low ache that was, to him, a curse.

He opened his eyes, and in the other room he saw what could only be a vision. He had to blink twice, not sure if he was seeing double. The front door had opened and in walked a shorter, more curvaceous version of Charlotte Godfrey. The woman was wearing a simple silk sweater and skirt ensemble in Charlotte's favorite cream beige color. As she crossed the shadowy living room, he noted that her golden hair was sleeked back in the same hairstyle that André had created for Charlotte, and the shoes, damn, those were the very same mile-high pumps he'd picked out for her at Charles Jourdan. He glanced out the window, stunned. In the garden, the other Charlotte was still dancing with the Mambo King. But waltzing straight for him in the kitchen was this other, curvy, dream Charlotte.

''Freddy,'' the woman breathed, pausing at the brightly lit entry shyly, hewing closely to the wall.

Freddy's brow arched. It was Melanie Ward—and it wasn't. She'd changed her hair color, her makeup, her clothes.... She'd remodeled herself to be an imitation Charlotte Godfrey.

He knew Melanie sensed that he was staring at her with lust, working it all out in his mind, and the strange thing was, she was letting him. She didn't do anything to break the spell. To his surprise, she was feeding it. Leaning against the wall, she twisted her hips seductively, thrust out her double D chest and pursed her lips. All the things he'd never expected to see Charlotte Godfrey do, but alone in the dark, imagined she would.

If he focused closely, he could see that her hair color was brassier, her skin not as smooth. But if he let his mind wander, he could just imagine for a moment it was Charlotte. Like seeing the double on a film—it was close enough to work.

He stepped forward, reached out and reeled her in, kissing her hard, with the same fierce passion that he'd seen Michael use when he kissed Charlotte. Melanie whimpered and it stirred him further. He was blind with all the fury, the frustration, the shame he'd felt at the hands of Mondragon. Roughly, he hoisted her leg up and around his hip, shoving her hard against the wall. Her head thudded but she kept on kissing him, rubbing against him, urging him on. He was dry humping her with all the violence he felt deep in his gut. Again and again he thrust against her. Melanie was panting now, calling out his name, fumbling for his belt buckle. Harder, faster, he pounded like a jackhammer against her, grunting by her neck while a thin trickle of saliva flowed from his open mouth.

Melanie's hand pushed down to his crotch and fondled him. Her hand stopped suddenly and she looked at him, her expression puzzled. Then she dropped to her knees and started unzipping his pants.

"Freddy, let me," she simpered when he tried to pull away. "Give me a chance."

Sucking in his gut, he grabbed her hand away so hard she yelped. Then he pushed away from her, in the same, disgustful manner that Michael had pushed away from him.

He zipped up his trousers, cursing her, cursing himself, cursing fate. In the harsh, unforgiving fluorescent light, he looked at Melanie while his breathing lowered to normal. Her sweater was hiked up over her breasts and her skirt was wrinkled and twisted like a rope around her full, rounded hips. Her face was smeared with runny mascara and lipstick. How did he ever think she was Charlotte? She was a crasser, more cheaply constructed version of the real thing. He hated her at that moment. Hated her for tempting him, for luring him into this sick game.

"Freddy?" Melanie had tears in her eyes and was tugging her sweater back down. She was looking for an explanation. He'd seen that look many times before with many other women. They all thought it was their fault. Better he let them think that.

"This never happened," he said, coolly tugging at his French cuffs. "You understand? I don't know what came over me."

Melanie's eyes reflected hurt before they hardened. She looked at his pants, straight at his package, sniffed, wiped under her eyes, then straightened.

"Yeah?" she asked, tilting one hip in a cocky pose. "Like hell you don't. What's the matter? Aren't I good enough for you? Only the real thing will get it up?"

"Shut up," he shouted at her, his fear strangling him.

Melanie looked at him hard and long before her eyes widened in comprehension and a spiteful smile spread across her face.

"Oh, now I see the way it is," she said, nodding her head. "It isn't about me. Or Charlotte. Is it? Or the way we look, or dress. We could rub up against you like a cat in heat and it wouldn't make any difference, would it? I heard about you, but I didn't believe it."

He stood rock still. "Heard what?"

"You can't get it up. Zippo. Kerplunk." She laughed out loud. "Well what do you know."

Freddy turned his back to her so that she wouldn't see how pale he'd become, or the panic he couldn't hide in his eyes. This was the secret he'd paid dearly to keep. His ex-wife, Ali, was sworn to secrecy in exchange for just about every penny he'd ever earned. If this got out he'd be joked about, perceived as weak. He'd be out of the circle. He couldn't let that happen. Not now, when he was so close to getting back in.

"You forget who I am," he said, his tone as cool as ice. "Keep your mouth shut and I'll get you a part in this new film I'm lining up for Charlotte. I'll make it a two-for-one deal. One word about this, though, and your career will be over."

He looked over his shoulder. Melanie's shoulders had slumped in defeat as she considered the offer.

"We both know that the vultures are circling already."

"Go to hell, Freddy."

He waited, looking out the window. Charlotte was walking her gardener out to the front. The wind tousled her hair, blowing off her straw hat. She chased after it, laughing like a schoolgirl.

"Okay," Melanie replied, sullenly. "It's a deal."

Freddy wasn't even listening to her anymore. He was totally consumed by his jealousy of the tall, handsome, masculine young man who was now reaching out for Charlotte's hand, reeling her in, gently kissing her forehead at the gate. Only a man who was so utterly sure of his virility could cause a woman to tremble as Charlotte was trembling with one chaste kiss.

For twenty some years he'd raged against God for that freak accident that caused his impotency. That anger festered in his soul, like a fetid cancer. Now that cankerous, foul, soul-crushing anger had a target.

The obvious virility of Michael Mondragon.

Twelve

The golds of early fall, like the golds of Charlotte's hair, were gone again. Michael tromped through the leaves of autumn, leaves that had sheltered him from the sun's scorching glare a few months earlier. "Nothing gold can stay...."

He missed her when she went away. She took a part of him with her, the best part. Their love had ripened over the summer months, and now that she'd left, he felt as dry and lifeless as the leaves that passed him on their fall to the earth.

He looked around at the tawny colors surrounding the nursery, shut up now for its winter rest. The crowds had gone; it would be peaceful till the madness of March. The pale ecru-colored cornstalks rattled in the wind by the makeshift roadside stand he'd set up to draw weekend tourists to the piles of fat, glossy pumpkins, bundles of dried everlastings, crisp red apples and a few crafts and jellies made by local women.

He trod on past the compost heaps, the sheds filled to bursting, up the road to the quaint stucco house with the bright green trim and yellow door sitting on the top of the hill. It had the best view of the valley. His father had built the house for his family fifteen years ago, once Roberto,

Miguel and Rosa were educated in the Catholic schools and he could leave the suburbs. It was a modest house, a happy house, always filled with Mexican music, the smell of Mama's cooking and the intimate sounds of Spanish. His father was more complacent since he'd returned and taken over the business. He was relaxing more in front of the TV, talking about taking a vacation with Marta—their first. The deep lines of worry were fading from his brow. Mama smiled more often, too, and took time to play with the grandchildren.

Like the seasons, however, Michael knew his time here was coming to an end. He'd be leaving soon, heading back to his job and his old life in Chicago. It was long overdue. He'd like to be back by the first snowfall. Now all he had to do was tell his father.

After taking a deep breath, he brushed a few leaves from his jacket, stomped the mud from his feet and entered the house to the warm calls of welcome in Spanish.

Maria Elena grabbed his hands and herded him with excited laughter to the fireplace. "Look Tío Miguel," she called, her face flushed from excitement and the heat of the flames. "Abuelo Luis lit the first fire of the season."

"In my honor!" Cisco informed him, his eleven-year-old chest expanding with pride. "For my birthday." Already the smell of chestnuts filled the room. Papa and Manuel were at the table, drinking beer and playing cards. In the kitchen, Mama and Rosa were preparing dinner. Often there would be an aunt and uncle visiting from Mexico, nieces and nephews, numerous cousins. Any family was welcome in this house.

Bobby hadn't arrived yet. Michael rubbed his hands before the fire. It pained him that Bobby had kept his distance not only from him, but from the entire family throughout this summer. He was probably afraid that Michael would say something, or accidentally hint at the truth, and preferred to eliminate that possibility by steering clear. It hurt that Bobby didn't trust his silence. It angered him that he kept away. He was missed by Mama at the Sunday dinners.

"Where is Roberto?" his mother worried as she looked out the front window. Her head bobbed every time she carried another steaming dish to the long wood table. "It has been several weeks since he's come."

"He'll be here, Mama," Rosa called back. "He knows it's Cisco's birthday. He won't miss the party."

"Won't he?" Papa muttered. "He has no *respeto,* that one. He likes his wild life-style with those painter friends of his in Los Angeles. Staying out late, going to bars. He's up to no good. He'd better behave himself if he ever does get here. Around these bebés. Manuel and Rosa, they are doing a good job teaching them to have respect for the family and our ways." He waved his hand brusquely. "Come away from the window," he commanded Marta.

"This life's five windows of the soul...." Michael muttered.

Luis looked his way, wary. "What is it you are muttering now in your English?"

"Bobby is a grown man and able to choose his own friends," Michael replied soberly, still staring at the fire. "If we're going to discuss respect here, we should respect him enough to honor, and welcome, his choices." He was treading on dangerous ground now and needed to be exceedingly cautious.

His father stared at him, gauging his meaning. "He doesn't choose us, his family," he roared, striking his chest with a loud thump. "He is a stranger to his parents."

"He's as he always was," Marta said softly. "A good and loyal son."

"Loyal? How can you say that? Is he here now, for Cisco's birthday? Is he here, in the family business like his brother and sister? No!" he thundered. "He *chooses* to help only in the summer. Because he needs the money, not because we might need him. He *chooses* to live in the city and paint walls with his friends who have purple hair and soft palms. I did not raise my son to be like this. He is the eldest. He should be more like the younger.''

Michael groaned and shook his head. "No, Papa. Stop."

"What? I speak the truth. You are *fuerte* and *formal*," he boomed, raising his hand to count off two fingers.

"Cisco, Maria," Michael called to the children. His voice was terse and brooked no refusal. "Go and watch television for a few minutes. I want to talk to your grandfather."

He had to talk to his father now. To tell him that he was leaving, as planned. He could see that his father thought otherwise. He was pushing him, relentlessly, to stay on. His decision would cause a divide in this family bigger than the San Andreas Fault, but the rumblings were beginning and the quake was overdue.

"I don't want to watch TV," Cisco whined, and moved closer to Michael, leaning against his chest, scowling. "I want to stay by Tío Miguel."

Manuel looked up from his cards and spoke harshly to Cisco in Spanish, ordering him to leave his uncle alone. Cisco only wedged closer to Michael, his face rebellious.

"I can stay if I want to. It's my birthday." It was an open defiance, unthinkable in Michael's day and age.

Manuel flushed and stood up in an angry rush, rocking the table and spilling the cards. Cisco ducked his head and Michael wrapped an arm protectively around the boy. Looking at his small, thin arms, he noticed several raised welts.

"It's okay with me," he replied in a calm voice, trying to douse the flame of fury in his heart. He abhorred any violence against a child. He'd felt the lash too many times in his childhood to bear its presence as an adult. He knew Manuel had a hot temper and a hard hand.

"Is that boy shooting his mouth again?" Rosa called from the kitchen. Her anger was palpable and he felt Cisco quake. When Rosa was in a bad mood not even the flies dared fly.

"Let him be," Michael called back. Then to Manuel, "I'll read him a story while you finish your game of cards. I'll talk to Papa later."

"If it's okay with you..." Manuel gave his son a warning look. "You must respect grown-ups," he added to Cisco.

"Enough," Luis shouted, waving his hand in the air to indicate to Manuel that he should sit down. "Stop bothering us, eh? We're playing cards here. Marta, hurry with the dinner. I am hungry. And after, we will have a big cake, no? I love the sweets, and I'll bring out cigars for your son's birthday. Come, Manuel, let's finish our game of cards and leave the children to the women."

"Rosa," Manuel called out to his wife, in imitation of his father-in-law. "Be a good woman for a change and throw some more chestnuts on the grate for the children. And some music, no?"

Rosa cast darts with her eyes at her husband, but out of respect for her father, did as she was told.

Michael felt Cisco's arms loosen, but in the boy's eyes he saw triumph. "Cisco, you little devil," he whispered in his ear, and wrapped his arms tighter around the boy. There would be a beating at home for sure, a few strikes from the belt at the very least for this infraction. But he knew Cisco wouldn't feel the pain. How often had he and his father played out this scene? And later tonight, they would play the same roles again. The rigid father and the defiant son. This time, however, the blows would be internal. They would both feel the pain.

"Feliz Cumpleaños!" Bobby swung wide the door and entered carrying a huge box in his arms. "Where is the birthday boy?"

Cisco leaped from Michael's arms to check out the gift.

Kids were as fickle as dogs when it came to handouts. "Nintendo! Wow, thank you, Tío Roberto!"

Latin music began blaring from the speakers, Marta clapped her hands in joy and the children were squealing for Tío Roberto to open the package. The moment of tension passed. Bobby made a successful entrance back into the family, and dinner was about to be served. For a while, all was right with the world. This skirmish was only a four on the Richter scale, Michael thought. A minor quake.

After dinner Michael followed Manuel outside, closing the door tightly behind him.

"A word, Manuel," he called out, catching up with him by Manuel's red Mercury.

Manuel, bent over the door key, looked over his shoulder, surprised. He stood up immediately, showing respect. Michael supposed it was because he was his boss.

"I'd like to talk to you about Cisco."

"*Aiiee.*" He made a show of moaning in distress, but he was smiling. "That boy he is a handful. A child of eleven and already he knows so much. He has too many opinions!"

Michael studied Manuel's face. It appeared he was proud of his son. He cleared his throat and began cautiously. "I think he has too many bruises."

Manuel's face clouded immediately, but he made no reply.

"Listen to me, Manuel. I know you may think it is none of my business, but I'm making it my business. I don't want to see any more bruises on that boy's body. Or on little Maria Elena's. If I do, you'll have to answer to me."

Manuel's porcine features turned red and puffed with restrained fury.

"Look," Michael said, putting his hands on his hips and steadying his breath. "I know these kids need discipline. If you must, spank them on their rears. But nowhere else.

Belts and cords, those are the tools of cowards. Not to be used on children. They are your flesh and blood, not donkeys!"

Manuel's face appeared crude and hard in the dark light, but he still didn't speak. He only nodded once, sharply, then swung open the door of the car and closed it. Michael stepped back from the spraying gravel and dirt, then stood and watched the red brake lights disappear down the drive.

Bobby approached him, his steps crunching in the gravel behind him. "What was that all about?"

"Oh, just trying to break a pattern."

"Speaking of which... Rosa told me what you said earlier. To Papa." He looked out across the land, as black in the dark night as the sea. He cleared his throat. "Thanks, *hermano*."

Michael felt his chest tighten. "You're welcome."

"Ah, Michael," Bobby said in exasperation. "Listen to us. So *formal*. You—I can understand. But see what's become of me? I'm becoming as stoic as you!"

They both knew that to be *formal* in the Mexican culture was to be steady. Serious. Women could be spirited and chatty. Men, though they could tell stories and laugh, were never gossipy. Men who were *formal* were careful of their words.

"No, you've got it all wrong," Michael replied with humor. "I simply can't speak so easily in Spanish, like the rest of you."

Bobby chuckled, but they both knew that wasn't true. Michael's Spanish had improved greatly in the past two and a half years, because he allowed himself to speak it.

"So, it seems they taught you something in that Ivy League college you went to, after all. I heard you quoted Blake tonight."

"Rosa told you that, too?"

Bobby's eyes sparkled with merriment. "Papa. He drew me aside and privately asked me what you meant by that 'windows' line. I almost burst out laughing in his face, but held back and told him I didn't know nothing. That, I'm sorry to say, he found easy to believe.''

The sound of his hearty laughter encouraged Michael to join him. When Michael stopped laughing, Bobby spread out his arms in a theatrical gesture. His tone, however, was no longer teasing, but heartfelt.

"This life's five windows of the soul, Distorts the Heavens from pole to pole. And leads you to believe a lie, When you see with, not through, the eye." Bobby paused, then said seriously, "I always thought of Papa when I read that.''

"Bobby, I'm sorry.''

"Why? Because Papa and I are estranged?''

"No. Because we are. I'm sorry for the distance.''

"Hey, man, it's not your fault.''

"If not mine, then whose?'' He shrugged. "I claim the fault. And apologize for it. I should have apologized long ago. It went on far too long, though you must admit you didn't make it any easier for me.'' Michael lowered his head and kicked the dirt. "I didn't know what to say. What to do. I felt—forgive me, but I felt like I failed you somehow. Crazy things like I should've hung out with you more.'' He ran his hand through his hair. "Set you up on dates.''

"Michael,'' Bobby said, throwing back his head. He took a deep breath. "Miguel, when we were little, while you were dreaming of little girls, I was dreaming of little boys.''

Michael was silenced. He looked at the drifting clouds as they covered a quarter moon. He always thought of the Cheshire cat when he saw that slivery smile.

"Mama said tonight that you were as you'd always been,'' he said. "It rang true. I don't know why it was so hard for me to accept that you're gay. But I want you to know that I do. And it changes nothing. You're my brother. I love you.''

He looked up then and saw the emotion tumbling in Bobby's eyes. They reached out to grab hold of each other, neither flinching, each hanging on to the history they shared, the name they shared. What did it matter who they dreamed of?

"You better be dreaming of Charlotte these days,'' Bobby said when they separated, happy in the easy laughter after a long summer's tension.

Michael's smile faded as he recalled Charlotte's last strained goodbye at the airport. "Dreams are all I've got. She's gone again. This is her second film, a period piece called *One Day in Autumn*. The last part was a supporting role, but this one is a co-starring role and will showcase her talent. She's really excited about it—and they're pretty excited about her. She's getting big money, and her third film is already being planned." He paused. "That one's even bigger.''

"Wow," Bobby said on an exhale. "Things are moving fast for her. How long will she be gone this time?''

"I'm not sure. She's been gone a couple of months already. Maybe another.''

"You know, I hate to ask you this, but is everything okay with you two? I mean, I've been seeing her picture a lot in the tabloids with these movie hunks. He's got his arms all over her. Are you two still together, or what?''

Michael nodded brusquely. "That's all publicity, Bobby. Her agent is setting her up with all these bankable stars so she'll be noticed by the press. Sort of create a buzz about her." He made a hissing sound, more of a curse. "It's working, too. Even when she's home, she's often out to a party or dinner at some studio boss's place. This new film she's in stars this heartthrob Brad Sommers. Charlotte told me Walen arranged for her to be seen dating this guy now, too. It's all harmless, but...''

He shook his head and stomped his boot on the floor. "I don't like it," he said in a dangerously low voice. "I believe her when she says it's just business. She might feel that way, but let's face it. We're talking about Charlotte Godfrey. I don't trust those men not to want her. I want to kill the guy who touches her."

"Easy, boy. Your jealousy will only get you in trouble." Bobby leaned against the porch railing and considered. "I should be enjoying this. After all the girls who cried on my shoulder over you in high school."

"They meant nothing to me."

"And she does?"

"What do you think?"

"Why don't you go with her to some of these parties, then? I've heard about those bashes. Caviar by the pound, champagne. Hey, I'd be there in a Hollywood minute."

"That Freddy Walen is a son of a bitch. He's doing his damnedest to turn Charlotte against me. I'm not sure if it's because he's simply jealous or he's prejudiced. Either way, I'm not on his list of suitable suitors."

"He doesn't want his pretty star dating a Latino, is that it?" He saw Michael's color rise and knew him well enough to let that sensitive subject drop. "It only matters what Charlotte thinks, and she doesn't strike me as the kind of person who is easily swayed."

"By this guy she is. He's got some kind of control over her. It's infuriating. She listens to him and does what he wants her to do. She says they have some kind of agreement."

"A pact with the devil, eh? Classic stuff there, brother. If I were you, I'd hold on to her tight."

"I intend to. But it's not entirely up to me, is it?"

"Sure it is. Fight for her. You have this crazy notion that you've got to prove yourself worthy of those blond, Protestant, upper class girls you're so fond of."

He smirked. "She's Catholic."

"Score one for our side. But the point remains the same."

Michael scowled and clenched his teeth like a man splitting hairs. "How does one compete against fame, fortune and millions of adoring fans?"

"Love, my dear brother. Simply love."

"We'll see."

"Where is she now?"

"On location in Maine. Somewhere on the coast."

"Go to her, man. Sweep her off her feet. Do the horizontal mambo and remind her of what you have together. Just give me five minutes, little brother, and I can come up with a thousand romantic schemes for you. Romance is what every woman wants—what she needs."

Michael's expression revealed he was far away in his thoughts. "I don't think so, Bobby. It's not my style."

Bobby coughed in frustration. "Right. Your style, as you put it, is to sit around and wait. And wait and wait. You are so boring with your stubborn patience."

Michael only smiled, knowing that to say anything to Bobby now would only get him going. He'd made up his mind to stay put and let Charlotte come home to him. He had other things on his mind to settle now, anyway.

"I talked to my firm in Chicago last week and they're not going to hold my position open beyond the end of the year. I can't blame them. Business is business. They have a schedule to maintain. If Charlotte and I are meant to be together, we'll find a way to meet between California and Chicago."

Bobby turned his head. "You're leaving? For Chicago? When did you reach this decision? I thought, well, we all assumed that you were staying on."

Michael straightened and met his brother's gaze. "Staying on? Here? I don't know why. I was clear when I came that I'd stay for two years. In a few more weeks the third season will be over. I've more than fulfilled my promise."

He squinted his eyes and thought of the phone call he'd recently had with a colleague in Chicago. Todd had made him heady with descriptions of a major new project.

"My architectural firm has a contract to design a new loft condo building in the River North area. It's a very big deal and they want me on it. It's a tall one," he said, his eyes sparkling with excitement. "Couldn't turn it down. I thought I'd stay here through Christmas. Less, depending on Papa's reaction."

There was no response from Bobby.

Michael wondered at Bobby's troubled face. "What's the matter? You can't be so sorry to see me go? You're not here much in the winter, anyway. And Rosa... Ha. She's counting the days."

Bobby let his beer dangle between his fingertips. "I was hoping you'd stay on. I like having you as my boss. I—I wanted to ask if you'd hire me for the winter season."

Michael's brows rose. "Winter? You can't stand to be around here during the summer much less the winter. Never have. You only work at the nursery in the summer for the extra money. What's the matter? No mural jobs?"

Bobby smiled ruefully. "Are you able to handle more secrets?"

Michael felt a coiling in his gut. His shoulders stiffened. "Do I have a choice?"

"Yes." Bobby's face was set. "You do."

Truth was, Michael didn't want to know more secrets just yet. He saw the wariness in his brother's dark, deep set eyes. He saw the tilted head, the straight, tense shoulders. He bore the look of someone poised to dodge another blow. Michael moved closer down the railing toward Bobby, his heart pounding heavily. He could feel the tension reach out to grab him.

"*Dígame,* Roberto," he said in the language of their childhood.

Bobby raised his chin a notch. "I'm HIV positive."

Michael absorbed the words. It was more a numbness. He imagined that this was what it must feel like to be hit by a bullet. A soft hiss. Burn. Then shock.

"AIDS," he replied. "Frankly, I'm not sure I know what that means anymore," he said, looking at his hands.

"Hey, let's not pretend that it's the flu. What I got I didn't get from a cough or a sneeze. When was the last time you saw the flu reduce a healthy man to a skeleton with the gait of a sixty-year-old?"

"You have AIDS," Michael repeated, ignoring Bobby's flippancy. He needed to get this straight. "But it's not active?"

"Oh, it's active."

Michael exhaled slowly, feeling a part of his soul was slipping out with the stale air. "I knew at some level," Michael confessed, sadness overwhelming him. "Of course, I'd hoped I was wrong."

He'd seen Bobby declining over the past few months, seen his hair thin, heard his breath shorten, heard his mother's pleas for her son to "Eat more!" Over the summer, Bobby had aged in years, not months.

"It's a plague out there, man. My partner died last spring. And friends. So many friends. People I used to know, see at parties, have simply disappeared. I pretend, you know, that they've moved. But I know. I know they're really gone."

Michael felt a slow-building panic in his gut. "But I've heard about new therapies. Research."

"Yeah, well... There are experimental treatments. Whispers of miracle cures."

"Then we'll do them. We'll try anything. I don't care what it costs."

Bobby smiled weakly, gratefully accepting the "we." "It took me a while to accept that AIDS wasn't necessarily a death sentence. I have friends who are taking different medications, handfuls of pills a day, and it's just not working for them. They get sicker and sicker. They're terrified that they won't survive. For me it's been different. I'm terrified that I will.''

Michael exhaled slowly, unsure of what to say next. He had no personal reference for this kind of pain. No wars endured, no gay friends. Nothing to help him shrink the distance between his own straight experiences and the horrors that his brother was experiencing as a gay man with AIDS. In fact, he suddenly realized how little he knew of his brother, his friends, his life.

"What was his name?" Michael asked. "Your lover?"

"Scott," he replied softly. "And thanks for asking." He cleared his throat. When he spoke, his voice was hoarse with emotion. "He was sick for a long time. By the time he died, he'd shrunk to a hundred-and-thirty pound shell, scaly and weak. You should have seen him when he was well, though. Man, he was beautiful. A bodybuilder who ate health foods and could dance all night.''

Michael reached out to place his hand on Bobby's shoulder. Bobby's head ducked to his chest. "I did the best I could to nurse him," he said, his voice choked.

After a moment he straightened, unwilling to share this private history. Michael's hand slipped back to his side while Bobby quickly wiped his eyes. When he spoke his voice was low.

"Do you want to know what his last words were? 'Tell my father I hate him.'''

Michael stared at Bobby's uncompromising stance, then slowly shook his head. There was no way Bobby was going to ask their father for help.

"What can I do?"

"Nothing." The answer came quickly. He was good at self-protection. "You're going back to Chicago."

"Come with me. I can get you jobs painting murals there."

"Ah, Miguel," he sighed. He seemed suddenly very old

and tired. His bony shoulders slumped, his large, coffee-colored eyes were rimmed with red, his once luxurious hair was now coarse and thin and sticking out at awkward angles from his visible scalp. "I can't paint anymore. I'm too weak. You don't realize how much strength it takes to do murals." He looked at his long fingers, thin and skeletal, with short, peeling nails. Michael remembered how vain Bobby was of his hands. He suddenly felt very frightened for him.

"I'm not doing so well," Bobby said obliquely, squinting at the distance like one looking down a long tunnel. "Everything's slipping away. I've lost most of my commissions. I just don't have the energy to do anything these days. Not even read. I can't digest food well. Me, the great gourmet, and all I eat these days is Campbell's tomato soup and dry toast. My teeth are bad and my breath is worse. None of my clothes fit and I can't afford to buy new ones." He shook his head. "I'm a mess...."

"I won't pretend that I know what that's like." Michael looked at his brother, alarmed at the level of despair he found in his eyes. Adding urgency to his voice he continued, "But you have to keep trying. We'll get you the meds. You'll start the experimental therapy. You've got hope. I want to be there for you. You don't have to do it alone."

Bobby waved him away. "I'm okay. I'm okay. All my friends are here. My support group. I'll get by. Don't worry about me."

"Shit. Of course I'll worry about you. How are you paying for the medication? It's expensive."

"That it is. Very. I've sold about everything I have. Scott left me a little money, but that's almost gone. My condo is on the market."

I have beautiful windows.

"Mama will take you in. And I can send you money."

"Live with Papa? I'm not that strong. I'd never survive living with them again."

"Where will you go?" He was frustrated now, feeling the pressure of Bobby's problem on his own shoulders.

"Listen, forget about it. It's not your problem. You're going to Chicago. I'll be fine. It was just an idea."

Michael steadied himself against the porch railing as he felt the power of the decision he must make shake and rattle his equilibrium. There was no way he could leave his brother now. He couldn't desert him a second time. He would stay here after all, give his brother a job, take care of him when he was sick.

Menso, fool! he called himself in two languages, laughing out loud into the night, ignoring Bobby's puzzled expression. He was not making this decision at all. Fate was kicking him into line, compelling him to move, one foot in front of the other, along the only path available. Time had no meaning for him. What was one year? Two? Three? A lifetime? What did it matter where he spent the time? California or Chicago? It was how he spent the time that mattered.

He moved to wrap his arms around his brother, hugging him without any awkwardness, ending with solid pats on his back of affection and a resignation he did not regret. At first, he'd thought his relationship with his brother was weakened by his homosexuality. But in fact, it was strengthened.

"Bobby," he said, still patting his brother's back soundly. "You just made your father a very happy man."

"My sons!" Luis called out, arms spread wide to embrace Michael and Bobby. "Can such a thing be true? Ha! Look out, world! Nothing can stop the Mondragons now. We are united. Strong as bulls on a stampede. Ha!" He tottered toward them, gripping them tightly in fierce hugs, the champagne making him more emotional than usual.

"You see, Marta? Your prayers to the Virgin have been answered. First one son returns," he said with pride, wrapping an arm around Michael, "then the other." He wrapped his arm around Bobby, squeezing him tight. "And it is the return of the prodigal son that brings his father the greatest joy, no? What? The Bible, it says so! Look it up!"

Bobby's eyes teared. Luis, overwhelmed by the news and the wine, began sobbing openly, a smile still shining on his face.

Marta stood beside them, nodding repeatedly, unable to speak. Tears of joy spread down her thin cheeks as she viewed the men in her life openly embracing. Manuel tilted his head and finished his beer, throwing his cards facedown on the table. Rosa, watching her husband leave the room, felt her world spin. She dropped her towel on the floor and walked from the room.

Michael followed her, catching up with her in the kitchen as she gathered her coat and the children's toys.

"You think you've been excluded again, don't you?"

"I don't think. I know. Nothing will ever change around here." She looked up at him, her eyes glittering with anger. "There were always only two children in this family. Roberto and Miguel. The precious sons. I was born to help Mama in the kitchen."

"It won't be like that."

"Why are you staying?" she cried, anguish mixed with anger. "You're supposed to be leaving. Two years, you said. You promised! What happened to change all that? Why do you have to stay and ruin things for me and Manuel?"

"There are circumstances. There's a lot you don't understand, but I promise you, I'm not here to make your life difficult."

"What do you know about difficult?" She wiped her eyes and sniffed. "Go to hell, Miguel. And Bobby. And Papa. Just leave me alone."

"Rosa..."

"I said leave me alone," she cried, swatting away his hand. "Just make sure you sign those checks on time."

Oh, Lord, he thought, wiping his face with his hand. We're just one big happy family. He put his hands on his hips and thought long and hard. He was home for the duration. Okay, that was set. There were fences to mend. Tempers to soothe. It would require everything he had. He needed some fortification.

Suddenly his scowl lifted to a smile as Bobby's ideas of romance came back to him. Well, why the hell not? he asked himself. If he was going to endure a few months of hell, he deserved at least a few days of heaven.

Thirteen

⤙~⤚

Charlotte died three times that day.

"Cut!" The director whipped the baseball cap from his curly hair and wiped the beads of sweat from his brow with his arm. "Good, Charlotte. Go take a break. We'll try again in a few minutes." He was speaking low, as though trying to contain an avalanche of fury.

He turned like a panther about to pounce toward Melanie, who teetered back and forth nervously on her high heels beside Charlotte. They were both costumed in prim, nineteenth-century maid's uniforms of black wool and white cotton, sweltering in the unusually warm October sun.

"Melanie, you're an idiot," he shouted with uncharacteristic venom. Usually George Berman was a pleasant, easygoing director who encouraged his actors to find their own way through a scene. Melanie, however, had ground his patience—and that of all the cameramen, extras, makeup artists and costume designers, not to mention the special effects people—straight into the ground with her foppish performance.

It was a very small part, only a few lines in an earlier scene and four lines in this death scene, but it seemed beyond her. Charlotte didn't think George was making things

easier by calling Melanie an idiot after the last failed take,
though she couldn't blame him. All Melanie had to do was
rush to Charlotte's side after she'd been shot by her lover
and hold her while Charlotte gracefully died. Charlotte had
hit the pavement five times in the past hour, the last three
bursting open the small vials of chemical blood that seeped
through her gown.

George called the costume folks over and spread his hand
out in Melanie's direction. "She looks like a goddamn
Rockette when she runs out of that house," he bellowed.
"Get her out of those heels. What? I don't care if she goes
barefoot, just stop her from mincing around like it's a fucking dance number!"

Melanie was escorted away by the costume assistants,
flustered and red-faced, mumbling apologies to George, to
Charlotte, to anyone who would listen.

Charlotte sighed heavily and walked to the welcome
shade of an old maple, resplendent in the golds and reds
of a Maine autumn. She leaned against the coarse bark to
catch her breath and rub the new bruises coloring her arms
and legs. A mild headache was beginning at the temples,
the nagging kind that she knew could go on for days. She'd
been having more of these headaches lately and nothing
seemed to shake them. What she needed was to get back
home—to Michael—and to the peace she always felt in his
arms.

She barely had a moment to herself before she was surrounded by assistants adjusting her wool maid's uniform,
hairstylists primping her hair, makeup people dabbing her
cheeks, and a slim-hipped boy whose sole job was to make
sure she drank plenty of water. Something Freddy had insisted on ever since her headaches had begun.

"I dunno, honey," the jockey-size makeup artist said as
he shook his head with disgust and dabbed more powder
on her arm. "That's gonna be one big mama of a bruise.
Can't you demand that they let you fall on the grass at

least? You're going to be black and blue from that pavement before that bimbo gets this scene right.''

Charlotte closed her eyes and tried not to be fed up with Melanie. Poor Melanie. She knew she was hurting. For the past few weeks since they'd arrived in Maine, Melanie had done nothing but complain about how few scenes she was in or how few lines she had in the film, all the while growing increasingly sharp-tongued in her criticism of Charlotte, whose own role was increasing in lines and scope.

The movie, *One Day in Autumn,* was coming to a wrap, but this scene was the worst yet. Melanie was missing her cues, stumbling and jiggling her boobs and bottom like a cancan dancer. She couldn't grasp that this was a serious period film. That this scene tragically culminated in the unrequited love of a besotted upper-class college student and his beautiful, long suffering housemaid. Not some bedroom romp.

"I don't think she can do it," George said, walking up to her with his hat in his hand. "Look. I know she's your friend and all, and Walen cut some deal. But I can't afford this shit.''

"Just give her one more chance," Charlotte said, her eyes entreating. Melanie needed this film. She hadn't worked in more than a year.

In response, George gave her a smoldering look. He'd been trying to seduce her since she walked on the set. For Melanie's sake, she stepped closer and put her hand on his chest. "Please, George? Let's do one more take?''

He leaned forward, placing his hand over hers. "You're not too tired?''

She shook her head, ignoring the pain in her leg where she'd hit a stone the last time she fell. Melanie had been right. Beauty was power, and the power of her beauty never failed to amaze her. She was only beginning to learn how to tap it.

"I'm fine. Really." She even batted her lashes. "Give

me a minute to freshen up and I'll be ready to die again. For you."

His eyes glazed over. "You're amazing, you know that? Not many actresses can work from six in the morning till six at night without whining." He patted her hand under his, the look in his eyes so full of intent it was embarrassing. "How about dinner after we wrap this up? You look like you could use some meat."

The assistants surrounding her turned away, rolling their eyes.

"Oh, George, I'll be exhausted after today. I think I'll just order a bowl of soup from the kitchen and fall right asleep in my room. Thank you, though. Maybe tomorrow night?"

He didn't even try to hide his disappointment. He let her hand drop and nodded once, so sharply she thought his head would fall off. Hollywood egos were as fragile as spun glass.

"Five minutes," he shouted to everyone. "I don't want to lose this light."

He passed Melanie as he stomped away, almost snarling at the too large, plain black flats she flopped across the gravel in.

"He hates me," she whined when she met up with Charlotte.

"No, but he hates the way you run, Mel." She reached out to touch Melanie's shoulder. The wool was hot and scratchy and Melanie was perspiring heavily. "Pretend you're a man when you run. Lead with your shoulders and don't move your hips so much."

"Why would I want to do that? The way I move is one of my greatest assets."

Charlotte pressed her fingers against her lids, relieving the pressure building there but ruining her eyeliner in the misty sweat. "Because you're a nineteenth-century housemaid who just saw her friend shot down in the street. You wouldn't be coy at a time like that, would you? You'd be terrified. Run like you're terrified.''

Melanie seemed offended and stepped away, out of Charlotte's reach. "That's what I am doing. Just because it isn't the way you would do it doesn't mean my way isn't good.''

Charlotte sighed, fearing for the worst. Melanie's resentment was clouding her judgment and there was nothing she could do about it.

"Let's do a take," George called out.

Too late. It was up to Melanie now, and she was already sauntering off to her mark, swinging her hips like Mae West. Her stubbornness only fueled her destruction. It was hard to stand by and watch it happen. Anything Charlotte said would come out sounding patronizing or shrewish, neither of which would be helpful or appreciated by Melanie. There was nothing she could do, Charlotte realized, frustration and worry mingling inside of her. She turned her gaze away, drawing together her wandering thoughts. Now it was time to close her eyes and begin her work. As the makeup artist dabbed her face dry of perspiration and repaired her eyeliner, Charlotte directed her razor sharp focus within, then called on the character of the young housemaid, Laura, to emerge.

When she opened her eyes, all thoughts of Melanie were gone. The scores of technicians and assistants, the hundreds of glaring eyes and trivial comments, all disappeared. She moved as though to inner music to her mark in the middle of the college square and serenely looked around at the ivy covered eighteenth-century buildings that surrounded her. At the horse drawn carriages, the long dresses, the bustles, the cravats, the walking canes and myriad other paraphernalia of the set. All helped place Laura into the time period. Ah, yes, she felt it now.

Laura moved into the scene. She was leaving the college, leaving the town, in a hurry. Her lover was obsessed, searching for her. She was afraid for her life.

Quiet settled on the set, the cameras began rolling, and there was her lover Charles, handsome, familiar, yet with a crazed look in his eye. He was coming at her with a gun. She screamed. He fired, and Laura fell to the ground, not wincing even once when she found the same stone she'd hit before. She lay motionless on the ground, not moving a hair while action swirled around her. Suddenly she heard George's anguished voice shouting loudly over the other noises.

"Idiot!" he cried.

Later that night, Charlotte couldn't find Melanie at the restaurant of the hotel the film company had taken over for the duration of the filming. Nor was she in her room, at the lounge, or at any of the other places frequented by the actors and crew. It was nine o'clock and there weren't many places to go. This was a small college town with one narrow street of businesses that shut down early.

Charlotte was troubled. An inner voice warned her to find her friend. George, totally fed up, had released Melanie from the film. Freddy was on his way from L.A. to deal with the fallout and she wanted to talk to Melanie before Freddy lit into her. What Melanie needed now was a friend, not a foe.

She searched the halls of the Gaslight Hotel, an old hotel that had seen better days. The creepy surroundings, with peeling wallpaper and fading carpets, made her feel uneasy. The smell in the air was stale, like old beer. Picking up her pace, she peeked into the small rooms where machines sold candy and dispensed ice, hoping to find Melanie. No luck. She moved on to the seedy lounge with dark paneling and neon signs advertising brands of beer. The film crew was gathered there playing pool and poker or just hanging out, bored and drinking.

"Anyone seen Melanie Ward?"

There were a few sexist comments about how everyone

had seen Melanie at some point. Someone broke through the snickering and said he thought he saw her headed toward the beach. Charlotte felt a shiver of apprehension and quickened her pace.

The hotel had a beach out back beyond the porch and down a rickety set of wooden stairs. It was a gloomy stretch of sand, littered with seaweed and broken shells and smelling of rotting fish. Salt air stung her cheeks, whipping through her thin sweater. She shivered and crossed her arms tightly around herself, narrowing her eyes and searching the blackness. Stars flickering in the crisp sky reflected in the ocean like hard diamonds.

She cast a look over her shoulder. No one was around. She descended the stairs and entered the eerie darkness of the deserted beach. She'd walked a few yards when she thought she saw a movement in the shadows, far down the beach. Charlotte squinted and caught a glimpse of pale blond hair, almost white in the moonlight. The figure was draped in flowing black fabric, probably the black wool maid's costume. It covered her like a blanket stretched over her knees. She was huddled on a long piece of driftwood, staring fixedly at the ocean.

"Melanie!" she called out, rising up on tiptoe and swinging her arm in an arc.

Melanie turned her head toward her, then slowly stood up.

Charlotte felt a huge relief in finding her. Now if she could just talk to her. She began walking toward her.

Melanie turned her head and was staring again at the ocean. Then she started walking at a measured pace toward the shoreline, not stopping when her bare feet touched the water. She moved like one in a deep trance as the water slapped up against her feet, her thighs, lifting the hem of the maid's dress.

"Melanie!" Charlotte cried out again, her voice raspy with panic. *My God, she's not stopping. She's going in.*

Charlotte took off on a run, fixing her eyes on Melanie so as not to lose her mark in the blackness of sea and sky.

"Your name, sir?"

"Michael Mondragon." He set down his bag and stretched his shoulders, getting a good glimpse of the Gaslight Hotel. He didn't know film people stayed at such dumps.

The clerk eyed him suspiciously. "I'm sorry, sir, but the hotel is reserved only for the cast and crew of *One Day in Autumn*."

Michael frowned, hearing the obsequious pride in the hotel clerk that he was associated, even at such a mundane level, with a film. He fixed the clerk with a no-nonsense glare. "I'm a friend of Miss Godfrey's."

The clerk smirked, eyes full of doubt. "Again, I'm sorry. But you can't check in until I talk to Miss Godfrey personally and get her okay. Sir."

"Fine," he said, cutting off the clerk before he could suggest other hotels. "Can you tell me where she is?"

The clerk's pale face suffused with pleasure. "I'm not at liberty to say."

Stupid little man, Michael thought to himself. He hated such games.

"I understand," he replied in a monotone. "Kindly leave this note for her. Is there a bar I can wait in?"

The clerk took his note with a blank expression. He was apparently concerned that Michael might actually be a friend of Miss Godfrey's and that he'd somehow offended him. Now he was all smiles and politeness, offering to hold his luggage behind the counter, guiding him to the bar and giving him a chip for a free first drink.

Michael thanked him and strolled to the bar. He took one look around the smoke-filled room and decided he needed a walk more than a drink. Flipping the chip, he tucked it into his pocket and headed out the back for a walk.

* * *

Melanie kept walking as the water covered her gently swaying hips, her waist, her back. Ignoring Charlotte's pleas, she pushed forward toward the stars. Charlotte saw the waves rock her upward in its swell. She kicked off her shoes, threw off her sweater and dove into the frigid ocean water. The cold momentarily stopped her breath, but she stroked after the bobbing figure ahead of her, swimming farther outward into the blackness.

She reached Melanie just as her head slipped below the surface. Charlotte held her breath and dove under the water, kicking her legs to add weight and speed to her descent. Down she went, her hands splayed in the murky depths, groping in the thickness of the frigid water for any part of Melanie. Her lungs burned and she felt the first stirrings of panic. This was her one chance. She'd never find her again in this blackness. Please, God...

Suddenly she felt a wispy bit of wool brush her fingertips, and lunging forward, she grabbed hold of a handful of fabric. Yanking hard, she got hold of an arm and pulled the body up. When she broke surface, her lungs burned and she took huge mouthfuls of air. Beside her, Melanie was coughing and flailing her arms. The back of Melanie's palm cracked the side of her jaw, sending a white pain shooting up to her brain.

"Stop it," Charlotte screamed, choking back the icy water. "It's me! Calm down!"

Melanie was like a cat in the water, all snarls and scratches. She fought with her, screaming, "No, no, no, no."

Charlotte felt her strength ebbing. The cold was numbing. Her jaw ached. She couldn't hold on much longer. But she had to.

Michael turned up his collar at the edge of the beach against the biting sea air. A cold front was moving in, putting an icy nip into the wind. Weather here in Maine reminded him of Chicago; he'd forgotten how bitter a cold wind could feel. He was about to turn back to the hotel when he heard a scream down the beach. He lifted his chin and scanned the sands, but the beach looked deserted. Standing quietly, he waited. The scream pierced the air again, and it sounded like it came from the water. He took off at a run, pounding the sand. As he drew closer, he could see two figures in the water, not too far out. Closer still he could tell they were women. It looked as though they were fighting. He'd heard that a drowning person could bring down the lifesaver with him in the panic, and it looked like that might be happening now. He ran harder. There was something about the women....

When he reached the water's edge, his heart slammed to his throat in raw fear.

"Charlotte!" he shouted, recognizing her. *My God, no, no.*

He whipped off his jacket and shoes and dove into the ocean, cutting through the waves with strong, arcing strokes, pushing hard, needing to reach her quickly. He grabbed hold of Charlotte, swinging her away from Melanie's flailing arms in one powerful push.

"Michael, no!" she cried weakly, coughing back water. "I'm okay. Stop her.... Stop her..."

Melanie was coughing now, too, in a wide-eyed terror.

Michael understood it all then. "Get back to shore," he shouted at Charlotte. "Now," he ordered when she hesitated. His face was grim.

Not wanting to delay him, not able to keep her head above water much longer, Charlotte obeyed, kicking through the icy water that numbed her limbs and sucked the life's warmth from her body.

Michael lunged forward, reaching out for Melanie. When she feebly flailed at him, he reached back and socked her in the jaw, stunning her. Then, grabbing the limp body around the neck and shoulders, he headed for shore. When they reached the safety of shallow water, he released Melanie into Charlotte's waiting arms.

Melanie wobbled on her feet out of the water to the sand, where she dropped to her knees, the picture of dejection. No one spoke. The shock of what might have happened stunned them into a morbid silence.

Michael moved to Charlotte and held her in his arms. She was shaking uncontrollably, from the cold and fear and realization. When he thought that he could have lost her, his mind went blank. It was beyond comprehension. He knew in that moment how much she meant to him.

"You're here," Charlotte kept repeating with surprise, wonder, affirmation. "You're here."

He squeezed her tight, murmuring reassurances. "I'll always be here," he replied, holding her tighter as his love for her grew more defined. "Always."

"Why didn't you let me go?" Melanie moaned beside them. She, too, was shaking violently in the cold night air.

Charlotte slipped from Michael's warmth to wrap an arm around Melanie's thin, fragile shoulders. She seemed so small, so childlike. Her heart went out to her. "I'm not going to let you end your life like this," she replied in earnest. "Not for a film. Mel, you have so much to live for."

"What? I don't have anything to live for." Her body swayed and her face twisted into a mask of anguish. "I'm all alone."

"You have everything to live for. I love you, Mel. I'm your friend. I'll stay with you."

Melanie wept briefly, then she wiped her face roughly with her hands. Struggling to her feet, pushing away Michael's helping hand, she walked a few steps away, staggering like a drunk, dragging her stretched black wool dress behind her in the sand. Mascara was running down her cheeks and her hair clung to her forehead in clumps.

Michael and Charlotte watched her warily when she stopped, weaving, not having anywhere to go.

"I'm so ashamed," she said in a high voice. This time when she cried, it was not with hysteria, but sorrow. Her wild tremors were reduced to a pitiful quaking of the shoulders.

Charlotte closed the distance and again placed an arm around her shoulder. "Let's go in and get warm. We can talk more then."

Charlotte looked up at Michael, who was standing in the dark, a lodestar, his dark eyes sparkling in the night. He was waiting, listening for his cue to do whatever was needed of him. She loved him more in that moment than she'd ever dreamed possible.

His gaze met hers and he understood what she needed without words. Nodding his head in affirmation, he walked toward the hotel with them, picking up their shoes, wrapping his jacket around Melanie's shoulders as he took hold of her other arm. They brought her to Charlotte's room, past the lobby and the prying eyes, ignoring those who had the insensitivity to laugh and mumble something about those crazy film people who had gone for a late swim in the ocean. At this time of year.

Much later, Melanie had soaked in a hot tub, dressed in Charlotte's Swiss cotton nightgown and settled into bed with a cup of herbal tea. Charlotte sat beside her on the bed, huddled under blankets that could not warm her. Melanie looked washed out, depressed, a small doll that had been cracked and not yet mended.

"I feel like I'm still in the water," she said softly, her eyes vacant. "I'm still slipping down into blackness."

"You're not," Charlotte replied, holding on to her hand. "I'm here. Don't let go."

She looked at Charlotte, questioningly. "Why are you doing this? You risked your life. You don't know me that well. You don't owe me anything."

"You're my best friend."

Tears welled up in Melanie's eyes and she reached over to set the teacup down, rattling the china. "I can't believe what I did. I could have taken you with me."

"Shhh, don't think about that," Charlotte replied, taking the cup from Melanie and setting it on the bedside stand. "You were panicked. You didn't know what you were doing." She paused. "Mel, suicide isn't the answer. You know that, don't you?"

"I'm more afraid of being alone than of dying."

"You're not alone. I'll always be there for you. That's what friends are for, right?"

Melanie looked away, crumpling the blankets in her fist and drawing them close under her chin. "Friends... Some friend I am." She sniffed, ending with a kind of hiccup.

"You're a wonderful friend. You're funny, spontaneous. You have a big heart. You have great makeup." She smiled when Melanie snorted. "I was such a curmudgeon, such a wallflower before you shook me up and made me laugh at the world and myself. I know I can count on you. With you I can blurt out what's on my mind and not worry that it'll come back to haunt me. I can laugh, I can cry, I can swear a blue streak or binge on potato chips and ice cream and feel safe. I know that, at any time, I can call you for help and you'll come running. You've taught me the meaning of friendship." She reached out to take Melanie's hand. "You saved me, I saved you. I'd say we're even."

Melanie squeezed Charlotte's hand, too choked up for a few moments to speak. When she did, it was with the air of a confession.

"I know I've been a bitch lately. I'm so sorry. It's just that everything started to fall apart at once. My looks, my career. And to sit by and watch everything turn to magic around you... I was just so jealous. It wasn't your fault. I know this, but I couldn't help myself. You have Michael.

You have talent. You're so damn beautiful. I think I'm most jealous of that.''

"Stop. You don't have to explain."

"Yes. Yes, I do." She paused, looking down at her hands. "Being beautiful is very important to me. I like looking good and getting glances from men when I cross the room. I never realized how much attention I did receive until the attention stopped. Now, when I look in the mirror, I can't believe what I see. The skin sags, there are angry wrinkles around my eyes. I look tired and worn-out. But the real fear is that no matter how many new hairdos, new face-lifts, tummy tucks or whatever, I'm still a middle-aged woman. I'm at the end of my career. I'm alone. I can't hold on to a relationship. Charlotte, I'm so scared."

"You're not alone, I wish you'd get that through your head. Just because you're getting older doesn't mean your life is coming to an end. That's crazy. We all age. It's life."

"Easy for you to say. When I was twenty-three, I never thought I'd age. Not really. I believed I would always look great. Ten years younger than my age, at least. Never tell your age, that was my motto. Well, I'm here to tell you, girlfriend, I'm forty. It comes sooner than you think. One of these days you're going to look in the mirror and not recognize the face that's staring back at you. You're gonna look at yourself under the bright lights and think, shit. What the hell kind of face is that? Just what do you think you'll do then?"

Charlotte looked away. She knew exactly what that felt like and exactly what she'd done.

"Oh, God, Charlotte," Melanie cried, covering her face. "What do I have to live for? My life has been a series of failed relationships and meaningless sexual encounters. I've given up on ever finding someone who will love me." She sniffed and wiped her eyes, smiling tremulously. "Except maybe you, Charlotte. You keep telling me how I'm your only friend. The truth is, you're the only real friend I've ever had.''

They cried and hugged and bonded as surely as if they'd cut their fingertips and become blood sisters. Charlotte thought of Dr. Harmon's warnings never to tell anyone about her surgery. She knew if word of her transformation leaked out her career would be over. Freddy would drop her in an instant. And Michael?

He was sitting in the next room, waiting for her. She was tormented by the irony of her dilemma: the truth for Melanie, lies for Michael? Deception was a cruel role to play, lies were foul lines to recite. Tonight, she vowed, she would tell him the truth. After she talked to Melanie, she would lie at his side, hold him close and remove the deceit from their relationship.

But first Melanie. Looking at her swollen eyes, her fingers plucking apart the tissue in her hands, her utter despair, Charlotte felt compelled to take a risk, for both of their sakes. Ignoring the voice in her mind that told her not to speak, she sat back, crossed her legs Indian-style on the mattress and took a deep breath.

"Melanie, I want to tell you about myself...."

Hours later, Charlotte tucked the blanket under her friend's chin, dimmed the light and, grabbing a few extra blankets from the armoire, tiptoed from the room.

Michael was stretched out on the couch, asleep, with her script in his hands. He looked so handsome her heart lurched with love for him. Did loving him make him more beautiful? His hair fell down across the angled bones of his face, exposing his unusually bowed, full lips. She sighed and leaned against the door, filled with the surge of desire to kiss that mouth. To feel his arms around her again.

She felt safe in his arms, protected and loved. She was drained and needed him desperately. But in a few hours, when the dawn shed its light, she'd somehow have to rally and reshoot two scenes with Melanie's replacement...and do the love scene with Brad Sommers. She wanted nothing more right now than to lock the doors, unplug the phone and collapse onto the sofa with Michael.

She closed her eyes, swaying with fatigue and the weight of her responsibilities. Her commitment to her career came first. George would not forgive her if he didn't get his shots tomorrow.

She marshaled the last of her energy to walk to Michael's side, remove the script and spread a blanket over him. She smoothed the hair from his face and placed a soft kiss on his cheek, allowing herself a moment to linger there, relishing the scent of his skin and the feel of his breath on her cheek. Then, yawning with the satisfaction that she was not alone, that she had two very special people in her life—a best friend and a man she loved—she cuddled into the armchair like a cat, wrapped a spare blanket around her shoulders and quickly fell asleep.

That night she dreamed of her mother, and when the telephone call came to awaken her for the day's work, she was surprised to find her cheeks were wet with tears.

The next morning, Michael stood just off the set, watching men and women scurry in preparation for the love scene. Charlotte lay in a four-poster bed, supposedly in the room of the wealthy young college student played by Brad Sommers. It was a skeleton crew; all unnecessary crew members were ordered off the set at Charlotte's request. She wasn't an exhibitionist and was nervous at performing a love scene.

"I won't be nude," she assured Michael when he insisted that he wanted to watch the scene. "But won't it be difficult for you to be there?"

It was only a perverse curiosity, an overwhelming possessiveness that made him stay and watch the scene. He'd read the script and knew the take would be tough for him to watch.

He stayed out of people's way. Just the preparation for the shot was a show. The director was in a snit, shouting and whipping off his cap in a fury as the crew scrambled to set up the shot. The cold front had moved in and threatened an early snow. They had to hurry, hurry, hurry. Two more scenes had to be shot today, reshoots of the scenes with Melanie's replacement, and George wanted to get it all in today before the overcast sky opened up.

Michael caught the director looking at him. He thought him a sour-faced sleaze, and when their gazes met, the director scowled at him, though he couldn't understand why. The director walked to the bedside and delivered a few last-minute instructions to his actors. Then he leaned over to Brad Sommers and whispered something private in his ears. He saw Sommers's eyes look up and search the room, settling on himself. The actor looked again at the director and nodded. Michael had the strange feeling that the words had been about him.

The cue was given. The set quieted, cameras whirred and the filming began.

Michael watched Charlotte intently, holding back the desire to cover her creamy shoulders, to throw the other man from the bed and to take her somewhere, anywhere, away from these prying eyes. She was wearing a white nightgown, embroidered with delicate rose-colored flowers and long, thin ribbons that encircled her breasts. One shoulder was bare where the gown slipped low, exposing her long, swanlike neck and the soft swelling of one breast.

The dark circles that framed her eyes when the phone woke them at five-thirty that morning had disappeared under the mastery of the makeup artist. Her head was resting on the pillow, her hair spread out over the pillows in waves. Long, slender arms, thrown up over her head in a kind of ennui, invited a man's lust. Her hair, her face, her body, everything was so beautiful he stared at her like one caught in a spell.

He was seeing her in the camera's lights as he'd dreamed of seeing her for the past few months while she was away. As he'd wanted to see her last night. The problem was, the man lying naked beside her wasn't him. The arms drawing her close, the hands caressing her cheeks, sliding down her neck to cover that bare, rounded shoulder, were those of another man. Michael knew it was acting, that this was a film, of course. But the scene was none the less galling, no less painful to watch.

The man—for Michael refused to give him a name— spoke fervent words of love. From the dreamy expression on Charlotte's face, he could swear that she believed him. Her eyes were soft with yearning and her breasts rose and fell with the passion he'd hoped was saved only for him. Michael could feel his own body stirring as he watched, like some cheap voyeur, as another man stroked, kissed, made love to the woman he himself loved.

What infuriated him was that he knew, as one man knows another, that this actor was physically aroused. He could tell from the trembling hands, the natural flush of his cheeks and the fervor of his kisses. At some point his acting had stopped and the passion expressed was very real.

Michael looked sharply around at the others on the set; the cameramen, the lighting men, the director. To his horror and disgust, each man bore the same rapt expression as they watched the love scene unfold. They breathed through parted lips.

Michael's hands rolled into balled fists as he felt his Latin jealousies rage inside of him. He wanted to rip the cameras away, throttle the man who dared to kiss the woman he loved and take Charlotte away from this unnatural place. He would seal his possession of her with his own mouth, his own body. Michael shook with restraint, feeling a slow burn of jealousy and the throbbing ache of desire.

The love scene continued relentlessly. He watched, transfixed, nailed to the spot, as the actor ripped at Charlotte's gown savagely and she struggled against him. Michael took a step forward, fists bunched. In one graceful swoop the man moved to straddle her and the sheet fluttered back, exposing Charlotte's full, rounded breasts and her dark, pink nipples, hard and erect.

Michael strangled a cry in his throat, turned and fled the room, seeking the refuge of the cold nor'easter outdoors.

The scene ended minutes after Michael left. The director called, "Cut and print," the crew sighed and applauded, and Charlotte pushed Brad away and curled up under the sheet, wrapping herself tightly with the fabric. Freddy Walen, standing in a shadowy corner, saw Michael leave and smiled in smug satisfaction. He'd been watching the way Michael suffered during the scene, relishing each grimace and the clenching of his jaw.

This was good, he thought to himself. Very good. He couldn't have planned it better. A man in his situation would react in only two ways: one, to be jealous—as this one was. The other was to puff out his chest and be pleased to see other men lust after his woman. Better that he was jealous. Raw emotions were always easier to manipulate. He followed him out, smiling again when he caught sight of Mondragon standing outside the door, his hands rammed into his pockets, his face a mask of pain.

"What are you doing here?" he asked Michael, sizing him up.

Michael glanced down at Freddy briefly, turned up his collar and looked away. "What do you want, Walen?"

"I was about to ask you the same thing. What do you want hanging around Charlotte all the time? She's doing her work. Work that doesn't include you. In any way, shape or form," he said pointedly.

"Anything that has to do with Charlotte's way, shape or form is my business."

Freddy was infuriated. The confidence of the man was galling.

"Well I've got a message for you from the director. He wants you off the set. You don't belong here."

Michael took a step forward, menacingly. Freddy pushed out his chest and stood his ground. The two men stood face-to-face, glaring.

"I've got a message for that pimp director," Michael said, his voice deep with anger. "You tell him I've read the script for that scene and nowhere does it say that Sommers character was supposed to tear off Charlotte's gown. You tell him for me that unless he wants his lead actor to get his fancy face rearranged, he'd better stick to the script. Got it?"

Michael turned on his heel and stomped away, not waiting for Freddy's reply.

Freddy bit his retort and smiled, satisfied. He returned to the set, anxious to check on Charlotte. He was furious about that stunt Sommers had pulled and was going to have words with George about it. He hurried to Charlotte's side, relieved to see her sitting up, wrapped in the sheet and arguing hotly with the script director.

"Nice work, babe," Freddy said, surprising her.

"Freddy, when did you get here?"

"Soon enough to watch this scene." He grabbed her robe from the costume assistant and handed it to Charlotte. "Here, put this on before you catch cold. You've got a break before your next two scenes. Then it's a wrap. I saw the dailies and you look great, just great. This is going to be a good film for you."

She slipped into the robe, barely hearing what Freddy was saying to her as her eyes searched the set for Michael.

"He left," he informed her.

She swung her head around to look at Freddy. "Who? Michael?"

"Yeah. I guess he couldn't watch, not that I can blame him. You and Brad make a nice couple. Are the sparks there for real?"

Her mouth twisted into a frown of disgust. "Really, Freddy. Get serious. I can't stand Brad Sommers. The creep attacked me in this scene."

"Hey, don't worry about it. I'll take care of it."

"See that you do."

"Calm down, honey. The man's in love with you and it has nothing to do with publicity."

"I don't care. Because I don't even like him. And I'm furious that he practically stripped me during that last scene. What was he trying to pull? Besides my gown, that is. That wasn't in the script. You go and tell him for me that if he tries anything like that again, I don't care if the film's running and they print it, I'm going to kick him so hard he'll be singing soprano. I won't even tell you what he was trying under those sheets. It's a good thing that Michael didn't see it or I think he would have killed him." She looked around the set again, worry revealed in her eyes. "Where did you say he went?"

"Who knows? Who cares?" He gripped her arm, staring into her eyes. "I thought we discussed this Mondragon guy. He's not good for your career. He's not good for you. He's not your type."

She yanked her arm free. "And just what is my type?"

"Someone like Sommers. Someone with class. Someone like you. Hey, Mondragon's a good looking guy. I can see why you had a little fun with him, but enough's enough. Drop him. We don't want his kind hanging around."

Charlotte turned on Freddy, anger shooting from her eyes like lightning.

"Michael Mondragon is not some fun that I picked up.

He is the man I love and I won't tolerate you insulting him that way. You manage my career, Freddy, not my life. I don't remember asking you for your permission, nor do I intend to stand here and listen to another ten-minute monologue on how to conduct my personal life. So far I've done everything you've asked and done it well. I'm living up to my part of the bargain.'' She pointed her finger at him. ''You just live up to yours. Now, if you'll excuse me, I want to change into some clothes and go find Michael.''

She took a few steps, then turned and added, ''Oh, by the way. Leave Melanie alone, too. She's not feeling well and doesn't need any lecturing, either.''

Freddy was furious with Charlotte's attitude, not just about Mondragon but about everything. She was bucking him, and he didn't like it one bit. He felt like slapping her in some way. Her affection for Melanie Ward gave him a perfect means.

''I have no intention of lecturing Melanie. I'm dropping her as a client.''

Instead of frowning in displeasure, as he expected, Charlotte's face brightened and she smiled.

''Good,'' she replied. Then she turned heel and strode from the room, leaving Freddy seething.

Charlotte dressed quickly and hurried outdoors, searching for Michael. She found him walking the gravel path that led to a small woodland not far from the hotel.

''Why didn't you wait for me?'' she asked tentatively, sensing his tension immediately. ''I looked everywhere for you.''

He kept his eyes averted, which bothered her a great deal. She felt the icy wall of his hostility wedge itself between them.

''I needed some air.''

She felt a sudden jolt of anger. ''I told you not to watch. But no, you insisted.''

When he looked at her she saw anger, then hurt in his eyes. It was the hurt that made her stay and not walk away.

"I didn't know how much it would pain me to see that man make love to you. It killed me to see you respond to him."

"I didn't," she cried.

He grabbed her by the arms, so tightly it hurt. "You did. I saw."

She tried to shake him away, but his grip only tightened. "That wasn't me, it was Laura. The character. I can't just turn off my body or its natural responses. Michael, look at me. I'm an actress. Love scenes are part of what I do. You can't be this way."

"Can't I?" He yanked her against his chest and planted his lips on hers in a kiss that was devastatingly possessive. Positioning her between his legs, he slid his arms around her and hugged the breath right out of her.

She clung to him, feeling her knees weaken. All that they had felt the night before, all that went expressed only in their eyes exploded between them, rushing forth like water released from a dam.

"You're *mine*," he growled, his fingers digging into her shoulders, his teeth bared at her cheek.

"Yes, yes," she responded, giving her heart and soul to him, an ancient instinct demanding that she choose him as her mate.

He pulled away, his eyes devouring her with a sudden impatience. She loved that sudden fierce desire that would overcome him, fill him with a single-minded focus. It could happen at any time. One touch could spark it, like a single strike of a match could ignite a fuse. It made her feel desirable. It made her desire him.

His face tightened, his mouth pursed as he looked to the left toward the hotel. People loitered about, talking, waiting for the next shoot. To the right, the path led to a small woods not far off. Grabbing hold of her hand he strode into the woods, walking fast, his heels digging into the soft earth.

She hurried by his side, clutching his hand, trying not to smile, all the while thinking, yes, yes, yes. He searched the woods for a secluded spot, far from the path where someone might disturb them. At last he found one. Suddenly he veered to the left to where a cluster of evergreens provided a tent and the earth lay hidden under a thick layer of leaves.

He walked her to this spot and, without a break in stride, swung her around, slamming her back against the broad bark of a glorious sugar maple. His hips pressed against hers. She could feel the hardness of his arousal.

He meant for her to, and ground against her, his breath mingling with hers in a vaporous cloud at their lips. His hands spread open her coat and slid beneath her sweater to feel the warm silkiness of her skin. He felt her stiffen as his cold hands explored her. He meant to touch each part of her that had been touched by Sommers, to burn away with his own skin, his own scent, any trace that other man may have left on her body. His hands rounded her breasts, cupping their fullness. Then, seeing in his mind's eye her hard, pink nipples, he squeezed them now with his own fingers. Her moan of pleasure sang like music in his ears.

He swallowed that sound with his mouth, hungrily claiming his territory. It was as if a fever burned through him; he couldn't touch enough, kiss hard enough, move fast enough. He wanted her now!

When his fingers entered her she was ready. He began to tug impatiently at her pants. She lowered her hands to help him, to undo his pants. Her eagerness at touching him, so hard and demanding, caused her to moan in impatience.

"Now, Michael. Now."

His hands cupped her rear, lifting her higher against the hard wall of the tree. She felt a burning scrape where tender skin met coarse bark, then a sudden, fierce filling when he thrust high within her. She gasped and clasped him tighter around the neck, wrapping her bare legs around his hips as he thrust again, harder and faster, pounding her against the bark. She bit his neck, stifling her scream as she shook and tightened around him.

He gave one powerful shove that pinned her against the wood, cried out her name, then shuddered against her.

Nearby, birds fluttered in the air, pierced the sky with their high calls, then gradually circled and slowly came to rest on overhead branches.

Michael stayed inside of her a moment longer, while his muscles relaxed, then slowly lowered her to the earth. Neither of them were inclined to speak.

Michael lowered his head and looked into her eyes, triumphantly.

She tilted her head and smiled shyly.

"I love you," he said against the crown of her head. A simple declaration of fact.

Her heart expanded so; it took her breath away. "I love you, too."

They both felt what this coupling had meant. They knew that here in the primitive setting of nature he had claimed her as his own—and she had accepted him.

Michael flew back to California that afternoon. Cruising high above the thick cloud cover, the plane suddenly lurched, causing him to shift in his seat. The movement released the faint scent of Charlotte's Joy perfume still lingering on his clothes and skin. Instantly he was filled with a rush of memories of the past twenty-four hours: their farewell, her beautiful face upturned, her luminous eyes soft with longing, her soft mouth pressing against his own. He got hard instantly. That was enough. Shifting again in the cramped space he smiled, imagining—hoping—that when she changed that afternoon for her next scene with Sommers, she would smell his scent on her as well, and remember that incredible coupling they'd shared in the woods. Sex was such a primitive act. He liked being akin to an animal, being a male and marking his territory. Even though he was traveling clear to the other coast of the nation, his woman bore his mark.

He leaned back in his seat, comfortable in the knowledge that he trusted her completely. No Brad Sommers or Freddy Walen or any other man would steal her away from him. Looking out his window, he saw the sunshine pierce the clouds.

Fourteen

❧

Charlotte didn't fly home to California right after the film had completed shooting a few weeks later. Instead, she took the short flight from Maine to New York, to keep an appointment with a financial adviser recommended to her by the producer of the film. Charlotte didn't have a great deal of money to invest, at least not by the producer's standards. By her standards, however, the post-tax, post-agent, post-expenses dollars she'd set aside to invest was a veritable fortune. At some point during the past few weeks her perspective on her life had crystallized. The eerie juxtaposition of Melanie's suicide attempt and Michael's declaration of love showed her how fleeting life was—and how precious love was. She wanted permanence in her life and had resolved to attain it.

Her visit to Bessemer Trust lasted two hours. In that time she'd set up a portfolio that invested a sizable portion of her capital in high risk ventures that would double her money quickly—or lose it even more quickly. Charlotte surprised Kenneth Clark with her ability with numbers and her keen sense of money. She was not the least surprised. She had been, after all, an excellent accountant. The fact that she was now investing her own money only sharpened her skills.

When she returned to California, she maintained her forced march. The first appointment she made was with Mrs. Delaney, the elderly widow who owned the house she rented. Mrs. Delaney didn't want to meet with her at first. She was a frustrated, irritable old woman who felt the world had done wrong by her. Like most people, however, she was soon won over by Charlotte. Together they walked through the garden. Charlotte helped her water the roses and threw sticks for Mrs. Delaney's two overweight Scotties. Mrs. Delaney seldom had visitors, invited no one, and other than her housekeeper, rarely saw anyone. Charlotte was patient with her, thinking of her mother, giving the older woman time to vent her frustrations and to talk endlessly about her sorry relatives. Eventually, Charlotte guided the conversation to pleasanter topics, such as the dogs, the garden, Mrs. Delaney's collection of Japanese porcelains. Given the opportunity, Mrs. Delaney could discuss these happier topics with more animation.

After the afternoon tea was served, she agreed to sell Charlotte the squat, postwar tract house on the bluff.

"You what?" Melanie's hands framed her face, the very picture of surprise.

"I bought the house," Charlotte replied with feigned nonchalance, setting down her purse on the front table. She cast a sidelong glance at Melanie's stunned expression, then burst out laughing, hugging Melanie with the sheer joy of her first house purchase. The two women danced and sang around the house, a tall, slender figure holding hands with a small, curvaceous one.

"Whatever did you do to make that old battle-ax sell?"

"She's really very nice, beneath that cold exterior," Charlotte replied. "She reminded me a lot of my mother, actually. A hard life and disappointments can sour a woman. She didn't even care about the house. Hung on to it for lack of anything better to do with it. She's got plenty of money, she's just lonely. I think we should invite her over once in a while for tea, or maybe a game of canasta. She likes to play cards. So did my mother.''

Charlotte felt a sudden pang of homesickness for her mother. She'd sent Helena a generous check every month with a long letter informing her of everything that was going on in her life. She never failed to include her dreams, her hopes and her successes. In every letter, Charlotte begged her mother to come live with her in California and never work another day in her life.

Helena never wrote her in reply. The checks came back, uncashed.

''When you want something, Charlotte Godfrey, you get it,'' Melanie exclaimed, setting her hands on her ample hips. ''I saw it in your chart right away. You are a Leo through and through.'' She didn't want to tell Charlotte that she saw a difficult time ahead for her as well. She'd found it best to keep that kind of revelation to herself.

''I am woman, hear me roar,'' Charlotte chuckled. Her eyes danced with excitement. ''Speaking of which, I made another stop today. For you,'' she said, handing Melanie a packet.

''What are these for?'' she asked, chewing her pouting lips while bringing the papers to the table. She absently shuffled through the brochures. ''Cooking school? You can't be thinking I'm going back to school? At my age? Don't be ridiculous. School is for young people. I'm too old to go back to school. I'd be laughed out of class.''

''Is this the same Melanie Ward I know? Talking about age?''

''No, it's not the same Melanie. And you know it. My body is worn out with rehab travails. Age *is* an issue.''

''No, that's not true. You showed me that. It's certainly not true when you're talking about going back to school. There are plenty of men and women in their forties who return to school. Older, too. In this day and age it's normal for people to change careers at least twice in their lifetimes. It seems to me that you've only had one career so far, so isn't it time that you open the door for another?''

"I can't," Melanie said, back-stepping. "You know me. I'm a bubblehead. I'm all body and no brains."

"Again, not true. Melanie, you always see the glass half-empty. It's time to look at the bright side. A positive outlook is good for the soul."

"What if I'm not a born optimist, like you? To me, the glass *is* half-empty somedays and half-full on others. Sometimes, it's bone-dry."

"Or overflowing. Optimists are made, not born. You can't always change your circumstances, but you can change the way you react to them. For one thing, depressed people bring you down. Spend time with people who are upbeat."

"Yeah, well I have you for my roommate. I'd have thought that was cheerful enough to last a lifetime. You and your lists," she muttered, sifting through the brochures.

"Exactly," Charlotte persevered, stubbornly refusing to back down. "I'm the queen of list-making. My favorite holiday is New Year's Eve just because I get to make new ones."

"I know what you're trying to do...."

"Try it," Charlotte said, linking arms with her. "I'll tell you what. Let's pretend this is our own private New Year's Eve. November ninth, the day we bought the house."

"We?"

"Absolutely, we." Charlotte insisted. "Let's make a list of all the things we want to do for the house and for ourselves. Like decorating. Cleaning out our closets. Finally starting that fitness program." She looked at Melanie with a wicked gleam. "Going to school."

"You're pretty clever, sweetie. A regular Pollyanna."

Charlotte laughed, delighted that she was catching Melanie in the spirit of the game, despite her protestations. She nonchalantly strolled into the kitchen to open a bottle of chardonnay. From there she watched as Melanie poked at the brochures with one finger, then felt a surge of triumph when Melanie bent over to open one up and scan the pictures. Her tiny nose drew close to the pages as she squinted.

"Hey," she called out, pointing to one picture. "That guy looks pretty old."

Charlotte walked in with two glasses of wine in her hands and peered over Melanie's shoulders. "Fifty if a day," she replied, handing a glass to Melanie.

"Do you think?"

"Go on. All I'm asking is that you go take a look at the place. For me."

Melanie frowned and sipped her wine. "Even if I did want to go, where would I get the money?"

"I'll spot you a loan."

"Oh, no." Melanie rolled her eyes. "I don't want to start that."

"It's no big deal. They're paying me an obscene amount of money for my next film. Who's to say what's fair? Why can't I do something with all that money that will give me pleasure and help my best friend? Besides, I consider it a good investment. I've been eating your cooking for years, and I'm a firm believer in your talents. You have a future as a chef, I'd bet my life on it. I'd like to bet my money on it."

"I don't know, Charlotte. It would be a big gamble."

"You know me, I'm very careful with my money. I've never made a bad investment and I don't intend to start now."

"I know what you're trying to do and I appreciate it. I admit I'm interested. I'd be a fool not to, considering my prospects. But I'd never be able to pay you back. If only I'd done this years back when I had money. Damn, when I think of all the money I wasted. It makes me sick."

"Half-empty..."

Melanie laughed.

"Seriously now," Charlotte said. "Lending you money will not be a hardship for me. After you complete your degree, we can talk about how you can pay me back." She sipped her wine. "I was rather hoping you'd do something exotic, like open a restaurant or a catering business. Something I could roll over the debt into."

Melanie's Kewpie-doll mouth twisted, considering the possibilities. Charlotte took hope from the way her eyes were dancing with the light. "I could do the housework, the shopping and the cooking to pay for my rent while I'm in school. God, I can't believe I'm saying that. Me, cleaning house. I don't even want to think about my nails. But I could do it, you know. You taught me a lot about how to clean a toilet bowl, sweetie. In fact," she continued, moving to the edge of her seat, "maybe I can do other chores, too, you know, like ironing or something."

"Before you turn into little Miss Suzy Homemaker, let's work out a loan program between the two of us that won't make you my personal slave." Her tone changed. "I don't want anything to ruin our friendship."

"No. Me, neither. Agreed."

"I'm going to be on location and on promotional tour so much in the next few months. And now that I'm a homeowner, I hate to leave the place unattended." She smiled. "I just thought of another job you can do. You can be the house sitter."

Melanie shook her head and threw up her hands, giving in. "Sure. Why not?"

"So," Charlotte put out her hand. "Does this means you'll go to school?"

Melanie took the hand. "When God closes a door, he opens a window, my grandmother always said." They shook on the deal, then hugged. Melanie slunk back in the chair and snorted. "And I always thought you were stingy. Turning off the lights, using coupons, tight budgets. But you're not. You're one of the most generous people I've ever met.''

"I prefer to call it frugal. So I can blow it on something I really care about. Like you.''

Charlotte moved to the sofa and leaned back into the pillows. Her whole body ached. Now that she was home, every muscle demanded that she take time to relax.

"You look tired," Melanie said, coming to sit beside her.

"I am.''

"Are you taking your vitamins?''

"I'll be better, I promise.''

"You drive me crazy. What's a mother to do? I'm going to pack them myself next time, and if you come home with a bag full of vitamins, I'm going to do something drastic. I don't know what yet, give me time to think of it.''

"I don't try to be bad. I've just been so busy....''

"All the more reason. Charlotte, you're not looking well. I'm worried about you. You're losing weight.''

"Just a few pounds.''

"Five, more like it. Are your headaches back again?''

"Mmm," she replied with a soft groan. "They come more often than not now. Migraines, the doctor says. I'm not so sure. My joints hurt, too. In tiny little spots, like those itsy bones in the wrist, the knuckles of my toes, the balls of my hips.'' She especially ached where Melanie had hit her in the jaw in the water, but she didn't want to mention that. No sense in making Melanie feel terrible, too.

"Now I know why you and Mrs. Delaney got along so well. You were a pair of old dotties, comparing aches and pains.''

"We did," she replied, a smile curving her lips. She stretched out on the sofa, kicked off her shoes and covered herself with a ratty old afghan her mother had knitted for her years before. "Could you dim the lights a bit, please, Mel? I need to rest for a minute before Michael gets here.

I don't want to greet him after several weeks hobbling about like an old woman.''

Melanie studied Charlotte as she lay on the sofa, her practiced eye picking up the details of her appearance. She was wearing a simple black dress with a fabulous cut, a Prada probably, a favorite of Charlotte's. The thick gold earrings and matching necklace were exquisitely braided and had the rosy luster of eighteen carat. No bracelets or rings cluttered her long, slender arms and fingers. Only a simple black Movado watch on a thin black leather strap encircled her slender wrist—a gift from Michael Mondragon. Melanie sighed, knowing that Charlotte Godfrey would look as beautiful in her own, inimitable way at forty as she did now. It was that timeless quality, more than anything else, that Melanie envied.

It was Charlotte's inner beauty, however, that made it impossible for her to begrudge Charlotte any good fortune that came her way. When she thought of what Charlotte had suffered as a child it put her own misery to shame. She was wise beyond her years. An old soul. If Charlotte could find the courage to make such incredible changes in her life, could she not at least try to make some changes in her own?

Melanie walked over to tuck the afghan under Charlotte's chin. How pale she looked, almost wan. Freddy put so much pressure on her, but then again, she put so much on herself. Charlotte Godowski...Charlotte Godfrey...the woman still remained a mystery. She had her beauty, she had success. What was it, she wondered, that still drove Charlotte so hard?

Later that same evening, Charlotte sat with Michael in front of the fireplace watching the embers flicker blue and red, the first fire in her new home. Earlier, Charlotte had laughed gaily and served chilled champagne for Michael and Melanie, her eyes sparkling as bright as her smile.

They'd raised glasses of champagne and toasted the purchase of the house, then Melanie had made a fuss declaring how there was a movie playing at the Biograph that she was just dying to see and slipped out the door, announcing with exaggerated tones that she wouldn't be home until midnight at the earliest.

Michael spent the next few hours making love to Charlotte in front of the fire, complimenting her on how the fire made her skin glow, then proceeding to make her glow even more by bringing her to climax once, then several times more, proving to her in actions as well as words how much he had missed her.

Afterward, the glow they felt was more from the gentle rocking in each other's arms, the sharing of dreams for the future and the comfort in knowing that what they shared was very, very special. They wrapped themselves up in a blanket and sat on a sheepskin before the fire, his legs straddled around her and his chin resting atop her head. She could feel the tickle of his coarse leg hair against her soft thighs, hear the bass of his voice, always so low after lovemaking, smell her own scent on his lips when he kissed her.

"Michael, do you think we'll always be this happy?"

"Of course. I don't see why not."

"These separations aren't easy for us. The next film will take me to France for several months."

She heard his low grumble of discontent. "It's the slow season. I can come visit you on the set."

"Only if you promise not to watch the love scenes."

He grumbled something in Spanish, tightening his arms around her and settling his chin in her neck. She cooed, feeling his evening bristle against her tender, perfumed skin.

"Michael, what did you do with those drawings you made for the house? You know, the ones you sketched when you first saw the site?"

She could feel his smile. "I've still got them. I never throw a design out. Let me guess. Now that you're a landowner you have visions of grandeur."

Now it was her turn to smile. "More like redemption. I seem to remember you called the house the proverbial sow's ear and how you could transform it into a silk purse. Something to compliment the garden." She turned in his arms, her face lit with excitement. "I want to do it, Michael. Really. I loved the drawings. Knew the minute I saw them I would do it if I could. Sometimes when I'm in the garden, when I look back at the house, I see your design. I make a few changes."

"You make changes, do you?"

"Of course." A smile twitched her lips. "I play little games in my imagination. I want a bathroom with a big mirror, so I can look at myself every day and not be afraid of what I see. And a dressing table, like I've seen in the magazines. One for Melanie, too. Such silly things I want, Michael, and I want them now. I don't want to wait. I feel like I've been waiting for things for most of my life."

"What's brought about all this? You won't even be home one week out of every four for the next several months."

She heard the frustration in his voice and cupped his face in her hands, shaking his head gently. "All the more reason why I need a home to return to. A base. I used to think that making movies was so glamorous. Exciting locations, fancy hotels, elaborate parties. It is all that, some of the time. Most of the time, however, it's trailers, carryout food, rise and shine at dawn and crash late at night, new lines to memorize and then publicity and promo interviews in between.

"Ah, Michael, don't you see? When I'm alone out there I need to think about this house, and how you've designed something special for me here. And it'll be good for Mel to be part of it. Getting her involved in the design."

"I'm sure she'll have plenty of ideas for the kitchen." He was warming to the idea.

"Yes," she said, clasping her hands together. "I want Melanie to design the kitchen to suit her. It's perfect. She won't feel so alone while I'm gone if she has something like that to keep her busy." She looked at Michael, her eyes entreating. "You will keep an eye on her while I'm away, won't you?"

"Yes, of course I will. It's just like you to worry about someone else. Who will keep an eye on you?"

"That's Freddy's job. He's always hounding me to eat right, to exercise, to get my rest."

Michael scowled. "I hate that guy. Don't trust him. He sees you as his meal ticket, Charlotte, not as his friend."

She pressed her fingers against his lips. "Shhh. I need both of you, so I'm going to ask you the same thing I ask him. Don't get on my case about him. He's my agent. He's doing a good job, and I can't do this without him." She took a deep breath. "My career means a great deal to me. I'm committed to it. And to him. Things are just beginning to take off now. I can't—I won't—let anything get in the way."

"Or anyone?"

"Why even draw that line in the sand? I love you. I don't see any reason why my career should interfere with what we have. You just have to be understanding of what it is I do. You can't be so jealous, Michael."

"Can't I?" He moved away from her and grabbed his champagne flute, drinking the contents of his glass in one gulp. "Maybe a career's not everything."

She looked at him, his dark eyes fathomless in the fire's light. "What do you mean?"

He told her then about Bobby and his battle with AIDS, and then in a halting voice, his own decision to stay in California, at least for as long as it took for Bobby to seek a way to stabilize. Or to help him face his death.

"But my career isn't as important as it once was," he tried to explain. "When I hear you imply, under all your goals, that you'd give up what we have for the sake of your career, of course I worry. Do I mean that little to you, Charlotte?"

"No, of course not," she exclaimed. "I'm not saying that. Michael, this isn't the same thing."

"Sure it is."

"No, it's not. You *are* an architect. Your training is done. You can build anywhere, anytime. It's not the same in my business. I have to make it now, or possibly lose my chance. This is my moment."

"Life is a series of moments, Charlotte. Don't deceive yourself into thinking that this is the only one. Believe me. The best-laid plans of mice and men." He took her hands in his. "What matters, Charlotte, is what we have between us. The love. The honesty. The complete trust. This doesn't happen every day. It has to be protected and guarded. Nurtured, like any plant in any garden."

"I agree, Michael. But my career means a great deal to me, too. Why do you think I must make a choice?"

"I thought my position at the architectural firm in Chicago meant everything to me. Then I came home again and realized what I had given up to achieve that goal. My brother and I were strangers. He didn't even call me when he found out he was dying. How do you think that made me feel? What did my career matter then, when I found out my brother was in trouble? I had deserted him when he needed me most."

Charlotte moved closer to him, holding him in her arms as he tightened his eyes.

"What's hardest now is that he is living a lie with my family. My father and my mother, they are blind to his being gay. To how sick he is—as I was. He can't bring himself to tell them for fear that they will reject him. Even if it kills him, which it might. I'm the only one who knows." He shook his head, clucking his tongue. "I hate living this lie. We are a family. We should be able to tell each other the truth."

Charlotte's heart pounded inside of her, beating out a death knell in her ears. She had to tell Michael the truth. Now. Or he'd never forgive her.

"You don't hate Bobby for telling you all this? For the pain he's caused you? And trouble?"

"Hate Bobby? Of course not. He told me the truth. He was honest. I hate my parents for doing this to Bobby. For forcing him to live the lie."

She shivered against him. She opened her mouth to tell him the truth hovering at her lips. "Michael, I..." She closed her mouth.

"You what?" He lifted her chin to look into her eyes. She faltered. "I love you."

His expression altered, became smoky with love and intent.

"Wait here." He stood up and walked to where his clothes were lying on the floor.

Charlotte watched him as he strode naked across the room. He was so beautiful. She loved him so much. He loved her. Why couldn't she tell him?

He bent double to dig into the pocket of his jacket and pulled out a jeweler's box. Flipping the top, he took out a ring and, returning to her side, cradled her back in his arms.

"This isn't how I'd planned to do this, but..." He lifted her hand and poised the ring above it. "I knew in Maine, when I almost lost you, that you were my life. Will you wear this, Charlotte? Will you share my life?"

Charlotte stared at the marquis diamond that glistened between his fingers, her eyes wide and her mouth gaping. She hadn't expected to make this decision so quickly. It seemed too fast. Too soon. She hadn't yet told him the truth about who she was. He had the right to know before he made this decision. But how could she risk it now? Risk not having him love her, honor her, cherish her, for ever and ever.

What matters, Charlotte, is what we have between us. The love. The honesty. The complete trust. This doesn't happen every day.

She did love him. He didn't know that his love was the bridge between the two Charlottes. That he made her whole. He only knew that she was Charlotte Godfrey, and that was how it should be. And Charlotte Godfrey *would* be honest with him. From this moment forward. Forever.

"Yes," she replied, her happiness bringing tears to her eyes. "Of course I will."

His eyes sparkled like the diamond he slipped on her finger. Then he hugged her tightly against him.

She held on to him, wrapping this treasured moment with joy and tucking it away on a high shelf in her mind to recall in the future. Looking over his shoulder, she stretched out her hand, wriggling the finger with the ring on it, admiring it.

"Mrs. Michael Mondragon," she said, feeling the words in her mouth. "Charlotte Mondragon. Mrs. Mondragon. Mondragon..." She paused, then laughed brightly. "My dragon. Of course. Why didn't I think of that before? That's what I'm going to call you. My Dragon. You *are* my dragon, you know."

"How so?"

"You challenge me. You made me fight my anger and loneliness." Her voice grew soft. "You made me believe in dreams again."

He kissed her cheek and tightened his arm around her.

"I was hoping it was because I lit your fire."

She laughed again, heartily. Then she turned in his arms, straddled his hips and proceeded to show him how right he was.

* * *

The phone rang four times before she heard Helena's voice.

"Mama? Mama, it's me. Charlotte."

There was no reply, but she heard a quick intake of breath. She held the receiver tightly in both her hands and closed her eyes, willing her mother to respond.

"Mama, I have some good news. I'm getting married! Aren't you happy, Mama? I finally found my *Someone*. He's wonderful. Kind, hardworking. He'll be a good provider, Mother. We want to get married in the church. And..." She rushed on, hearing no reply. "I bought a house. Isn't that wonderful? You can come live with me. With us."

There was no answer on the other end. Just a deathly silence. Charlotte clutched the phone tighter in her hands.

"Please say something, Mother. Please. I miss you so much." Tears sprang to her eyes and her voice caught in her throat. "Mama?"

She heard the click of a phone, then the harsh buzz of disconnection. Drooping her head, Charlotte lay the receiver back in its nest, lowered her head upon her hands and wept.

Freddy was seething with fury when Charlotte showed him the ring and told him the news of her engagement. This time, however, he was more careful to conceal it. Charlotte was due to start her first leading role, and the early reviews of her work in *American Homestead* was drawing critical acclaim. Word was also out that she was brilliant in the just completed *One Day in Autumn* as well. There was a definite buzz about her now. Her name was hot, strictly A list, and the offers were tumbling in. Big offers.

Her biggest break yet was this new film, the remake of *Camille*. Joel Schaeffer, director extraordinaire, had long desired to direct this project and Charlotte had won the role of Marguerite over Ryder, Thurman, Stone and a dozen other big Hollywood stars. It was a juicy part. A real plum. Charlotte was born for the role and Schaeffer was genius enough to see it.

So right now he wanted her happy. No sense in stirring up the mud—which was exactly how he thought of Michael Mondragon.

"Listen to me, babe," Freddy said, palm held out. "I've never given you bad advice. You've got to keep this engagement a secret."

Charlotte tsked and shook her head no.

"I mean it. The timing's all wrong." He felt panic and anger mingle in his gut, and he fought to keep it out of his voice. "We made a deal, you and me. I've kept my part of the bargain. I told you it was going to be rough. I told you that you'd have to trust me. You gave me your hand. You swore."

Her finely arched eyebrows rose up toward her temples like seagull wings. "Yes, I remember."

He had her. She was too decent a person to go back on her word. "Just for a while, babe. This film is going to be a blockbuster. Tell that matador of yours to cool it. The engagement's off."

She reared. "No, it's not."

"At least the ring is. Christ, Charlotte. With your looks, you could get a ring three times that size. Four."

Charlotte looked at the one-carat diamond and thought she would never want anything more. "I'll wear it around my neck," she replied stubbornly.

Freddy knew when to quit. He'd take what he could get. Mondragon was the enemy. He'd won this battle and he had every intention of winning the war.

Fifteen

~⊚⟋⊚~

Freddy sat in his office on Wilshire Boulevard, listening to a voice on the phone, frowning out at the bright May spring day. He didn't see the beautiful women strolling down the street as colorful, charming and plentiful as spring flowers. In his mind's eye he saw one face, the same one he envisioned each morning and each night. Charlotte Godfrey. And she was the topic of conversation of this international call to France—where *Camille* was being filmed.

"What do you mean she's in trouble? What kind of trouble? Is there a man or something?"

He didn't mind if Charlotte was sparring with one of the many men he fixed her up with for publicity. He even approved of the possibility of a fling with one of them. Hell, there should be a French lover in every girl's history, he thought. Anyone, as long as it wasn't that Mondragon guy.

"*Non,* it's not about a man," replied Jean-Luc, the assistant he put on the payroll to look after Charlotte. "Especially not *that* man."

Freddy wasn't happy when Charlotte was thousands of miles away from him on location, this time in a remote village of Provence. He liked knowing what she was doing, who she talked to. So he'd hired Jean-Luc, ostensibly as Charlotte's personal bodyguard. His main job was to act as

Freddy's eyes and ears on the set, and to block as much communication as possible between Charlotte and a certain Michael Mondragon of California.

"Make sure of it, or you're fired."

"I'm doing my job." He sniffed. "This Mondragon is...persistent." Jean-Luc was struggling with English over the phone. "He is calling with the phone and sending the letters every day. And now flowers. Every day with the flowers. I give them to the script girl. She is happy. Thinking they are from me, *oui?*"

"Yeah, whatever. I don't care who gets them as long as it's not Godfrey." He paused. "So what's the trouble?"

"She isn't looking so good. She is sick, I think."

Freddy sat up in his chair. "What kind of sick?"

"The doctors here they don't know. Headache and stomachache. Tired."

Freddy's hope *was* that after a few months away from Mondragon, what with being in a foreign country and experiencing the excitement of doing a blockbuster film, if she didn't hear from the guy her passion would die down. Sick, though, that wasn't good. Damn, she couldn't get sick now—or depressed. There was far too much riding on this film.

"Keep close to her. Don't let anything upset her, especially that Mondragon guy. Block communication coming in or going out, got it?"

Another California summer was approaching and a fourth season's cycle was well underway. The heavy chores of spring, done while the days turned long, the wind was cool and the spring rains watered, were beginning to pay off. The sharp rotating disks of the tractors clawed the soil to a loamy silt fit for seedlings. Now, when he looked over the rolling hills, Michael could see the beginnings of a fine, vigorous stock. It made him think of the secure future he was building here. Of planting seeds and watching them prosper. It made him think, too, of planting seeds in Charlotte and starting a family of their own.

Spring was also a time to mend fences.

Lord knew he was working on that, too. He and Rosa were on speaking terms again. It was a start. His father seemed to be mellowing, partly due to old age, partly due to the comfort of having his sons take over the business. And now he was building this log cabin for Bobby.

Michael wiped the sweat from his brow with his sleeve and turned to look at the log cabin he was doing the finishing touches on. He'd built it for Bobby to live in, to give him a place of his own. The cut wood represented a kind of mended fence, he thought. Fresh, strong timber, without rot or disease. A good omen.

He heard a shout of hello from the road and turned to see his brother walking up the hill from the main house. Michael had chosen this quiet spot near the pond for the cabin, a peaceful but friendly distance from his parents' house. Bobby might need close care if he took a turn for the worse. Seeing the improvement in Bobby's health, so readily visible even from a distance, gave him hope that invalid care would not be necessary. Bobby's face was fuller and his cheeks had a healthier glow. As his father exclaimed, "There's meat on the bones!"

"You're looking good, bro. How are you feeling?"

"I don't know," Bobby replied, rubbing his belly. "*Mamacita* just gave me my morning dose of rotgut. How many chili peppers do you think a man can eat before he burns a hole in his belly? 'The hot kills the germs!'"

Bobby and Michael laughed at Bobby's excellent imitation of Marta. Their eyes met, then they smiled and nodded, both knowing Bobby's improvement was due to drug trials with the new protease inhibitors. There was early indication that the virus was being reduced in the bloodstream. The hope was that it would be eliminated. A hope that was too breathtaking, too dear to be voiced.

So in addition to *Mamacita's* good food and chilis, Bobby took fistfuls of vitamins, minerals, herbs and other medications, natural and drug. During the winter, his nausea was almost constant, as was fatigue, but he held forth a strong front, only allowing Michael to witness his suffering. By spring, however, he was genuinely feeling better, even euphoric, as his health began to improve. Michael knew when he gave his brother the money to pay for the $15,000-a-year drugs that Bobby would never be able to pay him back.

"How about lending a hand?" he called to Bobby. "It's your damn house, after all."

"Oh, no, *hermano*. You're just looking for some free help. I refuse to accept your house, but I will help build it. Now, which one of those tools is a hammer?"

"Very funny." Michael flipped him the hammer. "Neither of us can live with Papa too long. And since I don't want to set roots here—" he met Bobby's gaze steadily "—the house is yours."

Bobby's eyes were sad. He shook his head and stepped forward, taking a beer from the cooler.

"I thought you were enjoying your life here. Everything is going so well for you. The business is just beginning to reap the rewards of your efforts for the past three years. You've brought in dozens of new clients. This spring the phone is ringing off the hook." He smiled crookedly. "All the suburban housewives are asking for that handsome Mr. Mondragon."

"Funny. I'm not getting those messages...."

"Charlotte would have my head on a silver platter if I put those through to you. I just pass them over to Papa. He thinks they're asking for him."

"That explains why his chest is the size of a barrel—it's so puffed up."

"His chest isn't the only thing that's puffed up."

Michael roared, thinking of how the cockiness in his father had indeed returned this spring. He leaned back his head, taking in a long swallow of the cool beer that Bobby handed him. "Boy, that feels good. My throat is parched."

"I'm not surprised. You've been working like a slave."

"I've had a lot of time to kill." He took another swallow, squelching the loneliness he felt for Charlotte.

Bobby, knowing the facts, adroitly changed the subject. "You should be pushing out your chest as well, Miguel. Look at the place. You've earned it."

Michael knew it was true. "The business is doing well enough," he admitted modestly.

"Well enough? The nursery is booming! You've more than doubled the business, and it's growing as strong as the stock in the fields. And Rosa and Manuel should be kissing your feet."

Bobby studied the expression on his brother's face. "You don't get any personal pleasure from your accomplishments here, do you?"

"That's a good question. Sometimes I walk the land at night and see the young trees growing straight and tall, smell the flowering shrubs, bend over to touch a sprout just emerging from the dirt, and I think, yes. This is good. Life is good."

"But…"

He ran a weathered hand through his hair, tightening the elastic at the nape of the neck where he had bound his long hair back. "But what am I doing here? I am an architect. I've spent a lifetime preparing for a real career, studying hard, planning my escape from all of *this*. I thought…" He looked over his shoulder at his brother and beyond to the winding pathway that led to his father's house. "I thought I was better than this."

Bobby snorted. "Spoken like a true academic snob."

"What's that supposed to mean?"

"Who ever told you that you were too good for the soil?"

"Nobody ever said it in so many words. But the message was clear enough."

"How old are you? And you still go on and on about what other people might have said once upon a time? I won't even begin to tell you what folks have said to *me*."

Michael heard no self-pity in Bobby's voice, and it shamed him.

"If I stay here, I've failed."

"Fascinating. You think that all the success you're enjoying now is beneath you. A novel concept, isn't it? Success in failure?"

"Actually, success in failure is an ancient Japanese concept. Achieving personal success—honor—even while the world views you as a failure is considered noble."

"Well put." Bobby flipped the hammer gracefully, placed it back into the toolbox and closed the lid.

Michael pursed his lips and looked at the rolling hills, freshly planted.

"I've promised Papa I'd drive him to Melton's farm to pick up the new chicks. Mama wants more eggs to fatten me up." He laughed, then walked past Michael, pausing to rest a hand on his shoulder. "I understand that stuff about success in failure. Look at my career. At my life. In a way, this disease has opened my eyes. I'm no longer condemned to die tomorrow, but I'm not cured, either. Each day could be my last. In this way, I am no different from you or anyone else. The way I see it, there is no success or failure. Only living. Every day. The best way we know how." He patted Michael's shoulder, then walked away down the path to their father's house.

Michael knit his brows and took another drink from his bottle, then leaned against the cabin, resting his head against the cool, coarse wood. Bobby was right—he was an academic snob. During his years and years of sterling education at the top institutions—Harvard, Wharton, Oxford—he stockpiled knowledge, building self-esteem as he was building this house, one log at a time. And in that time, other men's thoughts became his own. Other scholars' words became his own quotes. The community of scholars, of professionals, of educated men and women, had become his own. His family.

Returning home again, however, he realized that they were *not* his family. The stern faces of professors did not elicit the tender feelings of the beloved faces of relatives. A limp, polite handshake among colleagues was insipid compared to the emotional embraces with loved ones.

Why did he think that he was a failure if he didn't achieve success in the academic areas? Areas that all his life he'd been led to believe were somehow superior to work done with the hands. Academic fields, such as architecture, were superior to fields of plants or crops, or so he'd always thought.

Yet wasn't he getting as much satisfaction putting together this simple log cabin with his bare hands as he ever did building a structure on paper? It was no skyscraper, it was only two bedrooms. But it had a large center room with a massive stone fireplace and a wide front porch overlooking the sweet-smelling valley. He looked around and took in the acres of well managed lots before him. Compared to the drought-destroyed acres of two years earlier, these were lush with his new irrigation system and the stock was vigorous. And Bobby... His brother was healthier and more content now than he'd been in years. Weren't these successes?

He didn't know. He didn't know anything anymore. After spending a lifetime in pursuit of academics, he never felt more humbled by his ignorance.

Vicki Ray was in France to report on the shooting of the final scene of *Camille* for "Entertainment Tonight." As far as she could gather, the film had almost killed Charlotte Godfrey.

Joel Schaeffer, the director, in a fervor to create a masterpiece, drove the actors and crew at a fevered pace, demanding retake after retake until he got the scene just right. No one questioned Joel's brilliance once the shooting began. Scriptwriters were at the ready. Cameramen stood at attention. A small crowd of local people were allowed to watch from behind barriers. Even the proud and aloof inhabitants of Provence were eager to see the celebrated, beautiful new film star from America who was chosen to play their beloved Marguerite of the Camellias.

Vicki was standing on the sidelines with the rest of the press, taking notes, when she heard a cry of excitement from the crowd. Everyone surged forward. An excited nasal buzz in French hovered over the set as the trailer door open and Charlotte Godfrey emerged.

Even Vicki, as hard-boiled an entertainment reporter as they came, had to admit that when Godfrey stepped out of her trailer in her spectacular lavender-and-white gown, leaning heavily on the arm of her bodyguard, she felt awed. Everyone stopped and stared, eyes popping, hearts pounding. The fans, the crew—even Vicki Ray.

Godfrey's gown would win a Best Costume Oscar for sure. But it was the woman who had the luster and presence that caused eyes to widen, mouths to drop and hearts to sigh. Her golden hair was entwined with camellias, her face as waxy and white as their petals, her demeanor as fragile. Godfrey didn't acknowledge the crowd as she was escorted through it to the set. She looked straight ahead, serene and focused, like one hypnotized. Vicki Ray would later describe it better in her report. She said that Godfrey was "as one walking in a trance."

Her foreign fans accepted this as concentration and were not put off when she walked by without notice. They hushed in respect, whispering compliments, unlike her many American audiences who expected waves and smiles and resented being ignored. It was this concentration, Vicki thought, that gave Godfrey the reputation of being a conceited snob. In an odd way, it made Vicki all the more curious about the actress's personal life.

Because there was no doubt that her acting was pure genius. Either she was the best damn method actor she'd ever seen or the woman was really sick. And Joel didn't let up on her. He shot the scene first in master shots, then moved in for closer angles, mostly of Charlotte, but several of Leonardo DiCaprio's expressive face as well. The two worked magic together as the ill-fated lovers. But Joel wanted blood, and from the pallor on her face, it looked like he was getting it. No one believed for a moment her agent's bullshit about her having allergies. When the character coughed and choked during her death scene, even her bodyguard stepped forward, his dark, unreadable eyes sharply focused on his charge. What was the story there? Vicki wondered.

"Wonderful! Cut. Print," called Joel, beaming. The cast and crew clapped and cheered, as happy with the performance as the culmination of the scene. It had been a long day for everyone. Godfrey had to practically be carried back to her trailer by that hunk of a bodyguard. No one was allowed access to the star. Vicki was determined to get her story, however. The Godfrey woman mesmerized her.

"Hey, Joel!" she called out, trotting after the famous director. "Vicki Ray, from 'ET.' Any comment on the film? Or your star?"

The tall, thin, enigmatic director turned to scowl at his PR director, a sensitive-faced man with Ralph Lauren glasses and long, curled hair. Vicki had already run him over with her determination. The poor man cringed under the director's stare.

"Tell her I'll see her and everyone else tomorrow at four."

"What? You want enough time to get Charlotte Godfrey on a plane out from Paris?"

The press knew that the producers of *Camille* didn't want anyone to have access to their star until the advanced press releases came out. Editors were working on the clips before they even tackled the film. The push was on to get the "coming soon" excitement rolling as soon as possible. *Camille* was a winner; everyone could smell it. The producers, and Joel, wanted it out in time for the holidays—and the Oscars. Such was the way of blockbusters.

"Come on," Vicki Ray prodded. "Just one quote."

Schaeffer stopped and turned, his face tight. The PR man stepped forward, blocking her. For a minute Vicki thought she'd blown the interview. But then Schaeffer's eyes sparkled with pleasure and he waved away the assistant.

"I'm going on the record as saying that Godfrey's performance was nothing short of genius. Better than Garbo's. No, wait." He paused, glanced at his PR man, then a wide, self-satisfied smile eased across his face.

"You can tell them for me, Garbo lives."

Garbo Lives! ran the headline of *Variety* when the early publicity rushes came out. Talk of an Oscar nomination was already on everyone's tongues by the time Charlotte reached California.

Freddy's protective blackout and her penchant for privacy was perceived as merely a publicity ploy to recreate Garbo's reclusiveness, stirring the paparazzi into a feeding frenzy. The PR people at Miramax were thrilled with the comparisons with Garbo and played along, lip-synching Freddy's prepared press releases that Godfrey was a natural recluse.

"Well, yes," they conceded. "If the press insisted on comparison, Godfrey did prefer her privacy. Like Garbo."

As she traveled home, Charlotte wore an ill-fitting black velvet top, a baggy black skirt with a fringe hem, red sneakers and enormous black sunglasses. Freddy arranged for her to be met by cars so that she never had to wait in public.

This was customary, but he laughed at her perpetual dark glasses, telling her that she was defeating her purpose. She looked more like a star in this get-up than if she'd worn furs and silk scarves. Charlotte didn't see the point of telling him that her eyes were photosensitive now and she needed the protection.

She dismissed Freddy at the airport, insisting that she ride alone in the limousine from the L.A. airport through the winding hills to her home. Freddy had been insistent but Charlotte was firm. She would go home alone.

A trail of cars filled with photographers that rammed cameras in her face without any mercy followed her, but soon she would slip behind the tall, layered stucco walls that now surrounded her home and gardens. Freddy had insisted that the whole place get wired up. Electronic eyes and ears sensitive to body heat and motion made her house and gardens an impenetrable fortress. It was necessary, Freddy said, what with all the crazy fan mail she'd been receiving. Who knows what a stalker might do? She had called him eccentric, but now she silently blessed him.

The driver approached the secluded entry, made more so by the foreboding, heavy iron gates and intercom station. She focused on the lush hydrangea vines climbing along the stucco walls rather than the red blinking light of the sensors. The gates swung wide. She slid down her window, and as the car moved forward she caught the scent of jasmine from her garden. She was home. This small house on the cliff had come to mean so much to her, especially now that Michael had transformed it for her into this multileveled, open-space retreat overlooking both her lush garden and the valley below. It was a love letter from him to her.

She stepped out from the long black limousine, not waiting for the chauffeur's assistance, anxious for him to be gone. As soon as he settled her luggage in the house, she excused him, sighing in relief when she saw the heavy gates close behind the car. At last. Blissful solitude. No one was here to tell her where to stand, what to wear, prompt what she said. She was free from what was referred to as her entourage: Freddy, her agent, her personal maid, her hairdresser, her secretary, her press agent. Free from the badgering of her New York financier, her lawyer and her business manager. All of them doing their jobs. None of them concerned about her. None of them friends or loved ones.

A dull ache throbbed at the base of her skull, a signal she recognized now that a killer headache was not far behind. She'd have to take more painkillers soon. Perhaps when she ate. She'd feel better now that she was home, she felt sure. That's all she needed. To be alone in her home. She breathed in the sweet scent of her garden in the warm June breezes. How good it felt to be out of the trailer, out from the lights. In her own house.

Her house. The change was amazing. She had spent so little time here since the renovation, she barely recognized it. Once inside, she was confronted with the dramatic garden views that Michael had made possible. She took a deep breath and smiled.

"Melanie?" she called, but there was no reply. All was quiet. She dropped her purse and short white gloves on the front secretary, then sifted quickly through the mail set aside for her. Nothing from Michael.

She sniffed and caught the scent of Melanie's Shalimar. The whole house smelled of her. Looking around, she noticed that scattered here and there...everywhere...were Melanie's things. Her numerous collections of assorted crystals and delicate Herend china filled the shelves of Charlotte's étagère. The romance novel she was reading lay half opened on the sofa. There was very little in the house that indicated Charlotte even lived here.

In her bathroom she unpacked her toiletries, washed the voyage off her face and applied creamy moisturizer to her dry skin. She'd call her masseuse tomorrow. Ah, yes, she thought, rubbing the back of her neck. Some jasmine-scented oil and Ruth's magic fingers digging out the tension was exactly what she needed.

Michael had especially designed vaulted ceilings and huge windows in the luxurious bathroom so she could open her windows to the garden while she soaked in the whirl-pool tub. Bobby had joined in the project, too, painting sweet, chubby cheeked putti on the ceiling that peeked over at her with wide eyes and pointing fingers. He'd thought it was so amusing—just like the great murals in the pope's bathroom.

She dripped a few droplets of Joy perfume into the water, adding some to her neck and her wrist, over her sore joints. It was the scent Michael had given her. She closed her eyes, remembering the night he'd kissed all the small, secret places she had applied it on her body. How long had it been since he'd kissed her? Since they'd made love? Could it really have been four months?

The sweet-scented vapors filled the room. Suddenly she felt sick. Very sick. Moaning, she hurried to the apricot-colored toilet and slipped to her knees before it, just in time. The past four months of filming, the eight-hour plane trip, the two painkillers and her loneliness for Michael emptied out into the porcelain bowl.

Melanie knew the moment she entered the house that Charlotte had returned. One of her crazy operas was blaring from the speakers, her twelve pieces of matched Louis Vuitton luggage blocked the foyer and the scent of Joy and bath crystals permeated the house. She broke into a wide grin of delight and, after tossing her briefcase and purse into a jumbled heap beside the luggage, vaulted through the living room.

"Charlotte!" she called out. "Welcome home, sweetie! Charlotte? Where are you?"

When she walked into Charlotte's bedroom suite she

paused but saw no one. She was about to leave when she heard the sound of retching in the bathroom.

"Oh, sweetie, what's the matter with you?" she crooned, rushing to her side and holding Charlotte's thin, racking shoulders as she heaved. Charlotte's thinness alarmed her immediately. Her shoulders were little more than bones protruding through pale skin. Her hair was limp and without its customary luster.

When Charlotte leaned back against her, spent, Melanie wiped her mouth and face with a cool cloth, then helped her to her feet. When Charlotte stood, Melanie was stunned at the full sight of how much weight she'd lost. She hurried to wrap a shivering Charlotte in a thick terry cloth robe and helped her to the bed.

"I'm going to kill that Freddy." In her breathy voice, even a threat sounded sexy. Charlotte wanted to smile but couldn't. She felt boneless, muscleless. She slumped back into the pillows and closed her eyes. Deep, dark circles shadowed her eyes, and her cheekbones, already prominent, rose high and stark over gaunt, hollow cheeks.

"It's not his fault," she replied. "He hovers over me like a mother hen, even hired a personal bodyguard in France for me. Had a press blackout…he did everything he could."

"I'm going to get you something to eat."

"No, no," Charlotte moaned. "I couldn't eat a thing."

"What? Are you anorexic or something?"

"No, no. It's not that."

"Have you seen a doctor?"

"Oh, yes. Many. No one seems to know what's the matter with me. Except a therapist."

There were not many people she could admit this to. Other than Michael, there was only Melanie. "One psychologist said I'm suffering from an emotional disorder." She released a chuckle that was part laugh, part cry. "In other words, he thinks I'm nuts."

"You're the most balanced person I've ever met. Little Miss Cheerful. That's a crock if you ask me. Anyone can see you're malnourished. All you need is a few home cooked meals."

"Spoken like a chef." Charlotte pried open an eye and smiled at her friend.

Melanie had changed much more over the past several months. Gone was the tight, sexy, garish clothing. Gone, too, was the heavy makeup, brassy blond hair and high heels. Melanie had cut her hair, and now the soft, golden brown locks were styled in a soft bob that flattered her round face. She'd gained weight, too. At least ten pounds, filling out her soft, flowing pants and sweater in flattering curves. She no longer looked as trendy or as young as she did in her leggings and bunched socks. But she looked comfortable with herself, less pathetic and more alluring. She looked like a woman who no longer needed to flaunt her outer beauty, having found it within.

"So, enough about me. Tell me about what's going on with you since I've last seen you. How's school?" she asked, when she had climbed into her bed and covered herself with a mountain of blankets. Her body was still shivering.

Melanie beamed and flopped down on the bed beside her. "Great. More than great, actually. I love my classes, love going to school, love waking up every morning. It's probably as much *that* as skill that makes me really good at what I'm doing. My friend Junichi is just waiting for the liquor license and he'll be ready to open his new Japanese restaurant. We've done so much since you've been gone. The dock's been spruced up real good, and Junichi designed some wonderful Japanese-looking tables and chairs so people can nibble sushi outside and look at the sunsets. I know it's going to be a success. The stars and planets are all in alignment. And people are already knocking on the windows while we're working, asking when we're going to open for business. You'll be our first customer, of course."

"Of course. I can hardly wait. I'm just glad I didn't miss the opening."

"What do you mean, miss it? We wouldn't have opened till you got here. You're a partner."

"A silent partner."

"Whatever."

"You're spending a lot of time with Junichi. Outside of business, that is."

Melanie's brows gathered and she grew cagey. Charlotte knew that Melanie was more cautious these days. Her buoyant optimism was tempered, and she was working with a single-minded diligence at the Culinary Institute. She still had her sense of humor and her New Age ideals, but she also had a new self-esteem that was hard-earned. Melanie wasn't about to sell herself short again. Charlotte remembered the excitement in Melanie's eyes last winter when she'd described her wonderful sushi instructor, Junichi Takamoto.

"We're good friends," Melanie replied, looking away. "And he's very sexy. No big deal."

Charlotte raised her brow.

"Well, okay, there's a possibility he's a big deal. He's very special. Different from anyone else I've ever known. He treats me different, too. You know, he opens doors for me, takes my arm when I cross the street, puts his hand on my waist when we stand together. Little things that shows he cares. The kind of thing I see Michael do for you all the time. Every girl dreams of finding someone who loves her like that."

"And you've found that with Junichi?"

Melanie shrugged lightly and smiled. "I don't dare say too much. I'm just taking it one day at a time." She laughed lightly and plucked the pile from the blanket. "I will say that I knew when I saw his grocery cart there was hope for us."

"His grocery cart?"

"Sure. Carts send out powerful messages about the people pushing them," she explained. "When I see a guy with a basket full of beer and frozen hamburgers it's a real turnoff. It just screams couch potato. When I see fish sticks, I head in the opposite direction." She gave a shudder.

"Really?" Charlotte rewarded Melanie with a smile. "Okay, I'll bite. What did Junichi have in his cart?"

"Salmon. French bread. A can of dog food." She smiled smugly. "A bottle of wine. A good bottle."

"I've got a lot to learn."

"Too late for you, kiddo. It's tortillas and beans for you. Speaking of which, have you called Michael yet?"

"No. I just got back."

"Do me a favor and give him a call. He's been calling here almost daily, frantic to reach you. Asking when you were due to return. Swearing a blue streak in Spanish. I didn't even think of asking for a translation. He's usually the strong and silent type. In fact, I'm surprised he's not here right now."

A small smile curved Charlotte's lips. "You said he was frantic?"

"Insane. If he didn't build this place he'd a torn it down looking for you."

Suddenly, she couldn't wait another moment. Her hands shook as she stretched out across the bed for the phone. As she drew it into her lap, her heart was pounding again, this time in anticipation. It had been so long.... Her finger shook as she punched the number, forgetting the sequence halfway. Damn her foggy memory of late. She rubbed her temples and took a deep breath. Then, in a rush, she punched the numbers again, her memory clicking in.

The phone rang once, twice. On the third ring she heard his voice on the answering machine. She gave a soft sigh of disappointment. Still, the sound of his voice, even on the machine, made her toes curl. She waited until his message ended and the beep sounded. What would she say after all this time? The silence was filling the tape. Her hands tightened on the phone. She licked her lips, hesitant, then spoke into the phone.

"Michael... It's me. I'm home." Her voice caught. She was about to hang up when she heard a click.

"Charlotte?" It was Michael. His voice was sharp, urgent.

"Yes."

"I'm on my way."

When the doorbell rang a short time later, Charlotte felt much more in control—dressed in a Versace silk dress, her hair in a smooth chignon, her makeup artfully applied. A last look in the mirror, however, revealed her bare neckline.

"My ring—" She tore through her jewelry box till she found the small silk bag that held her diamond. The bell rang again as she pulled out the small, but to her, incredibly beautiful diamond, cursing when she saw the chain knotted up. There was no time to fool with it now. Making a decision, she slipped it on her finger, then hurried to the door. She felt suddenly shy, embarrassed. Taking a deep breath, she swung the door wide.

His face was suddenly before her. She blinked, it was so much like a dream. Months of wondering, waiting, agonizing. And now here he was in the flesh. His long, thoughtful face, his dark brows arched in scrutiny, his coffee-colored eyes bright with excitement, his dark hair, still damp, probably from a quick shower, tied neatly at the nape of his neck. He wore his customary crisp, long-sleeved white shirt rolled up, exposing tanned forearms covered with fine black hair. Black trousers, a thin leather belt. Leather sandals. She noticed each detail as her eyes roamed over the one face that she missed most in the world.

They both stood still, as though in shock, and stared at each other. Words that she had prepared in her mind while in the bath, rehearsed carefully, evaporated now in the emotion of the moment. She found she couldn't speak at all.

She saw his eyes study her, too. His gaze swept over her once, then again, as though to swallow her whole. Then it traveled more slowly, over her hair, her face, her body. She saw his brows knit in worry—acknowledging how thin and pale she was. Then she saw his eyes move to her breast and she knew the moment he noticed that she was not wearing his engagement ring around her neck. His eyes flickered, his brows rose, then his face fell in sadness. It was all very subtle and quick; no one else would have noticed but her.

Immediately she raised her left hand and rested it upon his chest, over his heart. He looked down, saw her hand, and though she couldn't see his eyes, she saw his lips curve in a smile.

When he raised his eyes to hers they were lit with joy. "I wrote to you," he said. "I called. I sent flowers."

"You sent flowers?" Her heart was light.

"You never received them? I don't understand."

"We'll figure it out later. But first, just hold me. Please?"

His face shifted. His eyes darkened and he moved toward her.

One step, just one, and she was back in his arms.

"I'm going to kill that guy."

"It doesn't matter anymore. I'm here now. With you. Nothing else matters as long as we're together."

"It does matter." Michael was resolute.

"I don't want you to tangle with Freddy. I'll make it clear he's not to interfere with my personal life ever again."

"You're not saying that you're going to keep the guy on? After this?"

Charlotte sat very still. "I don't want to talk about it."

"We *will* talk about it. He's not good for you. He's sure as hell bad for us. He wants to break us apart, don't you see that?"

"Of course I do. And I'm trying to tell you he can't do that. I can handle Freddy."

Melanie stepped into the room, her arms locked against her chest. "I'm glad to hear that. He's on the phone."

Charlotte felt a frisson of anxiety as she stood up. "I'll take that call," she said, eager to set things straight.

Melanie and Michael exchanged a commiserating glance while she spoke on the phone. Melanie leaned against the wall, her arms crossed. Michael reached for his glass but didn't drink. He swirled the ice until Charlotte hung up the phone and returned to the room.

Melanie pushed back from the wall, her gaze guarded. "Well? What did the creep want?"

Charlotte rubbed her long, thin arms, feeling suddenly cold. They'd had words about Michael. "He has a new deal he wants to discuss. It's a lot of money and he says it's a great part."

"When does it start?" Michael asked sharply.

"I'm not sure. Fairly soon."

"Damn, Charlotte," Melanie exploded. "He's going to kill you. You need a break. You can't go back to work yet. Look at you!"

"I know...." She had told Freddy the same thing, but he'd pushed it aside with his typical bravado. Everything was going to be great, he'd told her. Leave it to Freddy.

The deal was everything to Freddy. She also knew Freddy would apply relentless pressure. He'd hammer at her resistance like a tidal wave. Right now, she didn't trust that she had the strength to stand up to him. She needed a chance to recoup.

"I've got to get away," she said. "He's coming over."

"Good," Michael said, glaring. "There are a few things I'd like to tell him."

"I don't want to see him. I don't want another scene."

Michael stood up, his face intent. He moved quickly. "Then grab your bags. Let's go."

"What? Where?" She balked.

Seeing her shocked expression, he took her face in his hands and stared into her eyes. He did not wish to bully her, as Freddy did. No, he wanted Charlotte to make a choice. His gaze sharpened.

"Come home with me. I've a small house, a cabin in the woods. It's beautiful there, overlooking a pond. Surrounded by trees. You'll be safe at the nursery, it's private and secure. You can rest there and grow strong again, surrounded by flowers. My mother will cook good Mexican food to fatten you up. Bobby will make you laugh. And I—" His face hardened with intent. "I will stand between you and anyone or anything that threatens you in any way."

"I—I can't just leave. Disappear. I have responsibilities. There are people to notify."

"I'll take care of all that," Melanie volunteered. "That's what you pay those press agents and secretaries for."

"Charlotte," Michael said. "You're stalling. Yes or no."

"Your bags are all packed," Melanie prompted. "You just have to throw them in the car."

It was incredible to her that Michael would suggest such an impulsive act. He was not a man who acted without thought and deliberation. Neither was she. This made the invitation somehow all the more appealing.

"This is just like Camille. Marguerite was ill and her lover took her to the country to get well." She laughed lightly. "I don't suppose this is the time to tell you she died?"

"Write your own ending," Melanie said. "Go on. Be happy. I'll hold down the fort here."

Charlotte's breath came fast. Could she follow her hunch? Could she really just run away?

"Charlotte?" Michael was impatient.

Charlotte looked into Michael's eyes. Her accountants, lawyers, press agents, secretaries, even the vision of Freddy, zooming his way along the freeway in his vintage Mercedes, all vanished.

"Please, Melanie, call Mrs. Cookson and ask her to inform everyone that I am taking an extended leave. The numbers are all in her Rolodex." She paused, thinking that Freddy would track her down if he thought she was with Michael. "When Freddy arrives, tell him..." She thought for a moment. "Tell Freddy that I've gone to the country, to a spa, to take a well needed rest. It was, after all, his suggestion in the first place."

She spoke to Melanie, but she was looking at Michael. He was smiling.

Sixteen

Michael brought her to his cabin, a charming two-bedroom log home. Charlotte was surprised to learn that he'd built it himself. The living room was centered around a massive stone fireplace. The house was barren of any furniture, save for a new double bed, a large oak table and four chairs fashioned from twisted saplings. He put her in bed immediately, ordering her to rest. She felt safe, protected, in a cocoon. She muttered something about it being the most wonderful cabin she'd ever seen while she drifted off to sleep.

She slept for three days in the large four-poster while Michael slept on a cot in the other room. She vaguely remembered waking to drink water, eat thick chicken broth with crushed saltines that Michael brought to her on a tray, and stumble to the bathroom.

On the morning of the fourth day, she awoke to the sound of sprinklers outside her window, swishing out water in a circular pattern on the newly planted grass. In the distance she heard the rumblings of a tractor, the whistle of a mockingbird and occasionally a muffled shout from somewhere in the distance. She felt as though her bones were made of lead and her mouth of cotton.

"You're awake," Michael said, appearing at the bedroom door. "Would you like to test your legs?"

"I'm still so tired."

"Then stay in bed. It's your choice. You have nothing at all to do."

The concept was foreign to her. "I miss you. I think I'll get up."

And she did, if in a wobbly manner. He bathed her in the small porcelain claw foot tub, scrubbing her back vigorously with a loofah. Then he washed her hair with a rose-scented shampoo, his long fingers massaging her scalp till it tingled. After she was rinsed and wrapped in his navy terry robe, he offered her a tall glass of ice water with a slice of lime.

"You need to drink a lot of water. To flush out the toxins. Bobby has sent me a list of instructions and a hoard of vitamin pills for you to take." He didn't tell her he'd found the painkillers in her makeup bag. He would discuss that with her later, when she was stronger.

"You're spoiling me. I should be helping you."

"No, *querida*. Relax. Let me take care of you. Now you should rest. Drink your water. I'll make your lunch."

So it continued for another two days. She totally let go, letting him take care of her. She slept here as she'd never slept anywhere else. During the day he checked on her frequently, and when he was busy at the nursery or a site visit, Bobby stopped by to visit and chat. In the evenings, Michael cooked her meals and read Robert Frost to her while holding her in his arms. On the fifth day, she at last felt refreshed, well enough to go outdoors. Perhaps even well enough to feel a little bored.

It was then that she received an invitation to Sunday dinner from Michael's parents. It was a family tradition, Michael informed her. Every Sunday the family gathered at his parents' house for a meal.

"Quaint," she replied, sipping her echinacea tea and

raising her brow in query. "Have you brought many girls to this dinner?"

"No," he replied openly. "In fact, never. I've brought girls…women…to the house for a drink, or to say hello. But I've always preferred to keep my family and friends separate. They were—" he shrugged and looked at his palms "—from different worlds."

Charlotte hadn't expected this reply. She'd expected that he'd had loads of girlfriends to the house, what with his handsome looks. This made her own visit loom more ominously.

"Perhaps I should wait. Till I feel better," she hedged.

"If you wish. But—" he smiled at her, breaking her heart. "I'm anxious that you meet my family." He paused and she sensed his burgeoning impatience and excitement. "Charlotte, we've wasted so much time already. I'm thirty. I don't want to pretend any longer that we aren't engaged. I'm too old for these games and it doesn't suit my nature. I know what I want and I want it now. I've been patient for your sake. For the sake of your career. Now I say to hell…" He corrected himself. "Your career will survive. I'm not sure I will if we keep this up. My ring is on your finger. I want you to keep it there. I want to introduce you to my mother and my father. To announce our engagement." He paused and brought her ringed hand to his mouth, kissing it. "I want to tell the world that you're *mine*."

"Well, when you put it like that…" she replied, smiling warmly. "How about we just start with your parents?"

He smiled broadly, drawing her close.

"Do they know I'm living here?"

"Of course."

She frowned, thinking how her own mother would condemn a young woman for living with a man before marriage. At least they were engaged, she thought. "What does a gringa like me give her future mother-in-law for a gift?''

"A grandchild," he replied, then kissed her soundly.

When Sunday came, Charlotte dressed with great care. On the bed lay a tilting pile of rejects. She had discarded any dress with a plunging neckline or that was too short or clung too tightly. Bright colors might attract too much attention, strong cuts and lines of design might appear out of place in the rural setting. She stood before the bed in her slip, wringing her hands with worry, when she had a sudden memory of her cramped closet in Chicago, when she had only one good dress that had to "make do." That girl seemed so far away.

Michael stepped behind her and wrapped his arms around her, nibbling her neck. "I don't see why you're getting so worked up about this. It's just my family."

"Oh, you're no help," she replied, leaning back into his arms. "You just casually shower off the day's dirt, then swagger over to your closet and pull out your uniform."

"I like white shirts."

"How easy it is to be a man. As long as you're clean and cut your toenails, we women count ourselves blessed." She looked behind at his customary white cotton shirt and black trousers. "Ah, you're all dressed up. I see you've switched from Dockers to Armani."

"Well, it *is* a special occasion," he replied with a wry smile.

She settled at last upon a simple Chanel dress she'd worn to one of her promotional appearances. Her last costume designer had declared that one could always count on Chanel to set the right tone. Estelle had won two Oscars for her costumes so Charlotte decided she'd go with her advice. Michael warned her that his family was simple and not to dress too formally. But she was too intent on making a favorable impression to believe him. Meeting the in-laws required an Oscar-winning entrance. She placed around her neck a single strand of pearls, moderate in size so as not to be showy, and on her ears, modest mabe pearls encased in a ring of diamonds. The only jewelry on her hands was the diamond ring, which was as it should be, she thought.

The moment she walked up the steps and into the brightly painted Mondragon farmhouse she knew that she'd overdressed. Two men were sitting at a table by the window playing cards. They were wearing chinos and pale blue shirts, open necked, and heavy brown laced shoes. Two children in shorts and cotton T-shirts were stretched out on the floor playing Monopoly, their shoulders hunched over the board, intent on their game. There was only one woman in the room, a large boned, tall and assertive type shouting orders to one of the men at the table. Presumably the younger one was her husband. She was dressed in a long, casual, flowing red skirt of crushed cotton and a scoop-neck yellow cotton shirt that revealed many dark freckles on her fair skin. Her light brown hair was worn long and loose. The only jewelry she wore were large hoop earrings and a thick gold wedding band on her large hand.

Charlotte curled her nylon-covered toes in her Ferragamo pumps, wishing they were sandals. She was about to slip off the pearls and mabe earrings and stuff them into her purse when Bobby looked up and smiled.

"They're here!" he called out, leaping to his feet. He hurried toward them with his hands out to Charlotte. "At last. The troops were getting restless," he said, indicating with a nod of his head the children staring up at them from the floor with large round eyes the same color as Michael's. "I told them that an actress always likes to make a big entrance."

Charlotte blushed and smiled graciously, taking his hands. She looked beseechingly at Michael as Bobby drew her into the center of the room. She felt the old surge of anxiety reach up to choke her. Michael appeared at ease in the circle of his family, even amused by Bobby's show-manship. There would be no help from him, she thought, feeling that circle tighten around her in curiosity. She could tell he was eager to make the announcement.

The two men at the table folded their cards and stood as Bobby brought her near.

"Papa, Manuel, this is Charlotte Godfrey. *The* Charlotte Godfrey."

Luis, who was eye level with Charlotte, took her hand and smiled perfunctorily—a smile that did not reach his eyes. He studied her in the same manner that Freddy had when they'd first met. Charlotte looked at the man with the hair color and the demeanor of iron and knew that he was, in effect, making no apologies for so openly taking her measure.

"So, you are the famous actress?" the old man said in a loud, heavily accented voice. He said the word *actress* in the same tone he might have said "leper."

"I'm an actress, anyway," Charlotte replied, maintaining eye contact.

The other man was a younger, porky man with his shirt half open and his sleeves rolled up over sun weathered skin. He was shorter than Charlotte by a good four inches and seemingly overwhelmed, either by her fame or her beauty. He mumbled his greetings.

"I'm Maria Elena," the little girl announced with complete assurance, stepping closer.

Charlotte turned toward her, beaming with open gratitude for the child's warmth. How much easier to talk to children!

"Maria Elena, what a beautiful name. It rolls off my tongue like a song."

She seemed pleased. "I'm Tío Miguel's niece." She spoke crisply and with the unique poise of a precocious child who enjoys being on stage. "I want to be an actress, too, when I grow up. Or a dancer. Oh, and that's Francisco. We call him Cisco."

Charlotte's gaze moved to the boy still kneeling by the Monopoly board. She guessed he was about ten and the girl not much younger. He hovered near puberty and bore all the signs of awkwardness she remembered so well.

"Hello, Cisco."

"Hi." He looked down at the game.

Charlotte tried her best not to reveal how nervous she was. She wanted so much for Michael's family to accept and like her. It wasn't until she met Michael's sister, Rosa, however, that she realized it was going to be an uphill battle.

Rosa nodded brusquely when she was introduced, as close to a brush-off as she could deliver in a family setting. When she thought that Charlotte wasn't looking, she stared at her dress and her jewelry with undisguised envy, sucking in her stomach and fiddling with her hoop earring. Charlotte sighed, accustomed as she was to women's resentment.

When she met Michael's mother, however, she felt the first stirrings of hope.

Marta, as she asked to be called when Charlotte addressed her politely as Mrs. Mondragon, came from the kitchen carrying a tray of warm tortillas and salsa. There wasn't a trace of hostility in the petite woman as she approached, wiping her hands on her crisp white apron. A mother's warmth emanated from her smile and her outstretched hand; there was no pretense or veiled glances. When Charlotte accepted her hand, she noticed how small it was, and how well worn. These hands were no stranger to hard work. The hands instantly reminded Charlotte of her own mother and her heart melted.

For Marta was very much like Helena. Not in size. Unlike Helena, she was small and slight and wore modest, somber-colored dresses with buttons that reached high up the neck and hems that fell well below the knees. Her brown hair, streaked handsomely with gray, was worn in a classic bun, her skin was smooth and well lined with character, and her dark brown eyes sparkled with a quiet intelligence. Marta had the air of servitude about her, though not in the negative sense of a servant. Rather, it was more an air of someone who understood the true meaning of civility. That quiet politeness and thoughtfulness that prompted one to pour wine into an empty glass, to offer a seat to someone standing, to be kind to a stranger. Someone who knew that at the root of courtesy was a simple consideration for another's comfort.

The difference between Helena and Marta, however, was that Helena's air of servitude was often a posture of subservience. Helena was a fear biter who might lash out when cornered.

Marta, on the other hand, flanked by her strong, bullish husband, whom she obviously adored, her two handsome sons, a daughter and grandchildren, was secure. She could afford to share the warmth of her love as there was plenty to go around.

"I have an announcement to make," Michael said as the family clustered around them. "I've never brought a woman home for you to meet before. There has never been a woman in my life before who mattered enough to me to dare endure your scrutiny."

There was a smattering of polite laughter. Everyone was tense, sensing where this unusual jocularity was headed. Charlotte looked at her shoes, feeling the intense prickle of a brilliant blush on her cheeks.

"I've asked Charlotte to be my wife. And it's my great honor to announce that she's agreed."

There was a moment of silence broken by Bobby's whistle of joy. "At last! You've gone public. It's about time. Charlotte, I was beginning to think I'd never see that ring on your finger." He winked, and she knew instantly that Michael had pressed him into service as chief confidant about her wearing the ring around her neck. "He's not worthy of you, but since you're fool enough to marry into this family, come let your brother give you a proper Mexican embrace."

He hugged her warmly, patting her back and rocking her back and forth. Charlotte felt as high as a kite when Bobby spoke like that, including her in the family. The children danced on tiptoe, waiting to be hugged, first Maria Elena, then Cisco. Over their heads, Charlotte caught the raised brows and the surprised glance shared by Luis and Marta.

Luis stepped forward, clasped her hand between his two enormous callused ones and kissed her soundly on the cheek. "Welcome to the family," he said. He'd said the right words, but there was little enthusiasm in his voice.

Charlotte forced her wide smile and replied, "Thank you."

Marta leaned toward her son and whispered something to Michael in Spanish, low and furtive, and he replied in like. Charlotte wondered wildly if his mother was inquiring if she was pregnant or some such. Then Marta advanced in a hesitant shuffle, reaching up to kiss Charlotte on the cheek and repeating Luis's congratulations in a soft voice. Her large, dark eyes were round with worry despite the smile. Manuel stepped up, scrunching up his dry lips and kissing her briefly on the mouth. Rosa puffed up her cheeks and left the room without a word.

Charlotte bore the reserved reception with a grace that belied her hurt, because she wanted so much to be a part of Michael's family. It was only natural that they'd be hesitant about the first woman Michael had brought home.

The awkward tension was broken by the timely arrival of dinner, and it was with relief that Charlotte found herself seated at the table beside Michael and Bobby. His brother was one of those people who couldn't sit comfortably in a silence. She'd come across many like him in Hollywood. Bobby worked hard telling amusing stories about the family she was about to join, making everyone laugh. Michael frequently leaned over to pat her thigh or turn his head and wink with encouragement.

As the honored guest, it was she to whom all the stories

and questions were directed. She replied in answers she thought were not only polite but politic.

"When will you be married?" Luis asked in that gruff manner of his.

"I'm not sure. We have to talk about—"

"Soon," Michael interjected firmly.

Charlotte closed her mouth tightly, eyeing him across the space.

"Will you be married in the church?" This from Marta.

Michael shrugged. "I don't care where—"

"Certainly." This time it was Charlotte who interrupted. She met Marta's gaze and sensed from the gleam in his mother's eye that Marta approved.

"You're Catholic then?" asked Luis.

"I am. The Polish are staunch Catholics."

"That's good. At least she is Catholic." He nodded at Marta as if to say, "Maybe there is something we can salvage here."

Marta nodded in agreement.

Charlotte raised her brows.

Michael rolled his eyes.

Charlotte brought her hand to her head, rubbing gently on her temples. She looked up to see Michael staring at her hands with an expression of worry. Looking at them, she saw a tremor in her fingers. Quickly, she tucked her hands in her lap.

"So you are staying in the cabin?" Marta asked cagily. "Maybe you will be more comfortable living in this house? With us? We have a spare room. Of course he is your *novio,* but…" It was understood that Marta would be more comfortable with that arrangement. "I think Michael and Bobby can stay in the cabin, no?"

"No," Michael replied firmly. "She's quite comfortable where she is, Mama." Michael glanced briefly at Charlotte, who was stirring the food on her plate.

"Rosa stayed at home in her parents' house until the day

we delivered her to Manuel,'' Luis said, as though making a proclamation. ''At the steps of the church!'' He looked at Rosa approvingly, his eyes stroking her virtue as though it were a family jewel.

Rosa smiled then and raised a challenging glance at her.

Charlotte swallowed thickly, unable to defend herself. How could she blurt out that she'd been a very good girl, the best. That Michael was not only her first and only lover—but her first boyfriend! She glanced quickly at Michael. He appeared unconcerned about his parents' opinion. When he looked at her, his eyes brightened, as if to tell her not to worry. *He* knew.

''How did you get to be an actress?'' Maria Elena wanted to know. ''I want to be an actress, too, when I grow up.''

''Shhh, she doesn't want to talk about that,'' Rosa replied sharply. ''Can't you see she's tired?''

''I don't mind,'' Charlotte replied, smiling warmly at the child, grateful that she'd changed the subject. Her mind felt as though she were thinking through a fog, but she didn't want to disappoint the little girl who looked up at her with awe shining in her eyes. Too often in this business, once someone reached a certain pinnacle of success, he or she would ignore the questions of people they considered unimportant. She always thought it revealed lack of character.

''It all happened very fast,'' she explained. ''I wanted to be an actress when I was a little girl, too. Just like you. When I grew up, I came to California and was very, very lucky. And I worked very, very hard. I think that's the secret, Maria Elena. To want something enough, then to work hard enough. I hope you're lucky, too.''

''I don't want my daughter to be an actress,'' Rosa said. ''I have better things in mind for her.''

Bobby shot her a quick glance, his water glass stilled at his lips.

"Neither did my mother." Charlotte smiled sweetly. "But here I am."

"Where is your mother?" Luis asked. He spoke in an imperious manner, more demanding that questioning.

"She lives in Chicago."

"Ah, Chicago, huh? And your father? What does he do?"

"He passed away when I was a child. I never knew him."

A sigh of regret came from Maria Elena.

"I hope to meet your mother," Marta said quietly. "Will the wedding be here or in Chicago?"

"Here, definitely," Charlotte replied. "My mother—" She looked at her hands. "She probably won't come to the wedding."

Michael swung his head around to stare at her, surprise evident on his face.

"Not come? Not come to her daughter's wedding?" Luis boomed. Clearly, such a thing was incomprehensible to the family man.

Charlotte blushed and stammered, unwilling to begin another round of lies. Not with her soon-to-be family.

"My mother is angry at me for coming to California," she explained. "She doesn't approve."

"She doesn't approve of my Miguel?" Luis was thunderous.

"Oh, no," Charlotte hurried to correct him. She realized that he naturally assumed that since they'd both lived in Chicago, they'd met there. Well, they had...but Charlotte wasn't ready to explain that much at the moment.

"My mother's never met Michael." That was true enough. "I'm sure she would like him."

Luis nodded, appeased.

"She didn't approve of my becoming an actress." She cast a quick glance and smiled at Rosa, who was listening intently. "She thought it was wrong of me to travel to

California alone. She's not forgiven me. She refuses all contact with me.''

"*Virgencita,*" Marta exclaimed, her hands at her cheek and shaking her head. It was clear she would never abandon her own child, though she was too polite to say this at the table.

Oddly enough, this minor tragedy seemed to break the ice with the Mondragon family. Charlotte felt a bit like a lost puppy picked up by a kind family.

She managed to get through the rest of the meal well enough. There were, after all, plenty of props. There was a plate overflowing with food to push around, water to drink and the stem of her wineglass to fiddle with. It was after dinner, however, that she began to feel the strain. The family rose, chairs scraping, and settled into familiar after-dinner patterns. Charlotte watched as Luis ordered Manuel back to the table for a game of dominoes, and he quickly trotted to comply. Michael and Bobby fell in with them to Luis's hearty welcome. The children returned to their game of Monopoly while their mother, Rosa, sat on the sofa and made a show of reading a magazine, her back to the dining room.

"Rosa, go to the kitchen and help your mother," Luis gruffly commanded.

"Why should I? Just because I am a woman? I don't want to do it. You've got two strapping sons sitting around. And Cisco." She turned to her young son. "Do you think that just because you're a boy you don't have to do dishes?"

Cisco's jaw stuck out defiantly. "I don't have to. You can't make me."

"What did you say?" Rosa was inflamed, rising from the sofa.

Cisco visibly shrank inward but held his ground.

"He is right," Luis boomed. "This is not our way. Go on, Rosa. Set an example for your daughter."

"I *am* setting an example for my daughter."

She saw Bobby and Michael exchange glances. Interesting, Charlotte thought.

"Don't talk like that to your father," Manuel muttered, his dark skin coloring. He darted a warning glance at Rosa.

Rosa seemed unconcerned with Manuel's warnings. "It's nothing he hasn't heard before."

"Enough," Luis barked. The children flinched. "You shame your family with this behavior," he replied. Charlotte noticed that he glanced impatiently in her direction. Rosa, as stubborn as her father, attempted a careless shrug, but her eyes flashed in a dare and her jaw was set. She straightened her shoulders and continued flipping through the magazine.

"Why don't you ask our guest to do the dishes? She's a woman, too." She turned her head and gave Charlotte a cool once-over. "Or are her movie star hands too delicate for kitchen work?"

"Rosa," Michael exclaimed sharply. "Have you no manners at all? Charlotte is our guest. Man or woman, she doesn't have to lift a finger."

"Michael," Charlotte interrupted. Everyone appeared poised at the edge of their seats, waiting to see what move she would make. She sympathized with Rosa's feelings of injustice. This wasn't her fight, however. Charlotte had played so many roles in her life. She thought that this time she'd like to do what *felt* right. And what felt right to her was helping Marta clean up the mountain of dishes on the table. It seemed wrong to her that everyone else should sit and relax and leave all the work to the one person who had slaved at the stove to prepare the feast. Helping seemed the only decent thing to do, for a man or a woman.

"I'd like to help," she replied. "May I?" she asked Marta, walking to the table and picking up a large platter of food.

Marta looked up and rewarded Charlotte with a warm

smile without a trace of reserve in it. "*Sí*, if you wish," she replied.

Emboldened by her approval, Charlotte struck up a conversation with Marta as they carted stacked dishes to and from the kitchen and dining room. Marta replied openly in her broken English, making Charlotte feel enormously flattered. She sensed a real current going on between her and Michael's mother. They might only have been discussing the various kinds of Mexican peppers, a subject on which Marta was an authority, but it seemed to Charlotte that as they spoke, the words acted as the needle and thread that tied them together.

As she worked, Charlotte caught Rosa's hostile glare from the sofa. She obviously felt betrayed by Charlotte's action, for indeed, it worsened Rosa's position considerably. Beyond her, Luis watched her with a small smile of satisfaction carving his tanned cheeks.

To her great pride, however, Michael stood up and walked to the table. He picked up a handful of plates and carried them into the kitchen, commenting on how he still couldn't recognize one green pepper from another when he went to the grocery store.

She thought he'd never spoken sweeter words of love.

That night, while lying in his arms in the cabin, Michael asked her about her mother.

"What's all that about your mother?" he asked. "You never told me she didn't approve of your coming here."

"No, I didn't." She was being evasive. The walls seemed to be closing in on her.

"Or that your mother isn't talking to you."

"I was embarrassed."

"To tell me? I thought we told each other everything. It's one of the things I love most about our relationship. Our complete honesty."

She swallowed hard, his words cutting deep. "Some-

times the truth is very hard. It hurts. Does it matter?" She
turned to face him, lifting herself up on her elbows.

"Does what matter, *querida?* That you tell me everything? Of course. I don't want there to be any secrets between us."

"What if...well, aren't there some things in our pasts
that we don't need to share? I don't want to know about
every girlfriend of yours. You wouldn't want me to know
that detail about your past, right?"

He considered for a moment, then shook his head.
"There is a difference between uncovering, gradually, bits
of our pasts together and deliberately keeping secret a vital
truth. I look forward to growing old with you, taking long
walks along the beach and hearing you bring forth a story
of something that happened to you as a child. Some new
bit of information that I'll relish and add to my store of
knowledge. But secrets?"

He thought suddenly of Bobby and his father, how they
could never speak the truth between them. How shallow
their relationship was as a result of the lie.

"Let's make a vow. We will only speak the truth to each
other. No matter how painful. This is very important to
me."

How could she tell him now? He would hate her for sure.
No, he was wrong, she thought to herself. There were some
secrets that should be kept. What possible good could come
of his knowing about her surgery? About the pitiful creature
that was Charlotte Godowski? He loved her for who she
was now. Charlotte Godfrey. The woman she made herself.
No, she decided. There were some secrets that should be
kept.

Seventeen

"No, no, not like that. You're painting like the books tell you to paint, all in straight lines."

Bobby was teaching Charlotte how to paint. He sat in the shade of a ginkgo tree, his long legs crossed at the ankles and his broad forehead shadowed by his ubiquitous floppy panama hat, calling out instructions as she stood, in a wide stance, at the easel a few feet away. At various times, like now, he'd leap dramatically to his feet, moaning with exaggeration.

"Forget the books. Blend! Use your fingers. Don't be afraid. See? Go ahead, try it. A little more. That's right! Wonderful!" He panted with the effort.

Charlotte felt a thrill of discovery as she painted, even though she kept a careful eye on Bobby. He seemed more winded of late, not quite as bright in the eye.

"You don't have any role to play here, Miss Godfrey. Paint freely."

"I'm trying!" Unlike when she acted, she wasn't becoming someone else or losing herself in a role. This was more scary. She was probing herself, discovering and releasing hidden emotions and feelings that she released in bright, vivid colors.

"Bobby, can this be right? It looks so strange."

"What have you drawn? Tell me about it."

She cocked her head and frowned. "I haven't a clue what it is."

"You don't know what all those menacing black lines and evocative swirls are? Darling, I'm sure Freud would have a heyday. But let's not let him steal your thunder. Tell me what you think it is."

She narrowed her eyes, tucking her chin in her palm. "I think that box is my life. Or maybe…me." It was a large, blackened box, very foreboding and with defined borders, surrounded by black swirls like smoke. She looked up, her blue eyes very bright. "And that little white dot in the middle is me, too." She stepped back, laughing nervously. "Can that be right?"

He lifted his shoulders and smiled serenely. His voice was very gentle. "It is if you think it is."

A few weeks after she'd arrived, she came upon Marta in the small garden beside her house. The small, thin woman was bent double, pulling sprouting weeds around a four-foot-high full color statue of the Blessed Virgin Mary. Charlotte knew this model well. The blue cloaked BVM wearing a white wimple and carrying a rosary was a favorite of Catholic grammar schools across the nation. She felt a tug at her heartstrings, recalling how she'd loved to place the flowers she'd plucked from various yards on the way to school at the Virgin's feet.

Charlotte walked beside Marta and bent to tug at a dandelion. She felt much more at ease with Marta since she'd spent many hours with her in the kitchen, learning how to flatten *masa harina* in her hands to make tortillas, how to rinse the pintos and pluck out the bad ones before boiling them, and how to make a smooth mole sauce. She'd even learned the names of the many peppers that Marta cooked with, delighting Michael almost as much as she was delighting Luis. Her interest in the Mexican culture was going a long way in winning over the proud patriarch.

"You're looking better. Rounder. Not so spare," Marta said, looking up from under her wide-brimmed straw hat. Her gloved hand rested on a tough chickweed clump. "You feeling good?"

"A little better," she replied cheerfully.

"Sometimes," Marta went on, huffing a little as she struggled with the roots, "the healing must go on inside the soul as much as the body, no? I think you are still very sad about your mother."

Charlotte didn't reply, but tugged harder at the weeds.

"I was thinking, maybe..." Her hand stilled on the trowel and she raised her dark eyes to meet Charlotte's. "Do you like to come to church with me on Sunday?"

From the brush, a bird flew into the sky.

"Yes, I'd like that very much."

When she talked to Michael about it that night, he frowned, wondering aloud why his mother felt everyone had to go to church to be saved.

"I don't think she's worried about my immortal soul, except perhaps for the sin of us living together. That she's having a tough time with."

"You realize, of course, that the only reason she's putting up with the arrangement is because she wants grandchildren."

"I rather think she's concerned that I raise her grandchildren as Catholics."

"It doesn't matter to me," Michael said gruffly. "I don't want any of that breast-beating and finger-pointing in my household. I spent a lifetime lifting that guilt off my shoulders. I won't have my children shoulder it."

"I understand, but I do want our children raised in the faith. I can't imagine not... The sacraments, the tradition. The fabulous hats..." She laughed when he smiled. "Religion binds a family together.'' She paused. ''Michael, you do want our children raised as Catholics, don't you?''

He looked up at her, his dark eyes somber. ''You realize we're talking about our children.''

She looked off, imagining a chubby baby with Michael's dark hair and golden skin. The notion of being a mother suddenly became very real. ''I suppose we are,'' she replied, amazed.

Charlotte attended mass at Our Lady of Lourdes with Marta and Luis on Sunday. Marta wore a long black mantilla in the old tradition and looped a long black rosary with a wooden cross around her thin fingers as she prayed. Luis paged through his missal with his well-worn, tanned hands, his mouth moving over the words.

The smell of incense, the brilliant, meshed colors of the stained glass windows, the familiar statues of the Virgin and St. Joseph on either side of the altar, and of course, the large marble crucifix of Jesus hanging above it, stirred her as nothing had in a long while. She felt as though she'd returned home again after a long, arduous journey. She knew the proper responses to the priest's invocations, knew when to kneel and when to stand, knew the words of all the mass's litanies: the Apostles' Creed, the Our Father, the Hosanna. When she prayed the communion response, ''Lord, I am not worthy to receive you, but only say the word and I shall be healed,'' her face was wet with tears.

Marta looked at her with naked sympathy and compassion in her eyes, then reached over and patted her hand.

That night, as the crickets sang outside her window, Michael read Yeats on the creamy leather sofa they had purchased together from Gumps while Charlotte sat at the kitchen table. On the shiny oak surface she laid out a sheet of her best Tiffany stationery, an enamel Waterman fountain pen and a cup of chamomile tea. She sat with her hands still on the table, listening to Mozart's *Eine kleine Nacht-muzik,* trying to get in the mood, to find the right sentiment in her heart to be able to write this letter.

"You realize you've been sitting there for almost an hour, not moving a muscle," Michael said from across the room.

She startled, looking up and blinking heavily, as though waking from a deep sleep.

"Where are your thoughts?" His smile was beguiling.

"I'm just thinking," she replied, looking at his face. In the soft light, the many hues of his dark hair streaked like gold. "Of my mother."

He set down his book then, giving her his full attention. That gesture implied she was his top priority and meant a great deal to her.

"I was thinking of what words I could say in a letter that would cross the miles between us and find some way to bridge that gap. Being in a Catholic church again brought to mind happier memories with my mother. We spent hours every Saturday cleaning the church together. We'd polish the heavy brass candlesticks on the altar, dust pews, air out the priest's vestments, arrange flowers for the vestibule."

"Did you enjoy doing it?"

"I enjoyed the attention from Mom. I remember her teaching me how to scrub far into the corners. She has these large-boned hands, curved and worn from years of hard work. I was fascinated by them, and by her long fingers, puckered from use. It was very important to her that I not leave a mote of dust in God's house." She sighed and twiddled with the fountain pen. "It seems to me we spent so much time cleaning dirt out from the church that we didn't leave time enough to see to the mess in our own lives."

"Why don't you write that? Tell her now."

She startled in alarm. "What?"

"You've just told me what you really want to tell her.

If you want to start cleaning out the mess, roll up your sleeves and begin now.''

"She'd think I was blaming her.''

"Are you?''

She paused, examining her feelings. "No,'' she replied honestly. "Not anymore. I just want to be close again. Our happiness has changed me. Talking of our future, our children.'' She paused. "I miss my mother.''

"You might try telling her that, too.''

A week later, Michael and Luis rounded the corner of the cabin, hands gesturing in the air, engaged in a hot conversation. When they reached the front door they stopped short. Inside the house they saw Charlotte seated at the kitchen table, earphones on her head, books splayed out on the table before her. Her eyes were closed as she listened intently, then she responded to the tape, reciting Spanish aloud with a remarkably good accent.

Michael was both surprised and touched that she would make this effort for him, for his family. It had to be mostly for their benefit, since he demanded that the family speak English around her.

The two men just stared at her with a look of puzzlement mixed with awe on their faces. Anyone looking at them would have thought they were studying a piece of art. Finally Luis reached up to an itch behind his ear, giving the spot a thorough scratching.

"I admit she is not what I thought you'd bring home. A movie star. Humph.'' He rocked on his heels and rubbed the bristle on his cheek. "And she is so scrawny a bird, so rangy. Not much meat on the bones. But she has a big heart. And she makes a good mole sauce.'' He stopped to place his large, meaty hand on Michael's shoulder. "She maybe will make a good wife.''

Maria Elena and Charlotte were in Marta's big, homey kitchen preparing for Maria Elena's saint's day dinner. The yellow, blue and green tile border gleamed in the morning sun that was pouring in from the glazed windows. Marta had laid out on the long, heavy wood table bowls of warm, wrapped dough for rolls, and on the stove, several saucepans were simmering with the sauces they'd made earlier that morning. The air was redolent with the scents of sweet dough, spicy sausages, and cornmeal.

Marta was patting out the tortilla dough while Charlotte and Maria Elena cooked the fresh tortillas on the grill.

"Take it off when you see the first bubble," Marta reminded her.

"Sí, yo sé!" Charlotte called back, smiling at Maria Elena.

Marta grunted softly in appreciation. "Luis, he say you do good work at the nursery with Miguel. He is happy to see you in the family business. It is good for a woman to know the family business. To keep the accounts, no? A man might rule at the dinner table, but the woman—" She flipped the dough and pounded it with efficient strokes. "The mama rules the home. This she must do for her children. A man might gamble away the money, or drink."

"I doubt that Michael would gamble away his money. He works too hard at earning it."

"Miguel? No, but some, *sí,* it happens." Her small hands kneaded the dough while she glanced discreetly at Maria Elena. Charlotte had heard about Manuel's increasing drinking, and she nodded, remaining silent.

"In my heart, Mexico is my home," Marta continued. "It is the country of my family. My parents, my sisters and my brother. My culture, eh? But my children's home is here in America, so in my mind, it must be my home, too. Luis, he does not feel this way but—" she shrugged and caught Charlotte's eye, her own eyes twinkling "—the parents must suffer and endure so that the children can do better. It is the way it must be. I wanted my children to go to the

schools taught by the nuns. On this I was firm. I didn't
want my children to drop out of school or end up in jail
like so many other children that I knew in the old neigh-
borhood. Like—'' She fumbled with a word at the tip of
her tongue. ''What is the English word for when they have
numbers for an opinion?''

''Statistics?''

''*Sí,*'' she nodded, resuming her pounding. ''Statistics.
They were bad for Mexican children in Los Angeles. So
many drop out of school. Gangs. Not good for the children.
So we moved to the suburbs and Luis he worked like a
mule en el labor for very little money while I hired out as
a seamstress close to home. The nuns, they gave our children money for school...scholarships, eh? My children,
they were smart. *Sí.* Very smart. My Miguel, he went to a
college in Boston!''

''Yes, I know,'' Charlotte replied, thinking to herself that
Harvard was hardly just some college in Boston.

''I wonder now if maybe I made a mistake. That maybe
Luis was right. Miguel, growing up he had his heart torn
in two. For a long time he did not want anything Mexican.
Not the language, the music, the food. Not even his family.
He was very bitter about any prejudice against him, and
maybe when he rejected his culture...'' She shrugged. ''He
was prejudiced, too. He ran far from his family. Humph.
He was only running home again.''

''Did Tío Miguel run away from home?'' Maria Elena
asked.

The women laughed lightly, easing the tension. ''No, my
heart. No, but...'' She tilted her head and acknowledged
her granddaughter. ''In many ways it felt to me, his mama,
that he did. Yet I said nothing to him. It is better that your
children come home because of *respeto,* no? And love,
rather than duty. *Sí,* he came to California for duty, but he
is staying because of love.''

Charlotte watched Marta's gaze travel from the sweet

face of Maria Elena, as smooth and round as the ball of dough, to her own face.

"Now he is in the business, he speaks *español,* and sometimes with you he goes to church. I see his heart becoming whole again. It makes my own heart happy." Her eyes shimmered in water as she beamed up at Charlotte. "I think much of this is because of you. You are good for my son. For the family."

Charlotte pressed her lips tightly.

"Charlotte, a bubble!" alerted Maria Elena.

Charlotte turned quickly, sniffing, to flip a row of tortillas with expert precision while Marta watched approvingly.

"*Sí!*" Marta said, slapping another bowl of dough down on the floured table with gusto. "It is good for the woman to keep the accounts. Maybe you try, eh?"

Summer was coming to an end. Now she worked side by side with Michael in the nursery. Every day there were small tributes to the strong, binding relationship they were developing. A glance across the field as she tagged the young trees, a gentle kiss or pat on the rear when he passed her. The unspoken acceptance of them by the family and their co-workers delighted her, bringing smiles to her face and a lightness to her step. The past few months living with Michael and his family had been the happiest in her life.

Charlotte wasn't sure when or how she started becoming involved with the business. It was subtle at first. She helped out in the store, working the cash register, stocking the shelves. Her knowledge of gardening, the names of plants, both the Latin and the derivatives, paid off, and once again she thanked God for her excellent memory. When Luis, who liked to try and trip her up on occasion just for sport, begrudgingly accepted her as a member of the Mondragon team, the rest fell in line. Even Paco, the small, wizened foreman who'd been part of the team for as long as Michael could remember, tipped his hat when she passed him.

One evening, when she and Michael were too tired for passion and it was enough just to sit together on the porch, she asked to be allowed to do his books for him. "To keep the accounts," she told him. When he raised his brows, she bristled.

"I used to be a certified accountant, thank you very much," she said archly. In this area she felt confident that she was his equal. No, she decided, lifting her chin in a challenge. Even superior.

"You see? This is just what I was talking about," he replied with a smile of astonishment. "This is one of those interesting details about you that I never knew before. A pretty big detail, now that I think of it. You? An accountant?"

"I can add and subtract pretty good—for a girl," she replied with a wry smile. "Don't break down all my illusions and tell me you're like Luis and believe all a woman is good for is cookin' an' cleanin' and birthin'?" Her eyes were flashing.

"No, not that I find fault with that," he replied. "Okay, I concede." He laughed, palms up in defense against her jabs. "The books are yours. I bow to your professionalism. Gratefully."

"You'd be surprised just how much your mother does in this department, too."

"Nothing my mother does would surprise me. And since you're so keen to do the paperwork, you can do our taxes, too. We'll be filing joint returns very shortly, don't forget."

So Charlotte became involved in the financial details of the Mondragon businesses as well. She learned how his father had inherited the land from an uncle and clung to it tenaciously while others in the valley had sold off. The one hundred acres were extremely valuable now. If they sold off now, they'd all be rich beyond their dreams. She also learned how Luis had slaved in the squared-off yards of the California suburbs building up his lawn maintenance business. Rosa and Manuel managed it now, efficiently as far as she could tell, if not imaginatively.

Doing the books, she also knew exactly how much the growth of the lawn maintenance business was due to the flair and hard work of Michael Mondragon. He was more like his father than she dared suggest to him. He wooed new clients with gentle persuasion, knowing what and how to suggest, unlike Manuel, who waited for business to come to him and spent far more than his budget allowed. Already, Michael was talking about bringing young Cisco along next summer to learn new skills in the business.

When Michael talked about the spring that bubbled beneath their nursery land, his eyes became dreamy. "Fresh mountain springwater," he told her, with the emotion of a visionary. "An unlimited supply, just waiting to be tapped. That," he'd told her, drawing her near, "is where our futures lay."

She loved it when he talked about "their" future. It was as though he were paving the road ahead with gold.

On an unusually cool late August evening, as they sat rocking on the front porch of the cabin, listening to the cicadas singing their farewell songs, he explained to her about his father's desire for him to remain on the land, to inherit everything, to produce Mondragon heirs.

"To be honest, I never thought it possible that I'd want to stay. This was always someplace I couldn't wait to escape from. I hated it. The hard work, the coarse language of the men, the sharp orders from my father. But now—" he shook his head and looked at her, more perplexed than she "—it's changed. I'm building something here. The business, sure. But it's you that's made the difference," he explained, taking her hand and looking at her as she'd always dreamed a man would look at her someday. Not her face, not her body, but *her*. "You've made all the difference."

Charlotte felt the thrill of belonging to someone, to

something bigger than herself. She imagined having a life here, on this mountain, with Michael. Having his children here, Mondragon babies on Mondragon land.

She'd cuddled on his lap and wept, not able to explain what this meant to her. Here, she had a real family at last. She was part of a bigger circle, holding hands with others. Sharing, being included. It was like being a little child again, and finally, someone was asking her to play.

Later that same night, he brought up the subject that had been troubling him all day. She'd had another telephone call with Freddy Walen, and it, like all his other calls, left her nervous and agitated. He watched as she stood before the bathroom mirror, brushing her long blond hair with brisk strokes.

He never tired of looking at her. She had a vulnerability, a poignancy about her that made him feel like a caveman bearing a stick, ready to fight the enemy on her behalf. He'd never felt this for anyone else before. And to his mind, Freddy Walen was the T-rex of adversaries. He wanted that man out of her life.

"What did Walen want?" he asked as they climbed into bed.

Charlotte tucked the comforter under her chin and wriggled over beside him, rubbing her feet together in the cool, crisp sheets. Freddy was getting increasingly difficult to stave off. She'd told him that she went to visit her mother after her stay at the spa. That she needed time alone to settle family affairs and tend to her health. Freddy was antsy at first, but tolerant. Now he was chomping at the bit. She'd have to make a decision soon.

"He has a couple of projects he wants to discuss with me. In person." She sighed, bringing a knuckle up to her mouth. After a while she added softly, "I can't put him off forever."

Michael let out an exasperated sigh. "Why not give up the career?"

His answer was from the gut. She knew that Michael wanted her to give up her acting career and dedicate her life to him and his family.

"Which one?" she asked, striving for levity. "My career as an actress or as an accountant?"

"I should think an accountant's job would suit our life here very well," he said, pulling her up on his shoulder. "You could keep on as you are, running the books, expanding the operation. Yes, I can see it now," he added, stroking her arm. "Your first job would be to look after me, of course. I'd demand my share of time alone with you. But I suppose I could share you with the eight or ten little bebés we'd have."

Her laughter pealed through the air and she slapped his shoulder with feigned scorn. "We'll just see about that, Mr. Michael Mondragon."

"We'd have to add a few rooms on to the cabin, no doubt. Ten years hence we'll be lying here in our bed, on our well worn mattress, while the children crawl over us like puppies." He looked over at her, smiling innocently.

She wagged a finger at him, entertained by the fantasy. He was, despite all of his protestations, exceedingly traditional.

"I want children. Yours and mine," he said. "Now?"

She lifted her eyes to his and saw the sincerity. Such charm he had, she thought, stroking his chin. His dark eyes bright, his expression so fervent. Their life here together was charmed, like a fairy tale come to life. She couldn't bring the reality of children into this world until other decisions had been made.

"I'm not ready to simply chuck it all. And Freddy is beside himself, furious that I won't return immediately. He accepts that I'm taking a leave of absence to get my health back and settle my affairs, but he expects me back well before *Camille* opens for the holidays. So much is happening now.''

The mention of the name Freddy Walen was like waving a red flag in front of a bull. He colored and sat straighter. ''You're right. So much is happening. And I'm not talking about your film career.''

''I know,'' she replied, smoothing a long strand of black hair from his troubled face. ''I don't know what I'll do about my career any more than you know what you'll do with yours,'' she said. ''But I like to think you and I will follow the old Buddhist proverb. We'll be like two young trees with strong roots. And rather than stand rigid against the wind and crack, we'll bend.''

Her soothing tone worked. With a low mumble he settled back onto the pillows, drawing her close.

Eighteen

When Bobby came to the cabin for another painting lesson one bright September day, he was horrified to see her ashen face. She was sitting on the front steps, holding her head. The circles under her eyes were like black-and-purple thunderclouds.

"Good God." He stepped back and leaned on the door frame. "You're not pregnant, are you?"

"Spread that rumor around and I'll really be a scandal to your mother."

"Well, are you? Don't keep me in suspense, darling. I adore babies. Other people's babies, that is."

"I'm sorry to disappoint you, but no. I'm definitely not pregnant."

"Pity. Michael's prancing about here like a rooster. Well, whatever is the matter with you? You look like Linda Blair in *The Exorcist*. I expect you'll be twisting your head around in a few more moments, speaking in seven languages."

"I feel like it." She crossed her arms over her belly and moaned. "Oh, Lord, Bobby, I wish it was something I could exorcise."

"Is it something you ate?"

"I wish it were so simple. But you don't want to hear me moan about my aches and pains. Never mind."

He moved closer, extending his hand. "Come on. We shall take a walk, enjoy the sunny day, and then we'll talk."

While they strolled together through the rows of shrubs, he told her how he'd watched his lover grow sicker and then die, and countless other friends as well. He couldn't sit by and watch another human being suffer. He explained with enthusiasm about the protease inhibitors he was currently taking, about finding hope again after so much despair. Finally, as the shadows lengthened in the late afternoon, he brought up the name of his healer.

"His name is Xavier Navarro. He's a doctor, but he practices what he calls complementary medicine. Kind of a blend of therapies like nutrition, homeopathy, clinical medicine and old Mexican home remedies. I don't claim to understand it, but I do know it works. He is very smart, brilliant even. Up-to-date on all the studies. But more than all of that, he's a natural born healer. Do you believe such a thing is possible?"

"I do," she replied, thinking of the miracles she, herself, had experienced. "What have I got to lose? Do you think he could help me?"

"Yes, he could if anyone could." His voice was positive, full of confidence. It was very convincing to Charlotte, who was at this point grasping at straws.

"I won't waste your time trying to explain what he does. I'm not sure I understand it all myself. Why don't I make an appointment for you? As soon as possible. You can go in there, let him examine you, and see for yourself what he says. I really believe he can help you. Darling, I feel eons younger and stronger since I've been on his regime. A regular Hercules."

Charlotte laughed, amused as much by Bobby's dramatic

enthusiasm as by the image of his slight body in the pose of a bodybuilder. "Of course. As soon as possible."

Xavier Navarro's office was in his home, a small creamy building built in the Mediterranean style, nestled in the remote California hills. The office was nondescript but very clean. Outdated magazines lay neatly on a wooden table flanked by a few mismatched chairs. Near the glistening windows, several thriving plants flowered in the sunlight. This, she thought, was a good sign.

They stepped in and removed their jackets. There was no secretary to check in with; this was strictly a homey operation. She wondered again if she should have come. Michael was furious with Bobby for taking her to "that quack." Michael had little faith in anything that had to do with Mexican home remedies.

"Nervous?" Bobby asked.

"A little. I've been to so many doctors lately, and frankly I don't want to be poked and prodded anymore. You don't think he'll do a full examination, do you? After all, how much does he need to know to prescribe a vitamin regime but my height and weight? And my daily activities, exercise, that sort of thing, I suppose. Everyone these days seems to want to know about my stress levels." She glanced at her watch, impatient.

"You want some answers, don't you? Come on, just sit down and relax. Read one of these magazines and find out what happened in sports four months ago." He sat in a red chair and indicated an orange one for her. When she joined him he pulled a paperback novel from his pocket and within minutes was engrossed in the story.

Charlotte crossed her legs, stared out the window and counted the reasons why she should have just stayed home after all.

After a short wait, the door to the inner office opened and a squat, round, dark-skinned woman with Indian features and a flowing, riotously colored outfit strode from Navarro's office. She was beaming. The part in her hair was very straight, severe and almost two inches wide, exposing an alarming amount of bare scalp. Charlotte wondered if the woman was seeing Xavier Navarro about that.

Then a tall Latin man with thoughtful eyes, a dark mustache and a long, benevolent face appeared at the door. He was conservatively dressed in a tan suit and a yellow patterned tie. Everything about him was clean and orderly and his manner was polite, even courtly. She liked him immediately and felt almost a gush of relief.

"Miss Godfrey?" he asked. Her ears picked up no trace of an accent.

She nodded and stood up.

"I hope I haven't kept you waiting?" He smiled warmly, then turned to Bobby. He spoke to him in Spanish and Bobby responded in kind, obviously making some kind of joke because both men laughed.

"Won't you come in, Miss Godfrey? Let's see how I can help you."

"Go on," Bobby prompted, sensing her hesitation.

The physical examination was quick and impersonal. His nurse was friendly and efficient, and Dr. Navarro, although considerate, made no attempt at humor. Rather, he set her at ease by explaining what he was doing and why. His methods were practical, if sometimes a little unusual. The only time she felt nervous was when he studied her head, jaw and neck at length, bending so close she felt the brush of his jacket against her cheek and could smell the soap on his soft hands. She had to will herself to relax, to allow him to examine her there. It required the utmost trust.

When he raised himself back up, he placed his hands around her jaws, cupping them but not quite touching the skin, and closed his eyes. He remained motionless. Then something remarkable happened. She wasn't sure if she was imagining it or not, but beneath his hands she felt heat. A soothing warmth that tingled the skin, and deeper, especially in the jaw joints.

After the nurse completed a few blood tests, he joined her again, pulling up a chair informally to talk to her.

"Have you ever had any plastic surgery, Miss Godfrey?"

Charlotte expelled a quick rush of air. Denial was on the tip of her tongue, but looking into his eyes, so circumspect, she knew it was useless to lie to him.

"Are the scars visible?"

He shook his head. "Oh, no, not at all. I compliment the surgeon. He did wonderful work. No, I *felt* the surgery. Felt the energy change. It was quite clear to me, actually. What was it?" he asked gently. "The jaw?"

"Yes," she replied after hesitating. "And the chin."

"Ah, yes, I thought I felt something there as well. But it's much more pronounced at the jaw. Right about here." He reached out and pointed directly to the small spot on either side of her jaw joint that caused her pain. She jumped slightly at the touch.

"Yes. It hurts there."

He frowned and rubbed his own jaw in consternation. "I'm concerned about your symptoms. The aches and pains, the headaches, the nausea and fatigue. They're all connected, I'm sure of it. I'd like to do a little research. Would you come back? In a week or so? Good. In the meantime, I've worked out a program for you to begin immediately."

He spent a good amount of time advising her in an unhurried manner about her new health regime. Some of the advice was very simple, part common sense, part Mexican home remedies that he claimed had been handed down to him through generations. His family had always been healers, shamans in the old days. It was, he explained to her with a chuckle and a twinkle in his eye, both an inherited gift as well as a curse.

His advice also included what sounded like standard medical practices. He explained that like most things in life, healing was a balance of modern medical knowledge and ancient wisdom. She had a vitamin B1 and B6 deficiency, and a mineral deficiency as well, quite common today, he assured her. He prescribed some antioxidants for stress, some vegetarian sources of digestive enzymes, a little ginkgo biloba and a few other herbs that were given in neat little capsules, easy to take. She'd have to get used to taking a handful of pills, but if it worked, it would be well worth the gagging twice a day.

"We'll get you feeling better right off," he said to her as he saw her off at the door. "In the meantime, I'll go to the medical library and do a little research, get your results. I'll call you when I find something, all right?"

Charlotte realized how wrong she'd been to doubt Dr. Navarro in her early estimation. She left his office feeling more confident with his treatment than she had with anyone else's. In fact, when she watched him glide across the floor, she thought he walked on water.

Two weeks later, Dr. Navarro called and asked to see her again. Right away. It was a blustery day, overcast and rainy, the kind that if it continued, would signal an early fall.

"I'm sure it's just a follow-up," she said to Bobby as they drove together along the narrow, leaf strewn roads to Navarro's office. "I feel so much better on his regime. The symptoms are almost gone. Really, I haven't felt so good in months."

"No need to convince me of anything, darling."

She looked out the window, chewing her lip. It was herself she was trying to convince. Xavier Navarro had sounded so serious. There was a tone in his voice that hinted at bad news.

"I just know everything is fine," she said again, more

firmly. "Everything is so perfect. God won't let anything bad happen now."

Bobby, who knew better, kept his eyes on the road and said nothing.

Dr. Navarro greeted them at the door of his home office. The rain had begun falling in earnest, so they had to stomp their feet and brush the wet from their clothes after they scurried in. Unlike the first visit, there was no one else in the waiting room.

"Let's go into my office where we can talk," Navarro said after initial, polite pleasantries were exchanged.

"I'll wait right here," Bobby said, and he smiled encouragingly.

He couldn't fool her. The lines of his smile were tense over glittering eyes, and after he took a seat in the waiting room, he slouched low, crossed his ankle over his knee and began wagging his wing-tipped shoes and drumming his fingers, too nervous to read.

"I'm feeling so much better," she remarked when Navarro ushered her into the examining room.

"I'm glad," Navarro replied with a sad smile. "No, no, there's no need to change. Today we'll just talk," he said, and pointed to a chair.

Charlotte didn't want to sit in the orange cushioned chair. She didn't want to talk, to hear what Navarro had to say that made his expression so serious. Every instinct told her to run, but she sat in the indicated chair and held her hands tightly clasped. She'd imagined what he might have to say to her. That she had some disease that was causing all these symptoms, something debilitating. Or perhaps something horrible that would make it hard, or impossible, to have babies. My God, she thought, her heart pounding in her chest like a trapped bird. What if it was cancer?

"I've completed my inquiries and I believe I know the

cause of all your problems." He paused to look at his fingertips.

It felt as though the bird in her chest was flapping its wings wildly. She stared at the doctor's fingertips, struggling to hold on to her composure. He said he knew? There would be an answer? Could it be true, after so many dead ends? She stifled her questions and sat straighter in her chair, leaning forward in anticipation.

"I'm afraid the news is unpleasant. Do you remember when you came to see me last we drew blood samples for studies? The results reveal that you are experiencing an unusual reaction. That is to say, an unusual immune response. I believe your body is developing antibodies to the silicone or part of the constituents of your implants that were inserted into your jaw during your reconstructive surgery."

Charlotte heard the words but couldn't give them meaning. "Implants? What...?"

Dr. Navarro picked up a pen and quickly drew a sketch of her jawline. "When Dr. Harmon created your jaw, he inserted small pads here—" He pointed to two spots directly on the jawbone. "And here," he added, pointing to the chin.

Charlotte instantly knew they were the same spots on her jaw that caused her pain.

"The purpose was to project your jaw forward, to create a stronger, more defined line. It is a common procedure, and he completed it expertly."

"Then...why is there a problem?"

Dr. Navarro set down his pen and folded his hands on the table. "It isn't a problem with the surgery. I've consulted with someone I know who is doing research at the medical school. Your body is having a strong reaction to the implants. I'm afraid the implants must come out."

Her heart sank and she slumped in the chair. Oh, God, no, she thought, bringing her hand to her jaw. Did that mean she'd have to go through still another surgery to fix up her face? She never wanted to go through that kind of pain again. Or to smell the inside of a hospital again, or to feel that groggy, nauseating dizziness of the recovery room. And how was she going to get the surgery done without telling Michael?

"I'm sorry to have to tell you this."

"No, not at all," she replied slowly, letting it all sink in. She was having a hard time articulating words beyond a whisper. "Thank you, Dr. Navarro. I'm—I'm grateful you found the cause of all my complaints. Really. I've been led to believe my symptoms were all in my head."

"I admit, at first I was skeptical. Many of the illnesses and abnormalities reported with implants are anecdotal in nature. Nonspecific. In your case, it is clear the symptoms are real."

"But—" she stroked her chin, putting together what she'd heard "—there's one thing I don't understand. If I'm having a rejection of these implants, what will they replace them with? I mean, are there several different kinds of implants?"

Dr. Navarro looked at her with a puzzled expression, then it changed, slowly, as his brows closed together. He drummed his fingertips together.

"I think perhaps you don't understand," he began, shaking his head regretfully. "The implants... They cannot be replaced."

Charlotte blinked, uncomprehendingly. Surely she'd not heard right. "They can't be replaced," she echoed in a hoarse voice.

"No. It is most unfortunate."

Her world was slowing, slowing, grinding to a halt. This wasn't real. She was in shock. Numb. She looked around the room, moving her head with an effort.

"What if I don't do it?"

He drew himself up in his chair and looked her straight in the eye.

"You must understand, Miss Godfrey. High titers of antipolymer antibodies seem to correlate with greater severity of immune disorders."

"How severe?"

"These disorders get progressively worse." He paused. "They can be fatal."

"No. There must be some mistake," she said in a dazed voice.

"I'm sorry." Navarro sighed with sympathy and shifted in his seat. "This reaction isn't true for everyone. It is, in fact, rare. What you must understand is that in *you* it is clearly life threatening." He cleared his throat and leaned forward. "Let me speak plainly. Miss Godfrey, if you don't remove the implants, it is my opinion that you will get very sick. And die."

Suddenly she hated him, despised his kind, calm demeanor, the smooth skin, his full lips that turned down in a sympathetic frown.

"You're sorry? You don't know what you're talking about. You aren't even a plastic surgeon! I'm going to see Dr. Harmon."

"You should. As soon as possible."

"He'll tell me you're wrong. He'll fix it."

"Miss Godfrey," he began, tapping his fingertips together. "I've run several tests. There is no doubt. Dr. Harmon, any doctor aware of the facts, will corroborate what I am saying to you. I know this is difficult to hear and even more difficult to accept. But I don't want you to leave with any misunderstandings."

Panic began to grow in her gut as the possibility that what Navarro was saying might be true. In his white coat, sitting back in his chair, steepling his fingers with authority, he sounded too sure.

"If they are removed..." she began, thinking the impossible. "What happens to my jaw? To my face? What will I look like?"

"I can't really say." He looked uncomfortable and shifted in his seat. "I don't know the extent of your original surgery."

"If the implants are removed, then what will happen to my face?" she repeated with urgency.

"You should really talk to Dr. Harmon about these details."

"What...would...happen...to...my...face?"

"I..." He spread out his fingers and looked at them, and she felt as though her last shred of hope slipped through them. "I imagine your face, your jaw, would be as before the surgery."

She felt as though he'd just dumped a bucket of cold water over her. No, it couldn't be true. Her breath shortened. She felt a cold clutch in her heart, felt the little bird flutter and die, the breath squeezed out of it.

But death would have been too easy. She had to live through this.

Part Four

She dwells with beauty—
Beauty that must die.

—John Keats

Nineteen

~~~❧❧~~~

Bobby drove home from Xavier Navarro's office with none of his usual reckless speed. He took the numerous sharp curves and angled slopes of the mountain roads with care, not wishing to cause Charlotte any more discomfort than she already felt. He'd been worried about her even before they'd arrived for her appointment. Seeing her ashen face and wild-eyed stare as she walked out of his office however, he knew it was time for action.

He disguised his alarm with his customary detached humor, trying to bring Charlotte out of her desultory silence. Nothing was working. She stared ahead at the road with eyes that seemed to see nothing. Her responses were brief, noncommittal, strained. Finally, Bobby was at his wit's end. His self-confidence was shattered. There was nothing left but to be honest.

"All right, Charlotte, I confess, I can't stand this another moment. I'm a curious creature. I adore secrets and am very good at keeping them, especially if I like the person, and you know I'd do anything for you." He was gushing; his hand was lifting from the steering wheel, punctuating his remarks. "You've obviously had some bad news and I want to help. No, make that I need to help. I simply can't sit here and watch you suffer in silence a moment longer."

Charlotte turned her head. Then to his surprise, she said, "Yes, I need to talk to someone, and I think, yes, you are the very one I should talk to."

He felt momentarily giddy with self-satisfaction. A rush of gladness that not only would she confide in him, but that he was, for the first time in many months, needed by someone. He vowed he would not fail her.

"I know just the place to talk. It's on our way home. A sorry little café. The food is simply awful, but it has marvelous views of the valley, and what harm can they do to a bottle of good champagne?"

"I don't feel like celebrating."

"Champagne is not just for celebrating, *querida*. The bubbles loosen the tongue and lift the spirits. We shall go, look at the mountains, have our drink, and then you will cry on brother Bobby's shoulder."

Then, his efforts were well rewarded. Charlotte smiled, albeit weakly. He turned his head quickly back to the road, sniffing and blinking the moisture from his eyes, not wishing to appear maudlin. He didn't want her to know that he'd seen the sheen of tears glistening in her brilliant blue eyes.

Later in the café, they sat at a table by the window, watching the sun lower into the valley. As the shadows deepened in the darkening room, Bobby watched Charlotte's face as she talked about her love for his brother Michael. A myriad of emotions flickered over her lovely features as rapidly and unpredictably as the light of the candle stuck in the wine bottle on the table. She talked on and on about how she had never, even in her most secret dreams, ever believed that someone like Michael would ever love someone like her.

While she talked, Bobby listened patiently, knowing that she had to get through this prologue before she began the heart of her story. As the sun disappeared and the candle sputtered lower, however, her story began to take a turn.

She clutched the stem of her glass tightly, holding her lips tighter still as she paused and collected herself. Bobby sat up in his chair, moved his glass aside and leaned forward.

"When I was young," she began, looking off into the distance, "they used to call me Charley Horse...."

She watched him while she told him about her childhood. His eyes widened when she described how she was chased home by boys with sticks and, later, ridiculed by strangers on the street. He sat back in his chair with astonishment while she described how Dr. Harmon had cracked her jaw and rebuilt it, using her own bone and the implants to extend her jaw and chin. When she told him what Dr. Navarro had just finished telling her, she knew he believed her.

She imagined she was telling the story to Michael, and gauged Bobby's responses carefully. When she finished and his eyes softened with pity and total acceptance and love, she broke down. She didn't dare hope for this much.

"Why me?" she cried, bringing her face to her hands. "Why couldn't this have happened when I was old? I wouldn't care so much then."

"Oh, sure you would have. Beauty is never something one wants to lose. At any age, darling."

She dropped her hands and spread them on the table. Her anger flashed in her eyes. "What the hell does Navarro know? He's just some small town doctor. He doesn't even know what tests to order."

"He's very intelligent, Charlotte. He is well respected, does immense research at the medical school. If he's told you to have the implants removed, then I'd believe him."

"You'd believe anything he said because he's your healer," she shot back, cornered. "You're too afraid to think that his herbs and treatments won't heal you."

Bobby fingered his wineglass. "I do think the herbs are helping," he said softly. "But I know they won't heal me."

The guilt hit her full force. "I'm sorry, Bobby. Forgive me. I'm lashing out. I'm just so afraid."

"Of course you are. So am I." He leaned closer. "I love great art above all things," he said slowly. "I understand what a master this Dr. Harmon must be, and what a disaster it will be to destroy his masterpiece." He lifted his shoulders, draped in his raffish suit. "But you have to do it," he said, raising his eyes to meet hers steadily. "It is, after all, only your face. It isn't your life."

"Isn't it?"

"How can you ask that?" He appeared flustered, tapping his fingertips rapidly on the table in the same manner Michael might have.

"Michael," she replied. "How can I tell him about this? He loves my face."

"He loves *you*," Bobby said fervently. "You can't separate the two."

"You don't know how I looked. You can't imagine." She shook her head, bringing shaky fingers to her temples. "I wasn't just some lady looking for a chin-lift. I had a real deformity. Ugly, Bobby. There's no other word for it. Ugly."

He blinked slowly, trying to comprehend. "It's hard to imagine. That under that gorgeous face…"

"Exactly. I see how you're looking at me now. Trying to imagine. It's like I'm wearing some kind of mask. I know, you see, because I did it, too. When I looked in the mirror. That's how I know how hard it is not to feel that this face is something unreal. That I'm not real."

"But you said yourself you got used to it."

Her heart was in her throat, and she had to swallow hard. She suddenly remembered what it was like, when people at other tables stared at her, not with admiration as they did now, but with a perverse pity, as they would at any freak.

"You have no idea what it's like to be grotesquely ugly, to suffer, and to somehow accept it. Then to be given a second chance. To suddenly be beautiful, more beautiful than you'd ever dared hope. Only to have it all taken away. In one day. To be told, Sorry, it's all over now. It was just a dream after all—only now you don't want to wake up. You don't know what that's like, Bobby. You can't..."

"Charlotte, listen," Bobby broke in, squeezing her hands. "Listen. Beauty isn't about faces. People I've loved, handsome, healthy men.... I've seen them shrink before my eyes. Their beautiful faces scarred by disease, gnarled and pale. They were devastated. But to me, they were still beautiful. I didn't desert them because their faces had changed."

"Michael couldn't love me like *that*."

There. She'd said it. She'd voiced her worst fear. Losing her beauty was one thing. Losing Michael was far worse.

"He could. Loving someone, as Michael loves you, goes beyond the face." He smiled gently now. "You won't lose him. He understands how hard this will be for you, especially knowing all you've been through already."

"He doesn't know," she said, feeling sheepish. "You see, I've never told him. About the surgery. About all this. The time was never right. And then, well, it just became too late."

Bobby's brows gathered and he brought his coupled hands to his lips in thought. "He doesn't know? Any of this? The surgery, the deformity..."

She shook her head. "None of it."

Bobby's enthusiasm wavered, striking new fear in her own resolve.

"He'll be angry that you didn't tell him."

"Lied to him."

"You didn't lie."

"Not telling the truth is a kind of lie."

Bobby frowned and looked away. "Yes, I suppose it is."

"I'm sorry, I didn't mean to make comparisons."

"We both know that," he said, brushing off the apology. He thought a moment longer, looking at the last of the candle sputter at the mouth of the wine bottle. Then he looked up again, full of resolve. "Tell him. Soon. Tonight. If you delay, it will make him even angrier. It will appear that you've held back because you didn't trust him."

"I'm so afraid." Her eyes were wide. "If he rejects me, I couldn't bear it. I'd die anyway."

"He won't. Look at how he's been with me." His voice trailed away. "He's sold his condo in Chicago, given up everything, to pay for my medication. To stay with me. Sure, I'm his brother. And he loves me, unlovable as I may sometimes be." He glanced at her sideways, a devilish humor in his eyes. Then the serious intensity returned and he leaned forward over the table.

"Would he do less for you? I ask you, Charlotte. Give Michael the respect he deserves, the trust. Allow him to show you how much he loves you. After all, every man likes to think of himself as a knight in shining armor. Let Michael be yours. Tell him the truth."

Charlotte saw the light of appeal burning in his eyes, saw the light of the candle, shining brightly despite so little wax left to burn, and felt the first glimmerings of hope spark within her. Could it be possible that now, when all the other dreams—her beauty, her career as an actress— were crumbling around her, her greatest dream of all would be realized? That the dream, buried so deep she dared not even write it on a piece of paper, might come true. The one that she'd abandoned that fateful winter night in a Chicago garage.

That someday, someone could see beyond her face and love her for who she was inside.

Later that night, Michael returned home late from a site visit, his face flushed with excitement. He grabbed her close, swatted her behind and kissed her soundly.

"Made a big sale," he said, pouring himself and her a glass of champagne from the bottle that he'd brought home.

"I sold not only a landscaping job, but an addition for the house as well, one that would overlook the garden I'm designing. It's like everything is coming together for me, at last. The house and the garden, together. I can do both. *Both!* Do you see what that means to me? It's like a great circle. I'm finally old enough to see all the work I've done in the different areas of my life merge together. It's so much better. Ha! I'd never have believed that growing old could be so exciting."

Her heart broke seeing him so happy. Please, God, she prayed. Please don't let me ruin this. Let it be all right. She squeezed her eyes shut, feeling the pain of her prayer tight in her chest. She made a quick sign of the cross, then served her dinner.

She'd prepared his favorite meal especially for him—shrimp in a mole sauce, the way his mother taught her to make for him, a fine Montrachet wine, lemon ice to cool the palate.

While they ate, he leaned over the table to kiss her. She tasted the spices, then later, felt his tongue warming her cool lips during the kiss. He was feeling the wine, she knew. His eyes glassed over, his touches were more frequent, more urgent. He kissed her more and more insistently, interrupting his story. As the candles burned low, she was reminded of her conversation with Bobby earlier that afternoon. How different, she thought, is a good friend from a lover. Her heart was filled with love for Michael then, realizing in that instant that Michael was both a good friend and her lover.

The Mozart that Michael loved filled the room. They were like teenagers, necking at the table, rolling tongues, moaning deep in their throats, closing their eyes with each kiss. She grabbed for her wineglass. I need this, she thought, feeling a bit cowardly. I want to feel free, loose, uninhibited. To kiss Michael, to love him, to come again and again and to forget what it was she still had to tell him.

The lemon ice melted in the bowls. In the heat of their passion, he grabbed her hand and led her to the next room, to their four-poster bed. Laying her down on the sheets, his mouth on hers, he began making sweet, gentle love to her. Too sweet. She moaned, exploding in a need one step removed from desperate. The need to hold him, to kiss him, to take him in her mouth. There was a blackness inside of her she was digging her way out from, a swirling darkness that she climbed steadily to escape. Kissing, clutching, they rolled back and forth on the crumpled sheets, growing so blinded by their individual passions that they lost sight of each other.

She pulled back then, climbing to her knees, drawing him up before her. Their arms around each other, she looked at him, a mere outline in the darkness. So she traced his face steadily with her fingertips, over his broad forehead, his high cheekbones, his straight nose, his full lips. Sharp, strong lines.

He imitated her movements, tracing her face. A calm settled on them and they hugged. They rocked gently now, back and forth. No kissing. No more caresses. Just a deep clinging. This was, she felt, what she needed most from Michael. This spiritual, ancient rocking. Like a babe in her mother's arms. Or the ribbon of moonlight on a peaceful ocean.

The lovemaking that followed was tender, unusually sensitive and fulfilling. Afterward, she lay on his chest, feeling the lift and drop of his breathing, hearing the rumble of his body beneath her as they cooled.

"My dragon," she whispered.

"My Charlotte," he replied.

Her breath caught in her throat and she realized in that instant that all of her earlier intoxication was gone. She was completely sober now. Charlotte Godowski. That was who she was. That was who she had to tell Michael Mondragon all about.

It was dark. That was good. She could not see his face, nor could he see hers. She had to have faith. Yes, faith in him. Faith in herself. Dear God, help her. Her hands trembled and she ran her fingers up and down his arm.

"Michael," she began, as she had so many times before. "I love you."

"And I love you."

The response was pat. Comfortable.

"Michael, I—I need to tell you something."

"Anything, my love."

She closed her eyes. There was no backing down this time. No more lies, no more delays.

And then she told him. Line by line, word by word, she pushed out the same story she'd told only twice before. Never before, however, had the stakes been so high. He was silent during the telling; he didn't ask questions, or suck in his breath. He lay quietly, almost as though she wasn't there. She wondered wildly if she was using the wrong words. God, could she have told the story wrong? Did he not understand?

The CD clicked: Ravel's *Pavane for a Dead Princess*. It was all too appropriate. All too sad. She persevered, putting one word after another, beat by beat, like the moody music, keenly aware of Michael's silence. His breathing was ragged. His body was cool.

"Michael, say something," she cried. She rose up on her elbows and stared down wildly at his face. His eyes were closed. His brows were gathered tightly. Was that a tear that pooled by his eyes?

He brought his hand to the bridge of his nose and squeezed, grimacing as one in pain. "Charlotte," he said. Then stopped.

"What, what?"

"I don't know. Really. I don't know what to say." He opened his eyes and studied her face. "You say you're not who I see. That you're someone else. Another face. A face I'll have to learn to love.''

"It's still me.''

He didn't respond and she felt her world crumble.

"This doctor,'' he said, clearing his throat. "Dr. Harmon. Have you seen him?''

"No. Not yet. I'll call him tomorrow.''

He nodded, taking it in. "Okay. Good.''

His methodical calm unnerved her. "Navarro was pretty clear what he'd say.''

"He's just some Mexican quack.''

Her heart chilled. That was so cold. So quick. His denial was so far from the support she needed right now. She wanted to hear him jump up and declare his love—no matter what. Pick up the gauntlet, Michael, she thought. She needed to hear that. Her heart was breaking.

Her hands roamed his chest, back and forth, then slid up his neck to his face.

His hands remained at his side.

"Michael, I'm so scared. You're so quiet. I need to know you love me. Will love me no matter what. Please, tell me…''

"I can't.'' His Adam's apple bobbed and he turned his head away from hers.

She sucked in her breath and withdrew, moving from his chest to her side of the bed. She curled her knees to her chest, trembling.

He got up quickly, pushing back the covers. She saw his nakedness as a strong, dark shadow at the side of the bed.

"Why didn't you tell me sooner? Prepare me. Why weren't you honest with me?''

"I was afraid,'' she whispered. "Afraid that you wouldn't love me.''

"It was wrong of you, Charlotte. To lead me on. To tell me all those stories…''

"I know. I'm sorry, Michael, I'm sorry,'' she sobbed.

"I can't believe this."

"It's still me."

He looked at her, studying her, then raised his eyes to stare out the window. "Is it? Who are you, Charlotte?"

She saw in the moonlight the profile of his face. So strong and handsome, his nose as straight as an eagle's, his lips as full and soft as pillows. In his eyes she saw the struggle. He was trying to figure things out. To think of the right words. To be the Michael everyone expected him to be, that he expected of himself. When she saw them fill with tears, she was devastated.

"Michael," she said in a low voice, dragging herself to a sitting position. "Just tell me it doesn't make any difference. Tell me you love me. That it'll be all right."

He was silent.

"Please, Michael." Her voice rose and caught. She hated to hear the plea in her voice. "You don't understand!"

"I do understand! I understand that all that we had together was a lie."

"No!" Her stomach dropped. She felt ill. Cold. "Please don't say that. How can you say that?"

"I need some air." He turned and grabbed his pants. "I need to think."

In a frozen silence she heard the swish of one leg entering the jeans, then the other. The hum of a zipper. His arms going into the sleeves. Feet into sandals.

"I'm going for a walk." He started for the door, then stopped. His hand rested on the doorknob, hesitating. Then, without another word, he walked out.

She watched him leave, and it was like a door closed to her soul. He wasn't coming back, she knew. Not in the same way. Even if he did, it was too late. His silence spoke for him. The gauntlet lay in the dirt, abandoned. There was no knight. There was only the dragon, and that monster had devoured her.

* * *

Michael walked at a furious pace through the field of tall, brittle grass that left angry scratches on his fisted knuckles. He pushed hard toward the woodlot beyond. The hurt burned in his heart, bringing him real pain that made him wince. Only walking at a furious pace helped, fighting fire against fire. How could she have lied to him? Manipulated him. And what was all that about her deformity? And surgery? Charlotte ugly? Impossible. He couldn't grasp it. No, not his Charlotte. But was she his Charlotte?

He shook his head. What the hell, he didn't know who she was anymore. His heels dug into the soft earth as he strode on, walking far and long before he even noticed that he was deep in the woods. Michael slowed, then stopped, his long arms hanging at his side while he got his breath to steady and the sweat to cool upon his brow. Gradually, even his raging thoughts began to die down to embers. Standing still in a dark forest silence, he felt calmed by the noble trees that surrounded him. Ancient spirits standing straight and true.

Straight and true. God, the image shamed him. Could he say the same about himself? Michael put his hand to his face, squeezing his eyes tight. In the blackness he could see Charlotte's face, tearstained and bereft, when she'd begged him to comfort her. Fresh pain stabbed. How could he have left her like that? She'd suffered. She'd been sick. What did she say…that she could die? His fists gathered again, this time against himself and the fates. It was wrong! Not fair. How could God be so cruel?

Then came the harder thought. How could he?

He lowered his head. To say that he didn't love her physical beauty would be a lie. To lose the face that he loved made him feel *cheated.* And yet, to lose her was unthinkable—unbearable. He brought his fists to his temples. As he struggled, the babbling of a brook not ten yards away intruded on his thoughts. A line from a favorite poem by Robert Frost sprang to mind.

We love the things we love for what they are.

Michael dropped his hands. Of course, he had to go back to her. To talk to her, to try and make sense of it all. He didn't know what he'd say, he didn't know how to react, but he knew that he loved her. That was all he needed to know. What the hell was he doing out here thinking of himself while Charlotte sat alone in the cabin crying? He couldn't stand to think of her crying.

He strode with purpose out of the woods. As he made his way back across the field he looked up toward the small cabin on the bluff. Silvery clouds swam across the dawning sky, covering the soft glow of the pale moon's face like a veil. He shuddered, feeling a sudden sense of loss.

After a good cry, Charlotte felt a numbing coldness sweep over her. Like shields of lead surrounding her, her emotional barriers slammed down. All she knew now was that she wanted to leave, to clear out before Michael returned. She'd send a car for her things later. As far as she was concerned, she had her answer. There was no point in facing Michael again. None at all.

She wiped the tears from her face, dressed quickly, threw a few belongings into an overnight bag and called the one person who would come for her at any time, anywhere: Freddy.

A short time later she stood on the porch, bag beside her ankle, purse hung on her shoulder, one foot forward poised for flight. Within the hour, she saw Freddy's Mercedes pull up at the porch. She held her hand to her mouth, choking back a sigh of relief.

"Baby," he said as he hurried from the car to her side, wrapping her in his arms. She wanted to cry but could not. Would not.

"Let's go," she said. "Now."

"You got it." He grabbed her bag and turned to open the car door.

Picking up her purse, she noticed the diamond sparkling
on her finger. In the moonlight it shone bright and cold.
Charlotte remembered all the girlish dreams she'd had
when she'd looked at the stone in the past. Sweet dreams
of love and marriage, children, and promises to love and
cherish forever. She removed the ring with two tugs and
went back indoors long enough to set the ring on the
kitchen table. She couldn't look around in the spotless
cabin where they had spent an idyllic few months cement-
ing their relationship, building their future. It had all tumbled down around the eroding foundation.

Charlotte left the cabin, happy for the cloak of darkness
that masked the view of her vegetable garden ready for
harvest, of the clothesline on a pulley, of the tiny porch
with two white rocking chairs, of the pond just down the
slope, of the gentle rise and fall of the nursery's hills beyond. She closed the car door, then her eyes, and drove
away with Freddy into the black.

Twenty

Melanie was delighted to see Charlotte at the door, but squelched her cry of welcome once she saw Freddy right behind. She rose from the sofa and took the bag from Freddy's hand. Junichi stood awkwardly in the living room, looking at Melanie's face, then Charlotte's, then back to Melanie's.

"I think you should go, sweetie," Melanie told Junichi. "We can go over the wedding plans tomorrow."

Junichi recognized a crisis when he saw one and was happy to leave. He grabbed his coat, muttered a few cordial greetings to Charlotte and a quick farewell to Melanie, then beat a hasty retreat.

"I'll take over from here, Freddy," Melanie said.

"She called *me*," Freddy argued back. "I want to talk to her."

"She doesn't need to talk to you right now."

"I'll be the judge of that."

"Can't you see that—"

"Please," Charlotte said, her fingers at her temples. She took a deep breath and said calmly, "Please don't argue. I need both of you." Then, turning to Freddy, she said, "I'm exhausted, and I really need to get some sleep. You do, too, I'm sure. Why don't you go on home. I'll be fine here and I'll call you in the morning. We'll talk then. All right?''

He stroked his chin, but in the end nodded in agreement. ''All right. I'm just glad you're out of there. If I'd known...'' He stopped, seeing the terse expression on Charlotte's face. ''Okay. I'll call you tomorrow.''

''Thanks, Freddy.''

''Come on, sweetie,'' Melanie said, wrapping an arm around her shoulder. ''You look like you could use a nice hot bath.''

Melanie led Charlotte from the room. ''Don't let the door hit you when you leave,'' she called back to Freddy.

Freddy mumbled a curse at Melanie's back as he watched her lead Charlotte up the stairs to her bedroom. It suddenly occurred to him that the whole house had undergone a major transformation. Standing back and craning his neck, he took in the stepped windows, the addition that opened up to the gardens and the spectacular view. The first pink rays of dawn were stretching across the valley already.

Mondragon did all this, he realized with bitterness. That son of a bitch made a silk purse out of the proverbial cow's ear.

He decided that Charlotte would have to move. Every goddamn room would remind her of that guy. He couldn't have that. He wanted that man out of her life for good this time. How could he manage it? he wondered, walking to the bar and pouring himself a drink. Halfway through pouring the Scotch, he realized that the damn bar was new, too.

A bell ringing by the front door jarred him from his thoughts. Who was that at this time of the morning? The milkman or what? He hurried over to press the intercom button. ''Yeah?''

''It's me. Michael. Let me in. We've got to talk.''

Freddy felt his pressure zoom. That bastard followed us

here? Damn, won't he ever get the message? His fists tightened as he tried to formulate an answer.

"Charlotte?" came the voice from the intercom.

Freddy's gaze darted toward the staircase. Thank you, God, he thought, a smile spreading across his face. He had an idea. Opportunities presented themselves in life; you only had to grab them. He pushed the button and opened the gate for Mondragon.

He had to hustle if he was going to pull this off. Reaching for Charlotte's suitcase, he yanked it open and pilfered through the contents, pulling out one of her lacy bras, underpants, a pair of stockings and a dress. Yeah, these would do just fine. Closing the suitcase, he hid it behind the sofa. Then he scattered the undergarments across the floor, in a trail toward the sofa, ending with the panties at its base. He didn't have much time; he had to make do. Punching the pillows, throwing a few on the floor for good measure, he created a scenario as cleverly as any stage director.

Move fast, he told himself. Time was of the essence. Mondragon was going to be knocking on that door any second.

He spotted two used glasses of wine on the table next to an opened bottle. Perfect, he thought. There was even lipstick on the rim of one. *Brides* magazine had to go, he thought, stuffing Melanie's issue under the sofa cushion. Sweat beaded on his brow as he raced to the staircase to eavesdrop. Water was running in the bathroom and the door was closed. Good, he thought, removing his jacket and loosening his tie. He felt his excitement bubble. This might just work. While he fumbled with his buttons and yanked off his shirt, he trotted to the stereo and turned on music, loud enough so that the ladies wouldn't hear him downstairs. Just as he finished unnotching his belt, Mondragon rang the front door bell.

Just in time, he thought. Glancing up the stairs once more, he unzipped his trousers then ran to the door. He ran his hand through his hair to muss it as he swung the door open.

"What do you want?" he roared, taking Michael by surprise. He'd have paid admission to see the look on Mondragon's face when he spied Freddy at the front door. Mondragon's dark eyes flashed in instant animosity, mirroring the emotion in Freddy's own. It was a standoff, but Freddy knew he was the one holding the gun.

He watched as Mondragon's eyes roamed over his disheveled appearance: the messed hair, the bare chest. Freddy pretended to fumble at his zipper. He knew the impression he was setting, and by the fire raging in Mondragon's pupils, he knew it was working.

Michael pushed past him, his long hair flying. From the looks of his worn clothes, the mud on his shoes and the dark stubble on his cheeks, Freddy figured it had been a long night for that guy as well. Good, he thought to himself. How does it feel, Mondragon? I've felt like that for months.

"Where is she?" Michael demanded, stepping into the living room, his fists balled.

"Uh, I don't think this is the time for you to come in here and demand to see Charlotte," Freddy drawled.

"Get this straight," Michael replied, jabbing his index finger in Freddy's face. "All I'm asking you is—*where is she?*"

Freddy raised his brows and extended his hand, indicating the mess on the floor and the sofa.

Michael glanced over his shoulder toward the living room, paused, then slowly turned, facing the room squarely. Freddy watched the color drain from his face as he followed the trail of Charlotte's underwear and clothing across the floor to the sofa where his tableau was set. The wine, the flattened pillows, the silk panties.

Freddy wanted to giggle when he saw Mondragon's shoulders droop. Bessie Smith crooned in the distance. It was sweet indeed. He could have watched this scene for hours, but he didn't know how much time he had left. It was time for the coup de grace.

"You see how it is, Mondragon. Why don't you be a gentleman and just leave?"

Michael turned to face him. His lips were white and his eyes were wild with grief.

"I don't believe this."

"Why don't you ask her? She's upstairs, taking a bubble bath." He paused. "She wanted to freshen up."

Michael's nostrils flared, and for a minute Freddy thought he was going to lunge for him like before. But he didn't. He took a deep breath instead, then turned on his heel and left the room, left the house, and left, Freddy hoped, Charlotte's life for good.

"Hello, Dr. Harmon? It's Charlotte Godfrey. Godowski?" She prompted after the initial pause.

"Of course! Charlotte, how are you? It's been such a long time. I've been following your career. Congratulations. I knew you'd make it."

"Dr. Harmon," she interjected, her voice insistent. She didn't have time to chat about her career. "Something's come up." She briefly told him about her symptoms, the tests that Navarro had conducted. "He says that I have to have them removed. Of course he's wrong, but he did make me nervous. What should I do?"

There was a long silence. "It's difficult to say over the phone," Dr. Harmon replied slowly. "This Dr. Navarro, he said he consulted with Doctors Haverhill and Quinn? In L.A.?"

"Yes, but they never saw me. I can't believe they'd know the case well enough to make a diagnosis."

"They're excellent physicians. Navarro consulted the best. I've seen the paper that Navarro's referring to. Not everybody who has implants has APA, even in the study.

But your situation... Naturally I'd need to see you. Can you come to Chicago? Right away? I'll get my book.''

"Wait." She swallowed and took a deep breath. "You mean you think Dr. Navarro's right?"

"That the implants must come out? If your titers are as high as you read to me over the phone, then yes. All the indications are there. I'd want to do my own tests, of course. I feel terrible about this. There was no way to predict your reaction. Naturally I want to do the work myself."

"But I don't want them just taken out. Can't you put new ones in?"

"Unfortunately, no. Not in your circumstances. Any implant would be rejected, you see."

"You mean, if I keep them in, I could die."

The silence stung. When he replied, Dr. Harmon's voice was low and utterly serious. "Yes."

She sucked in her breath, covering the cry with her palm.

"Why don't you let me examine you? The best plan is for you to come to Chicago as soon as possible. Let me..."

"Goodbye, Dr. Harmon."

"What? Hello? Charlotte, don't hang up. You must—"

"I don't think you should start work so soon," Melanie told Charlotte when she saw her dressed in a smart cashmere wool suit and high heels a few days after she'd returned home. Charlotte jabbed her long fingers into calfskin gloves with businesslike, precise movements.

"Work is exactly what I need," she replied, her face haggard and her eyes puffy. When she looked up, she felt sure that her eyes reflected the bitterness she felt. "I'd say I've had enough vacation, wouldn't you?"

"What do I say if he comes looking for you? He will, you know. He loves you."

Charlotte knew she'd have to hear this kind of sympathy from several corners, but knowing it and hearing it were two different matters. "Please don't say that," she replied, her face grim. "It doesn't make this any easier for me."

"I'm sure it's not easy for him, either. You left him."

"No," she said, closing her eyes and resting her hands on her purse. She called upon the calm to quiet a faint stirring of pain threatening to erupt once again. "I didn't leave him. Quite the contrary. He walked out. I simply made things easier for him."

"But you love him, Charlotte! Fight for him."

"Whether I love him or not seems irrelevant at the moment." She sighed. "And I'm afraid the fight's gone out of me."

Melanie frowned and wrung her hands. "You don't sound like yourself. You're always the one with the glass half-full, remember? 'If you want something bad enough, work for it and you'll get it.' That's what you always tell me. Come on, Charlotte. Listen to your own advice."

Charlotte looked at Melanie, feeling pity for anyone who could believe such hogwash. "If I remember correctly, you're the one who's always saying that men are pigs and aren't worth the bother. I just happened to discover rather late that you're right."

"I could cut off my tongue. Charlotte, I was wrong. Well, sort of. Some men are pigs, but some are not. Michael is in the latter group. Really, Charlotte. Don't set your heart against him. You had something really special going. Go back to him."

"All I want to get back to now is my work."

"Charlotte..."

"Melanie." Her voice was sharp. "I know you're trying to help, but you're not. I don't care, don't you understand? I don't care about Michael, about my face, about anything anymore. My personal life is unpredictable and cruel. I can accept that. But at least I can control my work."

Melanie's face was white with worry. "You still haven't told me what to do if he calls or stops by. He will. You weren't here the last time when he was tearing up the town looking for you. He was a madman.''

Charlotte tightened her lips and looked at Melanie with eyes wide with frustration. ''You weren't there when he lay motionless on the bed, not speaking a word. He was cruel.''

Both women looked at each other without speaking. Stalemate.

''Well, are you going to call Harmon today?''

Charlotte shook her head. ''I'm not having the operation.''

This brought Melanie to her feet. ''What? Are you crazy?''

''I'd be crazy to have it. My beauty is all I have in this world. I have no intention of losing it.''

''You are crazy. No, I'm sorry I said that. You're just upset.''

''Yes, I'm upset. But I'm not crazy. I'm a realist.''

''This is wrong, Charlotte. Your beauty is just a shell. You can't sacrifice yourself to it. Life is precious. No matter what, you're lucky to have been born.''

''Lucky to have been born? Hardly.'' She thought of the character Marguerite in *Camille,* of how she ended her suffering by letting her illness simply take her away from it. ''It's just as lucky to die.''

Melanie's face paled and she clutched her throat. ''You can't mean that.''

''Oh, but I do,'' Charlotte replied with a deadly calm. ''But not to worry. I expect I'm not lucky enough to do either. I expect I'll simply endure.'' She lifted her arm, checking her wristwatch. ''I'm late for an appointment.'' She picked up her briefcase and strolled to the door. Opening it, she waved briefly at her driver, then turned to face Melanie. Her features softened.

''I know what I'm doing. And don't worry about what to say to Mr. Mondragon. I'll have my secretary call and cancel their lawn services. He'll have no need to bother you.'' She stepped across the threshold, then having a second thought, stepped back in and faced Melanie. Her voice was crisp and uncompromising. ''Promise me you won't call him.''

Melanie looked stricken. Obviously she had intended to do that very thing.

''Promise me,'' Charlotte insisted.

''Damn you, all right. I promise.''

Charlotte smiled briefly, nodded, then closed the door behind her and faced the morning, holding her head high.

Melanie watched her leave, clutching her sides with worry. She couldn't call Michael, damn to hell that promise. Damn him to hell for hurting Charlotte this way. But she'd sit by the phone, anyway. She didn't promise not to talk to him if he called her.

Michael thrust his shovel into the black earth and, giving a heave, hoisted another mound of soil from the ditch. Sweat glistened on his brow and soaked his shirt. He'd been at this damn ditch all day. He needed to work hard, to push himself physically to the limit. Pumping his muscles, exhausting himself to the point where he couldn't think, was the only way he found to help defray the pain in his heart. With each plunge of the shovel he imagined it was his fist and the earth was Walen's face. One after the other. Faster, harder, till the sweat poured.

''What are you doing?'' Bobby asked as he walked up the path with his long-legged gait.

''There's drainage work to be done.'' After one more shovelful, he rammed the tip of the shovel in the dirt and rested, leaning his elbow on the pole, wiping his brow on his sleeve. ''What do you want, Bobby?''

''Me, nothing. *Mamacita* wants you and Charlotte to come for dinner. You're late.''

''We won't be coming.''

He looked surprised, then his face darkened with suspicion. Michael looked bad. His hair was greasy, he was badly in need of a shave, and he looked as if he'd slept in the ditch he was digging. Bobby looked up into the cabin. Inside it was dark and ominously quiet.

"Where's Charlotte?"

Michael swallowed. His mouth felt dry and thick. "She's gone."

Bobby's mouth fell open but he remained uncharacteristically silent.

The next moment's silence told all.

Michael picked up the shovel and rolled his shoulders and neck. He didn't want to think of how he'd felt when he returned to the cabin to find Charlotte gone and the diamond ring lying on the bureau. Of how he'd chased her down, only to be confronted with... No! If he thought about it again it would swallow him whole.

"When did she leave?" Bobby wanted to know.

He thrust in the shovel, cutting deep into the earth. "Last night."

"And you let her go?"

"I was out walking. She was gone by the time I got back."

"And that's that?"

He remembered how he'd picked up the ring and sat on the bed in the darkness, twiddling the diamond between his fingers, staring at it as if it held the answer to why all this had happened. Why had she lied to him? Why had she left? And of course, how could she have betrayed him, so suddenly, so soon, with Freddy Walen of all people? When the morning light entered the windows, he still had no answers. All he had was a dead pain in his heart and an obstinate anger in his mind. The hell with her, he thought, stabbing the earth.

"That's that," he replied.

"I don't believe you! How could you desert her now? When she needs you most?"

Michael slowed, stopped and turned to look up at Bobby from the ditch. "You knew about her face?"

Bobby nodded. "I drove her to Navarro's. She was desperate. Afraid for her life, her looks. Most of all, afraid that you'd leave her. I was the fool who told her to tell you. That you'd pick up the gauntlet."

"Shit, Bobby. You have no idea what you're talking about."

"You know who you're like?" Bobby went on, heating up. "You're like one of those guys I know with AIDS who, once they get their meds and discover that they're not going to die after all, dance away, breaking up with their partner. Bye-bye now. I've got my own life to live. I don't want to stay here no more and see your ugly face."

"That's not fair. It's not about beauty."

"It isn't?"

"It's about her lying to me. Pretending to be someone she isn't."

"That is a crock and you know it. Can't you see you're repeating a typical pattern for you? You don't like something, something doesn't fit your standards, so you walk away from it. You couldn't deal with your Mexican family so you walked. You couldn't deal with my homosexuality, so you walked."

"I came back."

"Yes, you did. You made good. After you thought about it. But hey, that's okay. You're only human. I give you credit for coming around." He paused, and their gazes met. "I hope you can do the same for Charlotte."

"It's not the same." His voice was hard. His face was set.

"You are like a Mayan statue."

"I should be so lucky that my heart was made of stone."

Bobby threw his hands up in disgust and turned heel,

walking away with a great show of displeasure and clucking of his tongue. When he reached the curve of the path
leading away from the cabin, he stopped, thinking of a final
word he wanted to get in. Turning, he caught sight of Michael slumping against the dirt wall of the ditch, his arms
outstretched, holding on to the shovel. When he saw his
brother's head drop to his arms, and his shoulders shake in
silent sobs, Bobby's own heart broke.

"I want lots of work, Freddy," Charlotte said, storming
into his office and meeting his surprised gaze with a steady
one of her own. "Keep me very, very busy."

"That's my girl!" Freddy smiled broadly and clapped
his hands together before opening his arms and welcoming
her. When he stepped back, he peered at her face closely.

"You look good. Much better." Her hair was sleeked
back into a twist, emphasizing her brilliant blue eyes, and
she had the sleek elegance he'd come to expect from her.

"I always look well when I'm close to death," she
laughed, quoting a line from *Camille*.

"How are the aches and pains?"

"Boring," she replied briskly, taking the offered seat.
She plucked off her gloves in quick movements, eager to
get past the chitchat. "I'm on a strict regime of herbs and
vitamins. I've never felt better and I'm ready to work."
She gave him what she hoped was an enthusiastic smile,
one that said she was well in control of her mind and body
once again. She felt if she could act happy, she might be
able to climb out of this despair she felt in her heart and
actually feel happy one day.

"What have you got lined up?"

Freddy eyes gleamed in pleasure as he leaned over and
buzzed his secretary.

"How about some coffee in here?" He looked over at
Charlotte, his brows raised in query.

"Mineral water for me. No, nothing else. Thank you."

The order was made and Freddy joined her at the table. "I got to tell you, I was worried."

She noticed that he looked tired. The planes of his cheeks sagged, and she realized how difficult the past few months of her disappearance had been on him.

"I know. I'm sorry for that."

Freddy shook his head, almost sadly. Then he set a file atop the table and began to shuffle through it.

"Did I tell you how I closed a deal with John LaMonica and Paramount while he got his nose broke at Morton's?" He sounded eager to tell the story, eager to please her.

"No, Freddy, you didn't." She fixed a polite expression of interest on her face.

"No? Well, I was there eating my dinner with Michael Kuhn, hammering on about distribution, when in walks LaMonica, strutting like a short, collagen-filled peacock after his recent string of box office successes. Trailing in after him are..."

"Please, Freddy. Just the business details."

Freddy clamped his mouth shut, squinted, then said, "Sure. Okay..." He sat back in his chair and straightened his tie. Charlotte noticed he'd purchased a large diamond for his pinkie finger.

"The bottom line is, you're hot. Everyone knows you're poised to win the Oscar for *Camille*. LaMonica signed you for this action film called *Thunder Bay*, and wants to roll now. I thought it'd be good to get you into something a little different. Show your range."

When she didn't reply, he continued. "The deal's a sweetheart. Seven figures. Strong distribution. To star with Johnny Depp. You two look good together, everybody says so."

Charlotte listened to the story, watched Freddy ease back into his chair and lace his hands behind his head and thought to herself, *Is this what my life is? Deals and dis-*

*tribution, quips and gossip, grasping at opportunities like
wonder-eyed children chasing translucent bubbles?*

She shuddered and felt her blood thin and grow cold in
her veins. The cold drove inward, imploding, until she felt
an aching loneliness.

"So, what do you think?"

"Fine," she replied at length. "When do I start?"

Freddy dropped his hands and his mouth slipped open.
He lay his manicured hands flat on the table.

"Fine? When do I start? That's all I get after busting my
you-know-what out there?"

"What more do you want me to say?" she asked without
emotion. "Okay…I'm anxious to look at the script." She
spoke slowly and evenly. "I'll know more then. I like
Johnny. I'm sure we'll work well together. I've never done
an action film before but, hey, I'll do my best. There. Is
that enough?"

Freddy narrowed his eyes and tilted his head, considering. "You still upset about that Frito Bandito? I thought
that was all over." His face registered discomfort when she
didn't rise to the bait. "Don't tell me you went and got
back together with that guy?"

"No," she replied. "We're over. You don't have anything to worry about."

"Glad to hear it. I was beginning to think that you and
he…"

"Freddy," she interrupted sharply. "Let's stick to business, shall we? What else have you got lined up? I want to
work as soon as possible."

Freddy's face sobered, but he nodded and shuffled a few
papers on his desk. She knew he wouldn't argue with her.
After all, work was all he ever wanted from her, wasn't it?

Freddy took Charlotte's elbow and guided her from the
long, sleek limousine to the entrance of Cilantro, Junichi's
trendy new California-maki restaurant on the wharf. A

string of limos and Rolls-Royces lined the street like a Christmas parade. The two roommates had orchestrated the event to celebrate both the opening of the restaurant and the opening of *Camille*. It was strictly black tie and all the usual suspects were there.

Freddy stood at the entrance and surveyed the room while Charlotte chatted with Melanie at the door. He had to admit, Melanie looked pretty good these days. Softer, smarter. Not a bimbo anymore. He guessed success did that to a woman. She gave him the cold once-over when she saw him, but what did he care? She was a nobody.

Now, out there were the players, he thought with relish. He'd worked hard to fill the room, and it was standing room only. Too bad Charlotte had insisted she have the party at this joint. It was nice enough. They'd spared no expense in the decorating. Tasteful with lots of fresh holly and crisp white linen. Okay, he conceded, the location on the wharf was decent. But it wasn't Spago. Charlotte had insisted that everyone would be thrilled for a change in venue. He hadn't been so sure, but looking at the turnout, he was only too happy to admit she was right.

The power list was here. At the head table sat Joel Schaeffer and the various producers including the Weinsteins, basking in glory from the standing ovation the film had received at its preview earlier that night. Sitting nearby was a collection of master deal makers, super lawyers, producer-financiers, A-list actors...

Yeah, he thought, looking around at all the names and the tight, eager expressions on their faces. It was a good night for showbiz folks. Excitement was in the air. Champagne was being poured. Nothing stirred the blood like a box office hit. Tonight the restaurant was a marketplace.

And he was bringing in the hottest commodity. The buzz was already out that Godfrey was a shoo-in for the Best Actress nomination. Get your checkbooks out boys and girls, he thought to himself as Charlotte approached him, a dazzling smile on her face that eclipsed even the eye-popping diamond necklace around her swanlike neck.

He escorted her through the crowd with a proprietary air, nodding at people he didn't know, exchanging quips and barking laughs with those he did. He didn't blame the men who followed her with their eyes. They couldn't help themselves; they were getting hard just looking at her. When they shifted their gazes to him, their eyes asked, with obvious envy, how he'd gotten so lucky? Was she as good as she looked?

Glancing at Charlotte, he noted with pleasure that she had an innate sense of dignity. Either she didn't know that men were dropping like flies around her or she didn't care. Her brilliant blue eyes were fixed straight ahead, as though she were in her own world. It added to her allure. Freddy relished the attention, and his chest expanded as he fixed on the smug, satisfied look of a man who had already devoured this exotic dish and was sure to feast again. Mondragon was out of the picture for good. Charlotte was his now. And he was holding on tight.

Melanie's wedding was the highlight of the Christmas holidays. Charlotte helped her dress in a voluminous white gown with fur trim; she was determined to wear white. With Junichi, Melanie claimed she felt pure.

The ceremony and reception were held at Cilantro, their new restaurant. Charlotte, dressed in poinsettia red and standing beside her as maid of honor, thought Melanie was radiant with joy and happiness. That spirit was reflected in the face of Junichi, and in the faces of the circle of friends and family that surrounded them.

She beamed with pleasure for her friend as she listened to the exchange of vows. Melanie spoke clearly, with the voice of one who had overcome many obstacles in the past year and had emerged triumphant.

It was ironic, Charlotte thought to herself as she observed

her friend's luminous face, that the beauty Melanie feared losing with age had, in fact, altered and returned, one hundred times more enchanting. Each wrinkle was a badge of honor, the soft plumpness of womanhood was flattering, the shoulders straight and the gaze steady with confidence, indicating that she knew where she'd been and where she was headed. Most of all, her eyes were brimming with love for Junichi—and herself.

Charlotte cried into her hankie, sniffling more than Junichi's mother, who came in a close second. The guests were kind and thought she was merely sentimental. Melanie, who knew better, was reassured when Charlotte wiped her eyes and calmly greeted the guests in the receiving line.

"You are the most beautiful bride," Charlotte gushed when they were alone.

"Let me remind you of what you once said to me. That the best mirror for reflecting our true beauty is the presence of friends in our lives." Melanie hugged Charlotte close for a long moment, sharing a unique love that can only be shared by two dear friends. "You've been my best friend. You made me beautiful," she whispered in Charlotte's ear.

Melanie drew away, wiping her eyes. "And your gift was too much. Your shares in the restaurant... I can't say enough. Junichi calls it my dowry."

"Just promise me to be happy."

"I am. Deliriously. But don't think for a moment that I'm abandoning you, roomie. I'm only across town." She squeezed Charlotte's hands. "You're not alone."

Charlotte's vision blurred, but she hoisted a resolute smile. "Of course not."

Junichi came over and, after apologizing to Charlotte, escorted Melanie to another smiling couple for a photograph. The foursome exchanged pats and hugs and looked to Charlotte so couple-ish. Around her, people surreptitiously glanced her way, whispering. It was clear that they recognized who she was, were thrilled by it, but did not intrude and speak to her. They of course thought they were being polite by not approaching a celebrity. She was not one of them.

Charlotte stepped back a pace to stand in a quiet corner of the room and observe the party from a safe distance. As she watched the other guests form clusters and chat comfortably, she remembered another Christmas party four years earlier, in Chicago. She shivered from a cold blast that had nothing to do with the brisk December wind whipping the dock and rattling the wooden shutters. Charlotte realized with a sudden intake of breath that she was as isolated being beautiful as she'd ever been ugly.

Twenty-One

❧❧❦

Two months into the new action film, *Thunder Bay*, the cast and crew were sweating bullets, not shooting them. John LaMonica had finally managed to put this film together after two years of negotiating film rights, actors' and director's schedules, paying back favors and incurring new ones. Now, just when he got production under way and the cameras were whirring, his leading lady, Charlotte Godfrey, was crumbling.

"It's a hell of a way to start the New Year. You've got to do something, and do it fast," LaMonica told Freddy Walen in his steel gray office. The producer was in no mood to argue. "Or you leave me no choice. I'll release her from the film."

"What?" Freddy exclaimed, yanking the cigar from his mouth and leaning forward in his seat, elbowing across the acre of LaMonica's desk. "You can't do that. The film's half shot!"

"I can and I will." He leaned back in his chair and expanded his chest. He steepled his fingers and looked at Freddy from over them, each finger a loaded gun.

Freddy picked up his club soda and swirled the ice, eyeing LaMonica. The man was a bulky, square-jawed pugilist made to look elegant by a fabulous tailor. He was, Freddy reminded himself with a deep breath, the producer.

"What will you gain by that?" he asked, his voice conciliatory. "You'd lose everything."

"I'll close down the set and collect insurance before I go through another two months like this. She'll bankrupt the entire project."

Freddy champed down on his cigar, holding in the retort. LaMonica was part of a new breed of Hollywood producers who considered themselves honor bound to cut outrageous production costs. He'd built a reputation around his ability to do so, and as a result, was paranoid over rising expenditures. And there was no denying the costs were skyrocketing on the set of *Thunder Bay*. His mind was racing. He'd heard about Charlotte's problems on the set, but she was a consummate professional. He never dreamed it could get this bad. He leaned back in his chair, assuming a relaxed position.

"In all fairness, John, you can't dump this all on Charlotte. It's common knowledge the computer graphics imaging alone is running into the millions."

"Hey, the CGI I can handle. It's budgeted. It's your star's emotional life that's out of my range." He scowled, then said in a low voice. "What is it, drugs?"

"No, no, it's nothing like that. Frankly, John, I don't know what the matter is, except that it's physical. She's been sick, and it keeps getting worse. We've been to a lot of doctors, but they can't pinpoint the problem. After the film's done, we'll start with the specialists. Check her into a hospital and run the tests." He saw LaMonica raise his brows. "And I don't mean the Betty Ford. She's got something else. Arthritis, maybe."

LaMonica laced his fingers on the desk and stared at them for a moment, his face troubled. Freddy felt the sweat pouring down his back, but he kept his face cool by force of will. He knew LaMonica wasn't buying the arthritis line;

he didn't expect him to. He probably thought it was AIDS or something. The question was, would he pretend to buy it? When he cleared his throat, Freddy sat up, to show respect.

"Can you keep her stable long enough to finish the shooting schedule?"

"I give you my word."

LaMonica stewed this over, deliberately letting Freddy squirm. Fact was, Freddy didn't know what the hell was going on with her. Some of it was depression he was sure. He remembered the symptoms all too well from years of living with Ali. If Charlotte didn't pull her act together soon, she was going to be released from her contract. That was suicide in this business. In this case, a double suicide. He'd have to do something fast.

"Your word, Freddy." LaMonica was pointing his finger now, making certain there was no doubt who would be held personally responsible.

"My word is my bond and all that. Look, John, just keep the press away. They're starving for any information they can get on her since she's been nominated."

"Maybe if she talked to the press once in a while instead of fueling speculation..."

"We both know now is not the time for that."

LaMonica nodded and puffed on his cigar, deep in thought.

"Close the set." Freddy pounded his fist on the desk.

"It is closed."

"Then explain to me how Vicki Ray got that bit about Charlotte stumbling onto the set like a drunk? That woman practically stalks Godfrey."

"Vicki Ray has sources everywhere. And the fact is, Charlotte *was* swerving around, forgetting her lines. When we tried to prompt her she got downright edgy. Drew herself up like a queen and declared she didn't need prompting. That her memory was excellent. Frankly, Freddy, I heard that about her, but on this set, it couldn't be further from the truth. And when she does talk, she's practically inarticulate!''

His voice was rising. Freddy wanted to cool him down before he got carried away.

"Okay, I get the picture. I'll go see what I can do." He rose and snuffed out his cigar, eager to be out of the meeting before hostilities escalated.

"Freddy!" LaMonica called him back. He waved his hand to bring Freddy close, in a confidential manner. "We all know that this is a tough film—even for an actress in great shape. There's lots of physical stunts, and running. It's a high energy gig." He paused and studied his fingers. When he looked back up, his eyes were intense. He tilted his head and spoke sotto voce. "Go out and assess the situation. Then come back and set me straight. Today. In a couple of hours. Before I take your word."

Freddy held his breath. He was being given a second chance to back out, to let Charlotte sink on her own and not go down with her. Shit, he thought with a sudden panic. It must be worse than he thought. This offer was being made because he and John were friends, once upon a time.

Freddy met his gaze and nodded curtly.

He stepped forward and shook LaMonica's hand to cement the deal. Then he tossed the cigar in the garbage and walked out of the meeting, hoping to God he hadn't also just tossed his career out in the garbage as well.

Charlotte saw Freddy marching toward her cottage with the hunched-shouldered, determined gait of a man on a mission. He could have been a double for John Wayne.

She let the curtains drop and brought her fingers to her jaw, stroking the sore spots gently, feeling a quiver of anxiety stir in her chest. The first real feelings she'd felt in months. She knew what he was going to say. It would be nothing she hadn't already told herself. Shape up, kid. Buck up. When the going gets tough....

The one undeniable fact, however, was that she no longer cared.

She was in mourning. She felt an overwhelming sense of loss that no one could touch. A loss of her love, her beauty, her mother, her talent, of so many things, that she felt sucked into the vacuum of its density. A star, imploding unto itself, creating a dismal black star of suffering.

She'd written to Dr. Navarro several times for refills of his herbs, imploring him to send something new, perhaps stronger. For months his herbs had managed to pull her through, but they weren't working anymore. Nothing was working anymore. And the symptoms were getting worse, just as he had predicted. It used to be she had some good days and some bad days. Now they were all bad. Not long ago, she could pull herself together enough to remember her lines and rally through the day. The murky depression had crept in only during the nights. Now the bleakness seeped throughout the day as well.

She flopped onto the sofa and cuddled into the pillows, holding them tight, resting her chin. What were her choices? To tumble back into the life she once led was unthinkable. And that was what would happen if she had the surgery. To continue on as she was, getting sicker and sicker, condemned her to eventual death. Yet what was a life without love? Death held no power over her.

The challenge was to find a reason to continue living.

Freddy's face was ashen, his eyes were bulging from their sockets, and his mouth hung loose. "Are you telling me that this guy is telling you to take out the implants and what? Just leave it?" He colored and his voice rose with his blood pressure. "Hell, your chin will be scraping your chest!"

Charlotte clenched her jaw and jerked her head away.

Freddy was red-faced, and he slammed his hands on his hips. "That's bullshit. No way I'm gonna let that happen. Damn, why didn't you tell me sooner? Wait, I'm sorry. Let me cool down a minute and catch my breath. This is so much, so fast. Jeez, my head is spinning. I need to think."

Freddy put one hand on his forehead and paced the floor. After a while he sat down in the chair opposite Charlotte and took a deep breath. His eyes were focused, razor sharp, and she could tell he was exploring her face and jaw like others before him. She let him. She gave him his moment; it seemed only fair. This was no time for hedging or embarrassment.

They spoke for more than an hour, going over the details of her surgery, of her illness and of the doctors' reports. Freddy was relentless with his questions and she in turn answered honestly and completely.

"I'll tell you what," he said at length. He looked like he'd aged years. "I'm going to get on the phone to a famous plastic surgeon in South America that *I* know. He's world class. Takes only the best clients. This doctor knows what he's doing. I'll talk to him and we'll schedule an appointment for you, to take out the bad implants and put in the good ones."

She leaned forward, raising her hand to make him stop. "Freddy, I told you. It's not that easy. The research on this is very new."

"Yes, it is that easy," he shouted back, firm in his belief. "You tell me that you've had a major face job and that now it's got to be undone because one doctor says so, and expect me to say 'Oh well. Too bad?'" He slashed his hand in the air. "This is the whole ball of wax, baby. If your face goes, your career goes. Think of that before you take the word of one doctor."

"It's not just one doctor. Unfortunately."

"But you weren't examined by these other docs."

"No…"

"Well, there you are. We'll go see my doctor and he'll fix it. I'm telling you, babe, this guy's a genius. Listen to me, Charlotte."

Charlotte could feel the force of his will bear down on her. In the past, she'd been able to balance it with a firm, steady will of her own. She'd always known what Freddy was about. He wanted to manipulate her, and she let him think that he had. In the past, their goal was the same, and it was easier for both of them if she bowed to his experience to get them there. Only with Michael did she defy him. In this area she had closed the door firmly against him and his prejudices.

But...then again, that had been a mistake, she thought sadly. She had defied God, defied her mother, defied Freddy. Well, they showed her, didn't they? She didn't have it in her to defy anyone anymore. She wasn't angry. She wasn't depressed. She was just very, very tired.

"What should I do?" she asked quietly.

He tilted his head to one side, his eyes shining with a crafty gleam.

"Marry me."

She gasped and stared at him in disbelief. "Marry you?"

"Yes. It's the only way. I can protect you, care for you, the way you need to be taken care of."

"But...I don't love you."

He pressed the bridge of his nose and closed his eyes, then gave a short, impatient sigh. "It doesn't matter."

She felt a wave of despair sweep over her. "It doesn't matter?"

"No."

A muscle in his jaw twitched, and she sensed he was covering up some other, deeper emotion that she could only guess at. Freddy was secretive about his personal life.

"It doesn't matter," he continued in his matter-of-fact manner, "because the marriage will be in name only. In fact, we don't even have to go through with it if you don't want to. I figure we'll need to get to South America right after the Oscars, to get that surgery done. Naturally, that'll also be the time the press will be hounding you. We can use our marriage and honeymoon as an excuse to leave the country and rest up in Brazil until you're ready to come back. Leave it to me to handle all the details. By then, you'll be working on *Tess* and we'll be finishing negotiations for *Beauty and the Beast.* After that, we'll get another film lined up, and another. Cha-ching, cha-ching. No one will care by then if we're really married or not.''

"So we'll only *say* we're getting married...."

"I—" He exhaled slowly and, spreading out his hands, said simply, "If you prefer."

She tilted her head. "I do prefer."

His face flushed, but he only shrugged and said, "We don't need a piece of paper to bind us. You and I, we're a team. We're like that ying and yang, two halves of a whole."

Charlotte crossed her arms tightly around herself and studied him though narrowed eyes. He was sincere. He had feelings about her, stronger than she'd realized.

"You *do* love me."

He sighed impatiently. "Of course I love you, sweetheart. In my own way. There's always been something about you, from the first day you walked into my office wearing that awful suit and acting so prim. You had something special. It was something in the eyes. I don't know how to explain it. I see it now." His face softened, and he reached out to stroke her hair gently, as if she were a child, not a woman.

She leaned away from his hand, averting her eyes. She didn't want him touching her, stroking her. It somehow felt all wrong.

Drawing back, Freddy remained attentive, eager to make her understand. "I want to be your protector. I've created you. I gave you to the world. Don't you see? You—" He shifted his weight and clenched his fists, as though he were grabbing hold of her soul and cleaving it to his breast. "You *belong* to me."

Charlotte stared at his face while her mouth slipped open. My God, he meant it. He really thought she belonged to him. She felt a little afraid. And, though she hated herself for it, she felt a little safe. Most people didn't give a damn about her. They played sympathetic, but they were only interested in finishing a film that would bring in money. Or worse, they pretended to love her but walked away when the chips were down.

He loved her—*in his way*. What did that mean? She looked away at the drawn blinds blocking out the afternoon's light. Perhaps Freddy was right. What did it matter? What was love, anyway? An opportunity to be hurt and humiliated? To have her heart crushed and thrown away? This seemed to her to be so much more practical and efficient an alternative to lust and passion.

She opened her mouth to argue, but let it slowly close again. This was Freddy. He'd worked miracles before. Perhaps Freddy *could* find a way out of this dilemma. She was at her wit's end, grasping.

"Can you finish the film?" he asked, surprising her with the simple question.

She considered it seriously, forcing her soggy brain to think. "No. Honestly, Freddy, I don't think so. Not this one. I'm sorry."

Freddy dragged his palm down his face, miserable. "At least you're being honest. Well—" He slapped his palms on his thighs. "LaMonica's talking about filing a claim and blaming it on you. If we pull out now, voluntarily, he might be able to bring in a substitute and we might salvage your career. He'll appreciate being told up front. Right away."

Charlotte didn't say anything. She didn't have to.

"Now for damage control. We'll let word out that you're very sick." He raised his brows. "Which is true. But we'll

say it's something benign, like pneumonia. I'll get some
doctor to stand by the claim. Then we put you in hiding
until the Oscars. That's the main thing. We've got to get
through the Oscars. If you win there, then the rest of this
will blow over.''

"My health won't blow over, Freddy."

"Of course not. But let's take this one step at a time."

Charlotte leaned back, shivering with chills, while
Freddy explained all the plans that were under way for the
Oscars. He had obviously compartmentalized her problem.
Put it on the shelf in the "to do" pile while he focused on
the next issue. It was so uncaring, so businesslike, so ruth-
less. So Freddy.

She wrapped her favorite afghan around her shoulders,
the one that her mother had knit for her when she graduated
from college, and felt distanced from the event that was
cycling like a whirlwind somewhere out there. He talked
on and on about the music, the seating, the question of
whether she'd be a presenter, the schmoozing with anyone
and everyone connected with the Oscars.

Looking up she saw her face in the mirror: the wide-set,
luminous blue eyes, the perfectly chiseled cheekbones and
delicately protruding chin. The full, even mouth with its
slightly downward pout. Impostor! she thought, hating the
vacuous Beauty she saw reflected. She *was* the Beast!
There had to be some deformity still there, something hor-
rid and grotesque that was hidden in her perfect features
that prevented someone from loving her. She thought she
would be different if she changed her face. But nothing had
changed after all. She still felt the need to be recognized,
to be wanted, to be *loved*.

But she was not worth loving. Of course Michael did not
love her, she thought, burying her face in her hands. The
lack was not in him—but in her.

Twenty-Two

Michael usually loved the spring, the earth's awakening. In the distant hills the coyotes were in full cry. He stood out on his porch with his hands in his back pockets, listening to their songs of love. Deep, soulful howls that moved him deeply. Coyotes traveled in pairs, he thought.

Then he cringed. His own loneliness was oppressive. He'd thought by now, after months of separation, Charlotte would be out of his mind. But she'd sunk her roots deep, like the onions in her garden that were sending up soft green shoots after the long winter. What would it take to rid himself of her?

All throughout the winter her face was everywhere, in the tabloids, on talk shows, on billboards promoting her new film. She'd been nominated for Best Actress for her role as Marguerite in *Camille,* and the studio was going all out with publicity. He went to see the film—it was madness on his part but he couldn't keep himself away. He was tortured watching her—the face that he loved—light up the screen. When he felt charitable, he could agree with the critics that Charlotte was brilliant in the film. When he was feeling bitter, he felt that the role of the lying, manipulative beauty came naturally to her.

One line from the film, spoken by Marguerite to Armand,

kept coming back to him. *"I am not always sincere. One can't be in this world."*

Ha! It must have been so easy for her to recite those words. Like Armand, he had been betrayed. Even after all this time any trigger—a photograph of her face, a sudden memory, the scent of her perfume—acted as a dagger poised over his heart, waiting to strike.

And still her face was everywhere. She rarely smiled, however, in the photographs or during interviews. To others she might appear cool and aloof, but he knew better. He could pick out the small signals of distress: a tightening of her hands in her lap, a slight twitching of her lips, the slant of her head. Usually he would turn his head and pass, or turn off the television after she appeared on the screen. Occasionally, though, he would lapse into a kind of trance and stare at her and listen to her speak, and worry—why was she so sad? Those moments were the hardest. He was vain enough to think that she might miss him, or have regrets, possibly even remorse.

He often stared at her jaw and wondered, would it make a difference if her face was changed? Once he walked up to the television screen as she was talking to Jay Leno and covered up the bottom of her face with his palm so only her eyes were visible. Yes, it was still her. In the eyes. He felt he was looking through those brilliant blue orbs, straight to *her*.

The coyote's song pierced the softness of the night. Michael stared out over the mountains and the drifts of fog moving in. Might they have been able to work it out? he wondered. It was an exquisite torture, like picking at a scab.

"Hurry up, *mi'jos*," Luis called out as he drove up to the cabin, his face beaming in the dark interior of his truck. "Tonight these magnificent birds will make men out of you!"

Michael leaned over the porch railing and waved at his

father. Luis had insisted on taking his sons on a man's night out. Something to bind the men together after a long winter of mooning around, silences and avoidance. Luis was determined to bring his men together—no women allowed—women being the source of all this discontent, he figured. Interesting that he thought a cockfight would be the instrument of peace.

Michael was just as happy to get out of the house, to go anywhere. If he was home, he might weaken and watch Charlotte highlighted all evening on the television's Oscar coverage. He'd watch her dressed to kill in her couture gown, watch the photographers and fans clamor for a glimpse of her, watch her win—for he was sure she would. He didn't think he was strong enough to hear her thank Freddy Walen when she accepted the gold statue. Watching a gamecock rip the heart out of another had to be easier than feeling Charlotte rip the heart out of his own chest.

"And the winner is...Charlotte Godfrey for *Camille*."

The crowd roared their approval and Charlotte felt her heart spring to life. The cameras came in for the close-up, catching her face as it spontaneously broke into her trademark, megawatt smile.

Charlotte had heard that at moments like this time seemed to move in slow motion, and she realized it was true. The orchestra sounded, there was a thunderous applause and beside her she heard Freddy's urgent "Get up! Get up!"

She was rising now, feeling like her bones were made of lead, that her shoes were on backward, that her smile was frozen to her face. Her palms were damp in the long ivory-colored gloves, and she clutched the priceless gown of matching taffeta and silk, the color of camellias. Dozens of people had labored over the straight-bodiced, full-skirted dress that Freddy declared had "the magic of a star."

Freddy... She turned to him, breathless, her eyes wide

and bright. He squeezed her hand reassuringly, then kissed her cheek, smiling with relief and pride, his eyes brimming with tears. She felt him nudge her forward.

Charlotte took a deep breath, nodded, then marked her spot on the stage. Freddy had given her an amphetamine before she left for the theater to help her get through the long program. She could feel it racing through her veins and humming in her ears.

All around her were smiling faces, people pressing their hands upon her and murmuring congratulations, wanting to get close as she slipped past them in the row. The orchestra was playing the theme song to *Camille* as she glided up the aisle, up the stairs, gracefully skimming across the immense stage to where Mel Gibson was holding out a statue to her.

She felt the weight of the Oscar in her hands, a heavy gold statue that embodied so many dreams for so many people. An object of desire, even adoration—the golden calf.

She looked out over the elaborate art deco podium and didn't see the thousands of people, colleagues most of them in one form or another. She didn't think of the billion people watching her by satellite across the world.

Charlotte Godfrey thought only of Michael Mondragon.

Bobby came out to the porch just as Luis honked impatiently. Adjusting his collar, he waved to his father, then turned and rolled his eyes to Michael.

"Vamonos!" Luis called out. "We will be late! You think they wait for us? Get in, let's go!"

After an hour's drive to a remote valley, they arrived at their destination. It wasn't a place so much as an event. Under the blanket of night, trucks and cars clustered around a seedy-looking wooden structure. The Clubhouse, they called it. It was flanked on both sides by swarming men and long corridors of bird crates brought for the fights. Luis tapped the steering wheel with anticipation while Michael and Bobby exchanged glances in the back seat. Michael tied back his hair at his neck, on guard. Bobby was wary.

They made their way as one across the hard-packed field. All around them, tough, hardened men with beer bellies and muscled arms, most of them Mexican, were pushing shoulder to shoulder to squeeze into the Clubhouse. No concern for fire laws here; the joint was already splitting at the seams with shouting spectators, handlers and countless squawking birds. Behind them men were hissing in Spanish for them to get a move on. *"Andale!"* The fights had already started.

At the wide door stood a giant, bulky, full-bearded man. He was wearing a soiled sports cap, a denim jacket so greasy you could scrape it with a knife and a "don't fuck with me" scowl. Beside him, mounted beside the entrance, was a handwritten sign that read No Dopeheads, Faggots Or Bleeding Hearts Allowed.

Michael looked over his shoulder to check how Bobby was dealing with that. Bobby only winked and crossed his fingers, then slipped though the door. Michael followed right behind. Once inside, they marched through the soggy stench in a line behind Luis.

"Over there," Luis shouted over the clamor, pointing in the air to a cramped corner where Manuel was pacing, sucking a cigarette, beside a crate of birds. "Manuel has our birds. Beauties, they are. Come on."

"Your birds?" Michael hissed, moving close to Luis's ear.

Luis only sneered and pushed his way through the crowd to where Manuel was removing one large tricolor rooster rom the crate.

"At last! You got here just in time," Manuel shouted to Luis over the din. He ignored Michael. They had not been comfortable with each other since their words in October.

"The birds are tense," he said to Luis. "We lost two fights already."

"*Sí, sí,*" Luis responded with the calm of experience. He moved beside the crates, bending over with a grunt and checking his birds. When he came up, he shrugged. "What can we do, eh? We must lose a few. But no more. They cost me good money."

Michael could only wonder how much money. This activity was definitely not in his books.

Luis selected a long, straight blade from a row and scythed it through a page of a telephone book, then tried it against the callused skin of his thumb. He nodded, satisfied. Then, taking hold of the gamecock, he strapped the blade to the rear of its left leg.

"Look at him, Miguel," he said, calming the bird with knowing strokes. "He's magnificent, eh? A conquistador. No one teaches this bird to fight. It comes from God." Then he looked at his sons, his eyes shining. "It's in the blood."

Michael watched, fascinated, as his father handled the bird, stroking and kissing his head, oblivious to the roar of the crowd as one fight ended and men shouted and scrambled to cash in their bets. The signal was given and Luis moved into the pit, cooing to his bird, along with another handler sporting a cowboy hat. Michael drew nearer. The crowd erupted in a frenzy of renewed betting.

"Fifty bucks on the cowboy hat!" shouted one.

"Fifty on the red jacket!" shouted another, referring to Luis.

The men swarmed, frantic to place their bets while Luis and Cowboy Hat swayed rhythmically three times toward each other. The birds squawked and glared, catching the scent of the fight. Michael felt his adrenaline flow. His father was right. He saw that right away. The cocks were psyched. The room was close with the smell of sweat and blood, the heat of unwashed bodies pressing and the mounting tension of the kill.

For the kill was coming. One only had to see the crazed look in the eyes of the gamecocks to know that the fight was to the death. Michael looked from the eyes of the birds to the eyes of his father, then to the eyes of the men surrounding the pit. They were no different.

The birds were mad now; the crowd hushed. Luis and Cowboy Hat set their birds on the ground behind the lines in the sand. Instantly, their hackles rose and Luis's bird charged at the other rooster, pecking at his neck. The other bird attacked, missing, flying over the other bird's head. Then they were at it in earnest, all over each other, pecking at necks, stabbing at breasts, in a blur of feathers.

It was over in a few minutes. Cowboy Hat's bird was down. The crowd roared. Michael's stomach tightened. Cowboy Hat moved closer to make clucking noises with his tongue, entreating his bird to peck. It was no good. The bird was either dead or feigning death. Luis's bird flew up and perched upon the other bird's carcass, flapping its wings and stretching its neck while Luis crowed nearby.

Instantly, the teeming mass of men erupted into renewed shouting as money passed hands. Michael turned his head in disgust as Cowboy Hat grabbed hold of the vanquished bird and smartly swung it around, breaking its neck. Then he tossed the warm carcass onto a pile of other dead birds.

"So, this is God given, is it?" Bobby quipped, staring at the pile of discarded birds and beer cans.

Michael offered a wry smile in return, wishing he had a beer to wash out the stale taste in his mouth. "It's sure about blood, anyway."

"To think I've succeeded in avoiding this for thirty-three years."

"God, what a bunch of lowlifes. That son of a bitch at the door was spawned in a sewer. I can't wait to get out of here."

"Our mistake was to let Papa drive. Now we're stuck."

"How many more do we have to sit through?"

The crowd erupted again in a savage ovation. From over their heads, he could see a bird swirled by his neck in the air.

"Another one bites the dust," Michael drawled, scowling.

"I'll never eat chicken again," Bobby said, twisting his mouth.

"Don't bet on it. Here comes Papa with a plate of roasted bird and some beers. Hmmm, I wonder where the chicken came from?"

"Here you are!" shouted Luis. "I brought you some food."

Both Michael and Bobby raised their palms simultaneously. "Just a beer for me."

"How much longer?" Michael wanted to know.

Luis looked crestfallen. "It's just getting good."

"Great." Michael said, heading to the back of the Clubhouse, resigned to having to spend another hour or so in this hellhole. "Go on back to your birds," he called with a wave of his hand. "We'll be hanging around till you're done."

"Manuel is alone by the birds. Why don't you stand by him?"

Michael stopped and turned his head, his face hardened. Luis didn't argue and turned away. Michael was relieved to see his father's back.

Thunder rolled overhead as an evening storm moved in. Inside, the humidity deepened. The air grew thick and rank. A blue haze from the smoke of countless cigarettes hung low. Michael watched his father perform in his element. Even the most naive spectator could see that his father was a person held in great respect in this motley crowd. Through the evening the rest of his birds won, though one of the winners had to be put down, anyway. By the end of the fights he'd won a pot of dough, enough to replace the birds he'd lost and then some. Men gathered around Luis, admiring his birds, slapping him on the back.

You crazy old man, he thought to himself. Here in this visceral world of blood and guts his father felt right at home. Well, he wasn't like his father. Never could be. Never would be, he decided.

Michael looked over the heads of the crowd and checked on his brother. Bobby was resting against the wall. His face was pale and smudged with dark circles under his closed eyes. It was getting late. The crowd had thinned. The eyes of the men that were left were bloodshot and their breaths reeked of cheap liquor. Michael shook his brother's shoulder and set his mouth in a grim line. Blood and booze. A mean combination.

"Let's go," he said to Bobby.

Bobby stretched his shoulders and wiped a palm across his face, nodding. "None too soon. I feel like I need a bath. Maybe two. You go get Papa and I'll go get the car."

Michael fetched his father, where he stood laughing and joking with his cronies.

"All right," Luis snapped, lifting his hands. "Just let me count my money. Help Manuel carry the crates to the car."

He did so. Manuel helped him lift the crates without speaking, then led the way across the floor littered with brown and green bottles, cans and spit. Michael blinked wearily, eager to be gone. Outside, the fresh night air was like a welcome slap in the face. Thunder rolled; cool air was moving in. He gulped a few breaths over the crates, noting that the birds had quieted in the fresh air.

A few cars were clustered near the door. A few were cruising past, filled with laughing men, more drunk than not. Everyone was eager to get home before the storm broke. A few more cars were scattered like sleeping beasts in the brittle grass. Manuel's truck was parked only a few feet away. They went there first, delivering the exhausted birds into the rear of the pickup.

Michael scanned the shadowed lot, his brows gathered, his eyes sharp. His father was stepping out from the Clubhouse. A few men huddled by a maroon sedan, shoulders hunched, money and something else being exchanged. He swung his head from left to right, a sense of foreboding rippling through him. Where was Bobby and the car? He should have been here by now.

"Bobby?" he called out. Sheet lightning flashed in the sky as the storm rolled closer. He could smell rain in the air. He walked a few paces in the direction of where they'd parked, his gut tightening. These guys here wouldn't think twice about beating up a guy they thought was weak, much less gay. Wouldn't even ask. They'd consider it sport. Damn, Bobby was wearing those linen pants.

Thunder rumbled like a growl, and again lightning streaked the sky. He saw two cars parked ten yards off, his father's and a green low rider. Its doors were open. Someone was sitting on the hood. Farther out in the field, to the left of the cars, stood a circle of men, the tips of their cigarettes glowing in the black night. He heard a sudden swell of laughter. A shout. Then a few muffled grunts.

"Bobby!" Acting on gut instinct, Michael took off on a trot toward the noise, fists at the ready. He heard Luis and Manuel at his heels. Drawing near he heard the unmistakable sound of fist meeting flesh, and counted four men, maybe five. And one man was down on the ground, being kicked.

Michael picked up speed and vaulted into the group of men, ramming his shoulder into the chest of the one who hovered over his brother, pushing him off his feet to the dirt. He swung around to look at his brother. Bobby lay in the dirt, his arm over his face and his knees to his chest. Even in the dim light of the moon he could see that he'd been bloodied.

The vision cloaked his eyes with red. His months of well stoked anger bellowed from his mouth like a furnace of fury. He showed his teeth, raised his fists and lunged at the first man who was fool enough to get back up and fly at him. He was a big man, fat but soft. Michael felt his knuckles connect with jaw. Crack! He knocked the *delito* down. The pain felt good. Raw.

He threw back his shoulders, stretching his neck. "Come on," he shouted at the rest of them, waving them in. "Cowards! *Cholos!*"

The three other men, thin and edgy, danced on the balls of their feet like bantam cocks, then charged. Michael got a left hook into one before he felt a solid punch in his gut. The air whooshed out of him, and he staggered back two steps. But he ducked his head and lunged, swinging again and again, his fists meeting hardened muscle. Michael was bigger, stronger than this guy, but the dark-skinned man with a blue hair net and a tattoo was a skilled street fighter, as tough as taut leather. An uppercut made Michael see white. He walloped mercilessly and they tumbled to the ground, grunting and swearing.

Manuel and his father joined the fight, taking blows and giving them back, hard. Their heart was in the fight. This was more than honor; this was family. They fought hard and mean before the other men took off, shirttails flapping in the wind as they sprinted across the field to their cars. Luis had to hold Michael back from chasing after them.

"Enough," he called out, spit spraying.

The fight was over in a matter of minutes, but it had been bloody.

Luis was panting; his shirt was torn and his left eye was swollen shut. But he bore a wide, shit-eating grin that spread from ear to ear. "We fought them off, *mi'jos!* Together. Eh? The Mondragon men are conquistadors."

Manuel laughed and nodded, dragging his sleeve across his bloodied nose. "*Sí.* They better not come this way again, huh. We'll kick their ass.'' He stumbled over to Luis and wrapped an arm around him, patting his back.

Michael hurried to Bobby, who had lifted himself up on one arm. His head was drooped over his chest and he was breathing hard.

"Bobby, how bad is it?'' He was worried. This looked real bad. He bent down beside him and Bobby raised his head. Michael's breath caught. Bobby's beautiful face was a swollen, disfigured mass. His lips were cut, his eyes were black, his nose was bent, and blood flowed down his lumpy face like thick rivers through the Black Hills. Swallowing his bile, he gently took hold of Bobby's shaking shoulders and leaned him against his own.

"No,'' Bobby protested through broken teeth. "Blood.''

"I'll be careful.''

"I think—'' Bobby coughed, spitting out a tooth. "I think a rib is broken.''

Michael swore, sure much more was broken. Bones, ribs, his spirit.

Luis came up behind him and swore loudly when he saw his son. *"No lo creo...* Look what they've done to my boy! Call them back, Manuel. I want my hands on them!''

"Go get the car,'' Michael counter-ordered.

"Sí, the car. Quickly,'' Luis agreed, nodding. "We must get him home to Mama.''

"I think the hospital,'' Michael said.

"No. No hospital.'' Luis had a deep hatred for American hospitals. They were not for the Mexican people, he'd said for many years, ever since he was turned away when he was young and very sick. He stepped closer, taking charge.

"Does it hurt?'' Luis asked his son.

"No,'' Bobby mumbled.

"Can you endure?''

"Yes.''

Luis nodded, satisfied.

Michael saw a perverse pride in his father's eyes, looking down at his battered son.

"A conquered man has no face or heart," Luis said to Bobby. "But *mi'jo,* you have both." With eyes shining he stooped to hug his son.

"No, get back," Bobby cried, his palm outstretched. "There's blood!"

Luis hesitated, his hand in the air. He didn't understand.

Michael did. "You're cut," he said to Luis. "Your wound is open."

Luis touched his broken lip with his fingers, still not comprehending. He moved forward again.

"No!" Bobby shouted, scooting on the dirt, the effort causing him to wince. "Papa, get back. The blood." He coughed and lowered his head. "I have AIDS."

Luis's eyes grew round with understanding. He yanked back his hand as though burned and sat back on his haunches. He turned to Michael, seeking verification.

Michael nodded, eye to eye.

"How? When?"

"You know how," Bobby said, his voice soft and broken. "You've always known. You just wouldn't admit it." He lifted his gaze. He appeared resigned. Defeated.

Luis looked at Bobby, then Michael, with a dazed expression. This hit had been the hardest. He staggered to his feet and backed away.

Bobby squelched a sob and bowed his head. Michael felt the weight of him sag against his chest.

"Don't walk away," Michael shouted out after Luis's retreating back. "You son of a bitch. Don't you walk away! He needs you. Now more than ever. He's your son."

"He's not my son!" Luis shouted back. He had tears in his eyes, but his mouth, swollen and dark with blood, was chiseled. Thunder rolled in response. They all stared at one another, stunned, not knowing what to do or say next.

"He's not my son," Luis repeated in a mumbled voice, stumbling backward like a drunk.

Manuel trotted after him.

"No," Luis said in a slurred growl, waving him back. "Drive them home."

"Throw me the keys, old man," Michael called out, his voice laced with disgust. "We'll drive ourselves home."

Luis stopped and dug into his pockets, standing wide legged, head bowed. He pulled out his keys and threw them back. They skidded in the dust by Michael's feet.

"Hey, Manuel," Michael called out as he watched the two men walk away. "How does it feel to have some bruises, eh? You like it? Like you give Cisco?"

Manuel stopped like he'd been hit, bunched his fists, whirled around and stalked back, his face a red cloud in the darkness. Michael lifted his arm against him, expecting a blow.

"*Esse,*" Manuel spat out, stopping at Michael's feet. His eyes rolled in his head with fury. Then he bent near and ground out, "It isn't me. It's Rosa. Your sister."

Michael took the news like another blow, wincing with the shock. Manuel spun on his heel and hurried after Luis.

"Damn. Shit," Michael cursed, bringing his hand to his forehead. "What the hell's going on here? Has the whole world gone nuts?" He laughed, because if he didn't he would cry. "And Papa wants to make us men? This is machismo? You are cowards!" he shouted after them. "All of you! Homophobic cowards!"

Bobby drew himself up, clutching his ribs with his hand. Michael hurried to grasp his arm and help him.

"No, back off," he said, his face twisted with scorn. "You think the blood can't hurt you, too? You think you're some kind of a god?" He pushed himself up to his knees, groaning in pain. Still he pushed Michael's hand away.

"Christ, Bobby, let me help you."

"I don't need your help," he cried back. "I don't want your help."

Michael gave it, anyway, grabbing hold of Bobby's elbow and helping him to his feet. Michael led him across the grass, wincing inwardly as he watched each small, limping step Bobby made to the car a few yards away. He settled his brother in the seat, taking off his jacket and covering Bobby with it, then bending to swing his legs into the car for him. The linen trousers Bobby liked so much were torn and stained with mud. He closed the door, feeling the first fat drops of rain on his head and shoulders.

"Wipe your hands," Bobby told him when he got in. The car light was dim, but bright enough to reveal their cuts and bruises. "*Madre de Dios,* look at your knuckles."

"Don't worry about me. Put your head back. It'll stop the bleeding. Use the sleeve of my jacket to staunch the flow."

"It'll ruin the leather."

"I don't give a damn about the jacket. Use the lining, it'll be softer."

Bobby dropped his head back on the seat and brought the jacket to his nose.

Michael slammed his door and thrust in the key, determined to burn rubber to the nearest hospital. Where the hell was one, anyway? The engine roared and Michael swerved the car out of the field, sending a spray of gravel into the air. Catching sight of the Clubhouse in his rearview mirror, he prayed a silent prayer that the place would get struck by lightning and burn to the ground.

"I want to go home."

"I'm taking you to the hospital."

Silence.

"Maybe I'll get lucky and die there."

"Cut it out, Bobby. I don't need that." He stepped on the gas and pushed on. "You don't need that, either. Papa's not worth it. He turned his back on you."

"And you think you're so different?"

Michael swung his head around to stare at him, feeling stunned. "What?"

Bobby was barely able to move a muscle in his swollen face, but somehow he managed a half smile. "You always say you're not like Papa. Don't you see? You are exactly like him. In so many ways."

A muscle twitched in Michael's jaw as he heard this. He didn't interrupt, despite his gut urge to tell Bobby to shut up. The rain was coming down in earnest now. He squinted his eyes, flicked on the wipers and cursed the heavens.

"Go on," he said.

"I told Papa tonight because I had to. To protect him. Because I loved him. I didn't mind not telling him before. I know it bothered you. You thought I was living a lie." He closed his eyes and swallowed hard. "I was just living, Miguel. Surviving. I endured because I didn't want to cause him pain. Or Mama. Or me, either. I didn't want him to reject me. It's true, I was afraid. And when I saw that pain in his eyes tonight…" His voice hitched and his Adam's apple bobbed.

Michael's jaw worked while tears burned in his eyes.

"It hurts, man. Rejection bites." Bobby sniffed and wiped his nose again.

Michael passed a weary hand through his hair. "It's okay," he said, for lack of anything better. They drove on for a while down the rain-slicked roads, covering the miles quickly, heading out of the dark hills back into the lights of civilization ahead. Bobby moaned from time to time, especially when Michael hit a pothole or took a curve too fast. He wanted to make good time, even in this damned storm. He didn't like the pallor of Bobby's face. How could Luis have left his own son? Left him to die?

Then, not because he wanted to know, but because the comparison rankled so deep, he had to ask, "How can you say I'm like *him?*" He spat out the word.

Bobby turned his head, his eyes puzzled over the black leather jacket. Then he lowered the jacket from his nose, dabbing a few times. The blood flow seemed to have stopped. "You really don't know?"

"No, I don't know," he snapped back.

"A goddamn Mayan statue," Bobby murmured, his eyes blinking heavily. He tilted his weight, slumping into the corner. He licked his swollen lip, wincing, and sighed heavily.

"Miguel, Miguel, Miguel..." he mumbled, slurring the words. "You walked out on Charlotte, too."

Michael jerked as though shot with an electric bolt. "What?" he asked, turning his head to face Bobby. "What did you say?"

Bobby was still slumped in the corner, eyes closed and still. Michael's heart raced and he reached over to tap Bobby's thigh. But he didn't open his eyes. Panic set in and Michael leaned over, taking hold of his wrist. The skin was warm. The pulse was weak, but there.

"Thank God," he cried, leaning over the steering wheel and pushing the pedal to the floor, racing for the lights. He prayed as he roared across the slick highway in Luis's Buick, the rosaries jangling wildly from the mirror. "Let me get him to a hospital. Please, God, let him be all right."

His soul felt more battered than his body. He hadn't prayed in years, yet tonight he'd prayed like an altar boy, fervently and with utter faith in being heard.

At length he spotted an exit for the hospital and took it at breakneck speed, racing into the emergency room lot of the hospital. He squealed to a stop between two ambulances at the door. "He has AIDS," he informed the medical emergency team as they raced out.

"Thanks. We'll take over from here," one man replied, opening the car door. The team acted quickly, lifting Bobby to a gurney with their gloved hands and rolling him through the double doors into the emergency room.

The gray stone facade of the hospital was barely visible through the torrent of rain. Rivulets cascaded across the parking lot, soaking his shoes, plastering his long hair across his cheeks. Michael slunk against the car and bowed his head. No amount of rain would wash the blood off of this night.

Michael hated hospitals, but he loved his brother more. So he waited in the lobby throughout the night while Bobby was in surgery getting his jaw rewired. His own cuts and bruises had been attended to earlier, and he was relieved to find that there were no open wounds. But he would have an AIDS test, anyway, just to be certain. He nodded off a few times in the hard-backed chair, but sleep was elusive. By the time the night shift ended and a fresh batch of nurses had taken their posts, Michael was allowed in to see his brother.

Bobby was resting uncomfortably when he peered into the narrow two-bed room. He was relieved that the other bed was empty. It was more private and he could speak openly. He hovered at the door of the room, lest Bobby be asleep. His brother was hooked up to intravenous tubes and lying still. Peering closer, he saw Bobby's face and his own face fell in shock. Bobby's face... It looked like someone had tried to rearrange it with a mallet. His proud, beautiful nose was broken, his cheekbone was beaten so badly it caved in and his left eye was hidden in the massive swelling.

Michael stopped short, his hands clenching and unclenching at his sides, breathing heavily. He felt an urge to run outside, run all the way back to the hills and find the bastards who'd done this to his brother. He wanted to see them lying in a hospital bed, looking just like Bobby.

"You can go right on in. He's on some pretty heavy painkillers, so he'll be a little groggy." The nurse—a tall, dark woman with hair swept tightly back and glasses that slipped down her nose—nudged him forward. "You have company, Mr. Mondragon," she said in the cheerful, loud voice endemic to nurses.

Bobby pried open his right eye and made a muscle twitch, which Michael could only guess was a smile. "Hey..."

"Hey, big brother. You look pretty good for someone who had the stuffing kicked out of him."

"Look who's talking. Still, we did okay, eh?" His voice was raspy and hoarse, and he could barely articulate.

Michael chuckled and held back the tears. "Yeah. We're alive."

"Yeah, barely."

"I'm sorry, Bobby. I should've been there for you."

"It happened. I'm not a victim." Bobby's words were slurred because of the wired jaw and swollen lips. He closed his eyes with a twisted grimace. "Never again..."

"Has this happened to you before?"

"Not this bad. But the body remembers. Long after the mind has tricked itself into forgetting."

"Aw, Bobby..."

He sighed. "They got my nose. I was always able to save my nose before."

"It's okay. They tell me they can fix it."

"Good. I'd like to breathe through both my nostrils...."

Michael looked at his shoes, not wanting his brother to see the flash of tears. His face was a remnant of what it had once been.

"Does Mama know?" Bobby asked, his one eye visibly sad.

"Yeah. Sure. She's on her way."

"What does she know? About the other..."

"She knows everything. I talked to her on the phone. Papa was drunk by the time he got back. He forbid her to come. But this time—" he smiled slowly and patted Bobby's hand "—this time she packed a bag and left."

Bobby turned his head a bit, his bandages and broken ribs preventing him from moving far. "I didn't want that."

"She had to take a stand. She couldn't *not* come. Frankly, I'm damn proud of her."

"I don't want her to see me like this."

"How can you even think that? You're her son. She loves you. You'll always be beautiful to her, no matter what."

Bobby slowly brought his gaze to Michael, and when their eyes met, they both understood what was unspoken.

Will Charlotte always be beautiful—no matter what—because you love her?

"I heard she's engaged now," Bobby said softly. "To that agent guy."

"That's what they say."

"And you're just going to let it happen?"

"It's over, Bobby. Things have happened that you don't understand."

"All I understand is that you still love her."

"She left me."

"No. You let her go."

"It doesn't matter."

"If love doesn't matter, then what does?"

Bobby smiled then, that slight upturning of swollen lips in misshapen cheeks. But it was his eyes that held Michael. Deep pockets of sympathy—and a wisdom there that belied the few years' difference between them. Michael understood then that his brother had always been there for him, not the other way around. Whenever he needed someone to mend a bird's broken wing, to hold his hand when he walked into the first grade, to stand in the bleachers and cheer him on to victory when their father was too busy to go to his games—Bobby was there. Bobby had understood why he needed the leather jacket, why he had defied the family and taken the scholarship, and why, too, he had returned home.

Taking the punches to the body, that was easy. Michael had always thought he was doing the big favor, playing the hero when he stood, fists at the ready, between Bobby and whoever tried to hurt him. But as Bobby said, he was not a victim. He was the hero all along. Michael saw that now. The body blows couldn't hurt Bobby. His was a greater strength. He loved his father and mother, his brother and sister, unconditionally. He could endure, because he'd accepted who he was, after a long, bitter struggle.

And what of his own struggles? Michael thought. Why couldn't he know who he was? Michael's shoulders drooped.

"I don't know what to do," he confessed.

"You will," Bobby replied, closing his eyes.

A few hours later, Michael awoke feeling a nudge on his knee. He pried open an eye to see his mother bent over him, her eyes soft with concern.

"Miguel, wake up. Miguel..."

He mopped his face with his hands and yawned, then stretched his stiff shoulders. Looking around, he saw that he was still in Bobby's hospital room. Bobby was in the bed beside him, asleep. The room was a dark gray, rain still splattered angrily against the windows, and in the distance, he could hear the low rumble of thunder.

"I must have fallen asleep. What time is it?"

"It is almost noon."

"So late?"

"*Sí. Virgencita...*" She crossed herself. "The roads are very bad. Many are closed. It took forever to get here. *Si Dios quiere.* There is bad flooding in the valley. *Muy mal.* The water is rising in the river, and the rain, it shows no sign of stopping." She was wringing her hands and her face sagged with weariness. She looked worn and stooped. "The National Weather Service has issued a flood warning."

"Damn, when did they call it?"

"This morning. They say it is the flood of the century!" Her voice was high and her eyes were round with worry.

"Yeah, the third one." He scratched his head, waking up. "Okay, so where is Papa?" He sat up in the chair, alert now.

"He won't leave the land. When I left, he was putting plywood on the windows and stocking up on emergency supplies. He said he wasn't going to be chased away by a little water." She shook her head and clutched Michael's shoulder. "I passed the river on the way here. It is not a little bit of water, Miguel. I am frightened. The children are still there."

"Where are Rosa and Manuel?"

"They won't leave Papa."

Michael swore silently, not wanting to increase his mother's already overflowing anxiety.

"*Aiee,* Miguel. Cisco and Maria Elena— We must to—" she stuttered, too flustered to continue in English. She burst forth in Spanish, imploring Michael to save the children.

"Sit down, Mama," he said patting her hand, then standing. "Stay with Bobby. He needs you now. I will go out and make sure the children are taken to high ground."

She reached out quickly, taking hold of his shoulder with her small hand.

"*Mi hijo,* I am proud of you. Your father, he was wrong to do this to his son. I, too, am guilty. But Luis, he is a good man. He—" Her voice broke and she looked away.

"I promise you," he said, placing his hand over hers. "Everything will be okay. You don't have to worry. I won't leave him there. I'm going to drag that old man's stubborn ass off the land if I have to carry him to do it."

Twenty-Three

The storm was a hellion, screaming and hollering wind through the mountains and dumping a torrent of rain on the already waterlogged land. The speed and intensity of the storm was alarming. The river was cresting and the weather service was calling for families to evacuate immediately. Michael held the steering wheel to the Buick tight as he fought his way back up the mountains to the nursery, praying all the way that his family would have already heeded the warnings and left. In his gut, however, he knew his father wouldn't go. Damn fool, he'd risk the lives of his family over a plot of land.

He had to concentrate on the road. In spots, the car hydroplaned in several inches of water. Would he even make it back? The radio reported that, farther to the north, the levee of the Prajaro River had broken, sending eight feet of mud lurching through the center of town.

Approaching his exit, he spotted a yellow barricade. The police were waving people away, telling them over loudspeakers, in both English and Spanish, that they could not pass. That they should turn around and seek higher ground. Michael gritted his teeth, pressed the gas pedal and roared past them. In his rearview mirror he saw one policeman wave his hand, calling the other cop back in disgust. They no doubt thought that anyone who was crazy enough to head into the valley now deserved to die.

Common sense told him to turn back. Beyond the highway he could see the swollen river, already overflowing the banks and raging forward in a hell-bent current. But for once in his life, common sense made no sense at all. He was far beyond the constraints of rational thought. He had no choice but to go on.

The clicking window wipers barely kept the torrents of water from his windshield. Thunder raged overhead, daring him to continue. Squinting, he leaned far over the wheel to track where he was going. A long trail of cars were inching their way in the opposite direction, leaving the valley for higher ground. He had to swerve to avoid hitting two dogs that were running alongside a pickup truck crammed full with people. Children waved from the windows at the dogs, crying out their names. So, he thought, steadying the car and gritting his teeth, it has come to a choice between people and their pets. It had gotten as bad as that.

As he toiled past the long line of cars, many people called out to him, honking and waving wildly, "Go Back! Go Back!"

He bit down hard, ignoring them, seeing only the road ahead. For once he wasn't going to think, or analyze, or plan. He knew these hills. He knew the roads. His family was up there. He'd use his instincts. He just had to go on.

He pulled up to the house to find the windows boarded up with plywood and plastic sheeting, and Manuel's truck parked outside. Michael slammed the car door behind him and ran inside. Water was dripping down his back and from his head into his eyes, but he could still see Cisco and Maria Elena, sitting in front of the TV, watching the weather bulletins. They jumped up and ran to him when he entered the house, wrapping their thin arms tightly around his waist.

"Tío Miguel, they say we should leave the house now. We should go!"

"Yes, yes, I know. We will. Are you all packed up?"

"Yes," answered Cisco, trying to be manly despite the fear shining in his eyes. "Mama has our bags in the truck. And some food."

"Good. Where is your mama?"

"She's at the nursery. They're carrying the stock to the top of the hill."

"Okay. Listen up. I need your help. Maria Elena, go gather up some first aid supplies, flashlights and batteries. And a portable radio if you have one. Then listen to the news report for the road they're advising us to take to higher ground. Cisco, go downstairs and turn off the electric, water and gas utilities. You know how to do that?"

His chin went up. "Of course I do."

"Good. Do it. And see if Mama has any emergency drinking water down in the root cellar. If it's flooded down there, forget it. Stay out. Understand? Okay then. I'll be back."

Cisco nodded, relieved to have a job to do. Michael went to the back room, where he found himself a thick rain slicker and knee-high rubber boots, then, seeing that Maria Elena and Cisco were busy with their tasks, he went out in search of his father.

Michael found him standing on the deck of a Mondragon pickup, defying the rain, waving madly as he directed Rosa and Manuel in the loading of perennials into the back.

"What the hell are you doing?" Michael roared, climbing up in the back of the truck to stand in his face. He had to shout to be heard over the storm. "It's dangerous! We have to evacuate."

"It's not dangerous!" Luis roared back. "How's a little bit of water going to hurt me?"

"You stupid old fool, it's not you I'm worried about. It's those children!"

Luis slowed down and wiped the water from his face.

"They've called for an immediate evacuation," Michael called out to Manuel and Rosa when they approached, each carrying an armload of hosta. There was no time for petty squabbles. They had to cooperate to survive. "The river is cresting, and when it overflows, we won't be able to get out. There'll be water up to our necks."

"I'm not leaving," Luis shouted angrily. Lightning split the sky, illuminating the grim determination on his face. There was the glint of madness in his eyes.

"Then stay," Michael shouted back. "But you—" He turned to Manuel and Rosa. "You have to take care of your children. Leave now and take the recommended route. Go on!"

"I'm not leaving Papa!" Rosa shouted over the storm. She set the plants down in the truck, the mud leaving black streaks down her yellow raincoat. Her face was as determined and defiant as Luis's. "I've never left this place and I won't leave now. You go. You're good at leaving." Her eyes were flashing like the lightning overhead. She was shaking with the current of her resentment, unleashed now at this desperate moment. Her anger was a raw, frightening thing. A maelstrom raging inside her chest.

"You see, Papa?" she cried out. "It's *me,* your daughter, who stays by your side. Who does what you want her to do. Not your sons. Look at me, Papa!" She pounded her chest, the rain masking her tears. "*Me!* Not your sons!"

Luis climbed down from the back of the truck and held open his arms. Rosa ran into them.

Michael jumped down and walked past his father and Rosa to Manuel. His brother-in-law's eyes were dark with mistrust. Michael approached him slowly, as he would an animal with its teeth bared.

"Manuel," he said, stopping before him and speaking in a low voice. "Now is the moment not to be a son, but to be a father. Don't be like him," he said, waving his hand to indicate Luis. "Rosa won't go. You know she won't. Don't turn your back on your children now. You've got to take Cisco and Maria Elena to safety. It's not too late. Save your children, Manuel."

"I need him here!" Luis shouted angrily.

"Go," Michael urged. "I'll take your place here."

Manuel tightened his mouth in a grim line of determination. He stuck out his hand and Michael took it; they shook firmly. Then Manuel took off at a brisk clip to the house.

Luis raised his face to the sky and laughed out loud at the thunder in the clouds. "This woman, *she* is the man of the family. She is macho, no?"

"Man? Macho?" Michael called back with disgust. He saw the dark, insidious side of macho. It could turn ugly. "What is a real man? Does a real man turn his back on his son? Does a real man abandon his children to danger? If you don't protect your children, what kind of man are you?"

"I am a man who will fight for what is his," he bellowed loud enough for the heavens to hear. "This land is everything to me. Do you hear me? Everything! I will not leave it." With a wild fury, he began stacking the containers of hosta into the back of the truck, the rain pouring down his face as he labored.

"Nor will I." Rosa disappeared into the nursery, bound for more containers.

Michael swore under his breath. At least Manuel would get the children out to safety. The water was already at their ankles. In a few hours more, it would be slithering toward the house.

"Father, we should go!"

"You go! You are nothing. You have no culture. No language. No family. You go!"

Michael gritted his teeth, remembering his promise to his

mother. "I'll help you for a few hours. That is all. Then we'll all leave."

His father raised his eyes to meet Michael's gaze, triumph shining clear. But he didn't reply.

By four o'clock, they abandoned the rest of the nursery stock. They'd managed to transport a large number of pots to higher ground. Out in the fields, the winds had wrecked the orchards and the floods loosened the vines and dragged the stock out of the soil. By twilight, the containers were floating in the floodwater, a colorful flotilla of perennials, shrubs and ground cover.

Michael, Luis and Rosa stumbled through the thigh-high water up the hill, then waded through earth as spongy as chocolate pudding to reach the house, which was well situated on a high point overlooking the valley. They kicked off their boots on the porch and pushed into the silence of the darkened house, the storm still raging behind them. They stood panting in exhaustion.

"The electricity is out," said Rosa, testing the light switch.

"I had Cisco turn it off."

"Well, let's turn it back on! It's freezing in here. We'll die of the cold."

"Water conducts electricity like a wire. If we step into the water anywhere we'll be fried. The only way to be safe is to shut off all the power to the house."

"I'll wear rubber boots."

"No, that won't work."

"Miguel is right," said Luis in a low, tired growl. "Keep it off. Where's a goddamn flashlight?"

Michael found his way to the dining room table and fished around until he found what felt like a flashlight. His hands were stiff from the icy cold outdoors, but he managed to flick his puckered thumb on the switch. Suddenly, welcome light pierced the darkness. Good for Cisco and Maria

Elena, he thought. They'd gathered up a table full of supplies: jugs of water, tins of food, a first aid kit, four emergency lanterns and a stack of candles and flares.

"A radio," exclaimed Rosa, spotting one on the table. "Thank God. I'll turn on the weather."

The three gathered around the table, shivering, listening to the grim report. The day had seen record-level rainfall, double the biggest storm so far. The levee had broken, sending ten- to twenty-foot-high walls of mud and water lurching down roads and heading straight for the center of town. All the inhabitants had been evacuated. They were asking anyone who might still be in the area to seek the highest point and prepare for the worst. For a tense moment no one spoke.

"We'd better get out of here," exclaimed Rosa, her voice high with fear.

"We can't," Michael cut her off as she headed for the door. "The roads have changed to rivers. All hell's broken loose out there. Even the major arteries are cut off. We're trapped here now. We'll have to try to ride out the storm somehow."

"We can't do that!" Rosa exclaimed. "They said people were dying out there. It's worse than the storms before. The water almost got to the house then. It'll come for sure this time. I'm not going to sit here and wait to die! I'm calling for help," Rosa declared, running for the phone. She picked up the receiver and listened. Her face drained of color. "It's dead."

Michael saw her panic swell up and moved to wrap his arms securely around her. "We'll be okay, Rosa. We'll be fine. Look, there's plenty of supplies. We're on high ground. We might get wet, but we'll be fine."

He kept his voice calm, not feeling the least bit comforted himself by the empty words. He knew they were in trouble—big trouble. When he sensed that she was calm, he stepped back and smiled reassuringly. He was pleased beyond words to see her smile back, without any of the anger he had come to expect.

"Let's try and get dry at least. We're in for a long night."

Rosa nodded stiffly, trying to believe. "I'll go get some of Papa's clothes. I don't think either of us will fit in Mama's or Bobby's." She forced a choked laugh and headed for the bedrooms, her head low.

"Shit, this crazy California weather," Luis cursed, removing his coat. Underneath he was soaked to the skin. "One year there is no rain and we have a drought. Then there is too much rain and we have floods. In between we get earthquakes and fires. Goddamn fucking California weather."

Michael walked to the door and opened it, shining his light into the storm. What he saw made his heart lurch and his skin break out in a sweat, despite the freezing cold rain. Water was crawling up the slope of the drive—and it was moving fast.

"Papa, there'll be water in here in no time. Come on," he said, closing the door tight and heading for the supplies. "Grab this stuff and bring it upstairs."

"You don't think the water's going to get that high?" Rosa was walking back into the room, her arms filled with jeans and flannel shirts.

"It's just a precaution. We'd better get this stuff upstairs."

She nodded, but her eyes were wide with fear.

For once, Rosa did as she was told. Her light disappeared up the staircase. Michael thought to himself that this was the first time in the past three years that the three of them were working as a single team. That was something, he thought to himself. It took a natural disaster, but what the hell? He wasn't going to quibble.

Luis went into his back office and began stuffing papers and photographs into a tote bag. Michael ran into the kitchen, his light slithering across the cabinets as he ripped through the shelves and drawers until he found a plastic-coated tote bag, then hurried back to stuff supplies into it. The water was pouring in through the doors. It was already two inches deep on the first floor.

"Papa! Do you have a rubber raft?"

Rosa stopped on the stairs, her eyes bulging as she stared at the rising water in the house. She moistened her lips. "Oh, my God..."

"I have one of those blow-up boats in the garage," Luis replied, wading back into the living room, the tote around his shoulders.

"We can't go out to get it. Forget it, Papa. Go on up-stairs."

"I think Cisco has one of those Boogie boards in his room," Rosa cried.

"Go get it, and stay up there. Hurry up! Papa, come on!"

"Who is giving the orders around here?" Luis bellowed, rearing up and yanking his arm from Michael's grip. "I said I have a raft. I'm going to get it."

Before Michael could stop him, Luis strode angrily to the front door and swung it open. He was met with a five-foot tidal wave.

"Papa!" Rosa screamed as the water gushed in, sweeping Luis off his feet and swirling him madly around the room. Michael dove after him, stroking hard and furiously in the angry water that filled the small, dark space, crashing them both against the wall. As he swam through inky water up to his chest, he felt a bruising bump on his shoulder by something hard and stiff in the water. A broken branch? A piece of furniture? An animal? He didn't want to know. He pushed on, toward his father's voice, grabbing hold of his hand before he floated out the front door.

Rosa was screaming to them from high up on the stairs. "Where are you? I can't see you!"

"Grab his hand!" Michael shouted, pushing toward her narrow beam of light. "Pull him up."

Rosa was glad—for the first time in her life—for her size and strength. Bending far over, she grabbed hold of her father's hand and pulled him out of the water to the second floor. Michael climbed up right behind them.

Exhausted, numb with cold and weary to the bone, Michael slumped against the hall wall beside his sister and his father and lay his head back, chattering and breathing heavily.

"I'm sorry," Luis sputtered beside him. *"Lo siento."*

Michael draped his arms around his father and Rosa.

They huddled together for an unknown length of time, gaining comfort in their nearness. Outside, they could hear the storm roaring and shrieking, and the rain battering and shaking the roof. Inside, the water swirled below as black and thick as steeped tea. Michael could smell the sour stench of spoilage, and his shoulder and cheek were throbbing where he was hit in the water.

"We'd better see what's going on," he said when he'd caught a second wind. Turning on the flashlight, he shone it down the staircase. The beam of light revealed that the water was rising, step by step. Rosa sucked in her breath, and her hand clenched his arm. Luis swore softly in Spanish. Michael flicked off the light and leaned his head back against the wall, closing his eyes tight.

"Are we going to die?" Rosa's voice was shrill.

"Not if I can help it. *Ojala!* Giving my time to this place is one thing. I damn well don't intend to give it my life." He mopped his face with his palm, then ran it through his hair, pushing the long, damp tendrils clean from his face. "At least the children are safe. Thank God Manuel had the guts to buck you for once and protect his children." He swung his head to face his sister. "Think what would have happened if they hadn't left. Do you think you could have saved them from that water down there? Could you save them now?''

Her eyes widened in horror, then narrowed in self-defense. ''What business is it of yours?'' Rosa cried back. ''Don't stick your nose where it doesn't belong!''

He felt his fury rage like the storm. ''I'm making it my business. Ever since I came home you've been rubbing my nose in my efforts here. You've got a chip on your shoulder the size of California, and even though I can take what you dish out, I can't sit by and watch you take your anger out on your kids. I know about Cisco. I should have said something long before. Think of your children, Rosa. You put your need for Papa's approval ahead of your need to care for your children. If you've got a problem with me, deal with *me*.''

''Yeah, I've got a problem with you,'' she replied. Even in the darkness her resentment was easy to read. ''You come home and suddenly you're *El Patron*. The big man in charge. Just because you're a male, a son, you get everything.''

He thrust his jaw forward, unaware how much he resembled his nephew. Unaware that his sister was making that same comparison. ''I'm just doing my job.''

''Shut up, Rosa,'' Luis thundered. ''This is no time to go into this.''

''Again, you tell me what to do! This is the perfect time to go into this. We are forced together here. For all we know we might die here. I want you to listen to me for once!''

''Even now, at such a time, you talk to your father like…''

Michael cut him off. ''Papa, let her talk.''

She skipped a beat, registering his support. ''Miguel is right,'' she said in a calmer tone. ''I am angry at him, but it's really between you and me, Papa. I am never good enough for you. It was always Miguel and Roberto who mattered. The good sons. Always it was 'Rosa, don't yell, don't fight, don't be like a man. Listen to your mother.' Yet, just tonight you told me I was macho, as if that was the greatest compliment you could give me." She wiped her eyes with angry strokes. "Even my body was not good enough. It was too big. Too strong. A body that should've been Roberto's. All my life I felt I wasn't worth much. That a woman wasn't worth much."

"I always tell you a woman is worth her weight in gold, but you never act like a woman!" Luis cried back.

"But I *am. I do!*" She shook her head sharply, sending droplets of water across their faces. "Your ideas of what I should do as a woman are just as warped as your ideas of what Roberto should do as a man. Or Miguel should do as a son. They are ancient. Out of touch. Like telling us to endure. *Aguantar.*" Her movements rustled the dark. "When I was young, all I wanted to do was go to college, like my brothers. But you said, 'No. What does a woman need to learn besides how to take care of her family?'" She swallowed hard, gathering her control. "I did what you wanted, Papa. I got married. I gave you grandchildren. I worked for you in the business when your sons left you. And still that wasn't enough. When they came home, you took it all away."

She pounded the floor with her fist, lowering her head. "Do you know how that makes me feel? The anger goes deep into my soul. It blinds me. I try to hold it in. But sometimes I can't control it. I explode."

"And Cisco gets the brunt of it," Michael said softly.

Rosa's eyes widened with shock, then she averted them, turning her head and shrugging. "Just a few hits. It's nothing you and I didn't get from Papa."

"Do you want Cisco to grow up to hit his kids, too?"

Luis grumbled and barked out, "So it's my fault again. Always it is my fault."

"No," Rosa said in a strangled voice. "No, this is my

fault. When I think how I put my children in danger. They could be here now. My babies." The mountainous woman slumped to her knees and silently wept.

"Cisco is a lot like you," Michael said gently. "You should be proud of him."

She buried her head deeper into the crook of her arm. "I love him."

"Rosa, this goes too deep," Michael said. "You're so mad at Papa, at me, that it's eating you up inside. Love isn't enough. You need help. You need to see someone."

Rosa stretched out her hand in the darkness to grasp Michael's. Her hand was large and strong, her fingers damp and cold. The squeeze she gave him spoke eloquently of understanding and agreement. Of shame and forgiveness. Michael felt a rush of emotion and squeezed her hand in reply, sending her a silent message of love and support, from brother to sister, that needed no words.

Gradually the howling wind quieted and the pattering of rain silenced. Looking out the hall window, Michael saw that the rain had at last stopped, that the swirling black clouds were moving out. Though there was no moon or stars to illuminate the dark sky, it was clear the worst was over. Someone would be coming after them soon.

"We made it," he said to them, his voice hoarse and rough with fatigue. "We're alive. That's all that matters."

"We got through this together. The Mondragons," Rosa said, triumph audible even in her exhaustion.

Luis raised his head and met Michael's gaze in the dim light. "No, we are not all together," he replied soberly. "*Mi hijo.* He is not here. My Roberto. Or my wife."

Michael tightened his lips. Tonight, his father appeared humbled. Laid low, like the rooster that had fallen in the sand.

"You were right to tell Manuel and Rosa to protect their children," Luis continued in his low, gravelly voice. "I almost got you and Rosa killed with my stubbornness. I could have killed those bebés.''

His voice cracked and he shook his head. ''What kind of father would put his family in danger? Abandon his child? Break his daughter's heart? What kind of man?''

A week later the water had subsided and the families were allowed past the police barricades back onto their land. Michael, Luis and Marta drove in one car. Manuel and Rosa in another. They drove slowly across the mud strewn roads, a sad, defeated caravan, as the sun shone in a brilliant blue sky overhead. It seemed a mockery of the drenched and soggy earth below.

The nearby town was in ruins, the schools were ravaged, and it would take months to clear all the mud from the church. The pumping station had broken down and sent raw sewage spewing out, polluting every river in the county. Officials told the residents to disinfect everything, shampoo the rugs, wash the clothes and to boil anything that came in contact with their eyes or mouths.

It was hard to return to the nursery, to the house, to see all that they'd spent a lifetime in building destroyed in one night. No one said much as they walked around their ruined property, trying to determine what could be salvaged from the soggy masses littering their home and the fields. Everything inside and out was coated with a thick, gray, fur-like silt that stank to the heavens.

Marta, who had not been there during the flood and didn't know what to expect, stood at the front door to her home, tears streaming down her face. All her beloved possessions—her mother's clock, her photographs, her furniture—lay in ruins. The sofa was a mildewed lump on the front lawn.

Luis walked to the crest of the hill overlooking his beloved nursery and stopped, his hands clasped behind his back, his shoulders slumped. Rosa and Manuel followed him, flanking him on either side. Michael looked up from his work and saw them, a tableau of dejection, all slumped shoulders and bent heads. Laying down the sodden carpet he'd dragged from the house, he walked up the hill, placing one foot carefully ahead of the other as he traversed the slippery terrain. Reaching the top, he looked out over the nursery and saw what they saw. Acre after acre of rotting plants and marshy bog spread out before them. The nursery that he'd given up his architectural career for, that he'd spent the last four years building instead of skyscrapers, lay in desperate ruins at his feet.

Nature had stripped him bare. She had cheated him of any joy or satisfaction he might have felt at the end of this four-year rotation. It seemed to him as though she were mocking him and all his well laid plans. The Bible quote, *Pride goeth before a fall,* played in his mind.

Luis was devastated. He looked as though he'd aged ten years.

"I have seen this land, these plants, fail many times before," he said in a low, somber voice that seemed to come from deep inside. "But always I found something I could save. Something, eh? But this…" He stretched out his callused, wrinkled hands, then bunched them into fists at the sky. "Why?" he called out to heaven, his heart breaking. "Why did you have to take everything?"

"We're bankrupt," Rosa cried. "We have no stock left at all. Look! It's all just lying in the fields. The trees, the shrubs, everything!"

"Everything," Manuel agreed, walking to Rosa's side and slinging his arm around her shoulder in an offer of comfort. Rosa was taller than Manuel, but she leaned over to rest her head against his.

Michael expected to feel the same despair, or at least a fiery rage. These emotions he would have welcomed as old friends. Instead, he felt neither. He found, oddly, that he took it philosophically. Nature was an unpredictable mistress. A few years back she withheld her water from them. Now, on a whim, she poured it over them, almost drowning them. They could bunch their fist at the sky and cry out for vengeance, or they could shrug their shoulders and begin building again. He'd tried it the first way. Now, a little older, a little wiser, and a little more tired, he decided he'd try the other. Besides, all the swearing and cursing he'd done in the past had done nothing but make him all the more tired. It hadn't done a damn bit of good, as far as he could tell.

"My beautiful land," Luis cried out, dropping to his knees. "Look at her. She is ruined. Fouled. Her stench is putrid. I am lost. We have nothing left."

Michael walked to his father's side and bent down on one knee. He scooped up the earth and held it in his hand. The soil was damp but loamy, cool to the touch. He closed his fingers tightly around it, gaining strength, then brought it to his nose and inhaled the pungent scent. His face broke into a wide grin of satisfaction.

"Look, Papa. This land is rich and fertile. Smell it." He raised it to Luis's nose.

Luis looked at him suspiciously, but took a quick smell. He grimaced and turned his head away. "It is sour, *menso.*"

"No." Michael took hold of his arm and brought his attention back. His voice was low, but his hold was like iron. "I say it is sweet. Smell it again, Father. Close your eyes and think of the rows and rows of Mondragon stock, growing straight and strong. See the orchard in the springtime with blossoms bursting on the branches, hear the bees buzzing in the hives, the laughter of your grandchildren. Your family together. You and Mama, Roberto, Rosa and Manuel." He paused. "And me. Now smell this soil again. This beautiful Mondragon soil."

His father looked at him carefully, a gleam springing to life, before he closed his eyes and sniffed the soil in Mi-

chael's palm. Then sniffed again, while Manuel and Rosa
stepped closer, watching curiously. When Luis opened his
eyes again, he stared back into Michael's for a long time,
his face intent and fierce. Tears sprang to his eyes, then,
with a whoop of delight, he dug down and grabbed a fistful
of earth and raised it up to the sun.

"It does not smell bad. She is still sweet. Still beautiful.
She is still ours!"

"Yes, it is Mondragon land. Our land," Michael said,
his own eyes filling. "It is beautiful. And we will rebuild
our nursery here. We will rebuild our lives."

He felt a rebirth kindle in his soul as he spoke. He knew
he was speaking of far more than the nursery, or the land.
He was speaking of a certain woman who had been ravaged
by nature as certainly as this nursery had.

As he and the family worked to clean out the mud from
the house, he felt a lightness in his heart that he'd not felt
in many months. As he loaded the truck with curtains,
clothes and other items to take out to clean, as he dug
through the mud to find his mother's sterling silver spoons,
as he scraped layers of silt from the floors of the house, he
felt as though he was scraping mud from his own heart.

And beneath the anger, the hurt and the frustration, he
found the glowing, lustrous kernel of truth: he loved Charlotte. It was that simple. There was no point in shaking his
fist at the fates. He loved her, but he knew now that love
was not enough. He had to act on his love. No hell, no
high water, would deter him from his goal.

He loved her. He believed she still loved him. And if the
spring sun could dry this ruined soil and give birth to another season's growth—could their love do no less for
them?

Twenty-Four

It had been a long time since he'd driven the road to Charlotte's house. He took the curves easily, remembering them well. It was a beautiful spring day, perfect, he thought with a chuckle, to encourage a young man's fancy. In each cloud, he saw her face. In the color of the brilliant blue skies, he saw her eyes. As each mile passed, his conviction deepened. He would convince her that he loved her, no matter what. There would be no more veils between them. No innuendos, no more lies. Whatever fate dealt them, they could deal with it, as long as they were together.

He practiced the words he would tell her in his mind as he wound his way up the mountains. He would be plain. He would be direct. He would be honest. By the time he pulled up to her gate, he had it all straight in his mind. He rang the buzzer several times, impatiently. He'd already waited far too long.

"Who is it?" It was Melanie's voice.

"It's Michael Mondragon. I'm here to see Charlotte."

There was a pause, and his hands tightened white on the steering wheel.

"Thank God" came the reply.

The gates swung open and he drove on toward the house that he'd transformed. He'd designed it as a retreat for

Charlotte, a haven for the two of them away from the pressures of the outside world. He viewed the landscaped Eden, terraced with planes of baby's tears and brilliant bursts of flowers that changed with the seasons. White tulips were blooming now; soon, he knew, anemones would greet the summer.

The house, the garden, so much that they shared together here...seeing it gave him a shard of hope to cling to.

The front door swung open and Melanie almost threw herself upon him. He had to take a double look to make sure it was her. He hadn't seen her for nearly a year, and she was as transformed as the house. It was more than her softer, rounder appearance, or the sheen to her light brown hair, or the pink in her cheeks. She had a bright-eyed, contented expression that contrasted with the sounds of worry and woe pouring from her unnaturally full and rounded lips.

"I knew you'd come," she was blurting out, wrapping her arms around his shoulders and patting his back. The kitchen towel in her hand flapped in a wind redolent with the tantalizing scent of rosemary and garlic. "I just knew you'd come. But you sure took your sweet time about it!"

He strode past her into the house, his eyes scanning for Charlotte. "Where is she?" He heard the urgency in his own voice.

Melanie trotted after him, wringing her hands, her short curls and full breasts bouncing. "She's gone."

"Gone?" He wheeled around at her. "Gone where?"

"To Chicago. Oh, Michael, I hope you're not too late. You've got to stop her. He'll kill her!"

Michael felt his heart slam into his throat. "What are you talking about? Who?"

"Freddy. Charlotte is getting sicker by the day. She almost collapsed at the Oscar party and she's been hiding out here since then, not going anywhere. Not seeing anyone. Freddy hovers over her like a vulture. She won't listen to me anymore. She only listens to Freddy. It's like he's got some kind of grip on her mind.''

Michael felt as though a knife had just entered his heart. He exhaled a long breath, feeling bleak, defeated. ''Well, I see...'' He struggled with something to say. ''He *is* her fiancé....''

''No,'' Melanie exclaimed, moving closer to take his hand. ''That was all for publicity. Charlotte's not going to marry him. Marry Freddy? You idiot! She loves *you*. Don't you know that?''

Michael raised his eyes to Melanie's and began breathing normally. In fact, his heart began skipping a bit. ''Back up, back up. So, she's not going to marry Freddy? Then why is she going to South America with him? The tabloids are calling it a honeymoon.''

''Exactly. It's a smoke screen. Freddy's lined up some fancy doctor there to take out the implants and put in new ones.''

''Put in new ones? I thought she couldn't do that.''

''She can't. But Freddy's convinced her that this doctor in Brazil can, and she wants to believe it. She thinks her face is all she's got left.''

''That's ridiculous. She has so many other qualities. She...''

''She's not herself,'' Melanie interrupted angrily. ''And if you'd told her about all those other qualities before, she might not be in this pickle right now.''

There was a silent impasse as Michael brooded over her words. The truth in them hit their mark.

''Hey, I'm sorry, Michael. It's just that I'm so worried. Charlotte knew Freddy was a manipulator. He used her, but she used him, too. She always knew when and where to draw the line. She had this ability to drop a wall down between her and Freddy that he couldn't penetrate. But since you two broke up—'' She paused, and the look she gave him was part accusatory and part despairing. ''Now it's like she's given up. Michael, she's killing herself. Or letting Freddy kill her. It doesn't matter which. If she doesn't remove the implants like her doctor says, she'll die. If you saw her lately, you'd see it was already happening."

She gave him a rough push on the shoulder. She was like a curvaceous bull terrier, protecting the hearth. "Why didn't you come sooner? I waited by that damn phone for months watching her dwindle. Junichi and I spend more time in this house than we do in our own, because we're afraid to leave her alone too long." She jabbed his arm again. "What took you so long?"

Michael's eyes flared and his chin stuck out defensively. "I came. That first night."

Melanie's eyes clouded with confusion. "You came here? When? I was here."

"I doubt it," he scoffed. "When I showed up, it was only Freddy. Charlotte was upstairs taking a bath. Her clothes and underwear were strewn all over the living room, wineglasses on the table. Freddy was half-naked. I didn't need that bastard to explain the facts of life to me." He turned his head, seeing that scene again in his mind, feeling again the same burn of anguish. "It hadn't even been one night since she'd left my bed. It takes a long time to get over that."

"Wait a minute," Melanie said, holding her hand up. "Just hold on here. Something's not adding up. You walked in here the same night that Freddy brought Charlotte home?"

"Yes. After she told me the truth about her face, I went out walking."

"You ditched her."

He sighed and hung his hands on his hips. "Yes. It was a cowardly thing to do. I know that now, and I blame myself. I didn't know what to say. I still don't. She had months, years even, to come to terms with her transformation. I had two minutes. I'm not excusing myself. But hell, Melanie, I'm only human. I was angry and confused. When I came back, I found the ring on the table and I knew she'd left. The cabin was so empty, I felt so empty. So I followed her here."

"Well, I was here that night, and nothing went on between Charlotte and Freddy, I can assure you of that."

"What about the clothes? The wine. The scene was pretty clear."

"I'm telling you, I was here with Junichi earlier that night. He left when Freddy brought Charlotte home. I must have been up in the bathroom with Charlotte when you arrived. Yeah, I remember now. Freddy was supposed to go home. Charlotte didn't want to hear him tell her what to do just then, and I never do. So I told him to get out."

She brought her unpolished fingernail to her puckered lips and tapped. "And now that I think of it, I remember being pissed off at Freddy for making a mess of Charlotte's things. When I came downstairs, he was stuffing some of her clothes back into her suitcase. I thought it was pretty weird, but then again—" she rolled her eyes "—we're talking about Freddy. He's always had a thing about Charlotte." She snorted. "In fact, I remember telling Charlotte what a creep he was. That he probably took one of her panties."

The thought of that man fingering Charlotte's underthings made him clench his jaw before he let loose a string of oaths. "I can't understand why she stays with that guy."

"Don't even go there. Charlotte can be very stubborn. And she has a thing about Freddy, too. Not like a lover kind of thing. But there's a connection there."

His head began pounding again, and he placed his hand on his forehead to cool himself down. "So the bastard set me up."

Melanie stared back at him, shaking her head with incredulity. "Had to be. It would be just like him to mastermind the whole thing. He really hates you."

"The feeling is mutual." Michael was desperately trying to think past the red rage that blinded him. He wanted to hit someone. Bash something. Already, he could feel his blood screaming out for revenge. In his culture, it went beyond an eye for an eye. Disrespect demanded death.

Then, because his jealousy was a living, raging beast in his breast, he had to ask.

"It may not have happened that night. But they were close. It's been months. Have they ever..." He was struggling with his words. "Charlotte is a beautiful woman. And she was on the rebound."

"Are you asking me if they've had sex?" Melanie had no such delicacies. "Hell, no. Listen, Michael, let's get this thing out of the way right now. There never was, never will be, never can be sex between them. Freddy is impotent. Totally impotent, do you understand?"

He stood, stunned to the core. This came totally out of left field. He let it soak in a moment, wondering if he should question if she was sure, then, looking into her eyes, deciding she was. Melanie would know the truth about such things.

He thought of the lost months, the pain and agony that they'd both endured. He'd been such a fool. Bobby was right, he'd been as unmoving as a Mayan statue. No more, he told himself, his heart and soul springing to life.

"I've got to stop her."

"I don't know how. Freddy's got everything arranged, down to the last detail. He's not going to let anything or anyone get in his way—especially not you. He's waited too long for this. I'm sure he thinks he'll get Charlotte to marry him once she's vulnerable in Brazil."

"I'll find a way. Tell me what you know. Any detail might be helpful."

"Well...they're staying at the Drake Hotel tonight. Then tomorrow she has a live television interview with Vicki Ray. Do you know her? She used to be the 'Entertainment

Tonight' co-host. She has her own talk show now, and she's had this thing about Charlotte for a long time. Always writes and talks about her. I think she senses that there's something amiss there. So she's been after Freddy for forever to get a private interview with Charlotte. Freddy thought that if Charlotte did this one big interview, they'd get all those nasty rumors about her health and drug addiction out of the way. Kind of a clean sweep. Then they could skip town for a while and get the surgery. He's got Charlotte all prepped for the interview. Good ol' Freddy likes to cover his bases."

"When is it?"

"Tomorrow at two."

"When do they leave Chicago?"

"They have tickets for a flight out to Brazil tomorrow night. Michael, there's no way Freddy is going to let you see her. He's got her surrounded with bodyguards."

Michael ground his teeth as he looked around the house. It suddenly struck him how much the place was like himself and Charlotte. Their love was the inspiration for the relationship between the bold, dramatic lines of the house and the lovely, soft curves of the garden. Think, Miguel, think, he ordered himself, pacing the floor. He was an architect. Creating designs was his milieu, and he was a master at his job. Surely he could figure out a plan. He could outmaneuver Freddy Walen. He'd be damned before he'd allow that wily bastard to run off with his Charlotte, to destroy her inner beauty for the sake of a shell. He carved a path on the kilim carpet while Melanie stood, arms crossed against her breast, watching in uncharacteristic silence.

Suddenly he stopped, his eyes afire.

"Do you have the address of this Vicki Ray's studio?"

"Yeah, somewhere." Her voice rose with worry. "But what good would that do? They're not going to let you in backstage. Your best bet would be to try to see her at the hotel."

"Go and get the address—and the phone number. Then keep your fingers crossed."

"Why? What are you going to do? Freddy's got her every moment all planned out."

He offered her a wry smile and an affectionate pat on the cheek. "Then I'm just going to have to disrupt his plans, aren't I?"

The stage was set. The lights were ready. The "Vicki Ray Show" was about to begin.

Michael took his seat in the rear of the studio well ahead of the rest of the audience. He eased himself down into the narrow chair, the leather of his jacket crumpling against the metal back and his long legs bent into the cramped space. It was the first time he'd relaxed since leaving Los Angeles last night. So far, all had gone according to plan.

He didn't even try to reach Charlotte at the Drake. The paparazzi were circling the hotel like locusts. He knew the hotel and the Chicago police department well enough not to attempt the impossible. Instead, he went to visit Helena Godowski.

Michael repressed a smile when he recalled the brief, rather uncomfortable meeting with Charlotte's mother. Finding parking was more difficult than finding the building. Harlem Avenue was a major artery on the west side. The series of six identical buildings was a nightmare for an architect. The four-storied yellow brick monstrosities were each fronted with a variation of that imitation stone that was de rigeur for low income housing in the seventies. If he'd harbored any hope the interior would be updated, it disappeared when he walked into the green linoleum foyer with the chipped paint, plain steel mailboxes, buzzers with hand-scribbled names above them, and a metal-and-glass door void of any charm. Was it any wonder Charlotte had created an imaginary Frank Lloyd Wright-style home in Oak Park for her mother rather than this?

Helena opened her door a crack, suspiciously eyeing him while he briefly explained why he wanted to see her.

"I have no daughter," she'd said in a vinegary voice at the mention of Charlotte's name. When he began to question her, she stiffened her broad shoulders and tried to slam the door in his face.

Maybe it was his anger that she could disown her own daughter; maybe it was his desperation. Who's to know? But he held the door open with force and pleaded with the old woman to give him but a moment of her time. "Charlotte is very ill," he'd blurted out.

That gave her pause. And him hope.

She surrendered and let him in on the condition that he leave in five minutes. He stepped into the darkened apartment that reeked of Lysol and was crowded with heavy European furniture and doilies on every surface. He sat on her flowered sofa and, in polite tones, told her about Charlotte's illness. While he spoke he searched the walls, the tabletops, everywhere for some photograph, anything at all, to indicate that Charlotte once lived here.

Suddenly he stiffened, feeling that he'd been zapped by a bolt of electricity. No, it couldn't be. His heart began pounding in his ears. There on top of the television was a photograph of a young woman, a strange, odd, yet familiar woman dressed in a cap and gown. She had long, silky hair that he readily recognized, pale, creamy skin, and brilliant blue eyes that radiated warmth and intelligence and something else he could only think of as a challenge. She needed that look, he thought, feeling a sad pity for the girl. It didn't appear that the girl had a chin.

"Charlotte?" he murmured aloud. Could it be? It didn't seem possible.

Helena heard and followed his line of vision. "Yah, that is my Charlotte. When she graduated from college. Before she had that surgery."

He didn't want Helena to see the effect that the photograph was having on him. He struggled to keep his voice level. He cleared his throat and asked, "May I look?"

Helena dragged herself to her feet to bring the photograph to Michael. He held it in his shaky hands and stared at it like a man possessed, searching the foreign face for the woman he loved. It was familiar in some way, and not. The nose—that had to have been done, too. Where was Charlotte in this deformed stranger?

But when he covered her lower face with his palm and stared into the woman's eyes, he found what he was looking for. His breath came more easily, as though a tight fist had eased open. My Charlotte, he thought, and knew in that instant that he would love her forever.

He returned the photograph to Helena and put his heart into the task at hand. He cajoled, asked, begged Helena to meet him at the studio that day to confront Charlotte, to convince her to remove the implants.

Helena listened to his pleas with her back up against the chair, her feet flat on the floor and her hands over the apron in her lap, the vision of rigid self-control. She asked no questions. She seemed to him to be a lonely, worn-out woman, the kind that met the world with a frown rather than a smile. In this, she was so unlike her daughter, he thought, as he finished and waited for her response.

Ah, yes, the response... Even now, Michael couldn't believe the woman's coolness. She spoke to him with a formal politeness, as a maid spoke to a salesman at the door. How did she put it? She thanked him for his "interest." Then, standing and escorting him to the door, she told him not to expect her at the studio.

In that instant his heart went out to the little girl Charlotte must have been, growing up with this hard, exacting woman. Was it any wonder Charlotte always tried to please others before herself? To create that sad, bogus history filled with love and laughter? His love for her redoubled.

He was about to leave the dingy apartment in disgust

when he caught a glimpse of something in Helena's eyes—
eyes, he realized with a sudden softening of the heart, that
were so much like Charlotte's. She'd tried to hide it, but
those expressive eyes betrayed her. It was that faint glim-
mer of worry behind her rigid facade that prompted him to
tell her, kindly, that he'd have a limo waiting for her outside her door should she change her mind. Then he thanked
her politely and left. There was nothing more he could do
in that department.

Michael sighed and stared out at the stage. It was empty
save for one, solitary white chair in the center. He rubbed
his jaw, worried now that the grilling his Charlotte would
be put under once she sat in that chair would be too much
for her to bear. Doubt niggled at him. Had he done the
right thing?

A young man in an usher's uniform that was two sizes
too large interrupted his thoughts as he presented him with
his backstage pass.

"Miss Ray wants to know if you'll need anything else,
Mr. Mondragon," the usher inquired. "Some water? Coffee?"

"No, neither, thank you. Tell her all is set."

"They're opening the doors to the public now. The show
will be starting in about fifteen minutes."

Michael rubbed his eyes as the usher disappeared down
the aisle. A moment later he heard the high-pitched laughter
and excited talk of the audience as they began entering the
studio and taking their seats. He heard the name "Charlotte
Godfrey" and the word "Oscar" mentioned again and
again, like a litany. She was a big star now, "hot." These
tickets were hard to come by.

And if all went well, it would be one hell of a show.

Helena Godowski peered out of her apartment window
to the street below, careful to hide behind the curtain. The
long, sleek black car and its driver were still there! Unbe-

lievable. How long would it wait outside her door? Well, she wasn't going to the studio—and that was that. She let the curtain drop and fumbled with the buttons of her starched white blouse. Ach, the nerve of that young man. To send for that car even when she clearly told him she would not go to that studio. How much money did a car like that cost?

Humph, she thought, frowning. What did she care that the young man's face looked so crestfallen? He had no right to interfere in what wasn't any of his business. She knew who he was, even though she was clever enough not to tell him. He was that fellow Charlotte was supposed to marry. Well… She softened a bit at the prospect of her daughter finding a husband at last. She guessed he was a nice enough young man, handsome, and he certainly was polite. And convincing with those dark, unwavering eyes. But that didn't change things between Charlotte and herself. No, it did not.

As she crossed the room, she felt deep, deep inside the niggling of pain and guilt that she'd tried so hard to bury these past years. No matter what she'd said to others, Charlotte *was* her daughter. Her only child—of her only love. She'd handled that business of the surgery badly. But *her* Charlotte would never have said those things to her. *Her* Charlotte would never have left. Now her child was gone, as her beloved was gone, she thought, awash in self-pity.

Helena walked in front of the television and stood, wringing her hands, deliberating before the blank screen. What harm could it do just to watch her? she wondered. No one would know. She'd only watch a few minutes, to see if Charlotte was as sick as this Mondragon fellow said she was.

She turned on the program in time to see Charlotte walk across the stage to the thunderous applause of her fans. Helena sank back into her upholstered chair, feeling very small in the thick cushions. She'd felt this way the night of the Oscars, too, when she marveled at the poise and beauty of the woman they called Charlotte Godfrey. The big star. Her daughter.

She half listened while film clips were shown, for she was studying instead Charlotte's undeniably beautiful face and remembering the child. Then Vicki Ray was saying something about Charlotte marrying her agent, a Freddy Walen. Helena sat up in her chair, startled. What was that? Her agent? How could that be? Wasn't Charlotte going to marry that nice young Mr. Mondragon?

Then the camera shifted to focus just offstage on a barrel chested, handsome man in his fifties with lush graying hair slicked back, dark brows and a mustache below his long, distinguished, utterly recognizable nose.

Helena's face drained of color, her hand rose to her throat and she jerked forward toward the television screen. She heard nothing now other than the relentless pounding of her heart in her ears.

"My God in heaven!" she exclaimed, jumping to her feet, her breath coming in short gasps. She stumbled forward, reaching for the television, splaying her fingers across that face. The camera switched back to Charlotte, sitting alone on the stage, her legs crossed, poised, speaking in a soft voice about her coming marriage. Helena's stomach clutched and she took a few steps backward, feeling as though she were slipping into a deep, black hole.

What should she do? What? Was the world going mad? How much more could God test her?

Her feet tripped over the afghan that fell on the floor, a twin to the one she'd knitted for Charlotte. She ran to grab her coat and hat, her hands trembling, and scuttled down the stairs as fast as she could to the sleek black limousine that blessedly still waited at the curb. She panted as she ran, like one of the old steam engines she remembered in her homeland. Ah, Poland—it was all so long ago. As she slunk into the dark interior of the car and felt the lurch as it moved forward, she felt she was traveling not forward but backward, far back into the fog of her own history.

"Please, God," she prayed, feeling panic rise up in the darkness. Pressing her palms together against her wet eyes she implored, "Please, let me not be too late."

Twenty-Five

Heavy pounding on the door stirred Charlotte from her deep, semiconscious state. She pried open a heavy eyelid, cast a slow, drowsy look around the dimly lit room and remembered where she was. Vicki Ray's studio. How long had she been lying here like this? she wondered. So many memories she'd traveled through. So much material that she had forgotten, or had hidden somewhere in her unconscious.

The pounding resumed on the door, rattling the frame. Someone was calling her name. She winced, feeling as though someone was pounding her head.

"Go away," she called out, covering her ears. She felt like the little girl she'd remembered on Vicki Ray's stage, small and fragile. She used to hide in the back of her mother's large closet, behind the rack of shoes and the hems of her mother's long dresses. She liked it there where no one could bother her, or call her names, or see her face. The darkness made her feel safe.

Now there was a jiggling of the door handle and a rattling of keys. There was no way she could keep them from coming in now. Dragging herself up to a sitting position, she rubbed her fingertips across her cheeks, wiping away the moisture and sleep from under her eyes. She only had a second more, she thought, holding her face in her hands. Her fingers spanned the short distance from her eyes to the rounded curve of her inflamed jaw.

There was a whoosh of air as the door swung open, followed by the thunder of several pairs of feet entering in a rush. Of all the voices calling her name, she focused on only one: Michael's voice, low and urgent. And then he was there, kneeling beside her. She was aware of his hand, callused and strong, gently smoothing the hair from her face.

"Charlotte," Michael said, leaning so close to her she could feel his breath on her cheek. "Are you all right? My God, your face, it's burning up."

There was a humming noise inside her head at the touch of his hand. His scent, his touch, the sound of his voice... all were so near they were suffocating her.

"Keep away from her, you lousy spic," Freddy said angrily, stepping up to shove Michael away. She felt his hand jerk from her face as he lost balance. Opening her eyes, she saw the hand form into a bunched fist.

"Stop it," she cried, dragging herself up. "I won't have you two fighting in front of me. Not now, not ever." She was speaking to both of them, but her eyes were fastened on Michael. His dark eyes were burning into hers while she searched his, hoping to find, what? A sign that he still loved her? Still wanted her? My God, why was she still so vulnerable with him? she thought, frustration stoking her anger. She wanted him to suffer, as she had suffered. She wanted the anger now; she needed it to dispel the love she remembered a moment ago. From the corner of her eye she saw Vicki Ray step in front of Freddy, spreading her palms out in front of his chest.

"I didn't come here to fight him," Michael said, relaxing his hands at his side. "At least not in that way."

"Why *did* you come here, Michael?" She forced her voice to be cool.

"I came to stop you from ruining your life."

Charlotte wrapped her arms across her chest, her nails digging into her flesh. "I see," she replied crisply. "And you were going to achieve that by publicly humiliating me on national TV?"

"Hey..." He paused, visibly holding himself back while he looked at his shoes. "I'm sorry for the humiliation, Charlotte," he replied with deliberate calm. "It wasn't my intention to cause you pain but to save you from it." He looked up at her directly. "It was the only way I could think of, with so little time left, to stop you from going away with that man. He has everything planned to suit his needs, not yours. I had to expose him and his plans. To stop the lies." His face hardened. "No more lies, Charlotte."

She flinched as though struck. Immediately he put his hands out toward her, stepping forward. She took a step back, away from him, glaring at him with a look that forbade him to even consider a reconciliation. He stopped and dropped his hands.

"My life and my decisions are no concern of yours," she replied sharply. "You've only made things more difficult for me now."

"Charlotte," he said hoarsely, reigning himself in. "Regardless of what your feelings are for me, you must not pretend that some doctor in South America can cure you. That's just more of Freddy's PR bullshit. You know the implants must be removed. Look at you. You're burning up with fever, your hands are trembling. Don't fool around with your life. It's far too precious. If not to you—to me."

"What makes you suddenly the expert?" Freddy asked, his face set in an angry scowl. "You're a doctor now, too? For your information, I'm taking her to one of the best doctors in the world. First rate. You're wrong if you think I'd send my girl to anything less. Just because this doctor doesn't agree with the other doctor doesn't make him wrong. What's the matter? Haven't you ever heard of a second opinion?"

Michael looked at Charlotte and she saw the exasperation in his eyes, not that Freddy could be so obtuse, but that she could believe him and go along with it.

She colored, mostly because deep inside she knew he was right. She raised her chin defiantly nonetheless, refusing to answer him.

"Okay," Michael said through tight lips. "You're right, I'm not a doctor. If you'll wait right here…" He turned on his heel and went out into the hall, returning a moment later with a small-framed, boyish-faced man in an elegantly tailored suit.

"Dr. Harmon," Charlotte exclaimed, instinctively bringing her hand to her face. He was the last person she'd expected to see here, but still, she felt inexplicably glad to see him. More memories flooded back to her as he walked toward her: his calm demeanor, his wizardlike half smile and his pale piercing eyes. She suddenly felt as though she were back in his office, asking him to help her all over again.

"What are you doing here, Doctor?"

"Mr. Mondragon was kind enough to arrange for me to come." His eyes roamed her face as he spoke, focusing on her jaw and chin. "He's informed me of your intentions. Of course I wanted to come. You're my patient. And after all, you wouldn't return my calls."

The look he gave her was filled with warmth at seeing her again, and a glint of reprimand. She chafed and knitted her brows, knowing what was coming.

"Charlotte," Dr. Harmon continued in his levelheaded manner. "I'm here to personally tell you that to go to Brazil now is not only pointless but decidedly dangerous. Time is of the essence. I feel responsible, of course, for your reaction to the implants. Not that I could have changed it, but nonetheless, I'd like the chance to rectify the problem."

"No," she blurted. "That's impossible."

"I implore you," Dr. Harmon urged, "at the very least, delay your trip for a week. Come to the University Hospital and we'll run some tests. We'll get the information we need to make a definitive diagnosis.''

"No, no, we don't have time," Freddy argued with impatience. "After that bomb Mondragon dropped on TV today, we're better off getting out of here." He glanced over at Vicki Ray, who was listening intently to every word being spoken. "Come on, babe. We don't have much time. Our plane leaves in a few hours."

Michael stepped squarely in front of him, blocking his path to Charlotte.

"If you think I'm going to let her get on that plane..."

"Who's going to stop us?" Freddy snarled back. He pushed Michael's shoulder to pass him. Michael deliberately blocked him again.

Michael was several inches taller than Freddy, younger and more muscular. Charlotte knew by Michael's rising color that he wouldn't be able to hold in his temper for long.

He was, in fact, spoiling for a fight. "Stay away from her...."

"Who the hell are you?" Freddy retorted. "She's *my* fiancée, *bandito,* not *yours.*"

"No!"

The throaty, heart-wrenching cry soared from the doorway. Everyone froze and swung their gazes back to where a tall, stoop-shouldered woman with gray hair and a modest dress stood as though paralyzed, finger pointing outward.

Charlotte gasped and felt her heart beat double time. "Mother," she said, her voice a whisper in her clenched throat. She stared at her, slack jawed, wildly wondering what Helena was doing here now, after years of refusing to even speak to her on the phone.

But what was more odd was that Helena wasn't looking at her. Her blue eyes were rounded, stupefied, and she was pointing a shaky finger at someone to the right. Charlotte turned her head and saw that it was Freddy she was staring at so intently. He was looking back at Helena, his face scrunched with the look of someone trying to remember where he'd seen that woman before.

Helena seemed oblivious to the tense silence and gaping faces staring at her. Her eyes were fixed on Freddy, shining with a strange madness. Her cheeks were suffused with color.

"It *is* you," she exclaimed.

Charlotte looked from Helena to Freddy. He was squinting his eyes, leaning forward.

"Frederic, don't you know me? It's me—Helena. Helena Godowski. From Poland."

Freddy's face drained of all color as his shoulders rose. He shook his head. "No, no, that's not possible."

"It is. It's me! I've searched for you...for twenty-five years, Frederic." She took several steps closer to him, her hand still outstretched, as though unsure whether he was a ghost or an illusion. When she was very near, she halted her hand before his chest, wanting to touch him but not daring the intimacy. Instead she clasped it to her breast.

"Searched for me? Why?" Freddy asked. "How did you find me now?"

"Mr. Mondragon. He wanted me to come. I said no, but then I saw you. On the television. I was watching Charlotte." At the mention of Charlotte's name, Helena's doughy face sagged and she blinked several times. "Yes, yes...Charlotte," she said, agitated, bringing her fingertips to her cheek. "That's why I have come." Her eyes were wild again and she glanced over at her daughter. "You cannot marry Charlotte. It would be a great sin!"

Charlotte felt herself tense up and held her breath.

"What are you talking about?" Freddy asked.

"Charlotte, she is your daughter!"

Charlotte felt as though the floor had risen up under her, then opened up like a large mouth, swallowing her whole. Her legs felt watery, her equilibrium was spinning and she slumped down onto the sofa. Freddy her father? Impossible.

It was too crazy to believe. But why would her mother say that if it wasn't true?

Even while she denied it, from somewhere deep inside she sensed it might be true. Like one fighting her way through a dense fog, she tried to make some sense of this absurdity. After all, she knew she was born out of wedlock. She'd never seen a photograph of her father. And it would make sense of so many unexplainable things. Like why she and Freddy felt this strange connection with each other. Why he felt so possessive. Freddy's words came back to her: *I love you in my own way.* Like a father?

She looked up at him, standing white-faced with shock, staring down at her mother. My God, she thought. *His nose.* She'd never noticed it before, never had reason to, but his nose was like hers used to be. The nose her mother never forgave her for changing. She had Freddy's nose—her father's nose.

Freddy stepped back, far away from Helena. "You're nuts, lady. I don't have any children. I can't have children."

"You didn't know!" Helena exclaimed, frantic that he believe her. "I didn't know I was with child until after you left Poland. After the explosion. My family, they scorned me. The priest, he brought me to Warsaw. But they wanted me to give away my baby. I could never do that. I looked for your mother. It is she who told me you had fled to America. To escape the authorities. She helped me, Frederic. She bought me a plane ticket to find you." Her eyes filled with tears. "But I couldn't find you. I looked and looked, and then Charlotte was born. I couldn't look for you anymore. I had to find work to survive. Always, though, I hoped I would find you. But not like this!"

She reared up, pointing an accusatory finger at him. "This is a sin that you are doing. You cannot take your own daughter as your wife."

"God, no," Freddy replied quickly, white-faced and clearly shaken by the news. "I won't marry her. Shit, no,

I mean— I didn't know— Nothing happened.'' He was backpedaling now, fast, trying desperately to dispel the mud and murk that was swimming in everyone's minds at that moment.

Charlotte was swallowing the bile down her throat. She thought of Freddy touching her hair, of him looking at her in the mirror, of her going off to South America with him. It made her sick; she almost groaned aloud with what might have happened. She wrapped her arms around her stomach, as though to hold the nausea down.

"We weren't even really going to get married.'' Freddy was blabbering on. "It was all a hoax, an excuse to get us to South America for the surgery without the press hounding us at the hospital. I mean, Christ—'' he wiped his brow "—I never guessed....''

Freddy turned to look at Charlotte. Their gaze met and held, each exploring, each wondering, each finally coming to the same truth.

Michael's eyes were narrowed, and he was studying Freddy with an air of distrust and doubt. He might have accepted the story, but he clearly didn't have a change of heart about Freddy. He moved farther back into the room, taking a position as observer now in what had developed into a private family matter.

"Charlotte Godfrey,'' Freddy murmured, shaking his head as he calmed down, speaking more to himself. "Charlotte Godowski. Of course. You changed it.'' He raised his hand as if to touch her, then dropped it. "If you'da told me your real name, I'd have figured it out. I always knew there was something. Especially when I looked into your eyes. It's your eyes, you understand. They're so much like your mother's.''

He turned to Helena, allowing his gaze to sweep over the big, shabby-appearing woman with her short, straight gray hair, her pale, deeply lined face, her legs lined with varicose veins. Charlotte thought her mother seemed so stooped from the weight of hard times, so well past her prime. How would Freddy see her now, after all these years?

Charlotte was wondering this when she saw his lip turn up slightly in a sneer. When she'd been hoping for sympathy, Freddy offered disgust. She knew with a sick certainty that he was wondering what had happened to Helena over the years to change her so much. Charlotte's temper flared in defense of her mother. Helena had changed because she'd worked her fingers to the bone to take care of me, she thought. Because she'd been abandoned by her lover, by my father—by you, Freddy. He'd had his bit of fun, then run away, leaving the woman to pay the price. How dare he lift his nose at her now that she was old and tired, not the pretty young girl he'd ruined years before.

"So," he said, turning to her with a short, pleased laugh. "What do you know? I have a kid after all."

Charlotte lifted her chin, feeling very little tenderness toward him. She didn't know what she felt for him, exactly. That she was his daughter was still too fresh, too raw, to consider. Those emotions she'd have to deal with later. She was still grateful for all he'd done for her, but that was not love. She had gratitude; that was something. But certainly not enough. Certainly not love.

"I guess this changes everything," Dr. Harmon said in a solemn voice. "Surely, if you're her father, you won't want to do anything to jeopardize her health."

"No, Frederic," Helena said. "You cannot take her away from her doctor when she is sick."

"Of course I can." He seemed almost flippant. "I'm her father. I've got more right than ever now to see that she's taken care of. And I know what's best for my girl."

Michael pushed himself from the wall.

Dr. Harmon straightened his glasses, as if he wasn't sure he'd heard right.

Charlotte opened her mouth to reply when she heard her mother shout.

"No!" Helena's voice was imperious. It was the tone

Charlotte knew so well, the one that sent her shivering at attention as a child, the one that brooked no disobedience. Even Freddy stiffened when confronted with a full dose of Helena's righteous indignation.

"You are the same now as ever," she said, glaring at Freddy. "I see that now. I am not the young girl I once was. Life has hardened me, but it has also made me wiser. I see you now as you really are. You are the same," she hissed through clenched teeth, her hands bunched before her. "Selfish, uncaring, self-indulgent. You hurt me, but I will not allow you to hurt my child."

She turned to meet Charlotte, face-to-face. Charlotte's breath caught in her throat as Helena neared, feeling the enormity of the moment bear down on her in the form of this powerful woman. This was her first confrontation with her mother since that terrible night in the kitchen, the night before she left Chicago. They'd said terrible things to each other, unforgivable things. It all seemed so long ago, so meaningless now, in light of all that had passed since then.

"I'm sorry," Charlotte blurted out. Her pride no longer mattered. She simply wanted to stop the silent, hateful feud. This woman, for all her strengths and faults, was still her mother, and she loved her as only a child could.

"No," Helena said, bringing her strong, hard fingers up to gently cup Charlotte's tender face. She studied it, made peace with it. Charlotte was caught off guard to find repentance, not anger, in her mother's eyes.

"*I* was wrong," Helena insisted. "Wrong, wrong, wrong." She gathered herself up and cleared her throat, falling back on her rigid competence to get her through this unusual display of emotion. "I should have told you about your father. And how you were born. I made it dirty. It wasn't," she said, not in apology or as an excuse, but as a simple statement of fact. "It happened. Too long I spent wishing I had Frederic, when all that time I should have been happy to have you. I said you were my punishment. No, that is not true. You were a gift." She drew herself up and clasped Charlotte's long, slender fingers in her large, thick ones. "It is I who ask *you* to forgive *me*."

Charlotte gave a muffled cry. Her mother had asked for her forgiveness? Never had she heard those words from her, nor did she ever dream she would. She longed to rush forward and wrap her arms around her mother, so fierce were her feelings now, but she held back, remembering how her mother preferred not to be touched.

And then it was her mother's arms around her, clasping her tight. Charlotte felt herself slipping back in time. She was a child nestling her head on Helena's shoulder, smelling not the sterile scent of Lysol but the sweet perfume of soap and dusting powder deep in the soft folds of her neck.

Except—she wasn't a little girl. It was time to grow up. To put away the insecurities, the pensive worries, the dependency of a child, and to make a woman's decision. She straightened and wiped the girlish tears from her eyes.

Then she turned and sought out Michael. He was standing in the shadows, eyes on her. When she looked at him, he straightened and walked toward her, out of the darkness into the light. For a flashing moment she was transported back to the Mondragon nursery, feeling again the same love well up in her heart as when she'd stood on the cabin's porch, watching as he walked up the hill toward her, toward home, at the end of the day.

He was walking toward her now, she realized, after working to bring her mother and Dr. Harmon here, after orchestrating this unveiling. Might he love her, after all? *Her*—the woman behind the mask. She felt the fluttering of hope, and the tug of reservation. She had to know. For certain. She didn't want any more lies now, either.

"Why did you come back?" she asked him, staring into eyes the color of the earth. "The truth."

He was standing very close to her. He knew what she was asking. She could tell by the muscle working in his jaw and the way his fingers twitched along his thigh.

"Because I love you," he replied.

"Even without this face?"

He moved forward, placing his hands on her shoulders. "I said I loved *you*. I might have been attracted to the face, but I fell in love with the person. So if your face changes, Charlotte, I know that my love will not."

She refused to be swept off her feet. She nodded, accepting this statement as she would a precious gold coin given by someone she cared about deeply but didn't completely trust. She studied the declaration in her heart, flipping it back and forth, her doubt biting down on it, to see if it was real.

"Don't believe him," Freddy said, closing the distance. He was red-faced, worried that he might lose everything.

She sensed Michael tensing up.

"Wait," she said to Freddy, then turned back to Michael. "I know of only one way that will prove to me if you could really love me, no matter what."

She turned and went to her purse, digging into it till she found her wallet. Then, opening it up, she took from behind her driver's license a photograph of herself that she always carried with her, to remind her of where she came from, of who she was.

"This," she said, holding the picture up like a banner, "is a photo of myself before the surgery." She turned her hand and looked at the photo for a moment, feeling a fondness for the poor unfortunate girl with a chin that looked like a mud slide. Girding herself for whatever might come, she walked toward Michael. Her stomach was roiling, but she'd had enough of lies and fairy tales.

"Take a good look. For both our sakes, be honest. I wouldn't blame you if you walked away." She held out the photograph. "Could you love this girl?"

Michael didn't take the photograph. Instead, he smiled. "I told you, I already do."

"No, I mean the girl in the photograph."

"I've seen a photograph already. In your mother's apartment."

Charlotte made a strangled sound in her throat, and she covered her mouth with her hand. She wanted to believe him, so desperately.

"I knew I'd seen that girl somewhere before," he continued. "It stuck with me, but I couldn't place it until I saw you on the stage today, besieged by Vicki Ray's questions. You had this stoic expression in your eyes, this endurance. And I suddenly remembered where I'd seen that expression before. It was that girl I met in an elevator one cold night. It was the eyes I remembered, not the face. I asked you if you needed help. And you said *no.*"

"I *did* need your help," she exclaimed. "I should have said yes."

"Say yes now," he said, his emotion trembling in his voice. "I let that girl down once before. I'll never let her down again."

"Let me look at it," Freddy said, shouldering his way closer. He took the photograph from Charlotte's hand and stared at it.

She watched as his jaw slackened, then he raised his eyes to look at her, then back at the picture in disbelief.

"Are you kidding me?" Freddy asked. "And you have any question whether or not to go to Brazil? One look at this picture should be enough. Harmon, you're a frigging genius."

"Shut up," Helena snapped. "My Charlotte was always beautiful. I told her that then and I tell her that now. She has a beautiful soul."

Suddenly the room erupted with shouts. Everyone was telling her what to do, pulling her in several directions. Freddy—her agent, her father—telling her to go to South America for surgery. Dr. Harmon, the man who'd started this transformation, telling her to stay. Helena, telling Freddy to be a good father for once.

She shifted her gaze toward Michael, instinctively going there for support. He waited silently for her to make the decision. Her memories—her life—had come full circle.

Looking at Michael, she realized with sudden clarity that it all came back to him.

She turned on her heel and faced down the others as the circle tightened around her.

"Back off!" she shouted, her hand held out in an arresting gesture.

Everyone stopped talking at once.

"I don't want to hear what any of you want me to do," she said. "This is about *me*. *My* face. *My* life. Go on out. All of you. I need time alone. I have to make this decision on my own."

There was a stunned silence and no one moved. Freddy was clenching and unclenching his fist. Then Helena nodded her head and said with her heavy Polish accent, "You heard what she said. Out!"

"No," Freddy said, digging in. "You've got to understand one thing. If you lose your beauty, you lose everything. Your career will be over."

"Better her career than her life," Michael retorted.

"Michael, please. Let me handle this myself," she said, holding out her hand. She faced Freddy.

"I said out there on stage that I'd do anything for beauty. I was wrong. What I should have said is that I'd do anything for love."

Freddy's face contorted with rage. "You want to throw it all away? All that we've worked for? For what? So you can be a nobody? So you can get married, have kids, grow old and worn out like your mother?" He tightened his lips and for a moment she thought he was going to cry. Instead, he exploded in anger, pointing his finger at her accusingly. "When we started this thing, you swore that you'd do what I told you to do. You swore it!"

"You had no right to ask that of me, nor should I have agreed to it. I'm sorry. My first responsibility is to myself."

"I made you who you are!" he cried, his hand raised in an angry fist. "You owe me. You belong to me."

Michael stepped forward, menacingly.

Charlotte shivered, feeling the overwhelming force of Freddy's possessiveness. It was an obsession. It was unhealthy, and she backed away from it as she would from any dangerous disease. With sudden clarity she realized the dependence that she'd felt for him during the past months was like the thorns in the fairy tale that held the Beauty captive while she slept. But looking at him now, awakened, she felt those thorns slip away, leaving her feeling oddly apathetic toward him. Strangely free.

"In order for me to belong to you, I would have had to give myself to you. I never have, Freddy. I never will."

"So you give yourself to that loser instead?"

"I think," she said, her voice reflecting that she was finished with this conversation, "it's time for you to go."

"If I go, he goes," he said, glaring at Michael.

"I told you to leave," Charlotte said.

"If I leave now, I leave for good."

She took a deep breath and cut the tie forever. "As you wish. Goodbye, Freddy." She would never call him father.

His face flushed an angry red, his mouth worked, but for once he did not speak. They both knew there was nothing left for them to say. She thought he looked very old suddenly, every bit as worn and spent as Helena. When he turned his back on her and walked away, she thought of how he'd once walked away from her mother, too. Mother and child.

The moment the door closed, she slumped, feeling a tremendous relief. She'd just been through the mill. She closed her eyes, gently rubbing them. There was so much she would have to think about—later. When she was rested and alone. Right now, she had to keep her wits about her. She had a serious decision to make. Charlotte looked up and saw Michael's face.

Suddenly, the answer came easily.

Twenty-Six

❧⦂∞⦂❧

Three weeks later, Charlotte paced the floor of her hospital room, wringing her hands, waiting for Dr. Harmon to arrive and remove the bandages from her face. The implants had been removed, the surgery was a success and all that was left was the unveiling. It was déjà vu.

"Charlotte, relax," Michael told her. "He'll be here any moment."

"I can't relax. You don't understand."

"I understand that you're worried about what you'll look like. Anyone would. What's the worst thing that could happen?"

"I'll look the same as I did before the first operation."

"Dr. Harmon already told you that you wouldn't. Removing the implants can't undo the reconstruction. At most, you'll have a receding chin line. No big deal. You're lucky."

"I'm not worried about that," she blurted out. Four years ago when she waited for the unveiling, she had only herself to worry about. This time the stakes were even higher. Despite his avowals of love, she couldn't help but worry how Michael would respond to the face.

"Oh, I understand now. It's about me again."

"Yes," she whispered. "I'm a survivor. I'll live through

whatever happens. But that doesn't stop me from worrying if you'll still love me.''

He sighed and shook his head. "Come here," he said gently, extending his hand.

She ducked her head and took his hand, expecting to be reeled in and comforted in his arms. Instead he stood and led her to the bathroom and placed her before the small, industrial, chrome-lined mirror over the sink.

"Charlotte, look at yourself in the mirror."

She looked into the mirror and saw her reflection. Her head was completely covered, from crown to neck, with a swaddling of white gauze bandages. Only her eyes were visible, along with openings for her nose and her lips.

"I can't see myself."

"Wrong. Look again," he urged, stepping away. "If you can't love who you see right now, then whether I love you or not doesn't really matter."

Against all that sterile white, her blue eyes seemed to possess even more color, even more vibrancy. They seemed to beckon her to look deeper, beyond the facade, to where the real Charlotte lay sleeping. When she did, she caught a glimpse of the beauty that had eluded her for so long. All her life she'd been playing roles from behind a mask. That night in Chicago, she'd vowed to change her life. She began with changing her face. She didn't know then that she also had to change how she felt about herself. Like the Beast in the fairy tale, she never believed that she was worthy of love. The magical transformation from ugly Beast to physical Beauty never rendered the ultimate prize of love. This glorious reward was hard earned by qualities that had nothing to do with physical appearance after all.

When she turned, she saw Michael, tall and confident, shaking hands with Dr. Harmon at the door to her room. When she stepped back in and faced them, they couldn't see that behind the bandages she was smiling.

Epilogue

'Beauty is truth, truth beauty'—
That is all ye know on earth,
And all ye need to know.

—John Keats

Epilogue

Charlotte rode in the plush darkness of the sleek limousine from the L.A. airport toward the rich, fertile hills and valleys of Southern California that she now called home. The roads were bumpy after the limo turned off the highway onto the small, winding back roads that would lead to the Mondragon property. She rocked and swayed on the soft cushions while looking out at the vibrant greens of the landscape she knew so well. Over there was the open meadow where Michael had taught her how to shoot skeet from a shotgun, and up ahead was the woodlot where, deep within, grew a cornucopia of morels, a secret she shared with no one, not even her husband.

She smiled, thinking of how rich her world had grown in the two years since she'd had her second surgery. Richer by far than the lush nursery that Michael had rebuilt on Mondragon land. Expanded land, when one considered the additional hundred acres she'd purchased for Michael as a wedding gift. It was a piece of choice real estate that bordered the nursery, one that the family had dreamed about every spring when they walked the land. Her investments had paid off well, her house had sold for an enormous profit, and it gave her more pleasure than she could imagine to give everything she had to Michael on her wedding day.

He had, of course, given her everything she wanted. Love. She remembered the answer she once gave to Vicki Ray during an interview. "Everything, anything, for beauty." She'd learned since her marriage that love transforms even ugly things into something beautiful.

Looking out the window, she caught a glimpse of her shadowed reflection in the dark window glass. She still was an attractive woman, though not the ideal of physical perfection she might have once been. What a relief, she thought with a sigh. She never wanted to be a great beauty. All she really wanted was to be normal, to be loved. Dr. Harmon had been right when he'd told her she'd have, at most, a receding chin. She tilted her head to get a better view of her jawline in the mirror. Nice, she thought. Maybe even pretty. No, her face was beautiful, she amended. This was the face that Michael Mondragon loved.

It was also the face that millions of people across the world had wanted to see on television yesterday. She'd granted an exclusive interview with Vicki Ray, her first since her disappearance. A disappearance that, like Garbo, whetted the appetite of the tabloids and the public. Vicki had done the decent thing after that tumultuous confrontation in the green room after her show. She'd had enough to feed the tabloid gossip machine for months. To her credit, she kept mum, allowing Charlotte her privacy. It was because of that human decency—kindness from one woman to another—that Charlotte called her and asked if she could do an interview.

Her purpose was to bring to the public's attention the miracle of reconstructive surgery, especially for children with facial deformities. Charlotte hoped that by going public with her history, she'd help increase donations and support for organizations that provided surgery and care to children around the world. If she could help one child escape the childhood she'd endured, it was well worth it.

She ran her hand along her jawline and cupped her chin

in her palm. Not that she'd change a single thing about her past. It had, after all, led to this present.

Charlotte dismissed the car at the entrance to the Mondragon nursery. She wanted to feel the cool, early evening breezes brush her cheek as she strolled the rest of the way home on foot. She dumped her suitcase in one of the nursery's sheds, slipped off her jewelry, let loose the pins of her hair and let it fall, shaking the long tresses down her back.

Ah, yes, now the crowd of the city felt far, far away; the stale air of the plane was carried away by the soft breezes of a California twilight. She sniffed the air and caught the intoxicating perfume of night jasmine. Her heart skipped happily in her chest, and her skin glowed as soft as the early moon overhead. She was home. Excited now, she started a brisk pace up the hill to the house, to where Michael and the family would be waiting for her.

As she made her way along the gravel road, she envisioned Luis and Manuel sitting at the small table, sipping beer and playing dominoes. Cisco was probably parked in front of the television with a mountainous bowl of ice cream; there seemed to be no way to avoid it during the lazy summer months. Cisco was well in the throes of puberty now, a handsome young man, tall and dark, like his Tío Miguel, whom Cisco adored.

Marta no doubt was bustling in the kitchen, humming over her sauces as she prepared the Sunday dinner with Maria Elena, who decided she liked cooking and was her grandmother's best helper. As for Rosa... Well...she'd never be happy in the kitchen and no one tried to force her anymore. Instead, she'd started college, and when she wasn't working at the lawn maintenance business that she and Manuel now owned, or going to class, she had her nose in a book. Michael had stipulated that Manuel and Rosa go through family counseling before handing over the business to them, and though they resisted at first, they thanked him later. Now Rosa was Bobby's favorite target—he teased her mercilessly, claiming that she was the true academic in the family after all.

Dear Bobby, Charlotte thought, pausing at the edge of the woods to catch her breath. He was doing all right, having reached peace with his father and himself. As for his AIDS, well, they were all optimistic. And with Dr. Xavier Navarro's help and the protease inhibitors, he was maintaining his health while living in the cabin beside the spring pond that Michael had given to him—along with the sweet springwater rights. In time, the proceeds from the fledging springwater business would support his medicine and allow him to continue painting.

The woods were already deeply dark. Up overhead, a bat swooped and glided in the twilight. Michael, she knew, would be standing on the porch, looking down the road, waiting for her return. The thought of him sent her back on her path, onward and upward, past a dense thicket that, if she crossed, would lead to a small rock-strewn stream the horses loved to sip from during a summer afternoon's ride. In the distance she could see the rolling hills filled with neatly cultivated Mondragon stock, vigorous once again.

In the two years since her marriage to Michael, they had built the foundations of their own family here, on this land, with the same hard work and prayers that Luis and Marta had more than a quarter of a century earlier. They watched the seasons come and go in their natural rhythms, attuned to the signs and capricious whims of nature. As much as they loved the land, were sentimental about it, they never slipped under the spell of the delusion that nature was all harmony.

They both knew better. They had learned and accepted that nature was change, and change meant uncertainty. If the nursery, or their looks, eroded in time, they knew they would persevere. Because what they shared transcended the mortal bonds of time and space.

She passed the stone wall that marked the border of their

house, a broad, California Spanish stucco with deep red tiles on the roof that reflected the twilight colors enveloping her now. She turned the curve and her lips rose in a similar curve, spying Michael's broad form standing on the front porch, looking out at the drive, leaning against the wood pergola. A deep bark sounded in the air, alerting them of her arrival. Next came the high-pitched squeal of a little girl's voice. Charlotte laughed aloud, watching her daughter's chubby legs kick the air in excitement for her daddy to put her down.

"Mama! Mama!"

Charlotte hurried to the porch, running, dropping her purse as she neared the stairs. Bear, their big black-and-white dog, practically knocked her over as he barked and ran in excited circles around her, tail wagging, whining in pleasure. Charlotte opened her arms to her daughter, relishing Marguerite's beautiful, creamy skin, her glistening black hair like her father's and her mother's brilliant blue eyes. It was her delicate, perfect chin, however, that Charlotte loved to look at the most, to kiss, to thank God for.

Charlotte brought her year-old daughter to her chest, rocking her, kissing her forehead, hugging her as she always dreamed she'd hug a child someday. She lifted her eyes and saw Michael, so proud, so strong, his eyes filled with a deep and abiding kind of love. He had answered her dream. He was her Someone. How nice to believe again in fairy tales and happy endings, she thought, smiling at him.

He smiled back, communicating millions of words of love in that one glance. They both knew that in a short while they'd put their bundle of energy to bed and make love in their own bed, in their home, on their land. Afterward in those quiet, close moments, he'd lift her to his shoulder and stroke her hair while she told him of the time she'd spent away from him—he'd want to know every detail. All this they understood with that one smile, that one knowing glance. She sighed with a contentment that went beyond description.

Moving her line of vision beyond her child, past Michael's broad shoulders to the mountains beyond, she saw the infinite power and glory of nature's sunset. The majestic colors swirled together, light and dark, brilliant and mysterious, unique and different, blended in harmony.

She smiled, lifting her face to the sky, welcoming the light into her heart.

A random predator is terrorizing Southern
California. After children start disappearing, it's
up to the FBI's finest to stop a killer...

RANDOM ACTS

Criminal profiler **Laurel Madden** is at the top of
her field. But Agent Madden has a dark side and
even darker secrets—which is why she understands
the criminal mind so well.

Claire Gillespie is a reporter assigned to cover the
case. She has another more personal agenda: to rip
away the veil of secrecy that surrounds and protects
Madden. Claire has evidence that the FBI top agent
committed murder—and got away with it...until now.

Dan Sprague is the veteran FBI agent who stands
between the two determined women—torn by duty
and loyalty to one woman and an intense attraction
to the other....

From the bestselling author of
The Best of Enemies...

TAYLOR SMITH

MIRA BOOKS

Available mid-September 1998
where books are sold.

From the bestselling author of *Suspicion* comes a tale of romantic suspense certain to deliver *chills and thrills*!

CHRISTIANE HEGGAN

Accident or Murder?

Simon Bennett—one of the country's most talented and controversial architects—is dead.

Everyone believes it to be an unfortunate accident—everyone *except* his daughter Jill. And in her quest for answers, she finds lies and evasions.

Jill needs help. Ex-homicide detective Dan Santini would be the perfect candidate, except that he's also her ex-husband. But as they begin to delve into the past for answers, Jill starts to suspect that the truth is more frightening than the lies!

DeCEptiOn